Henry F. Keenan

The Aliens

A novel

Henry F. Keenan

The Aliens
A novel

ISBN/EAN: 9783337000516

Printed in Europe, USA, Canada, Australia, Japan

Cover: Foto ©Andreas Hilbeck / pixelio.de

More available books at **www.hansebooks.com**

THE ALIENS.

A NOVEL.

BY

HENRY F. KEENAN,
AUTHOR OF "TRAJAN," ETC.

NEW YORK:
D. APPLETON AND COMPANY,
1, 3, AND 5 BOND STREET.
1886.

TO

DAVID GRAY

AND HIS WIFE,

MARTHA GUTHRIE GRAY,

𝕿𝖍𝖎𝖘 𝖁𝖔𝖑𝖚𝖒𝖊

IS AFFECTIONATELY INSCRIBED.

CONTENTS.

CHAPTER		PAGE
I.—The Helot's Hand		5
II.—The Cup that Cheers		24
III.—The Dregs of the Flacon		41
IV.—Niobe		53
V.—A Village Hampden		65
VI.—"Wars of Rose and Shamrock"		84
VII.—A Tale from Boccaccio		101
VIII.—Young Barbarians at Play		122
IX.—An Eldritch Comedy		142
X.—Visions of Delight		155
XI.—A Text from Leviticus		173
XII.—Lady Molly falls into Brogue		188
XIII.—New Masters at Marbury		201
XIV.—The Tell-tale Treasure		216
XV.—Friends at the Blue Jay		231
XVI.—A Mystic Romaunt		245
XVII.—Darcy Gains a Victory		258
XVIII.—The Handmaid of Boaz		268
XIX.—Coward Conscience		281
XX.—Between Two Loves		295
XXI.—Briseis		310
XXII.—The Curse of the Alien		322

4 *CONTENTS.*

CHAPTER	PAGE
XXIII.—A Woman's Reason	331
XXIV.—Sweet Bells Jangled out of Tune	340
XXV.—An Army with Banners	354
XXVI.—The End of the Dream	370
XXVII.—A New Love	388
XXVIII.—A New Life	404
XXIX.—Norah Reaches Home	417
XXX.—Consequences	427
XXXI.—Sorrow's Crown of Sorrow	441

THE ALIENS.

CHAPTER I.

THE HELOT'S HAND.

IF my pen were a ray of sunshine, or the ink flowing from its point had the actinic quality of the fabulous fluid wherewith the scribes of the Ptolemies created to the eye the thing of the thought, I could hardly give you the reality of the sylvan loveliness that captivated the eyes that fell upon Warchester in the early days of this century. Eyes dim with tears and hearts heavy with yearning grew bright and light in the re-assuring serenity of the scene, as the jaunty canal-packet Red Jacket shot through the gleaming water-way to its wharf in the heart of the town, one rare June evening. long, long ago—so long ago that the children of that day are patriarchs now. Measured, however, by years, that June evening was not so far away; measured by change, it was an age in the processes of science. The cyclonic forces of enterprise and invention had not yet begun their mad swirl over the land. Life was not a battle, nor wholly a burden, to the least favored. Simple manners, sincere aims, homely joys, modest ambitions, re-

ceived as a heritage, were cherished as a faith. Few were
very rich, and few cared to be ; none were very poor, and
none feared to be. Want was an incentive, not a burden;
wealth was a slave, not a master. Handicraft was primitive, for science had not then unrolled the ample page
that makes the miracles of the past the needs of to-day.
Art had not found the Aladdin lamp, that reveals the
dynamic forces of heat, steam, and electricity.

This was when New England was the center of population, and Boston the metropolis of taste and learning ;
when New York was but a straggling patch upon the rocky
ribs of Manhattan Island ; when a day's ride southward
from the city of Penn brought the heir of all the ages of
civilization into a land of legalized helotry, sordid and
soulless as the feudalism of Rome ; when a voyage to the
Mersey was an affair of fateful resolution, that the prudent
prepared for by making their wills and setting their house
in order ; when the overturn of a throne on the Continent
was news in New York three months after the event ;
when the telegraph was as much a marvel in enlightened
circles as the telephone to the nomads of the Congo to-
day; when the journals were didactic pamphlets, and
compared to the diversified pages we see as the mind
of a Bœtian to that of a cultivated Athenian; when the
stage-coach was still the popular express, and the pillion
the favored locomotion of the genteel ; when no one read
American books, because few were written, or, if written,
unknown, until the stamp had been put on them by English taste ; when, even in the enlightened circles of New
York and Boston, the play was a godless diversion, and
the player an outcast from the most liberal groups, and
the actress a sinner whose feet took hold on the pit of
wickedness ; when novel-reading was of the deadly sins,
and dancing damnation ; when at many a chimney-stone

might be heard the piping treble of veterans whose eyes had seen the British ensign dipped before Washington at Yorktown; when the last expression of political and social opprobrium was the taunt of Toryism, and to be a Federalist was as loathsome as in 1865 it was to be a Democrat; when the elderly among affluent men clung to ruffles and laces, silver buckles, high stocks, garments of gay color and ancient form; when silk gowns were the mark of gentility, and strong liquors part of the family feast.

The unlovely in man was less obtrusive, and the caprices that impair the angelic in woman less in evidence, in the diversions, occupations, and even frivolities that divided the feminine mind. Gain was not then the scheme of chance it is now become, and, though there was less affluence in the groups that held sway among social forces, wealth brought the ease and refinement we associate with it now.

These were some of the slowly changing conditions at the moment we enter Warchester that tranquil evening long ago. The deciduous glories, that now make Warchester the "enchanted city" to the stranger, were then merely its natural vernal plumage. Then, as now, the site delighted the observing. Nestling in a wooded valley, lulled by the melodious murmur of the Caribee, or stimulated by the feverish rush of its waters as they swept over the crags and cascades lakeward, Warchester was crowned with beauty and endowed with the resources of thrift.

In the days when the credulous population, that grew rich by its traffic, held the Erie Canal to be a stream, mingling the golden marvels of Pactolus and the sacred functions of the Nile, Warchester was the most considerable if not the most populous inland city of the Middle States. Spread out in roomy squares and broad avenues, on the banks of the Caribee, the town from its infancy had

been remarked as an ideal situation. Rivals to the eastward and westward disputed the pre-eminence of Warchester, and, as the census was then in its infancy, the indignant dwellers of what was called the "Sylvan City"
were forced to leave the dispute to Time to settle. Wrangling and disputing on other points, the rival towns joined
in calling down blessings on the head of his Excellency,
George Clinton, to whom that Romanesque masterpiece,
the canal, was fondly believed to be due down to the last
sod on the bank at Lake Erie. Joined to this artless faith
was a deeply rooted sentiment that the new channel, creep-
ing over the fields and winding sluggishly through the
towns, was a stream of more definite beauty than the purple waters that bathe the stones of St. Marc's. For years
the stream justified the simple faith of its adorers. It
scattered plenty through a smiling land, until the railway
came, like a brawny youth taking the burden from totter-
ing age. Luxurious maples grew in profusion to the very
edge of this wondrous water-way. Indeed, the abundance
of foliage in the business quarters gave the stranger the
impression that the city had been surveyed in the recesses
of a primeval forest, and the axe had been forbidden the
vandal hand of greed. Warchester spread along the river-
bank, nestled under the hills, and sent suburban offshoots
far into the rich fields, unconscious of the dynamic forces
that to-day makes it an industrial Venice. Even in those
early days the Warchester builders seemed not unconscious
of the open volume of beauty Nature laid before them,
for the wooden structures were reared with a simple grace
and less harshness of form than befell later urban archi-
tecture. There was something of harmonious design and
color in the secluded homes nestling in the gleaming foliage that made Warchester an Arcadia.

If the canal did not turn out the Pactolus of the people's credulous dream, neither did it steep their disappointed senses in the languorous repose of the lotus-bearing Nile. The cumbrous bottoms that discharged a diverse traffic on the city wharves brought the seeds of the fortunes that to this day maintain the patrician group that rules the town. Midmost the mountains and the lakes in valleys of fainting richness the city prospered and throve, until it grew out of the memory of its founders. Even in those early days it was acknowledged to be the fairest inland city of the Union. In truth, Nature seemed to wanton in the beauties offered the greed of man—where the founder's mill was perched upon the edge of the cataract, and the yellow prize of the valley was ground to the ceaseless music of the Caribee's waters. The spot selected for beauty and repose had not yet become a mart, teeming with the appliances of the artisan and the needs of the pioneer.

Through the beauties thus faintly outlined, the packet glided gayly cityward, as the mellow afternoon sunlight fell upon the tender green of the trees and the limpid ripples of the canal. Six fleet horses moved the vessel at a lively jog as she drew nearer the wharf. The packet's arrival was evidently something of an event, for the people in the streets near the canal gathered in groups and waved amicable tokens toward the company on the foredeck. As it entered the famous aqueduct that carries the waterway across the river, there were loud cheers from the center of the town, and waving flags were descried near the main wharf.

A wheezy cannon could be heard from a distance, its ratchety detonation drowned in frantic huzzas for " Governor Darcy—Huzza for Dick Darcy." The Governor was plainly the large man in the group that filled the prow of the packet. He removed his hat with stately delibera-

tion, and stood with serene countenance, bowing greetings
to the right and left. Turning to a lad standing at his
side, the Governor said, graciously :

"Mark, some of this welcome is for you! Warchester welcomes a Warchester; you must make your bow
manfully, for honors come naturally to a Warchester!"

The youth, watching the faces on shore with glistening
eye, blushed as the great man called the attention of the
others to him, and shrunk into the throng behind the
Governor. The packet meanwhile had slacked speed, and
was careening gayly toward the well-worn planks of the
Rialto wharf—as the dock at the end of the dromedary
bridge was suggestively called in those days. Facing the
boat and the bridge, the city displayed itself in a pretty
square, flanked by the bank, the post-office, the Blue
Eagle tavern, and St. Mark's Church. The quaint *ensem-
ble* of pointed gable, Gothic spire, and truncated arches on
the bridge, gave the scene a vivacity of the picturesque
which redeemed it from the disheartening rawness of
primitive towns. Meanwhile there were movement and
joyous expectation on the shore, and answering demon-
strations from the crowded deck.

Warchester was so young in corporate dignity that the
civic machinery creaked in its newness. Colonel Warchester, the founder's eldest son, was serving his first term
as Mayor, and the City Clerk, Captain Wellsly, who had
been an alderman in New York, was depended on to
coach the raw hierarchy in municipal forms and the eti-
quette proper to such occasions as the present. It was
vaguely felt that some extraordinary ceremonial should be
prescribed for the reception of the Governor, but the
Captain had given up the attempt to school the raw
aldermen. So after all the ceremonies were left to hazard,

Colonel Warchester remarking dryly as the puzzled committee stood beside him :

"Dick Darcy wouldn't know what to make of fuss and feathers in his own home—where, man and boy, he never saw anything more of show than the Fourth of July fireworks."

The reception was therefore more a *fête* of friends and neighbors than the formal event the indignant Captain had set his heart upon. But there were color and life notwithstanding. The solemn chariot of the Warchesters stood in the center of the throng, and in it sat the "Mayoress," Mistress Warchester, very grand and overpowering in satins and laces. Grouped about this stately center were the "ladies" of the councilors and the chief dames of the city's greatest. But far more conspicuous than the elders were the small son and daughter of the house of Warchester, the Governor's namesake, Master Darcy, and his sister Mildred. The pranks of the boy and the solicitude of the girl fascinated the attention of the waiting throngs, while the mother was as obviously distracted by the lad's recklessness and impulsive forays from the nursemaid's keeping. Twice he had barely missed tumbling into the water, and, just as the signals of the Red Jacket were seen, he was ignominiously dismissed to the rear of the carriage in the stout arms of the harassed Abigail.

Expectation had reached its most vivacious pitch. The brand-new home guard, drawn up in the Athens road, that runs east and west through the town, came to a clattering "present." The Governor is putting the last step on the gang-plank. The band gives all its lungs, and not much art, to "Hail to the Chief!" The Mayor steps to the triumphal dais while the preparatory piping is going on, and everybody waits distractedly to see how the affair will end! Certainly Darcy can't kiss all his kinsfolk nor shake hands with his constituents before sundown ? If he can't, the reception is a sort of deception, for what did Warchester make a governor for if he were not to be filial, and homely, and affable when such occasions come about? But Darcy, ignorant of the expectations of his compatriots, moves forward smiling—"Jacking" one, "Toming" another, and "Dicking" familiarly, where the Toms and Jacks came to an end—with jovial delight until he reaches the Mayor, to whom he bows with grave dignity and shakes an official rather than friendly hand. Then a great shout breaks out and dies away in shamefaced and untimely incoherence, the abashed enthusiasts not quite sure whether such a salutation is the proper observance; whether the acclaim which did honor to Darcy the candidate were quite in keeping for Darcy the Governor! But the affable statesman soon re-assures all who can reach him, and the shouts break out hilariously again as the gleam of satisfaction is seen in the great man's eye. Having saluted urbanely all the personages of the civic throng, the Governor makes his way to where Madam Warchester sits in state. He bows low over the white jeweled hand she extends, kissing it in the old-time fashion; whereat there is a pleased simper among her train.

"I have brought your young kinsman safely back to you, Mistress Warchester. You'll hardly know him for the sly rogue of four years ago. He has turned into a monk for studiousness, and I make no doubt he will do the family great honor!"

Marcus had pushed forward, but, blushing furiously as this encomium drew the eyes of the group upon him, he shrunk behind the carriage, refusing the embrace of his aunt before so many eyes.

"And how our young city has grown!" continued the statesman, addressing the group, in a joyous, paternal sort of rapture. "I protest I shouldn't have known it if I had waked suddenly inside the limits. If we continue to spread out in this fashion we shall be the principal city of Imperia by the time Warchester's turn comes for the next governor!"

"Why not?" interposed the Mayor, confidently. "Is there any other city has such advantages? We have the canal, the lake, and the river, to fetch and carry, to turn our wheels and grind our wheat. The mines of Peru hold no more gold than the surface of the Caribee valley; we have the most intelligent population in the State, the best families in the country!"

"And a Warchester for mayor," slyly interjected the Governor, as the other halted in his complacent enumeration of the infant city's aptitudes.

"And—and—with such blessings and advantages," continued the Colonel, a reproving seriousness in his tone, "Warchester should be the sustenance of a vast population before this generation passes away."

The salutations were ended, the militia had begun its march, and the company was ready to form behind the Governor, when a sudden movement toward the edge of the water, a stifled shriek and scurry arrested the Mayor and his guest. Mrs. Warchester, looking down, seemed to mark the absence of her son. He was nowhere to be seen. A cry from the edge of the crowd enlightened them as the derelict nurse darted wildly among the soldiers in search of the strayed urchin. The girl had lost sight of the child only an instant. Agitated by the amorous glance of a gay trooper in uniform, she had forgotten that eternal vigilance is the watchword of the nursery as well as the State. At all events, when the questioning, awful eye of the mother found her, she cowered in terror.

"Where is Darcy, Margery? Surely you have not let

him go among the crowd again?" Margery fled wildly in pursuit. The child, quite naturally, made for the object of his curiosity, the packet. Here, partly concealed by a large post, he watched with wonder and delight the amazing sights of the deck and the gangway, as the great hulk gave up its treasures. Marcus Dunn, the lad whom the Governor had signalized by his attention, fell out of the official center and stood in the shadow of the warehouse, watching the debarkation intently. He seemed to expect a familiar face, and his eyes darted quickly from the strange squads that came out, specter-like, from the low steerage doorway. The group was in suggestive contrast to the Governor's following preceding them. They were a frightened file of emigrants, confused and disheartened by the movement of the packet and the abuse of the officers, who hurried them out without much regard for age or sex. They streamed out over the narrow gangplank, laden with the motley and nondescript belongings that the humble transport laboriously when seeking new homes. They were clad unseasonably in fabrics of curious shape and texture. Whether it was the humorous contrast in the reception, or curiosity to witness their dispersal to new destinies, Marcus remained at his post until the last laggard straggled out. The little ones, who seemed to outmember the company greatly, were soiled but ruddy, full of unbridled curiosity and infantile delight, with tongue and eye eloquent of the naïve surprise that befits the small but observant traveler on an occasion so momentous as the selection of a country over which to rule in the fullness of time. The train did not move fast enough to suit the energetic supercargo, and he remonstrated urbanely:

"Here, you allfired Micks, hustle yourselves kinder spry, and give us a chance for the freight some time to-night. Hurry up there; you're slower than the wrath of the Lord, and not half as sure! Come there, Paddy, you ain't on your ould sod, where the shamrocks grew between your feet.''

The company to whom these benign remarks were addressed straggled forward, all ages and sizes, in a frightened scramble. The first to reach the shore was a man in the prime of young manhood, symmetrical of figure, brawny limbed, with the outlines and port of a drummajor. By the hand he led two little boys, the eldest, perhaps seven, red-haired, blue-eyed, with tawny patches of freckles, unbridled curiosity and mischief equally mixed in the expression of his face. The other boy, younger by two years or more, came haltingly, turning his eyes wistfully backward to see that his mother followed, was distinctly unlike his elder. His eyes were dark gray, his thick shock of hair a sunny brown, his complexion like the first turn of the maple-leaf in fall. Behind the boys came a woman, perhaps twenty-five, with a figure whose beauty the shapeless gown and ill-fitting covering could not wholly disguise as she reached and rested dejectedly on the large boxes piled on the wharf. She was the realization of the mourning, martyr-like Madonna, Murillo painted in his Sevillian reveries. As the crowd grew more clamorous, her large violet eyes opened wider and filled with blinding tears; she looked back in terror toward the packet, clutched the hand of her husband, and pointed to the train still coming over the plank. As she raises her arm the head of the younger boy is pillowed under her shawl, and the attitude emphasizes the resemblance to the Murillo Virgin.

By careful management the straggling urchins were gathered within reach of the father, sitting on the boxes, watching curiously the people of the New World, where he had come to seek his fortune. Evidently re-assured as to his right to be there, he deliberately opened a capacious pouch, and, filling a short clay pipe, held a lighted match until the flame reached his finger, meanwhile surveying his distracted brood.

"Mind yer oi there, Nan, ye divil's own get!" he broke out as a hoydenish merry romp of a girl came down the plank with a babe on her arm, stopping to joke with one of the deck-hands. But she landed her charge safely in the mother's arms, and the pipe sent up little puffs that seemed to signalize peace in the bosom of the smoker.

"O Hugh, dear! th' byes 'll fall in th' wather—sure I know they will if ye don't spake a word to them," and the mother arose in alarm as the lads skirted the edge of the bank. A nod from the father brought them under the mother's wing, who, turning in frightened solicitude, asked breathlessly:

"Nancy, girl, are the childer all here? I don't see Norah."

Nancy took her laughing eye from the stalwart boat-man, and, counting the little ones hurriedly, nodded. Meanwhile another group debarked, ranging themselves near the waiting mother and her children. The father of these distinctly contrasted Aliens, a stumpy, blue-eyed, tow-haired Saxon, led his little ones, but, unlike the Celt, made no attempt to lighten the mother's burden. Even the boatmen stopped to comment on the strange spectacle. The mother came down the plank with an infant at her breast and another strapped on her back, which was painfully bent, as she descended the steep incline to the shore. By the hand she led a small urchin, staring with large blue eyes and wide-open mouth at the strange new sights opened to his infantile wonder.

The placid patriarch of this group, unconscious of the

unkindly curiosity excited by his shirking of the family
burden, seated himself tranquilly just beyond his companion Aliens, and, as if reluctant to intermit the joys of his
pouch, adjusted a long porcelain pipe upon the bundle
under his arm and fell to whiffing the white smoke with a
serene content that drew smiles from the natives, as yet
not familiar with the German in his primitive condition.
The man himself, apparently indifferent to the labors attending his kith, stared about in meek wonder, untinged
by anything like concern.

When the exodus of the human freight came to an end,
the emigrant belongings, heaped upon the deck, were
pitched out in vicious volleys by the robust crew. Then
the packet was cast off and moved a length forward to the
overhanging warehouse to unload her wares.

At the same moment the first mother, missing her
smallest boy, turned in terror to the stout girl near her,
crying, "Nancy, dear, mind the childer; don't ye go near
the wather. Holy saints! Denny's drowned."

Now, the small boy called Denny, released from the
paternal control, had taken the hand of the little Norah
and toddled in ungovernable curiosity to the water's edge,
where his eye had caught the gay figure of the Mayor's son
braced against the capstan or rope-post. The two children, about the same age, eyed each other shyly—Denny
with timid curiosity, Darcy with wonder not unmingled
with a placable arrogance: if a boy of five might be capable of that instinctive assertion of condition. The pretty
costume, the well-combed hair of the other, excited such
wonder in Denny that he boldly stretched out his hand to
touch the glittering buckle of the belt that fastened the
child's tunic. Norah, shrinking behind, also fascinated by
the lad's finery, stared wonderingly as Denny put his
hand upon the shining clasp. Discomfited at this, Darcy

turned and fled, looking inquiringly over his shoulder as
he ran. It was but a step to the water's edge, and the
loosened rope tripped his little feet; before a hand could
be reached out to stay him, he rolled down the shelving
bank and into the water, fairly under the bulging side of
the boat. Denny, probably thinking it a game, followed,
tripped, and he, too, rolled down the bank, and both were
in an instant lost under the clear water. The screams of
the emigrant mother startled the great folks just ready to
drive off.

"Where is Darcy?" Colonel Warchester asked in sudden alarm. The loud cries near the water and the rush
of those nearest the place warned him. But before he
could get to the spot the athletic form of Hugh clove the
crowd, as, with ready presence of mind, he tilted the gang-
plank on edge, and slid it between the boat and the bank,
in the form of a wedge, to keep the packet from grinding
the little bodies on the stones of the shore. Dropping
down along the smooth wall, Hugh dived under the children and soon re-appeared with one on each arm. As he
reached the top of the bank, both mothers stood together,
by the curious irony of nature, equal before the altar of
calamity, terror, and the devotion of motherhood. The
proud lady never looked at the brawny rescuer; unmindful of the dripping garments, she snatched the terrified
child to her breast, turning her back on the abashed instrument of her darling's safety. He relinquished the
little fellow with a word of good-humored but apologetic
earnestness:

"It was this bould little brat that did it, ma'am; yer
little boy was as paisable as a kitten with a bowl of new
milk!"

This was an implied censure of Denny that his mother
resented in her way. She seized the dripping culprit,

soothed him on her breast, and, as she turned away, shot
an arrow of such pathetic reproach as Marcus thought
must have followed the eyes of the saint when Caiphas
gave the innocent to the malice of men. The lad felt an
impulse to go to the despised mother and make up for his
kinswoman's ungraciousness and ingratitude. His sentiment was so strong that he presently felt a sort of com-
punction when his uncle bade him enter the carriage and
come to the feast.

The incident hastened the departure of the throng.
The dripping child was packed off with the guilty nursemaid. The band began a joyous march, and, between
open lines of militia and citizens, the *cortége* hurried off
to the imposing mansion of the Warchesters. It was a fine
pile of brick, covered by white plaster. It was adorned
in front by stately Doric columns of white, supporting a
single-pointed gable on a wide projecting architrave. The
house stood far back from the street in a park of noble
maples, and from the porch great vistas could be seen,
bounded by the distant Holly Hills, that made the city a
vernal amphitheatre. A great company had been invited
to banquet in honor of the Governor, and afterward half
the town were to join in a reception. The pleasant
grounds presently echoed to the strains of the military
band, and, as darkness fell, the company sat down to the
feast.

Darcy's adventure was the topic of the supper-table,
for the late dinner was not in those days the sign of professional condition or social standing.

"Who was the man that leaped in after the children?"
asked the Governor, who had not seen the episode.

The question seemed to embarrass the company. No
one, it appeared, had ever thought of the agent of the
rescue. Madame Warchester, to whom the company cast

a questioning glance, looked appealingly at her husband,
the Mayor, as if invoking his official address to shield her
from confessing the plebeian means that had dared save
her son from drowning.   The Colonel, clearing his throat,
and, with a glance.that said things were not really so bad
as they might be, made answer :

"I am quite sure that it is the brother that James
Boyne has been expecting the last fortnight.   There was
just enough family resemblance to make me sure of that.
He was a fine stalwart fellow, and his arms came in good
play."

"It was a manly act, and the man deserves recognition.   I like to see these brawny recruits filling up our
ranks.   With a few thousand like this Boyne, in this fer-
tile land of promise, we shall be the greatest nation and
happiest people in Christendom," and the Governor beamed
cordially upon the company.

"It didn't occur to me to remark this person," Mrs.
Warchester said, frigidly, meeting the Governor's eye
before turning to give an order in a whisper to a domestic.

"Well, Governor," remarked a young lawyer, anxious
to display his parts in such fine company, "if that's all the
country needs to make it prosperous we won't have long
to wait ; there were fifteen children, by actual count, between two mothers on the wharf to-day."

"That was the reason I was surprised at this Boyne
person taking the trouble to fish out his infant," retorted
a rival lawyer, bent on keeping Mrs. Warchester on his
side in the social combat.   The witticism fell rather heavily on the table, but Mrs. Warchester came to her *protégé's*
rescue.

"O Mr. Hapgood, how can you be so wicked !   No
doubt the babies of these Irish persons are as dear to

them, though they do seem to come in litters, as our own."

This was said with such an air of benignant raillery, and just the shade of equivocation, which left the first satirist in doubt whether his sally had been understood in all its exquisite humor, and he continued :

"I never realized the humorous inspiration of Swift's plan for the utilization of babies until I remarked the rabbit-like fecundity of the Irish mother!" This was successful in eliciting a burst of merriment, which incited young Gideon Meadows, an attorney in the employ of the city to contest the claims of the Poultney heirs for a large tract of water-front, to say :

"No wonder Ireland has a famine every few years when the baby crop beats the potato crop!"

The Governor, who had listened with evident surprise to this conversation, drew a long breath, and, raising his glass to the hostess, said, genially :

"We'll drink to the boy's immersion, though we don't believe in the Baptists."

This excited a ripple of laughter, as everybody understood the allusion to a Baptist seminary and college just incorporated in the city.

"But, my friends," he continued, "I'm sorry to see that you let prejudice stand before your senses in dealing with the question of peopling this country. You make no objection to the negro coming in? Why draw the line at the Irish? If our ancestors had been of your mind, I should have been toiling in the bogs of Kerry to-day, for my grandfather, as you must all know, was Irish. That, however, is neither here nor there. A man that did the thing this Boyne did to-day deserves some notice. If he is, as you say, James Boyne's brother, I will make it a duty to go to the mill to-morrow and stimulate the man's pride by telling him whose son he rescued, and that we are all grateful—eh—Mr. Mayor?"

As a large mill-operator and leading politician, the Governor might be expected to hold views of this sort, but the company was careful to give no indorsement of them, especially as Mrs. Warchester compressed her lips in a manner that every guest at the table knew the significance of.

"The truth is," the Mayor said, reflectively, "I wish we could check the inflow of foreigners. I think we could get on very well without them. In our business the market is glutted. There are more mill-wrights in Warchester than there are mills this side of the Ohio. We have the best craftsmen of Belfast and Manchester, and with these we can educate enough apprentices to carry on all the mechanical trades of the country. I lament the changes wrought in our morals by this influx of foreign peoples, with their curious habits, their lax religions, their noisy merry-making, their Sabbathless weeks. Why, the result is as manifest already in Warchester as the water of the well when the spring freshets come. I remember when there wasn't a liquor-shop inside the corporation; when cider was the strongest beverage known to men of all degrees. Now there are fifty 'saloons' or tap-rooms where alcohol is sold. I remember when man nor beast was seen on the street on Sunday, save at the church-door. Now the streets are a fair on Sunday; the fields along the river are filled with young and old. We have become as godless as a French city. I have been reflecting soberly on the problem, and I want to take further counsel with you before you go back," concluded the city father, looking at his guest with earnest thoughtfulness in his gray eye.

"I'm afraid you'll not get much comfort or food for

your present convictions from me, Warchester," the Governor broke out cheerily. "I believe in the emigrant. God bless us, a hundred years ago we were all emigrants. Suppose the Mohawks had set up the same principle, where would our fine old families be now? No, no; we must welcome cordially the nomad of every land, and give him welcome and the means of enriching himself and us. But there is a broader question involved. This country is, in a certain sense, a refuge for mankind. That the eternal destiny of the race was so ordered, the history of the continent proves. It was reserved by the universal rule of things, until the known world became so crowded, corrupt, and intolerable, that the ways and deeds that heaven orders were lost sight of, and could only be resumed by the vast tranquillity of this virgin continent. Here is a land where the distressed shall come for all time and pitch a tent of peace. No, Warchester, you can't swing back the gates heaven has flung open. The Irish and German customs may not be to our taste, but men are insensibly molded by their surroundings, and you will be surprised to see how soon these strangers conform themselves to such ways of ours as are worth imitation. The children of the present generation will be wholly of us, with no trace of their alien origin in mind or manner."

"But their ways are so abominable," interrupted the young lawyer. "The Irish are such a tipsy, whisky-guzzling lot—never sober, never peaceful; always wrangling, beating their wives, pillaging their homes, and dispersing their families to the common refuge of strangers. The Germans are not so repulsive. They do not ruin their families by drink. But, on the other hand, they drive them brutally to labor, and, as for their wives, they make them bear the burdens of the household and the fields. When I was in Europe I saw German women harnessed

2

to carts with cows, asses, and dogs, and I am constantly expecting to see the same thing here."

"Oh, those are mere phases of certain forms of foreign life, that do not survive long residence in this country. I have no doubt educated Germans or Irishmen would find habits and ways in us quite as repulsive as those you remark, if we were forced to choose our homes at random among the Europeans."

The subject, however, had become much more serious than the company relished, and the young people demanding music, there followed a merry reel, Mrs. Warchester leading off in great splendor with the Governor, who was known "to fling the lightest heel in twenty townships !"

CHAPTER II.

THE CUP THAT CHEERS.

THE prim festivities came to an end at midnight—an hour bordering upon the unseemly, in any other than the grand Warchester mansion, in those times of primitive diversions and Puritan aftermath. In the sallies of the company it was remarked that Marcus Dunn had been curiously reserved for a favored lad of his years. He was known to be a sober youth by habit, and not quite unconstrained in the presence of his aunt. The young damsels, who had looked forward with lively expectation for his return from the East, agreed among themselves that the youth's wits were not so lively as those of his less-favored companions who had ended their schooling in the Warchester Academy. There were significant glances when

Mark, in answer to a question, said, abstractedly, that he was not sure that he should remain in Warchester.

"Ah, Master Mark, your heart used to be here ; surely you have not left it with any of the favored lasses in New York ?" Hapgood said after one of these sallies.

Mistress Warchester, at the head of the table, heard this jest and pursed her thin lips resolutely.

"Boys of Mark's age have other business than thinking of hearts. I hope my sister's son knows the duties that lie ahead of him, before he gives way to follies of that sort ! "

Mark blushed, and his interlocutor shrunk back guiltily, for didn't everybody in Warchester know that four years before Master Mark had been banished to West Point because he had given his boyish heart to pretty Molly Myrickson, the daughter of the rich banker who had begun his career in Warchester in the grimy blacksmith-shop near the Blue Eagle tavern ? Molly's pretty, bright, and roguish eyes had captivated the boy of fifteen, and it was not until they had passed tender words in the cherry-lane behind the Warchester mews that the amour came to the horrified ears of Mistress Warchester. There was a dismal combat between the angry aunt and the quavering boy. He vowed eternal fidelity to the charmer ; but presently the decree came to go to West Point, and he finally succumbed, pledging his honor not to write or in any way renew the courtship until such time as he was his own master. He had cherished the sweet agony during his first years in the Academy ; but evil tidings came that Molly had given her hand to another—the great Lord Poultney—and Marcus retained the sting of the disappointment as well as the bitter-sweet of the first passion— a taste of the fruit of the tree that is not knowledge nor life.

When the guests had gone, the young man found the sleeping-rooms hot and intolerable. He passed out on the veranda, and set off down the dim, deeply shaded roadway. The heavy air swooned with an odorous burden —enervating, soothing. Pygmy armies of fire-flies filled the night like showers of glowing coals on the background of leafy green. The gleaming spray rose and fell before him as he sauntered on, lost in delight. Many of his aunt's guests still lingered in the grounds, and he resolved upon a moonlight ramble if he could get a congenial companion so minded. The dispersing groups wandered streetward, chattering freely of the *fête*, the personages, and the thousand and one trifles that interest womankind —and sometimes mankind, for that matter. The company was made up from what, even in those days, was instinctively regarded as the Court quarter of the town ; for, from the first, Warchester's social demarkations were as distinctly drawn and enforced as the well-born in Bogenberg or De Vereville. Marcus caught the drift of the comments upon Governor Darcy. They were vivaciously condemnatory, and it was generally agreed that the "low social surroundings and common atmosphere" of the "Capital" had obscured Governor Darcy's former fine perceptions. Others again were "surprised" that a woman favored by such rearing as Mrs. Warchester should have set such a feast before young men ! Wine and peach-brandy on the table ! What if it were from the hand of the Washingtons ? Wasn't it well known that George Washington loved the bottle too well ? Hadn't he passed days roistering with my Lord Marquis de Lafayette ? Hadn't he ruined the stock of this country by begging his dear marquis to procure him a brace of jackasses from the king of Spain ? Hadn't he wickedly sent to Malta for these odious beasts and paid as much as a Christian would pay for a house? Worse than this. Hadn't Mrs. Warchester set off an apartment for the men to play and smoke in? What were the God-fearing of Warchester coming to if such European excesses as this were to be encouraged?

Marcus was not edified by the tone the comments began to take, and though he was not fond of his aunt, nor congenial to his uncle, he resented the baseness that made their hospitality the topic of demeaning tattle. But the young fellow really had something else on his mind. The scene at the debarkation of the emigrants haunted him. Indeed, the eyes and form of the martyr-like mother had never quitted him during the week's journey from the sea. He wandered to the wharf, idly wondering if he should find them there.

Meanwhile the personage whose presumptuous humanity had precipitated this discussion was by his conduct amply justifying all the strictures expressed by the severe social Areopagus at the Mayor's mansion. Hugh had put on dry raiment under the friendly shelter of the warehouse as a tireing-room, and in his Sunday corduroys and smart, green frock presented an appearance in sharp contrast to the figure of an hour before.

"Why doesn't me brother James come? He must have got me letther long before this? Sure he knows we don't know where to seek him?" he said, as his wife sat sad-eyed, with the children huddled beside her.

Darkness fell, slowly and softly, on the lonely Aliens after the crowd had gone. The elder children wandered about, lost in wonder at the strange sights of the new city. Hugh strode back and forth, looking impatiently at every one that approached from the street—expecting the brother that was to induct his brood into their new home and eagerly anticipated future. Letters had been dispatched from New York, where the family had been detained, warning the kinsman of the arrival.

James Boyne had given his brother small encouragement to quit his native land; but when he found that it was decided, he wrote to say that he could find work for Hugh, and would prepare a place for the family or give it shelter until a home could be chosen after the mother's own mind. Hugh had set out with high hopes and joyous anticipations of the future for himself and his boys in the new and wonderful land beyond the Western sea. But Kate was sorely against the change. They were happy in the old home. Their stone cottage and well-tilled fields were known throughout the county for thrift and tidiness. Here she had been courted and won, and every furze-bush, every violet in the ditch, and every holly in the hedge, had a tale for her soft eyes that echoed deep into her senses; and now, as the hours passed, and there was no sign of the expected kinsman, anxiety and terror sank deeply into the mother's heart.

"Come, Kate, don't be down-hearted," said the husband, stroking her hair fondly. "Sure there's nothing to fear. It's a fine night, and we may as well be here as anywhere."

"Ah, Hugh, dear, I can't draw a free breath while we're this way. It's a hard, cold country we've come to. Did ye see the woman, when ye handed her the boy? Sure my lady of Louth wouldn't give a navvy a look like it."

"Well, never trouble, Kate, dear: little we care how she looked; we'll never set eyes on her again, praise God! James is kept late at his work, likely. He'll be sure to come, for he knows the ship came in. Luk at the Dutch divil, beyant," he added, jovially. "Be me sowl, he'll have a shebeen over him and a ditch turfed before he's

a week older"; and he burst into a low, frank laugh at
the expense of the guileless Saxon alternating vast whiffs of
smoke with copious drafts of beer, and wedges of black
bread, larded with sticky white cheese.   Soon there was a
bustle in the German group.   A noise of hearty greeting—
much explosive kissing on the part of the men as well as
the women, and presently, with their goods packed on two
large wagons, the fair-haired Saxons drove off, chattering
briskly.   The release of these companions in misery ac-
cented the loneliness of the remaining exiles.   However,
there was nothing to do but await the appearance of the
brother.   As the twilight deepened one of the children was
dispatched to a neighboring grocer's for food, and, when
it came, the table was spread on a large box, the children
gathering around joyously, as though the open air were
their normal state.

The young stars came out in gleaming webs of light
above their heads, as they had never seen them before in
the low horizon of the fatherland; the crescent moon
hung on the deep misty edge of the neighboring hills; the
water plashed murmuringly under the softened outline of
the Rialto; and the lessening bustle of the town sank into
summer-night's silence.   As the moon was obscured behind the hill, a thick, transparent darkness succeeded.
The town was buried in shadows.   Still the brother did
not come.   The children had bestowed themselves on the
soft luggage, and lay in various postures, peacefully sleeping, when ten o'clock tolled from the neighboring steeple.
The mother, dozing fitfully, started as the sound fell on
her ear.   She counted the strokes aloud, and then cried
anxiously:

"Hugh, ye'll do better to get beds in some near public house for th' night; it's clear James'll not be comin' to
us at this hour.   We can search for him th' morrow.   I'm

beat with worry and heart-ache th' night, and I must get rest ! "

Hugh agreed with the suggestion, and went off to get quarters for the homeless brood. The children, meanwhile, with childish adaptability, were sleeping peacefully as the night went on and Hugh didn't come. The bells of the big stone church over among the trees, whence the chief business mart of Warchester has long since driven it, tolled the half hour. The three women clustered in a group, silent and desolate.

"Surely, Nancy, Hugh can't be all this time seeking beds ? Something must have come till him. Oh, sorry's th' day the farm was sold and we come till this cold, cold country ! "

"Keep your heart, Kate, darlin', an' sure it's all rich we'll be afther we're here awhile, an' go back till th' blessed land and live like squireens."

"It's cold comfort to smell the furze on the hedge when yer up till yer neck in the bog, Nancy, dear. Where in th' name o' God can Hugh be ? Oh—sorrow—sorrow th' day we did it—sorrow—sorrow ! "

The babe woke at this, and added its plaintive cry to the woful symphony.

"Larry, boy, do you come with me and we'll see what's happened to dada "; and Nancy, rousing the elder of the boys, set off in the direction the missing parent had gone. Midnight was ringing from the church-tower before the two returned. Nancy was crying softly and Larry was laughing.

"Did ye find him ? What is it ? Speak up ! " cried Kate, starting from a doze.

"O mammy, he's drunk as a lord in the shebeen of Teddy Donigan of Dundaff—that was beyant the hill of Ballinasloe "; and Larry, very much amused at the spectacle he had seen, and won by a bright-hued "stick of sugar candy," felt rather proud than otherwise of the reception the exile had been given by his compatriot.

"Teddy says we're to bring th' childer and stop with him. He has beds enough for all."

"And what's to be done with the boxes and luggage?" asked the mother peevishly. "We'll be robbed out of house and home if we leave them here."

"Mag an' the' byes might stay by them till some of th' men beyant culd come for them," suggested Nancy doubtfully.

"Divil a wan o' me'll stay," interrupted Master Larry promptly.

"Ye'll do as ye're bid, or I'll tell th' father on ye."

"'Twas me da, himself, bid me come back till him," muttered the youngster, skulking behind the boxes.

"Mag, are ye there?" (Mag was a neighbor's daughter, under the care of the Boynes.)

"I am; be me sowl, I was fast asleep as the saints in Wicklow," and Mag, yawning, cheerfully hustled forward, and, being informed of her assignment, assented readily.

"Larry, ye'll stay with— Where are ye, Larry, boy? Larry, I say, d'ye hear me?"

But there was no Larry; and, as the mother began to sob at the disobedience and perversity of her first-born, his brother, who had been aroused by the clamor, came to the mother's side, pulled her skirt to attract her attention, whispering timidly:

"Don't tell dada on him, mother. I'll stay with Mag till they come. That's a good mother; don't cry!"

The babe had been taken by Nancy, and Kate, stooping down on her knees, caught the child passionately to her heart, hugging and moaning convulsively, "Oh, ye are mammy's boy. God—God in heaven bless him, and

God pardon me that I have a heavy heart, when he sent me this child for comfort."

"Sure, it'll be mornin', Kate, if ye don't haste, an' we'll be a show for all th' people!" and Nancy, bending with the babe in her arms, touched the kneeling woman's shoulder. The mother rose, lifting the child with her.

"There, Mag, darlin', keep the childer safe till Teddy Donigan comes fur them."

Nancy led the way, the cross and sleepy girls staggering along the dimly lighted street, for Warchester did not then present the illuminated splendor that may now be traversed for a circumference of five or more miles. The rush of falling waters could be heard as they made their way through the silent street. Turning to the left, Nancy pushed on until at a light shining in a window she stopped.

"Here it is," she said simply, and drew back to give the mother precedence. It was a wooden structure but little less shabby than most of the unpretending edifices that lined the river street of Warchester. Through the thin walls could be heard the jovial chorus of "The Night before Larry was Stretched," scored by emphatic clinking of glasses. Kate, lifting the latch — for there were no knobs in that quarter in those days—entered a large room lighted by candles and thick with smoke. A long table, serving as a bar, occupied the whole side of the room nearest the door. Behind this stood the rosy-faced compatriot who had given Hugh such exuberant welcome.

"And sure it's the wife hersel'!" he exclaimed heartily, coming out from behind the table and taking her hand cordially. "And Kate, dear, yer as bloomin' as th' day I kissed ye, when ye was gatherin' shamrocks in the paddock of Dundare. Well, well, and to say yer th' mother of five fine childer!"

"I've a heavy heart, Teddy. I wish I was back in

Dundare, instead of here. 'Twas a sorry day that I quit it
—a sore day!"

"And is that yer notion? D'ye moind me now: ye'll
not be th' length of yer arm in the land till ye'll love it;
ye'll not know th' people a day till ye'll find thim all as
near ye as Barney Boyne's pigs in Down Patrick sty—that
were so thick, bedad, that th' wan scratched the others'
back and left each other nothing to do but ate. Sore are
ye indeed, Kate, dear? Ye'll not be here a month till yer
that glad that, if th' parish of Dundare was at yer back
dure, ye'll be that proud ye wouldn't dig the praties for
the pigs."

· He laughed and winked in affable comradeship, and
laid his large red hand on the astonished woman's shoulder in the glow of this revived amity.

"Och, indeed, be me sowl, 'tis true for me! It's a foine
land this. Th' money just makes itself, me dear, and
Hugh 'll be as rich as me Lord Louth before ye tache the
wee childer to lisp the spache of the land."

He looked about and winked irrepressible knowingness at this delicate stroke, and, finding Hugh listening,
continued, "It's niver a poteen or praty a mon wants
here. There's niver a mon satisfied till he knows whether
ye have a mouth on ye! Niver a bailiff to whisk th'
leather from yer fut, th' straw from yer flure, or th'
praties from yer pot. Niver a lard to luk big or moind ye
that yer only made from the bogs, while he's of the marble of Dundalk! None to make bastes of th' childer and
drabs of th' wenches! No," added the social student of
international differentiations, as the company acclaimed
these proud periods, "no, bedad, nor a gintry to rid the
rood of ye as the dogs drive the pigs!"

Then, observing that Kate was pulling at Hugh's elbow
and urging him to arouse himself, he added jovially,

"Arrah, let th' lad alone. It's a long day since he sat
down ferninst a friend. He'll be all the better for a wee
spree the first night he puts fut in the place. He won't
be here a year before his chist 'll be as full of gould as
Biddy Maguire's ditches of yellow gorze."

Hugh was wholly overcome. Stretched almost at full
length on two chairs, the rest of the company were clinking glasses above him in a sort of clan rite unknown to
his wife. She strove in wild terror to rescue him from
the maudlin company, but every one joined in friendly
rivalry to "keep the lad a bit to enjoy himself." Unable
to endure the atmosphere longer, and dead with fatigue,
Kate fell upon the floor in a faint. The elder girl
screamed as she saw her mother falling, and the soberest
of the company threw the door back to give air to the
swooning woman. The suppressed cries and movement
of the place arrested the attention of Marcus Dunn, who
was sauntering back from a view of the cataract after he
found the wharf deserted. He hastened over, not altogether certain of the wisdom of entering such questionable
quarters. When he saw the Madonna of the voyage lying
in a swoon, he recognized the need of a cool head, and, lifting the limp figure from the floor, he carried it to the door,
and then, with the aid of hartshorn, soon restored the victim to the miserable consciousness of her surroundings.
As her large eyes rested with a flash of recognition on the
strange face, she murmured :

"No, no, my lord; you can't mean that for the truth
—talkin' to the likes of me."

· "Kate, dear," said the servant Nancy, clasping the
recumbent figure, "sure it isn't Lord Louth at all. It's
a strange gentleman, ye don't know at all, at all !"

With a hasty glance at the interior, where the tipsy
father now lay sprawling on the floor, Marcus Dunn, not

caring, not daring indeed, to await the woman's complete
consciousness, walked away, reflecting bitterly on the significance of the phases of life he had seen since sundown.
The sum of these midnight reveries would not have been
accepted as just or tolerable by the fine company with
whom the young man had spent the evening. But he was
young. He had just passed years of generous emulation
among the opening intellects of youth and in the broader
thoughts of an old community. He had read Rousseau,
studied Jefferson, and was much given to the whimsical
doctrines of the then dominant schools abroad.

As Kate passed back through the stupefying fumes of
the tap-room to her chamber, Hugh was lying prostrate,
half on the floor and half on an overturned chair. He
was babbling incoherently of flowering deeps and the
cresses that grew in the brook of Derrydell, where his
darling Kate had given her pledge across running water,
and he had carried her away from the envious courting of
the young lord of the land. She tried to lift him, to
arouse him, but the orgy had gone too far. Teddy was
outraged by this reflection on his hospitality, and animated
the victim sufficiently to prompt him to put his paternal
mandate upon the mother. Kate remonstrated tearfully,
but the tipsy father, crazed by a tipple new to his palate,
became morosely imperative, and ordered her to take the
"childer" to bed and leave him in peace. She was forced
to stand by helpless and see her weary little ones hilariously toasted and fondled by the reeking bacchanals. Her
weary mind went back to other days and other scenes,
when men made merry, but in no such reprobate uproari-
ousness as this: the memory of gorze-lined ditches and
blooming bogs, where Hugh and she had gathered the
shamrock and woven the primroses in chaplets, where with.
the merry-makers they had danced on the green, kissed

over the All-hallow-een tub, while the pipers piped, and
the lads and lasses tripped in measure over crossed twigs
and under holly bowers. But there was no grog to madden, nor such hideous speech as here. Oh, how she
longed to be back in the dear cottage, with the soothing
ripple of the brook and the children at play !

The next day Hugh was too much prostrated by his
debauch, and too ashamed, to make inquiry for his
brother. But the second day James came himself. He had
been in the country at Millville, and had not received the
letter announcing the arrival of the exiles. He gave them
cold welcome to his own house until they could find one
for themselves; and, with a heart light for the first time
since she had touched the shore of the country, Kate
gathered her little ones and hurried from the dreadful
place identified with Hugh's downfall.

"Darcy must be bent on renomination," said Colonel
Warchester to his neighbor Hapgood, a day or two later,
as they walked homeward from the council-chamber.
"When we went to the mills yesterday he made inquiry
for the hero of that exploit, and left word, if the man
were found before his departure from the city, that he was
to call at the Governor's house. The men gave him a
lusty cheer as the news spread, and I could see that his
long-headed excellency was not dissatisfied with his afternoon's work. Of course the story will spread, and, whether
this particular fellow ever hears of it or not, Darcy has
gained his point."

Dunn heard this version of the Governor's good offices
the same evening, and repelled the insinuation vehemently.

"My father knew Richard Darcy since boyhood, and
he never knew a selfish or unmanly trick in him. I don't
believe the Governor ever thought of self, in seeking to
commend a brave fellow for a brave act well done. But

I tell you what it is, unless you change your methods with these foreigners you will certainly bring about the condition of things you affect to fear. You claim that you resent the intrusion of other nationalities, because they bring débauchery and sink into squalor here. Very well; how can they do anything else when you, the ruling caste, turn your back on them, and actually assign them the same place in the social economy that the Southerners give their slaves? Take one case in point : I was deeply interested in the people surrounding this man for whom Governor Darcy made inquiry. The wife is a woman of the rarest and most exquisite beauty—even under the disadvantages of clumsy drapery, and the disorder of a long sea-voyage. I studied them during the trip from New York; as they straggled on the wharf the day they came ; and by a chance, perplexing as it was disagreeable, I saw them again after midnight in a wretched groggery on River Street, where, owing to the absence of a brother, they had ignorantly taken quarters with a compatriot, not knowing the dubious surroundings or character of the place. Now, if this family is wrecked by the dissoluteness of the father, whose fault is it? Yours and mine. We should have agencies for the protection of these homeless wanderers, which on the arrival of an emigrant vessel should direct and provide until the helpless victims of ignorance and rascality could look about and help themselves."

" I think if we give the creatures work and the protection of our laws, we are doing a great deal more than their conduct or their character, as exhibited from day to day, gives them any right to expect," said the Rev. Dundas Vernon, with a sneer of benignant pity for the error of his friend Dunn; and with that the young man ceased, ashamed of obtruding his opinion where it was so obviously unwelcome.

Weeks later, Dunn, passing down River Street, in the early dusk, stopped with some curiosity before Teddy's "shebeen." A rollicking chorus could be heard from the inner room, and an occasional clatter of heels keeping time. He was turning away, when two figures came into the doorway. Even in the twilight he could not mistake the supple grace, the meek dignity of the emigrant woman. The man was hardly recognizable. His open, frank countenance was swollen and bloated ; he swayed uneasily as he walked and clutched at every available object, as if to brace himself against further advance. Dunn heard the soft voice pleading ; then the tearful urging turned to gentle force. But, when the two had gone a few steps from the doorway, a leering Silenus thrust his head out, and, spying the two figures making away, shouted :

"Hi, byes, luk at this. There's Joan scuttling off wid Darby at her tail, and divil a drop in the kittle at home. I say, Hugh, dear, is it hot wather or holy wather that puts the cock's comb on the hen ?"

A shout of hiccoughy laughter followed this sally. Hugh turned unsteadily, looked at the speaker, then down at the slight figure of his wife.

"Don't ye see yer makin' a show o' me, Kate ? Leave me, I say, and go home ; go home, d'ye hear me, ye drab, go home!" But she clung the more desperate, murmuring piteously ; he shook her off roughly, and made a plunge for the doorway, where the outlines of a dozen leering faces could be seen framed by the green posts. In an instant she was before him with her two arms about his neck, pleading. He thrust her off again, and, as she made a dart to return, he raised his mighty fist. Even the dazed intellects in the doorway were aroused by this piteous little tragedy. She fell prone to the jagged curb, the blood streaming from her mouth. A second time Dunn's arms supported the miserable woman; a second time her tremulous breath mingled with the hot rage and impatience of his own. The crowd, attracted by the fall, brought a constable from the neighboring fire-engine house, and the husband, moodily out of view of the prostrate victim, was arrested and hurried away to the lock-up. Finding that the family were housed some distance away, Dunn aided Kate to a neighboring apothecary's, where her wounds were washed. She cowered in sobbing anguish until told to get up and go home. She never raised her eyes, but arose meekly to do as she was bid.

At the door she did not recognize who took her hand, or how she got into a carriage that was waiting. Even the novelty of riding for the first time in a hackney-coach did not rouse her from the lethargy. She never looked at the young man who sat silently in the seat before her. Presently the carriage stopped before a square cottage, sitting far back in a trim fruit-garden. Dunn opened the door, got out, and stood waiting. She never stirred, but sat quite collapsed in the corner, moving her hands as if counting.

"Come," he said gently—"come, Mrs. Boyne; your children are at the window waiting for you."

She never moved; she didn't even seem to hear. Dunn turned in perplexity to the driver, and asked him to go to the house and bring the youngest son, Denny, to his mother. He had remarked the mother's fondness for this child, and he rightly judged that if anything would rouse her from her stupor it would be the prattle of the boy. When the little man came shrinkingly, he could hardly be induced to get into the carriage, but, seeing his mother, he was in her bosom in an instant. She started, wearily, pushing him from her, and then looking about her astonishedly.

"Where in the world are we, Denny, dear? Is it in Dundare, and is this Lord Louth's coach that he promised me when—when—" Her voice fell, and she looked in startled surprise at the child.

"No, mammy, we're here at Uncle James's, and you must come to the house."

He led her out—led her past her benefactor, of whose presence she was as oblivious as she seemed to be of every contemporary thing. In an instant the door closed upon mother and child. Dunn paid the coachman, and slowly betook himself cityward, filled with reflections that he would hardly have cared to define. He was obviously less puzzled than indignant with himself in his inextinguishable compassion for and interest in this hapless mother, whose fate it needed no prophetic vision to foretell. To say that the angelic endurance and serene beauty haunted him would be but a poor statement of the fact. Her fate and the destruction of her family dwelt with him with a baleful pertinacity that would have driven him mad had he not relinquished his place in the law-office that he had just come to fill.

The face of the woful mother haunted him. He couldn't understand it. There was no possibility of the love that makes men mad. Could it be that he, a lad barely twenty, loved and longed for the mother of a family of children? But what was the restless longing to see her—to guard her against the wretchedness that must inevitably fall to her lot in the condition her husband held her? He was a "most sober mind," as his uncle often described him, this sage Marcus Dunn, but there was surprising fire in his eye and swift action in his young limbs when he thought on the "Murillo mother," as he insisted on calling the helpless Kate.

She, poor thing, falling deeper and deeper under the

burden of her poignant woe day by day, never even saw
the shy benefactor that in many a way spared the mother
afflictions, until his very goodness became a danger, for the
malicious made a mock of the "gentleman's" solicitude
for the drunkard's wife.   Then he realized the madness
of the feeling gnawing in his heart, and he resolved to fly
—as many a wiser never had the constancy to do.

He arranged to travel for a time; and, when the Governor returned to the capital, Marcus Dunn accompanied
him.   He put the sea between him and the haunting face:
but he saw it in the galleries of the Louvre; he saw it
among the orange-groves of Seville, where Murillo had
found and loved and painted it; he saw it on the purple
hills of Sorrento ; he saw it by day and by night.

At first he had been filled with a sense of triumph over
temptation resisted ; then, as the months changed into
years, his mind insensibly shifted the conditions, and he
saw his flight a shameful cowardice, an ignoble surrender
to airy specters, that no man of resolution would heed.
Then he conjured the wretched family.   The father, with
the guardian-spirit of self-respect stifled by the disgrace
of prison, lower and lower deeps, until death in the gutter
ends the woful history.   And she ?   What of her, with
her radiant beauty and child-like ignorance of the world
and its ways ?

CHAPTER III.

THE DREGS OF THE FLACON.

It will, I own, be mostly my fault if "grandeur hear
with a disdainful smile the short and simple annals" of
these poor personages.   Even so plain a man as Carlyle

loved better to tell the story of a Frederick the Great,
Marie Antoinette, or the kingly in letters, than the pathetic vicissitudes of a Rousseau, a Marat, or a Bunyan.
Purple and gold make us so much more human, so much
more engaging, so much more worth one's while reading about! However, it is not my business to rail at
the world or its worldliness here; there seems to me so
much that illustrates the human heart, in some of its most
trying perplexities, in the destiny of these Alien people,
that I can not resist the impulse to portray the pathetic
incidents of the old-time tragedy. A race transplants its
virtues, as well as its vices, to a new soil, and it depends on the conditions that surround their growth whether
it be the virtues or vices that flourish—whether it be the
worst or the fittest that survives.

Within a week of his arrival on the Rialto, the Saxon
Ritter, the Boynes' fellow-emigrant on the Red Jacket,
was lodged in a tidy tenement in a part of the city that
was known in those days as "Dutchtown." The children old enough to swing their arms were in the cotton-
factory, which, even at this early day, was one of the
wonders of Warchester. The father was at once taken
into a brewery—a modest beginning of those vast edifices
which now make Warchester the Munich, Pilsen, or Stras-
burg of America. The first floor of the house was given
up to a beer-counter, where the old friends and neighbors
of the new-comers gathered of an evening to revive the
pleasant amities of the fatherland, Frau Ritter dispensing
the cheese and pretzels with a thrifty eye to her small
profits. Oswald and Ruprecht, the boys, were already at
task on English grammar, which they studied at their
work and in the long evenings at home. There was no
sense of expatriation in the burden of their new life.
They had merely changed one field of thrift for a kinder

one. The roof that covered them was better, and the advantages ready at hand were greater, than they could have gained by a life-time in the crowded Meissen village they had quit on the tranquil banks of the Elbe. Instead of black bread and blood-sausage, they might now have flour and beef; the mother and little ones, instead of dragging a cart, harnessed side by side with a mastiff, might now on small capital reap such profits as were only known to the rich and favored in their Saxon home. Fuel which had at Meissen been gathered twig by twig, carried on bended back for miles over the hills, might here be picked up free, or got for so little that winter was no terror to the homestead. *Heimweh*, that palsy of nerve and muscle, they never knew. All was Arcadian in this new land, for plenty smiled on every hand. Here the fields were greener, the skies bluer, and the air clearer, than in the Valley of the Elbe, buried from October to May in cold fogs and chilly blasts. Then the reality of prospering obliterated all regret, if they ever had any, for the breaking up of old associations. Here they were part of the activities of society —social and political ; at home, helots, not even equal in the common law of conscription. Here already the vote of Herr Hans Ritter was carefully recorded by the German leader, who had his naturalization papers in their first stage the day after the family arrived. This alone gave the family a sense of personality never before felt. In a few years they too would be of the gentility, the rulers of this rich land ! Servile, with a servility born in the bone and bred in the long life of emphasized class distinction, they turned as naturally to the ruling party as the Puritan to the Church when arriving in New England. The revolutionary spirit which had arrayed the Prussian and Baden Burschenschaften, a few years later, against the German despots, had not penetrated the Saxon valleys. There divine right was as implicit a creed among the poor as it was a tenacious doctrine among the rich. The Ritters had changed locality, not nationality; the power that ruled in the new *Landschaft* might not be *König* or *Kaiser*, but the essence was the same—a divine thing to be spoken of with awe, implicitly adored and unquestioningly obeyed. Housed in walls of fragrant pine, sleeping on straw or husk mattresses, the memory of the rough-plastered stones, the brick-tiled floors, and prison-windows of their Saxon home, was one they looked back upon without regret.

But the other family, that had been the companions of their long journey from Liverpool on the sailing-vessel, and then on the canal-packet to Warchester, did not find such circumstances of happy assimilation. The evil planet that arose in Hugh Boyne's destiny was at its apogee when his brother's absence from town that night of the family's coming made him a prey to the convivial assiduities of his compatriot.

The Celt has the vanity of the Gaul: he loves to love, he loves to be loved; he loves to admire, and he loves to be admired. He loves to be praised, first for his wit, if he have any—if not, for his strength; if he have neither of these, then for his fidelity, piety, or any of the more admirable traits that come from the heart. But if he have none of these, no mental or moral pre-eminence, he is apt to abandon himself with imbecile improvidence to any dullard temptation. He riots in the excess of weakness. Refused the lead in admirable traits, he must be the intrepid law-breaker. He must shame the Ashantee in moral squalor when there is no play in his wit that extracts praise. Tiger and monkey, Voltaire called his countrymen, the Gaul. Abdiel and Hecate, the Celt might be summed up. None so faithful when trust is given them; none so rancorous when doubt is instilled.

Hugh Boyne missed the Abdiel *rôle* by the merest chance. Had Governor Darcy's kindly inquiry for him come to the alien's ears ; had he heard that the Governor of the State had come into the mill to ask for him—Hugh Boyne—he would have found a way—frail it might be as the Moslem's Al Sirat—a way of light and faith to the destiny he was fitted for. Had any one—had James, who knew of it—but told Hugh that Governor Darcy, before the whole mill, had praised the brave fellow and promised him his countenance and protection, one man would have been spared a life of regretful misery, and many innocent souls saved such sorrow as it tears the heart-strings to retell.

James, through jealousy, neglected to tell his brother ; and, the men, through ignorance or indifference, never took the trouble to hunt up the new-comer ; and Hugh, burning with the shame of a detention in the city prison, avoided the sight of those who knew him. When he found himself in the gaol, after that melancholy scene at Donigan's, he was too much humiliated to go home. He resolved to quit the city—to seek a farm far away in the country, settle the family, and send the children to school. He still had four hundred pounds of the five hundred he had when setting out from Belfast.

That was enough to make payment on a modest place, and, far from the haunts of the deluding companions of his past excesses, he would grow up, as his father had done, a man of repute in his neighborhood. But the money was in his brother's chest at his house. If he went there he should see Kate, and he wasn't able to face her without breaking down, and if he broke down he knew that he would fly to the bottle. He wandered aimlessly through the streets, not knowing what to do.

It was noontime, and the men were hurrying homeward

from the mills. A coherent plan worked through his bewildered brain. James, his brother, would be going home to dinner presently. He would get him to fetch the money. He walked along more briskly now; but as he saw his brother, he lost some of his confidence. James was his senior by six or seven years. He had warned him sternly against his late misdeeds, and, as he came up now, the glance he bestowed upon the prodigal did not encourage any effusive confidences. Before he could frame a phrase to pave the way to his object, James said, without halting in his swift stride, which obliged Hugh to move so quickly as to disconcert his already feeble purpose:

"Kate's dying. I suppose you know. It'll be small loss, but you've no call to make a show of us all."

The eyes of the brothers met; Hugh stretched out his mighty arm and stopped the other as though he had been a child.

"Dying, James? Kate? What do ye mean? Ye've not been hard with the ‿poor girl for what's past? Ye don't bear a grudge for the old quarrel?"

"I mean just that. I suppose she's dying. She came home yesterday in a hack and went to bed. She was in a fever all night, and was worse this morning when I came away. Why don't you come and see for yourself how she is? Shut your mouth about the past. She made her bed; what's it to me whether she likes it or not?"

The two resumed the rapid stride the sudden announcement had interrupted, and in a few minutes they were at the house. Kate was very low. The doctor prescribed quiet, and forbade the intrusion of any one in the invalid's room, outside of the person who attended her. She must, as much as possible, be kept from seeing any one who would bring up the immediate past, until the unsettled mind was stronger.

"Unsettled!" Hugh echoed, gasping. "Is she mad, doctor, dear?"

"No, she is not mad; but she might easily be made so. She has been in great trouble; of what nature you of course know. If it recurs she will be a raving maniac, and will have to go to the asylum."

Hugh sank into a seat, and, burying his head in his hands, sat stolidly in the same place from noon till nightfall. When James came home, his heart relented, and he urged the unhappy man to cheer up. After supper he took down his fiddle and, going into the garden, played the songs they used to love in their old home. The children stole out and formed a group about them, and for a time Hugh forgot his guilt and the victim of his weakness lying in the room beyond.

Kate's critical condition lasted a month. The instant that Hugh learned that she was out of danger he asked James for the balance of the money, and explained his purpose to go at once to the country.

"You will do better to put it in the bank," said the prudent senior, "and if you find a farm that suits you, send for the money. It's dangerous to carry such sums about on you."

"There isn't much danger for me," said Hugh, stretching out his sledge-like arm. "It'll be a bowld man that'll run agin that."

In the end Hugh set out with the money. He meant to strike for the rich country south of the city. On his road he passed the Rialto wharf. A packet had just drawn up, and recalling his own melancholy plight on the same spot months before, Hugh stopped a moment to look at the immigrants. With a cry of surprise he recognized a townsman, and running down brought joy to the poor soul. The young man had a letter to Teddy Donigan, who was

3

a relative by marriage; could Hugh show him Donigan's place? Hugh, in the joy of a kind turn, could and did.

It was a fortnight later when Hugh found himself in a condition to think. He was in the same confinement that had brought him to himself before. This time he had been thrust in durance for a more serious offense. He had half killed Teddy Donigan, whom he accused of robbing him of nearly four hundred pounds sterling. Teddy didn't die, and, as no one appeared to prosecute, Hugh was set at liberty. Then James heard of him off on the canal; then he had been seen with a party going to the southward from the nearest lake port. Then all trace was lost.

Kate recovered health, but I doubt if her reason ever resumed its clear play. So soon as Hugh had disappeared James made Kate understand that he could not keep such a houseful about him. He was willing to retain the second girl, Agnes, as housekeeper, but the rest must shift for themselves; useless to ask what she was to do in a strange land, among a stranger people, many of whom regarded the Irish as a race of helots, hardly to be trusted to hew the wood and draw the water that this superior civilization made use of; she was ignorant of their household ways, their internal methods; useless to point out the dependence of her little boys and girls.

She pled all this, and she pleaded in vain. There was fierce rancor in James Boyne's heart. Hugh had been the indulged darling of the family. It was he who was favored of the lasses in the dances and merry-makings on the green and under the hawthorn. He, the elder, was asked to fiddle while Hugh whirled the girls in the dance. It was for Hugh that Kate Claymore had rejected his own long-cherished love — scornfully he thought — and the memory rankled deeper than the prick of all the thorns in his lonely and loveless life. Kate, too, was a Catholic of the hated Stuart line, and she had turned Hugh into half-hearted devotion to the sober creed of the Boynes.

She was an evil breed of evil blood. Her great-grandfather had been driven from France in '93 for his popish faith. Why should a Boyne stretch out his hand when the curse of Heaven was so plainly working vengeance? She had brought the hated creed into the breed of the Covenanters; and, now that Hugh had forsworn her, why should he impoverish himself to stay the ruin that must come sooner or later? He was doing more than most kinsmen in keeping the younger children until they could work into homes of their own. But deeper than all this lay a reason that James Boyne would hardly own to his conscience. Hugh was far cleverer in mind and ways. He had been rated a first-rate mill-wright in Belfast, and if he should return and come under the notice of Governor Darcy—who had spoken of him before all the men in the mill—how soon would it be before Hugh leaped into the place of foreman over James's head?

When bidden to prepare to go, Kate didn't in the least comprehend that James was serious. Hugh would soon come back and provide a home.

Until then surely James could not be in earnest in asking her to seek a refuge elsewhere, without means and without power of earning her bread? She dimly suspected the possibility of his rancor, for she had been repelled in the days of his wooing by something sinisterly selfish in his somber moods and acrid criticisms of more favored lads, but she did not suspect the vigor of his prejudices or the implacability of his hate. She could not ignore the fact that he had never welcomed her cordially, but he couldn't mean to turn her out destitute while she waited to hear from her people at home and from the absent husband. Oh, no, such odious cruelty could not happen between kin. In this miserable uncertainty a month passed. One night, James, calling Kate aside, asked harshly :

"When are you going?"

"Going where, James?" asked Kate, not for the moment understanding.

"To the devil, for all I care, but go you must from this house. To-morrow I will call in the constable and have your duds set in the street. Now do as you like. This is no poor-house."

He was harsh as his word, cruel as it was. The constable came in promptly after the noon meal; Kate's belongings were pointed out, and the family impedimenta set on the edge of the sidewalk. The wretched mother sat supine, bewildered, incapable of realizing her woful plight. When the luggage had been carried out to the last box, the constable touched Kate on the shoulder and pointed to the open garden-gate. She rose humbly, Denny in her arms, and, without a word, walked firmly to a chest on the edge of the curb, where she sat down, looking wistfully at Larry, who stood frightened and uncertain in the doorway. The girls, too young to comprehend, stood in awe-struck silence. Nancy, the children's nurse, had taken a place in another family, and the mother sat in the street, homeless, helpless, friendless. Deaf to the reproaches of his neighbors, callous to the spectacle of the mother's misery, the harsh kinsman sat at the window as darkness fell, unrelenting. The outcasts would have passed the night in the open air if an indignant neighbor had not compassionately thrown his hearth-stone open to the mother and her brood.

Through the endeavors of this Samaritan a small house was found, and the landlord induced to postpone the rent for a time, until the mother could look about her. Kate summoned fitful energy. She was a fair musician. She had been carefully trained in the Belfast Latin School, and was able to teach ordinary branches. In a few weeks she had a class of children, and the future seemed secure when, one luckless day, an inquisitive parent, lingering about the window, heard Kate expounding tales from Irish history to the small disciples. To the dismay of the mother the Irish rebellion was made to appear the work of patriots, the English were represented as butchers, robbers, and tyrants, who had pillaged the land for centuries! Heresy of this sort, in a community that boasted of the directness of its descent from the Englishry, was more than enough to ruin Kate's venture. The children were at once withdrawn from the school, and the only resource left was sewing. Kate was an accomplished seamstress, but no one who could afford sewing in the town would consent to have it done by such a heresiarch as the misguided Irishwoman!

Then followed miserable months of harder and harder effort. One by one her children were taken away until Denny alone remained. The youngest child, in the dead of the long cruel winter, dropped its emaciated body into a pauper grave, unmarked and unrecorded.

The mother and Denny were taken from the frozen walls, where Death hovered expectantly, and were carried to the almshouse. Kate was placed in the rude hospital, where she hovered on the verge of madness, until the soft odors of the lilacs and the fragrance of the May air lulled the wild blood into tranquil enjoyment of the lovely days and nights of spring. With restored mind began keen solicitude for her children. Larry, Mabel, Agnes, Norah, where were they? Dead? No, she knew that only the baby Bessy had died.

Even Denny was not at her side in her convalescence. He had been placed in the overseer's family to play with a little fellow of his own age. For a time they refused to let the child be with his mother. It was only when Kate made plain her determination to leap from the window that the boy was restored to her. Then she began to inquire for the others, but was met by evasive and disingenuous answers. She listened with dreamy, dilating eyes to the stereotyped phraseology of the guardians of the establishment, who read to her the transactions concerning the disposal of her flesh and blood. She merely asked to look at the book when the reading was finished. She made a mental note of the names of the families into which her children had been adopted, and thenceforth spoke no more of the matter.

Finally, pronounced sane in mind and restored in body, she took Denny by the hand and began the world anew, simply equipped as Tubal in his quest, moneyless, friendless, helpless. She found herself on the highway, lulled by the sensuous summer sounds, joyous in the shrill carols of the madcap birds. One thought, haunting, burning, vivid, sustaining, lighted the dark recesses of hallucination that rose and fell with her hopes and fears.

Her children—her helpless darlings were the current of her thoughts—motherless. What were food and drink and raiment to them while the mother's heart was not beating near them? She would gather her darlings about her and make her way over land and sea to her father's house, where she had been the indulged, caressed darling —where, on Halloween, she had been queen for all the lads and lasses of leafy Dundare. But she must keep this holy mission a secret. Even the small Denny must not know it, for in his joy he would blab it to the birds, and didn't everybody know that what the birds knew the world knew? So the pathetic secret was locked in her own troubled breast unutterably, and the fateful quest was

begun in faith so touching, so confident, that I am convinced of the clairvoyance of unsettled intellects, and I
think it was the dim perception of this that gives to the
mad recognition as seers and prophets among the more
searching intellects of the Oriental races.

CHAPTER IV.

NIOBE.

OUT of the charnel-house, and on the highway to Warchester, Kate stopped to take her bearings. The city lay
two miles distant over the hills. There were some of her
darlings there. She would see them first. The resolution
gave her strength. The delicious softness of the green
sod made walking seem flying for a time. The atmosphere
was intoxicating. The air was a vision of paradise with
flitting butterflies, darting wrens, cooing doves, and piping
robins. Her mind was far away. She saw the white blossoms of her father's hawthorns ; she heard the lark over
the primrose spring ; she saw the stalwart lover leaping
the hedges that separated the farms ; she saw herself a
wife at sixteen—at twenty-six a widow, or worse. Before
she reached the city limits her strength failed her. She
was forced to sit down and rest ; but the longer she sat
the more incapable she felt of resuming her journey. A
farmer driving city-ward stopped to ask a question. Denny ran in alarm to his mother. She answered faintly that
she didn't know, and her voice prompted the man to invite her to get up in the wagon. He kindly aided her to
mount, and made a reclining place for her on bags of oats

he was taking to mill. He stopped within a few squares of James's house. Larry, who was playing in the garden, recognized his mother before she opened the gate. Running toward her he closed it, and, standing on the inside, said, in an eager, shamefaced way:

"Uncle says you're not to be let in. That if you come about here he will turn me away!"

Kate looked at her son in a coaxing, yearning incredulity. She had to bend down to catch his eye through the slats, and the boy started back as if she were about to seize him. But she was only looking at the little ingrate, and whispering to herself, "Larry, Larry"—she had dropped on her knees outside the fence—"Larry, do you know me? I'm your mother, child. I—I—O my God, my God, my God—I'm mad!"

Denny at this began to sob in quick gasps. That restored her in an instant. Soothing him in her arms, and rocking back and forth, she, relapsed into silence. Larry skurried off sidewise toward the house, now and then casting back an eye to see if the interdicted mother were following. But the dark group remained discernible through the slats until he had summoned the inmates of the house to testify to his obedience to his uncle's orders. Hours passed, and the mournful mother held the post by the gate. People passing thought the poor woman resting. James Boyne presently came along, and was quite upon the crouching figures before he noticed them. He started, but, recognizing the mother and child, harshly bade the woman get up and begone.

She arose slowly, helping herself by the slats, hugged the little Denny to her breast, and, without a word, stepped firmly away, looking straight before her. That night she slept on the common, near the river, and in the morning bathed the child in the limpid stream. Water-cresses grew plentifully at the edge of the merry brook. These she picked, and, washing them in the water, ate and gave to Denny. But the child could not eat them, and she cast about for something more nutritious. A lad came along singing, with a steaming pail of milk, the fluffy foam dripping over its edges. Denny eyed it hungrily. Kate felt in her ears, on her breast : for the first time she seemed to miss her simple jewelry, which had gone months before. She looked longingly at the milk, then at her wedding-ring. Slipping it off she held it up to the boy, saying, hoarsely :

" Give my little boy some of your milk, there's a darling. I have no money, but you can get what the milk's worth from this and give me the rest."

"Oh, pshaw ! I don't want your ring, missis. I guess you can have all the milk that cub'll drink. Here, fire away, buster," and, relishing his facetious readiness of wit, the youth held the pail to Denny's frankly longing lips.

"Have some?" he said, proffering the pail to the mother, as the child's small need was supplied. Kate looked longingly at the milk, then at the boy, and shook her head.

" Just as well have a swig as not. Milk ain't much account now; every one has a cow, and no one buys."

Kate allowed herself to be persuaded by this specious reasoning, but suspected that he was giving them the milk through pity. He went off whistling cheerily, and Denny, enlivened by the example, began to run in chase of a swarm of yellow butterflies. Near noon Kate made her way again toward the house of her kinsman. Instead of going to the front gate this time, however, she put Denny over the fence and clambered over after him, near the house. She opened the door and walked into the living-room. A strange young woman, engaged in some household service, started up with a scream.

"Where is Agnes?"

"Lord, ma'am, she's not been here for many a day."

"Where is she?"

"I can't justly say, but I think it is in Holly Hill, a great house near the river."

"And who are you?"

"I am James Boyne's wife; we were married in April," said the young woman, suspiciously, beginning to comprehend who her interlocutor was. With this evidence of recognition Kate turned, quit the room, and went in search of Larry. She was tired and Denny was heavy. She set him down on the door-step and called her elder son. She went in search of him about the neighborhood, but the boy was not to be seen. Returning to the steps to get Denny, she saw her brother-in-law, James, hurrying up the path and into the house. She hastened her step to get the child, when suddenly her kinsman appeared in the doorway with a heavy double-barreled rifle in his hand.

"Now, you crazy devil, if you don't get out of this, and keep out, I will shoot you down like a dog."

He raised the piece to his shoulder and pointed it over the head of the child, which sat between them on the steps, at the mother advancing in the walk. She never made a cry, but with her eyes wide open, shining with the gleam of madness, she advanced to the very muzzle of the gun, stooped and picked up the child, and then, with a wild cry, fled, fled, fled, until she fell lifeless under the very feet of a horse driven by the doctor who had attended her in her first attack.

Then the tragedy deepened. The miserable mother was found irreclaimably insane. She was separated from her boy and confined in an asylum. The child was sent to the Home for Homeless Boys. In the asylum the mother was ironed, to keep her amenable to the regulations. She was perfectly quiet save when the officious agents of the institution willfully plagued her with tales of the death of her children. Then she broke into fury, and the tortures invented by the crude science of that time to allay the afflictions of the mind were applied with remorseless vigor, the agents apparently delighting in the experience and practice their malignancy secured them.

It was fully a year later when Kate, more Madonna-like than the day she stepped out at the Rialto, was transferred to the convalescent chamber. Here all the cunning of insanity came to her aid, and one morning she was gone when the doctor came to make an examination. How she ever learned the whereabouts of the boy no one knew; but one afternoon Denny, walking with his little fellows in the street, saw his mother beckoning him from the covert of a rose-bush. He ran to her, the guardians in full chase after him. They were separated, the mother following the child with moans of anguish to the Home door. Poor thing, perfectly ignorant as to forms, regulations, and the laws of the Home, she hadn't the remotest idea how the child could be obtained, seen, or communicated with. But she resolved doggedly not to quit the place so long as he was there.

How she ate and slept an all-knowing Power alone can tell. Denny saw her from his dormer-window one morning, standing under a leafy maple, before the sun was up, gazing wistfully toward his prison. He slipped out as the scullions were cleaning the kitchen utensils, and, crawling into an empty barrel in the grocer's cart, was jolted out into the lane behind the brick walls. The driver stopping to fasten the gate, the child leaped out and ran to his mother, whom he felt sure of finding under

the trees. Sure enough she was waiting, and there was
no surprise in her joy at seeing him. In her school she
had shown the girls how to make Irish lace—in which she
was deft and nimble. Whenever she could submit to re-
straint, she was welcomed in rich farm-houses to teach the
girls and work on these coveted housewife fabrics. But
the longing for her children, and the sleepless suspicion of
the stranger drove her forth at the end of a few weeks,
leaving no token with her wondering hosts to account for
her flight.

Wrapping her darling Denny under her shawl, she fled
to the open fields. How she supported life during these
vague intervals of time was never known. She was found
always where the farm-lands sloped into green dells with
running water. Here she seemed absolutely without care.
Decking Denny with the flowers of the hedges, she sat
by the water-side for hours, the child playing contentedly
with the pebbles, the frogs, or any animate thing or inanimate thing; for birds or beasts, kine or whatsoever living
thing came to know these woful intruders, had no fear
of them. Kate's wavering sanity had become a subtle
power. She knew she was not in her sane senses; she
doggedly refused to think, lest she should lose the only
weapon left the bereaved—cunning. With infinite adroitness she fabricated reasons to the not over-inquisitive
world she encountered in her rambles. But this nomad
life covered an inextinguishable purpose. She would keep
on wandering through the pleasant country roads, sleeping in the hay-fields, and lurking where the berries grew
or accept hospitable proffers in the farm-houses, until she
had gathered all her lost brood.

One sunny morning, when the birds seemed mad with
joy and the wheat stood sheaved in tasseled cones through
the fields, Kate, turning out of the high-road, came upon

a gate leading to an affluent farm-house. Children came
down the lane shouting at the cows, as the tramp leaned
wearily against the fence. She inquired the name of the
owners, and, on hearing "Dr. Marbury," she set Denny
on the ground and led him by the hand, flying with eager
steps toward the comfortable porch. As she passed from
the small gate up the path, a little girl, perhaps nine years
old, came out of the rear door, going toward a small stone
building between the house and the lane. Kate gave a
great sobbing cry when she saw the child. She was carrying a large wooden dish with a gleaming pat of butter in
the center. Startled by the cry, she turned, and, catching
sight of the wild, strange figure, halted and let the dish
fall to the ground.

"O Norah—Norah—my darling! Come to me, Norah! It's your mother!"

For an instant the child's eyes dilated in wonder, and
then lighted in gladness, as she saw Denny smiling at her.

She flung herself, sobbing, into the mother's arms. It
was in this tender plight a tall, severely prim matron presently, coming hastily from the house, discovered them.
Norah timorously explained that it was her mother, and
the wanderers were kindly taken in, bathed, and fed, and
a family council was held as to the future of the mother.
But in proportion as the solicitude of the good family increased, the terror of the mad woman grew. In spite of
all urging to remain until something could be devised,
Kate quit the house the following morning before the
Doctor had returned from consulting a neighbor in her
behalf. She fled down the lane, and, coming to the uttermost verge of the Marbury estate, halted, stripped her
body of a new gown forced upon her by Norah's kind
patron, threw it far over into the masses of still uncut
wheat, and, resuming her frayed gown, took up her march

to find her other children. She believed, in a wild, unreasoning way that the Doctor had bewitched Norah, as the child broke into wild sobs when the crazed mother urged her to fly and live the nomad life of herself and Denny. The gown, she felt, desecrated her. What she meant to do when she had gained knowledge of all their whereabouts, Denny never knew. She confided most of her mad projects to her little confidant ; but when in later years he strove to recall her purpose, he found that she had no definite plan.

Before the gold-dust of autumn had powdered the green tresses of summer, Kate's quest brought her to her youngest daughter but one, Agnes. She was but five when the family was broken up, and her uncle James had given her in adoption to one of the great families of Warchester. She lived at first as a dependent, then as a daughter of the house. Her family name was dropped ; indeed, it is doubtful if her new family knew it, and the little Agnes had but the vaguest recollection of any other than the luxurious life in which she was now growing. It was on the edge of Warchester that Kate came upon a group of children in a merry picnic. Agnes was among them, and the mother, with a delirious cry, rushed at her and clasped the little one to her heart. But the child struggled and screamed. The governess haughtily waved the mother back, and threatened to send for help if she did not go away. Agnes looked at her mother with cold, unrecognizing eyes.

Whether she recalled her or not, I can't say. It is not unlikely that she dimly remembered the past. Images fade in some young minds completely, while others retain infantile pictures to old age. The wretched mother brought back, if she recalled the kinship at all, misery, unrest, and squalor. But to the mother there was only one hideous reality, that drove the blood back to her heart and threw a blinding mist into the feeble processes of her brain. Her child—her darling, brought to a child's most lovely age in sore travail—refused her; refused a mother burdened with cruel woes and undeserved misfortunes. Ah, it was too much. God was not good. He should have spared her this bitter, bitter bruise.

Denny never knew distinctly what the fortunes of his mother were during the days and months that followed this miserable scene. He recalled in after days that she seemed to fade fitfully out of his troubled life, and that he was very unhappy in a great red brick farm-house where noisy overgrown boys and coarse girls beat him and reviled him. The elders were morose and stern. Then he recalled the slow growth of a terrible resolution, and the infantile art with which it was carried into execution—to run away and find his mother, who was always present to the sight of his mind, hovering by running water or weaving nosegays under the wild crab-apples.

He fled back to the mad-house, where something told him he should find the lost mother. He never afterward forgot the wasted face of the mad woman he found cowering in one of the maniac wards. Her lustrous auburn hair had faded to a subdued dead-gold hue; the large eyes were still clear and most wonderful—untroubled. She was thirty now—a vision as fair in maturity as she must have been when as a maid she stood before the altar. The little boy fled to her with rapture, and the attendants, who had before found her irritable and unmanageable, were astonished at the transformation wrought by the child's presence. The paroxysm of tears seemed to clear the confusion of the brain. The mad woman met the officials as tranquilly thereafter as though her brain had never been touched. Again she was enlarged from durance; again the old nomad life began. But the end was near. The craving to see her children drove her in quest of Mabel, the elder of the three girls. She found her at last, after such persistency as would have disheartened a Hindoo devotee.

When Uncle James married he had put away the last of the "tribe," as he said grimly to his wife. One of the rich mill-owners had lost a girl about Mabel's age, and, seeing the child one day bringing James Boyne's dinner to the mill, he had taken a strong liking for her, and in the end asked the kinsman to give her to him in adoption. He was a man of strong prejudices, holding the Irish in the loathing and hatred he had learned in his childhood, in Londonderry, where once a year the alien English celebrate the conquest of the hated Celts. Mabel was taught to detest anything bearing the Irish name, and warned that the recognition of any tie with her kin would end in her expulsion from a home of plenty. She shared the education of the sons of the house, and was in all respects treated like one of them. As she was returning joyously one day from the fashionable select school in Warchester, Kate saw and recognized her lost darling, her first-born. With a great cry of thanksgiving and rapture, she flung herself on the startled girl.

"My Mabel, my darling—"

But the mother's rapture was not returned. The girl, large for her age—she was nearly fourteen—disengaged the clinging arms, uttering a little shuddering cry the while, drew herself back, blushing crimson as her girl friends looked on in astonishment. Denny toddled up to her and caught her hand. She pushed both mother and child from her with the air of a person who has been mistaken for another.

"Why, Mab, who is it?" exclaimed her friends. "Any one you know?"

The girl looked resolutely into the face of the other, half laughed as she said:

"Yes, it is a crazy woman I used to know when I was a little girl."

"Poor thing! perhaps she's hungry; let us give her some pennies."

A small sum was made up, Mabel adding a few coins, and the kind little maiden who had proposed the gift handed it to the dazed figure that had shrunk back against a timely tree.

"Here, poor woman, buy your little boy bread to eat," and the girl held out her hand timidly with the pieces of silver glistening on the pink palm. But Kate, with her yearning gaze fastened upon her daughter, took no heed of the child's well-meant dole. The girl laid the money at Denny's feet, and ran after her comrades in fright. The pretty group passed on. Mabel was the only one that didn't turn her head to take account of the staring, miserable mother, transfixed as Niobe in the dispersion of her children.

A few months afterward the sad, sad drama came to its natural end. Kate left the mad-house again. This time forever. A coarse box of pine held the supple figure, a common cotton sheet covered the wondrous beauty, supernaturally emphasized by the years of mental coma before the soul joined the mind in flight from the body.

She was laid without comment or proclamation in the flat lowlands that mark the lowly from the favored dead in the lovely cemetery of Warchester. Possibly harder clods fell on the coffin; possibly humbler agencies of decay invaded the cerements. Be this as it may, the grass grew green and tender over the low mound; the blossoms from the neighboring shrubberies drifted over her; the royal robin, and the whole train of warblers, not knowing that it was a pauper spot, sang all the day in the branches, and poured forth ineffable requiems as the night fell, and gentle and simple were reduced to common colors and shapes; on the greensward the moon poured down beams quite as impartial of the silver that fell on the lowly as on the rich; the sun shone as warmly as if the grave had been among "the storied urns and animated busts" of the consecrated spot beyond, where the more fortunate permitted their clay to mingle with the soil, no more refined than that in which the Alien moldered.

Perhaps, too, in that other company beyond the grave, beyond the woes and wrongs of the world, the outcast from her kin and kind found the grace, mercy, and peace man denied her; perhaps in the heart of a juster, tenderer kin beyond the grave she found the indulgence of a father, the benignance of a God!

It was with considerable difficulty that, a year later, Marcus Dunn found the mound of the woman whose beauty had filled him with such strange unrest. It lay deep in a hollow, where the mighty hill rose in almost precipitous plateaus cloudward. A peaceful brook babbled by, but no name was on the unsodded mound when Marcus identified it, after long questioning the sexton. Presently an iron rail inclosed the place; a stone slab containing a brief memorial of the victim's life was reared at the head, and the world might read that Kate Boyne slept beneath. Years later, when the fashion of the city coveted this lovely dell, the authorities gladly relinquished the "God's acre" to become the sepulcher of the rich. The desecrating graves were all dug out; monuments there were none, save on this one, where the babbling water seemed to creep more familiarly and murmur more tenderly. A workman, removing the slab, threw it against an iron bar. It broke, and revealed the story of the Alien mother's life and death as I have herein sketched it. Marcus Dunn made inquiry for the little Denny, whom the mother loved; but he got only vague answers. The family was dispersed over the land. The father had never been heard from since his flight; the uncle, James Boyne, was dead or had moved elsewhere.

CHAPTER V.

A VILLAGE HAMPDEN.

HAD Denny been the son of affluence, the course of his life thereafter would have needed no commentary, nor made an instructive tale in the telling. His inheritance was bitterer even than the penury his young mind could not understand. Given house, not home, with his harsh kinsman Uncle James, he soon learned the misery of dependence where there is no fraternal instinct, no common bond. Larry had been unruly, and sternly turned over to a distant farmer, known for his decisive training of vicious boys. Denny, his uncle told him ungraciously, could find a home with him as long as he conducted himself well. A lad of Denny's years is not apt to regard admonition so little definite as this with much attention, and Denny was never quite sure what behavior was unholy in his kinsman's eyes.

He soon learned that whatever he did, his aunt found him a troublesome boy, of no sort of use in the house. Hence, he was generally kept outside the door, while this disciplinarian was alone, or if admitted, only to do the menial labors of the day. Rendered reckless by the lack of sympathy between himself and the household, Denny formed fierce attachments with the neighboring boys, whose pranks were indignantly denounced by Aunt Betty. When the wickedness was laid before Uncle James, that Spartan remonstrated with the child with links of clothes-line on his wretched little body, early in the morning, before the child was out of bed. These flagellations finally became so regular that the neighbors remonstrated, and the uncle then savagely bade the boy seek a home elsewhere. The child, vaguely troubled by the new misfortune, quit the house in broad day—Aunt Betty resolutely locking the door to show that she looked on the going as final.

Whether misfortune sharpens the wits at the expense of the sensibilities, I am not prepared to say; but that vicissitudes make the intellect retentive, the surprising vividness of Denny's recollections of these wretched scenes long afterward is proof. Confiding his hopes to a friend, that misfortune made and that death alone could deprive him of, Denny himself presents these fateful epochs in his life.

"When the box with my mother's body in it was put in the ground, I could not understand that I wasn't to go in with her. The men that had lifted the box and lowered it into the grave caught me roughly, and called to the sexton at the gate. I was carried away; I didn't know where, for, as I struggled in a wild passion with the man who held me, some one struck me a stunning blow on the back of the head. When I came to my wits again, I was in my Uncle James's kitchen. Aunt Betty, his wife, was mixing batter. I was on a low cot under the window, and watched her a long time before she saw that I was awake; for I supposed I had been asleep.

"She was a stout, good-natured looking woman, with a very red face, and small, dullish blue eyes. She spoke kindly to me when she saw I was looking at her, and asked if I was hungry. She gave me some bread with dark molasses on it, and, all recollection of the grave having gone, I ate with great satisfaction. Then I suddenly saw the graveyard, with the red wet clay in great gashes seaming the green turf, and I began to cry bitterly. Aunt Betty grew angry at this, saying that a boy that was so lucky as to have an uncle to take him in and give him a home ought to be thankful and happy. But as the face of the dead came to me, more and more clearly, I hated Aunt Betty, and broke into louder sobs; so that, as I couldn't control myself, I jumped up, and, running from the kitchen, made my way to the bedroom, and, crawling under the bed, sobbed myself to sleep.

"How long I lay there, I couldn't tell when I awoke. The place was dark. I couldn't for a good while recollect where I was, quite sure that I was dead, and that I should see my mother. Voices presently sounded in the next room, and I heard my own name. Then I knew where I was. I crawled out of the place, and sneaked into the light. My aunt uttered a little shriek when she saw me, and my uncle turned on me with a frown. He was a man of stern, unsmiling face at all times, but now he seemed to have that dry, soapy look one associates with marble figures. He looked over me instead of at me, as he sternly reminded me of my wickedness to my aunt. I was to have a home with him so long as I behaved myself; but if I did not, what had happened to Larry would happen to me. Larry, I afterward learned, had been unruly to Aunt Betty, and had been articled to a farmer, noted for his way of managing headstrong boys. At nine years one is not apt to define terms such as my uncle used very precisely, and I know I was a great deal puzzled to imagine what would be considered good or bad.

" I came to comprehend later that boyish goodness or badness bears the same comparative relation that every abstract thing does. In those days coal was not much used in Warchester, and I learned that one form of badness was neglect to keep the kitchen wood-box supplied with fuel seven days in the week. Aunt Betty having no maid-servant, I learned that goodness meant relieving her stout limbs of all the work usually done by a servant. Of my uncle I never knew much. I held him in such terror that, if he let his eye rest on me at the table, I nearly choked with fright. I don't know whether the life I had led with my mother in the fields, or a native tendency led to it, but I was fond of wandering, and whenever I could slip away I trudged off where the trees grew and the brooks wandered pleasantly over the shining stones.

" These expeditions sometimes led to angry outbreaks from Aunt Betty, who from a luxury soon came to regard my contributions to the kitchen work as a necessity. Often when I had been off for an afternoon, on getting home I would find the table standing from dinner—no fire in the stove, and Aunt Betty in bed. This happened a great many times, and occasioned quarrels between the husband and wife.

" At last the quarrel involved me. Aunt Betty complained that she was deprived of the help of one of her nieces because I was kept in the house; that I was an idle little brat and no use to anybody, 'as odd in his ways,' she added, 'as that crazy jade, his mother.' My uncle said nothing further, but the next day, at noon, finding me alone in the garden, he reminded me of my aunt's complaint; cautioned me to do the work and save her every step I could, or he would have to send me off on a farm and get one of Aunt Betty's nieces. I did not answer, but I did for a time strive to save her all the work I could.

"The worst of it was that Aunt Betty, whose father was agent for a wholesale liquor-store, began to drink a good deal. She began it in a curious way. When the church fairs were starting, she had many church women in the house sewing. They drank a good deal of tea, but I noticed that when I came to wash the pot for supper there never were any leaves in it. I soon discovered that it was only hot water, sugar, and some liquid from a keg in the cellar that they drank.

"After a while Aunt Betty used to sit by herself and sip this stuff. At first she was very merry, and joked and petted me, even giving me money, and telling me that when uncle and she died the place should be mine. After a time the drinking didn't make Aunt Betty merry. She became fretful, and scolded me on the slightest cause. I never was more miserable than during this year. I could not go to school, as I had been doing, because Aunt Betty's drinking brought on illness, and I had to do all the work of the house.

"This went on perhaps a year, when Aunt Betty insisted on having her niece, as she couldn't get the wash done to suit her. When the niece came my miseries increased. She was a snub-nosed, red-haired girl of fourteen or fifteen, very stout and big for her age. She began to persecute me from the first, and I could see by my aunt's manner that she was making ground against me. One day, after I had been off to the woods, Meg, the niece, met me at the door with a storm of abuse.

"There was no wood cut; the work of the house had been delayed all day that I might go traipsing about like 'your mad mother before you.' I don't know what I said in the passionate rage of the moment, but the girl fled up the steps to the kitchen. I stood at the bottom, panting and trembling with shame and anger. As I turned away, I felt a sudden darting pain in my head, and knew nothing more. When I did come to know where I was, it was dark, and I felt my head swathed and throbbing. I couldn't move my neck. In time I learned that the back of my skull had been fractured; my aunt, standing on the steps, had thrown a heavy carving-knife down at me as I turned my back, and the blade had cut through the skull.

"When I had recovered sufficiently to get about, my uncle told me that he couldn't afford doctors' bills for a big boy like me, and announced his intention of sending me to a farmer until I was of age. The threat threw me into a fever. I couldn't eat or sleep. The terrors of that unknown destiny—all the more dreadful that they were unknown—made me a ghastly shadow of myself. When the person came, and my uncle called me into the room, I fell into convulsions on the floor. What happened after, I didn't know; but when I was conscious of my existence again, I was in a wagon under the stars, rolling noisily over a country road; a hearty voice was singing a stave of a negro melody then much in vogue.

"I waited, in wonder and dread, the end of the affair. I conjectured that I was with the farmer, and that he was driving home. It was very solemn and quiet when the horses stopped at a high-barred gate, and the man, jumping out, let them pass into the yard. I made no sign of consciousness, and kept resolutely in the bottom of the wagon, until, the horses having been stabled, the man climbed up, and, shaking me by the shoulder, exclaimed, not unkindly:

"'Come, skeesicks, here we are home.' I got up without saying a word; he lifted me down, and we went under the thick shadow of a great mass of trees. The house was quite dark, but a light was soon struck. I could see the man now. He was the same that had come for me in the afternoon. He disappeared for a moment, and left me in the darkness. I could hear a clatter of dishes, and presently he returned with a great platter of corn-bread, blue delf bowls, and a pitcher of milk. He asked me a great many questions as we ate : whether I had been to school, if I liked to work, could I husk corn, and what not. He laughed good-naturedly at some of my answers, and, when the milk was finished, he slipped off his boots and directed me to do the same, setting them with great care behind the stove. At the head of the stairs he led me into a room where there was some one already in bed.

"The room was large, deliciously odorous with the faint perfume of bergamot ; the windows were hung with gayly colored dimity ; the floor covered by a smartly variegated home-made carpet ; a crane-legged bed, with a purple valance, was almost the only article of furniture—at least its long legs and high posts prevented the eye from taking in any other details. In the bed I could catch sight of a shock of black hair, and one ruddy cheek that fairly glistened in the flaring candle-light. With the words :

"'Get into bed, youngster,' the man quitted me, taking the candle. I was so startled by the sudden darkness that my first impulse was to run after him ; but my terror of him was too great. How I ever undressed I can't imagine, but, wretched and hungry for companionship, I fled under the bed-clothes, snuggled to the red cheeks, and sobbed myself to sleep on the unconscious stranger's shoulder.

"I was aroused in the morning by a gentle shake, and, opening my eyes, the ruddy cheeks of the night before were over my face. Two very bright black eyes were regarding me with wonder. It was barely daylight ; the

4

birds outside the window were chattering and chirping
like an orchestra preparing an overture. The fresh scent
of honeysuckle came through the open window; the sun
was so young that its first beams were purple rather than
yellow. I made friends with red cheeks—a grandson
of the house ; and I found that the man who had brought
me thither the evening before was not my new guardian,
master, or whatsoever relation my condition implied. But
another surprise was in store for me. While I was timidly
questioning my little comrade, some one entered the room
very softly and stood beside the bed. She was a young
girl in her first teens, with liquid, earnest eyes, and hair
that seemed woven of the dusky-bronze gold of the dande-
lions. I lay with open mouth and eyes, vaguely remembering the face, but it seemed in some other state of existence. Tears came into the deep-gray eyes as she looked
at·me, and, bending down so that her soft lips pressed
mine, she sobbed :

"'O Denny ! don't you know—don't you remember
Norah ?'

"I knew her now, but a child's memory at first isn't
very trusty. She told me that it was her work and her
urging that had finally induced the kind people who had
become parents to her to go to the city and take me from
Uncle James's unwilling fireside. 'There never was any
one so kind as my dear Doctor Marbury and Aunt Selina.'
I learned afterward that 'Aunt Selina' meant Mrs. Marbury, but she was universally known as aunt, because, as
I afterward found, she had so many grandsons and nieces
and nephews. The Doctor was her second husband.
They had married late in life, when grown daughters were
married and settled near them. They had been divided
in the loves of their youth through some family feud, and,
coming together long after death had obliterated the causes

of the quarrel, they were tranquilly going down the vale together, serene of spirit and kindly of soul. These were the new parents Providence had raised up for me. Under the lovely teachings of this best of women, I passed from the emotional Nihilism bred of a loveless kinsman's charity to the beneficent inspiration of tenderness and love. Life, which even in those young years I had begun to perplex my untutored mind about, became more meaningful. I understood, or seemed dimly to comprehend, the use of loving something different from my dear friends the birds. I didn't know for a long time when nor what first gave me the impulse to make all the use of my faculties, that it dawned on me boys even less favored than myself had often brought to great ends.

"Ah! I realize it all now, when I think of the serenity and joyful growth of that life ; when I recall the miles of fields, every tuft of which became as familiar to me as the foreground of a painter's canvas ; when I recall the days spent in the heart of the solemn woods—far, far in, where the melancholy pines seemed to shrink from mingling their weird monotones with the joyous voices of the gayer foliage ; when with companions or alone I was equally content ; when alone, I filled the woods with the fairies of the 'Midsummer-Night's Dream,' the savages of 'Robinson Crusoe,' or the elves of the 'Fairy Queen.' Never, I believe, did a boy, not an Indian, live so much in the woods, or comprehend so intimately the miracles that pass under the leafy recesses ; where the world we see so little of teems and toils much as men do, but to less selfish gains and less ignoble ends. Life was a joy to me ; the tranquil fields, where I toiled or played, were equally endeared to me ; the fragrant orchards, where on Sundays I sat far up in the ample arms of a friendly giant, living the joys, suffering the sorrows, or gloating over the marvels of my childhood's heroes. It was a vast world, this of my first years of imaginative growth. Children live wholly in the imagination, and I count it a priceless chance that placed me in an atmosphere where Nature herself joined in keeping up the exquisite comedy. It was as impossible to exclude the animate wonders of the Marbury meadows from the prosaic doings of my daily life, as it is for the priest to omit the solemn atmosphere of the church as a part of his ministration.

"Then the dear home life! The gardens, gay with holly-hocks, dahlias, and a hundred other simple blossoms; the groups of nodding sunflowers behind the dairy windows, whose heads turning to the sun we watched with solemn wonder; the four-o'clocks, whose regularly closing petals excited our awe; the lustrous currant-hedges, where, like young Bacchuses, we gorged the luscious berries; the wonder of wonders, the 'Jack and Jill' brook, that comes from ever so far off in the West, and was lost in the Alleghany Mountains. Who shall count the joys of these fairy realities to us, at a time when the mind was plastic and the habit of doubt was not known? I learned that brook by heart—miles of it, I mean—from the great pond over beyond the school-house, where the black snakes lay coiled in the sun, to the cavernous gap far below, where it branched off southeastward. I knew every sylvan secret of the Marbury meadows before the year was out, though I never shirked my chores, nor missed the school tasks. I haven't spoken of my little bedfellow, the grandson of Dr. Marbury. He was one year older than I. His mother had died the year before, and his father had left him with his grandmother. The boy was an affectionate little fellow, and we got on with but few wrangles, and these, I think, were generally my fault, though I didn't think so in those days. Sometimes he would return from a visit to his cousins, who lived in the city, and so soon after these as he happened to fall out with me he would run off a safe distance and call me 'Paddy!'

"Now, I had been tortured by this nickname at school; whenever the boys had a quarrel with me, they poured wormwood on my sensitive wounds by calling me this ignominious term, indicating Irish : and in those days to say that meant to embody the race most contemned of all the aliens settling the country. I couldn't understand the reproach, or why Irish was so repulsive or intolerable, but it became my horror by day and my torture by night. Once, hearing Mrs. Marbury alluding to some one who had offended her in the neighborhood as a 'good-for-nothing Irishman!' I grew quite white with suffocation as I turned and asked her:

"'Aunt Selina, why is it low and wicked to be Irish?' She was sitting in her high-backed arm-chair knitting, the sunlight falling over her shoulder, and framing her kind old wrinkled face in such peace as you may see in some Flemish portraits. She dropped her knitting on her knees and looked down at me below her spectacles. Norah was standing in the pantry-door, and Byron—Aunt Selina's grandson—stopped spinning a top, with which he had been disturbing the afternoon dreams of a lion-like cat that remonstrated with him from time to time by a sharp gruff noise like a growl, and a slap with the flat of her paw, very like a human stroke.

"'Why, Denis, child, come here.' As I sank at her knees, hiding my face, she patted me on the head, and said gently :

"'My child, I was wrong to make use of that word in that way. It is not low and wicked to be Irish, but people have come to look on all who are low and wicked as Irish. It is wrong, no doubt. Indeed, it must be wrong, for my grandfather was an Irishman, and my son's wife was Irish. But generally, since the canal came through the country, people have associated ignorance and lawlessness with the gangs that dug the canal, and most of them were Irish. When your comrades call you Irish, you mustn't mind it; they don't know themselves what they mean, and, if it were not that, it would be something else.'

"I was soothed, but not satisfied, with this specious explanation; and the next time I was called Paddy I gave my tormentor such a thrashing that the affair came up in the class-room. The teacher heard the story, and, when it was ended, said grimly:

"'Well, Denis, I don't see why you object so fiercely to being called Irish: you *are* Irish. Of course you can't help it, nor can any one help calling you what you are, especially when you act so like an Irishman as to black the eyes and bruise the body of one of your playmates.'

"It was thus officially proclaimed that my race was a disgrace. During the years that I remained in Marbury, 'Paddy' was the name I was known by, and I found it better to answer good-naturedly than resent it. I should not have been so easily reconciled, had it not been for a scene that happened one day at the end of the third summer term, when I was in my eleventh year. The whole family had attended the closing exercises, when Denis Boyne was called up to receive two prizes in scholarship and one prize for conduct, and was loudly applauded for a recitation by the visitors. Norah was very proud, and talked of her brother all the way home, and you may be sure that young fellow didn't suffer much on finding everybody praising him. At supper-table my dear Doctor, looking kindly at me through his great round goggles, that at first made me laugh when I looked at him, said, in his cheery, benignant tone:

"'Who knows, mother, perhaps our little Paddy may be a great man some day—President or Governor: Jackson is an Irishman.'

"It was too much to have the hateful name and reproach brought against me in the glory of my triumph. It was more than my excited mind could bear. I choked over the mouthful I was swallowing, and, with a bursting heart, bolted from the table, and, flying madly to the spot where the plantains were high and thick, I flung myself prone on the ground in a passionate outburst of misery. Norah came out presently and called me, but I never answered. It was nearly time for my evening work, and I was thinking miserably of facing the rest, when Aunt Selina came upon me from the currant-bushes. She patted me gently on the head, and rather made me ashamed of my foolish griefs. That night, when I was sneaking off to bed—(in those days we all went to bed by twilight; I never remember a candle lighted in summer, and I never had a light to go to bed with even in winter; such indulgence being regarded as an effeminizing luxury) —as I was sneaking off to bed, the kind Doctor came out after me, and said, with something very like sternness:

"'My boy, you must get over this silly shame about your origin. It is not what a man is called, or what he is born, or what his fathers were, that make him either good, or useful, or to be admired or hated. You must learn to look upon men just as though they were all cut from the same piece, and were worth just what they made themselves worth; or, like your figures in arithmetic, of value only as they take place in a column. It doesn't make you one bit better or worse to be Irish, German, or French. In the days of the Romans, all the world, not born in Rome, were barbarians. But we aren't people of their lordly ways. When I was a college boy in Baltimore, I was made miserable by being pointed out as a Yankee, while the most arrogant spirits in the town were the descendants of the Irish, who had been great families when the English ruled the province.'

"I can't say that the Doctor's philosophizing eased my anguish, or that I bore the taunt with equanimity until many a year after, when I came to comprehend and estimate at its just value the vulgar prejudice against the Celt as a citizen in the New World. But I redoubled my work, determined to employ all my faculties to make such a man of myself that my race should be no reproach to me. Events soon came to pass that changed the current of my existence, and altered the shaping factors in my career; and, please God, though I have endured sorrows since, it has never been for any act of mine that could be justly called disgraceful or unworthy. But, as I look back upon those years, I sometimes wonder that my heart wasn't wholly hardened, and that I didn't become the outcast and reprobate that the harsh and thoughtless, who had much to do with me, prophesied. For I think now that, though I was an affectionate and tractable child, I was difficult to govern, for mischief was as natural to me as the brogue to Donnegal. That I didn't fulfill those dark predictions was, under the good God, the wondrous chance that gave me the friendship and, finally, love of a being so rare and pure and perfect that I shrink from even naming her at this miserable epoch of my life.

"My first days at school were marked by the trials and anguish inseparable to an introduction to companions of one's own age. Shy, and, when not shy, reckless to the utmost limits of impudence, the Irish in me was a well-spring of malicious pranks and tests on the part of my comrades. One day, when they had exhausted every other artifice to worry me, it was proposed that I should kiss all the girls when the school closed, under penalty of being dragged in the mill-pond. Now, this pond, which spread to limits of fascinating terror to me, far away among the gloomy swamps, was filled on warm afternoons with monstrous water-snakes—the very sight of which to this day turns the marrow in my bones to ice. It was agreed that the boys should hold certain girls near the gate, and that 'Paddy' should 'smack' each one loud enough to be heard by the whole band. Sure enough, when the teacher had disappeared, as the girls came trooping out a dozen of them were caught, and I was ordered to do my duty. To tell the truth, I didn't mind the matter very much, as most of the girls had shown me profound disdain and contempt. But, as I was thrust forward by two stalwart young ruffians, and the girls, who had made but little objection to the other lads seizing them, began to rain down blows on my bare head for my presumption, the fun was too good for the leaders to give up at once, and they kept me at it, blinded, scratched, and now angrily struggling to be released. But the more I was buffeted the more in earnest the rest became, and it was resolved that, as I had not succeeded in kissing one girl, I should be flung into the pond at the roots of the willows, where the snakes were biggest and always sure to be found. I was bleeding and helpless, and unable even to kick at my tormentors as they dragged me over the sand and sod to the water's edge. Some of the girls became compassionate at this, and cried out against it.

"'Pshaw! it'll do him good; they don't have snakes in Ireland,' cried the leader of the merry-makers, Arthur Kennel.

"The pond was across a wide field from the school-ground, and they dragged me along, shrieking. Once I must have fainted, for, when I became conscious, I was

lying quite unmolested on the ground, the boys staring at
me in a sort of fright. As I opened my eyes slowly, Arthur exclaimed :

"'Oh, fudge, he's only shamming : these Irish are
coons for tricks. Heave him along. I can see the snakes
uncoiling to welcome him.'

"O my God ! the horror of that moment. I sprang at
the nearest boy and buried my teeth deep in his cheek ;
a hand came near me : I think I must have bitten a finger
quite to the bone. I was mad with fear and rage—princi-
pally fear—and, before they bore me down by force of
numbers, three of them were howling with pain and quite
bloody. I was blinded with blood, and I never knew how
they got to the edge of the water. Here I had regained
strength, and made another fight; but Arthur, by a sharp
welt across my eyes with his satchel-strap, quite blinded
me, and I lay on the ground kicking and striking out in
an agony of horror. They were too tired to resume for
the moment, and I had just time to catch a glimpse of
great monstrous coils of scaly serpents wound around the
limbs of the willows that grew perhaps ten feet from the
water's edge. Then I yelled, 'Murder!' but Kennel and
another boy, throwing themselves on me, stuffed a hand-
kerchief in my mouth. My terror now gave zest to the
purpose, and they seized me again by the shoulders and
feet, a boy holding each arm. Then, as we reached the
water's edge, Kennel said suddenly :

"'Paddy, can you swim ?'

"I thought they were going to relent, and I clutched
at the chance of escape. I told a lie.

"'No, I can't.'

"'So much the better. But you're too foxy, Paddy.
I saw you swim down at the Devil's Pool. You can't fool
me, Irishy!'

"Then, before I realized his purpose, my arms were strapped under me, and the rest halted to take breath before flinging me in. I held them at bay with my legs, kicking viciously, and squirming around in the soft soil until I could feel even my skin, through the clothes, wet and muddy. They threw themselves on me, however, and were lifting me for the plunge, when a terrified voice said :

"'Why, boys, what are you doing?'

"They turned, and some of them relinquished their hold. I looked eagerly. It was Cordelia Dane, the daughter of the Deacon, one of the rich farmers of the country.

"'Ah, Dilly, you're just in time for the fun. We're going to throw Paddy in among the snakes; he never saw any in Ireland, and we want him to see what we've got in this country.'

"'But what has he done to you? It is very cruel. He is bleeding and hurt,' and she came nearer to me and shuddered as she saw the plight I was in.

"'It's all perfectly fair, Dilly,' Arthur Kennel said. 'We'll leave it to you. We gave him his choice: kiss the girls or be ducked. He wouldn't, or couldn't, and we must keep our word. If he had kissed one girl we would have let him off. Wouldn't we, boys?' asked Arthur, winking at the others.

"'Oh, of course,' they chimed in

"'You are wicked and dreadful boys, and I shall tell the teacher of you,' she said hotly. 'You're cowards: all of you against one. Go away; let the poor boy go home.'

"She came quite close to me now, where I sat on the ground, all sense of danger quite gone, and lost in wonder at the interposition of this, the most timid and shrinking girl in the classes; for, though I had seen and sat near her on the benches, she had never noticed me nor did I dare speak to her. She bent down and tried to loosen the strap, but it was tied with a cord.

"'Come, come, Dilly, we're bound to have our way. This is no place for girls; go home and tell the teacher that we've given the Irishman a bath. He needs it, doesn't he?' and Arthur pushed her roughly from me, while the rest laughed.

"'You say you'll let him go if he—he—kisses one girl?' She blushed scarlet. The boys gathered nearer with grinning curiosity.

"'Yes, if he'll kiss a girl we'll let him scoot. What do you say, boys?' and Arthur looked at the rest.

"'Agreed!'

"She came to where I sat, and bent down until her rosy cheek was quite at my lips, and said:

"'Denis, kiss me.'

"I touched the soft flesh timidly as Aladdin the hand of the princess.

"'But the bargain was that it was to be a "smack" that we all could hear. No one heard that.'

"'Yes, that's so, a smack, a smack, or no fair,' was the unanimous shout.

"Dilly looked from one to the other in gentle entreaty; but the young cannibals were remorseless. She came close to me again, and as she did so I saw the handle of a short case-knife in her dinner-basket. Though my arms were tied, my hands were free, and I seized this quick as a flash. In a second I had cut the strap and was free.

"'God bless you, Dilly!' I said; 'but I won't let you do that again for me, to please vagabonds like these.—Now,' I said, 'if you want to throw me into the water, come on!'

"They saw the knife; it had been ground down, and came to a sharp point; it would have been a dangerous weapon in determined hands. Then they slunk away, and we were left alone. They kept up jeers and taunts until they were out of sight. I was afraid to go near the water to wash myself, for I thought the great limbs were snakes. I was too shy to speak to the little maid; I walked along behind her. She never said a word, but once, as I caught up with her, she silently handed me her hand-kerchief to wipe the blood from my face. I was too abashed to take it, and shook my head. We walked to the forks of the road together, nearly half-way to the Doctor's, and never a word was spoken. The bobolinks were singing on the rail-fences, the red kingbirds fluttering in the elders, and she seemed to be intent only in watching and listening to the pleasant summer sounds. I knew a spot by the brook that crossed the road where violets and yellow cowslips grew, and I noticed that the girls had little bunches of these on their desks, and sometimes gathered them for the teacher. As she walked on ahead of me, I furtively plucked a pretty handful of these, and, as we reached the parting where she turned to the right, trembling with shame, I came silently to her side and held them out. She blushed prettily as she took them, and said :

"'Thank you, Denis Boyne ; I think you're a very good boy.'

"I stood rooted to the spot as she walked away, and glowing with wonder and admiration, as she turned, after she had gone a little way, and looked back. All the way home the bobolinks kept saying :

"'Good boy, Denis Boyne ; good boy, Denis Boyne,' until I thought that the birds knew me, and knew what was in my heart.

"And that I have loved good, and hated wrong, and cruelty and baseness, and am come to the esteem of my kind, is due to that tender heart, that spotless soul—the

God-sent minister in my misery, the consoler and inspirer when the heavier hand came upon me. I look in her sweet eyes now, as I looked that dreadful day, and all is peace and benignance, and I bend humbly and reverently to Him that softens or turns the wrath of the cruel, and sends the angel, men call woman, to make the mightiest as a little child."

CHAPTER VI.

"WARS OF ROSE AND SHAMROCK."

IN the days when Denis played dryad in the Marbury woods, Malvern, the neighboring spa, was not the sumptuous assemblage of summer hotels and city traffic it is now become. The springs, where Denis sat many an hour dreaming of classic superstitions, gushed from shining sandy beds under leafy recesses, where marble basins now hold the water and gay pavilions cover the thirsty at its shrine. But, though the hamlet had not taken on the airs of a resort in fashionable favor, the famous tavern, known far and near for its excellent cheer, counted on a regular summer visiting-list that made the woodlands gay for three months. There were merry-making and good cheer, if not the dissipation and splendor of a later time. In those days, however, the stately families that came for rest and the waters were content with accommodations that their effeminate descendants would reject as hardships.

In those days a fine reader was a courted person, and to talk agreeably, listen discreetly, and bow with grace, were held to be accomplishments which adorned any man, young or old. The tourist who lounges in the magnificent pavilions of the Malvern of to-day can form but a vague notion of the place as it was seen by the personages of this history. Where long lines of pilastered colonnades gleam through stately sweeps of branches now, the visitor in Denis's day found the husbandman's barley, buckwheat, oats, or the robin scattering the apple-blossoms that covered the young blades. The tavern, kept by Major Waffle, was the joy of the unfastidious city men, who settled down to its venison patties, its wholesome roasts, and well-flavored game, with an enthusiasm that is lost on the culinary triumphs of to-day. So soon as the summer set in, Major Waffle put the neighboring Nimrods —all held in renown for cunning—to supply his table for the *gourmets* that drank the waters and ate—as an occupation—between July and September. Royalty itself, in the days when whole oxen were set before Queen Elizabeth, never encountered such hospitality as made the renown of the honest Major.

Had the super-sensitive Vatel spared his life, when he over-salted the Grande Monarque's soup, and lived to taste the Major's masterpiece, he would certainly have choked himself with chagrin on encountering that famous partridge pot-pie that drew a tribute from the great Lafayette when he passed through the country. It was only on gala occasions that the Major gave himself up to the creation of this toothsome triumph ; but the feast was long remembered, and events were dated from it as of old from the feasts of the rich Romans ! Nor, though lacking the ostentatious proportions of its prodigious successor, was the Devon tavern lacking in homely comforts and even luxury. Wide halls divided the house into rooms of equal size, front and rear, forever fragrant with the odors of flowers and foliage.

Front and back the rooms opened upon green vistas of

leafy aisles or billowy water. Of an evening, in lieu of
the modern concerts and feverish movement, cards were
brought on in the great parlors, and the groups, dividing
into fours, played a decorous whist, until the ladies gave
the signal for retiring. The younger folks danced the
old-fashioned reels, or the cotillions of the day, to the
primitive strains of a flute, violin, or harp—an orchestra
made up from the hotel boys, or wandering minstrels entertained by the kind Major. Nor did the pretty feet of
our grandmothers trip any less gracefully to the measures
piped and scraped on these instruments than do those of
our own daughters, sisters, or sweethearts to-day, with full
string bands and puzzling profusion of essentials that take
up the time our ancestors gave to merry-making. For,
though you may doubt it, there was infinite pleasure in
these primitive summer jaunts of the old time. Women
as well as men were fond of the excitement of cards, just
as they were in the grave societies of the Old World.

Colonel Warchester, whose family were lords of this summer haunt, never became so charmingly convivial as when
he was able to get a new listener to that famous anecdote
of his father and General Washington playing for a night
and a day, until the father of his country was obliged to
stake Madame Washington's finest brew of peach brandy,
pledged to Madame Lafayette at that, to keep up the
game; how, not daring to tell his thrifty dame, the father
of his country made a pretext for carrying her off on a
visit to her kinsman, Custis Lee, and, while she was gone,
sent the brandy to Colonel Warchester at Annapolis!
·The Warchesters held their heads even above the Lord
Poultney who had made Malvern his summer home regularly during his sojourn in this country. Lord Poultney
had bought a great tract of land not far from Warchester,
on the southeastern shores of Lake Montaria, founded a

town which bears the glory of his name to this day, and in everything but naturalization had become an American.

Malvern waters had restored the wasted tissues of the gouty earl, and he was its most devoted and delighted patron. He was never tired of telling how his youth had been restored by its springs, a miracle which did not excite the enthusiasm of a family of poor relations settled in my lord's straggling colony. They were still less charmed with the wonder when, in his fiftieth year, the rejuvenated lord, falling in with the bewitching Molly Myrickson, married her off-hand to the indescribable indignation of Warchester's "best people," who had not as yet come to regard riches as equal to a hundred years' quarterings. Michael Myrickson had applied his modest energies to the development of the resources that finally made the town imposing and himself rich, first, by swinging a pick in the bed of the canal, and afterward in shoeing the unshod feet of the horses that passed the Rialto corner of the town. Michael's trained eyes taught him to mark the phenomena of soils, and, revolving the matter in his mind, he was convinced that the mineral signs he found on the feet of certain horses would pay examining.

He went to the lands where the horses wrought, and sure enough a slight scrutiny developed deposits of coal and iron. The land was near Lord Poultney's purchase. He made an arrangement that insured him two thirds of the usufruct, and by Lord Poultney's aid began working the lode. This was the first case of the kind in Warchester. Everybody waited to see how Madame Warchester, the social arbiter, would decide the rank of this upstart opulence. Colonel Warchester, who had often stopped in the shop, where Michael stood with some neighbor's horse's hoof between his knees, and conversed affably, found himself considerably embarrassed one day on discovering Michael elected to the presidency of a bank in which the Colonel was a stockholder. The scene was a good deal relished by Governor Darcy, who good-naturedly satirized the pretensions of the original settlers in the young city, and was regarded with aversion by the more tenacious votaries of family caste. As banker and millionaire, the Myricksons were generally conceded equality among the less tenacious advocates of the divine right of social precedence entailed in native birth. There was great curiosity to learn the result of the contest between Lady Molly and Mistress Warchester. My lady had not passed much time in town after her marriage. The field of the cloth of gold upon which these social pretenders came to settle their rivalry was, to the joy of their feudatories—Malvern.

In equipage, the Warchester family-coach rather eclipsed the Poultney *calèche*. My lord clung to his English ways in this as in the regulation of his daily affairs, and even Lady Molly couldn't ridicule the cumbrous yellow-bodied Berlin out of his affections. So, while the Warchesters descended into the ample arms of Major Waffles and the honest Mistress Major, from a carriage of shining ebony and lusterless argentry, the Lady Poultney skipped out of the lumbering yellow chariot that had held beauties of George II's time, when the young Poultneys made a great figure at the masques of my Lord Walpole near Twickenham. The stout blacksmith, in his character of partner and Crœsus, refused to make part of his son-in-law's establishment, and came to Malvern on the stage-coach quite simply, as though his newly acquired wealth might fly if used too lavishly.

Madame Warchester bowed with a prodigious dignity to the company gathered on the shaded piazza, and swept into the wide hall, her children following her, with such

an air as I imagine Queen Bess assumed when she alighted
at Kenilworth, and, giving her hand to my Lord Leicester
to kiss, sailed into the stone doorway. My Lady Molly
stopped and waited for her lord to clamber down ; he had
been sitting on the seat with the driver, and, as she spied
old friends, saluted them good-humoredly. One young
girl, starting up, was caught in Lady Molly's arms with
loud kisses that sounded along the balcony and made
every one adore the honest soul.

" Me darling ! Oi'm delighted that ye're here. I was
afeared ye'd go to Niagara, and me lord wouldn't go there
for love or fear."

Kind glances followed my lady as she disappeared, and
even my lord, as he hobbled in, came in for some of the
good-will his jolly wife excited. It was a remarkable
trick of Lady Molly's speech that when she was in certain humors the brogue betrayed the origin of her wit and
lively humor. When she was at ease she rather encouraged her tongue in the drollest vagaries of her father's
copious brogue : possibly because the play upon the vowels displayed the richness and flexible delicacy of her un-
dertones, which fell upon the ear with a delicious reso-
nance.

It was remarked by those who knew her well that,
when she chose, Lady Molly could slip the brogue from her
ready tongue and replace it by an accuracy of accent that
would have driven a Dublin grammarian mad with envy.
Molly's wit and beauty made her a favorite, even before
the glory of a coronet came to decorate her dark auburn
hair.

There was a good deal of politely subdued excitement
and expectant *qui vive* among the three-score guests of the
" Devon," when Lady Molly's coming was known, to see
the encounter with " My Lady Warchester." She was al-

ways called "my lady" behind her back. She must give place to Mrs. Paddy, it was said, for by all social laws the titled lady must take the *pas.* Lady Molly, coming down through the corridor to dinner, was stopped in the doorway by a personage just arriving. As she stood blocking the way, Madame Warchester, with her daughter Mildred, and her son Darcy, the cadet, moved swiftly forward from the drawing-room of the hotel. Lord Poultney stood facing the hallway, and my Lady Molly stood with her back to it. Madame Warchester gives my lord a lofty bend of the head, which he responds to by a sweeping bow, and asks after her own and her family's health. She barely murmurs a grimly polite reply as she pushes past the elderly nobleman, who says, with stately emphasis :

"Lady Poultney ; Mistress Warchester."

Madame looks him straight in the eye, as if to mark the event more unequivocally, and, gathering her flowing robe, passes with frigid ignoring into the dining-room. Lord Poultney looked after the valiant campaigner in helpless perplexity, and then, as the full significance of her action came upon him, his mild eyes bulged in apoplectic incredulity. He made a gesture as if about to seize the serene figure sailing past him ; but the arm of Lady Molly, slipped within his own, recalled him to the conventional amenities.

"'Pon me word, I believe he'd have boxed her ears, as Phil Dougherty did the Duke of Wicklow," said his wife, talking of the encounter afterward. "Me friend the madame is hard to plaze," added the countess, laughing at the scene. "She wouldn't know me, when I was plain Molly Myrickson, because I didn't have enough rank ; now she refuses to know me because I've too much."

Mrs. Warchester's repugnance to the good-natured countess was not shared by the male members of the family. Colonel Warchester never omitted an opportunity of saluting her; while his son Lieutenant Darcy Warchester, just graduated from West Point, declared her irresistible. The Lieutenant indeed would have found Malvern tiresome the first week of his stay, if Lady Molly had not encouraged him to join her forces; for the place was divided into two distinct camps—the elderly folk owning allegiance to the imperious Warchester, while the younger gayly cast their fortunes with the countess.

Dr. Marbury, who had been a school-fellow of Colonel Warchester, gave a humorous sketch of the wars of the rose and shamrock—as he called the feud—one day, on returning from a dinner at Malvern, to which he had been invited solemnly by his old-time comrade. Denis listened to the account of the stately dame and the husband, and vaguely recalled such persons, but he couldn't remember where he had seen them. The Colonel and his wife were coming over in state to visit the Marburys, and the house was full of preparation. To do honor to such distinguished people, the leading citizens of the township were invited to tea. It was late in the afternoon when the gorgeous Warchester coach, flashing back the yellow sunlight, rolled up the sequestered lane of the "Marburys."

The whole company was ranged on the porch to receive the great city folk quite in the style of royalty. Madame Warchester had changed little during the years that have passed since we saw her, divided between devout joy and irrepressible loathing on realizing that the sacred bone and sinew of her loins owed to one of a proscribed and alien race the life that came from blood so blue as the Warchester's. She was, if anything, more impatiently imperious as she stepped into the old-fashioned parlor that Aunt Selina opens only on state occasions—rooms in which no member of the house ever ventures to enter unless the presence of a very deeply honored visitor unlocks the sacred portal. Mrs. Warchester is a woman of too much breed, ing, in spite of her exactions, to betray the amusement she feels in the primitive decorations and antique furnishing of Aunt Selina's cherished apartment of state. The walls were papered with the gentle shepherds and shepherdesses that seemed beings of radiant beauty to our grandfathers and grandmothers. The floors were covered with a home-spun carpet, in alternating strips of the brightest green, yellow, purple, and what not, of an incongruous inhar-monious hue, that the unæsthetic taste of that time indulged.

Upon the mantel gleamed plaster figures of cupids, angels, and fauns, revealing the wandering Italian image-boy—the only agent of art in those days, and the precursor of the "chromo" of to-day. The window-shades of thick green paper were lurid with parti-colored scenic effects that suggested earthquakes and fiery hurricanes. To add to the exquisite incongruity, in various points of vantage stood pasty bunches of waxen flowers, sedulously displayed under glass cases, to keep their hideous bloom from the dust. This, too, in sight of lovely blossoms growing in profusion outside in the garden and on the lawn.

Mrs. Warchester betrayed by no sign the merriment this archaic interior caused her. She inquired affably for the numerous relatives of Mrs. Marbury, affected a deep interest in the crops, which became an early topic, and, by the time the tea was served in the homely wainscoted dining-room, where the cooking was likewise done in win-ter, she had captivated, so far as that is possible with such awe inspired, all the modest matrons about the board : captivated them much as a royal lady who graciously, wandering abroad, condescends to rest informally in a cotter's kitchen to refresh herself with his humble fare. The tea over, the great lady withdrew, begging that her children might come over and examine the wonders of the farm.

The Colonel, by no means disconcerted, presents his children to the rural group, who admired them without venturing to speak to them. A prettier girl than Mildred, his daughter, the dazzled eyes of the Marbury magnates had never seen. Just turning in her later teens, Mildred was the ideal of the sensuous beauty our grandsires used to rave over, to sin for, and fight for, and, God help us! die for. I don't mean to make the catalogue of her charms, but, if you are satisfied with Byron's picture of Gulnare, I have always imagined that Mildred Warchester must be the exact counterpart. Nor was her brother Darcy less marked in his way. A more comely youth than the lad in cadet regimentals—he had just been graduated from West Point—could hardly have been found west of New York.

The Colonel found it very difficult to make conversation with the shy farmers and their still shyer wives. He learned that there was capital fishing in the wide water of the creek and good boating behind the old mill near at hand.

" We have excellent fishing hard by, and, if the Lieutenant likes the sport, Denis—a lad we have with us—will be glad to help him." Dr. Marbury said this cordially, looking around for Denis, who had not been seen during the afternoon.

" Darcy will certainly take advantage of the chance, for he has been complaining that there was no fishing near Malvern." With this the great carriage was driven off, the whole company standing in a reverential attitude as it rolled away.

" A very proud woman, Mrs. Warchester," said Aunt Selina, confidentially, to her husband. " I never knew such a one who didn't come to misfortune."

"What misfortune can come to her, my dear? She has everything to make the world pleasant. She has great wealth, social pre-eminence, a charming family; her daughter is beautiful, her son is a youth of acknowledged parts. What but death can mar the pleasure of such a one?"

"I never knew a proud woman yet—I mean that hateful pride—that didn't come to sorrow, and I have a feeling that that woman is inviting misfortune upon herself. Do you know, every minute she sat here I thought I saw an expression of disdain and mockery in her eye."

"Selina, you are too old to be notional. I'm afraid you are envious; you think our sleepy sorrels a poor team compared with the dashing bays that drag my lady about, eh?"

"If no woman envies Mrs. Warchester more than I do, she must be a very unhappy person; for, unless I'm mistaken, to be envied and feared are the ruling ideas in her life."

A day or two after this famous visit, Denis, wandering on the banks of the brook toward Malvern, was startled by snatches of singing mingled with merry peals of musical laughter, and presently there emerged very near him a vision of youth and beauty such as he had never dreamed: a girl in white, clinging to a capricious pony that seemed bent on throwing his pretty mistress into the deep mosses of the wood. Following this vision, a young man in careless hunting-dress, the collar thrown open sailor-fashion, and a bundle of fishing-rods under his arm, alternately caressing and teasing the pony. As the couple spied Denis, laden with the floral spoils of the forest, they called simultaneously to the pony to halt, and then turned quite calmly to question him. The young man, advancing a few steps and flinging his burden down, said, taking his hat off:

" Perhaps, my lad, you can show me the wood-path to Dr. Marbury's ? "

Denis, a good deal startled by the spectacle of such beauty, admitted awkwardly that he could show the path, but made no motion toward doing it.

"Well, will you be kind enough to do it ? " said the young man laughing, as he picked up his rods and resumed his hat. " Knowledge in this world is a universal heritage ; ask and ye shall receive. That's the law : isn't it, Milly ? "

"Wicked fellow, do you know what you're quoting? I've no doubt you think you are repeating a line of Shakespeare ; you are not."

"Dear me. You don't mean to say that the lore of my baby days is returning, and I am getting my scripture lines back ? Because if you do I shall revive the black in my mother's hair by adopting the gown instead of the sword as a profession."

"Are we going to reach the Marburys? Does this boy know the way?" interrupted the girl impatiently. Denis had stood quite dumfounded as the foregoing badinage passed between the radiant figures illuminating the beechwood. But, his wandering wits recalled by this last query, he hurriedly set out, saying simply :

"If you want to go to Dr. Marbury's, please to come this way."

"Is it much farther, my nimble Narcissus ? " Darcy asked, as Denis, accustomed to the recesses, shot through the shrubs and over the mosses like an Indian. He heard the voice, but didn't distinguish the words, and waited inquiringly until the questioner came up.

"Only a few minutes more and we shall be there; you can see the chimneys through the trees over the orchard yonder."

5

When Denis had conducted the visitors to the porch, he didn't know what devolved upon him. In grave doubt, he called Norah. That young woman's voice rose in clear soft tones from the dairy, and as Denis's call reached her she ceased, and a minute later her head appeared above the granite steps.

"Here's somebody to see the Doctor," said Denis, quite unequal to the novel occasion.

Norah was hardly less agitated or at fault. Girl-like, her personal appearance was the first condition of the problem. Had she been called upon in the beautiful French cambric, sacred to the most solemn festivals, on rare Sundays when missionary celebrities crowded the chapel, she might have confronted the young man, even under the trying ordeal of a better-dressed girl in the contingency; but to appear before this bewilderingly handsome youth, with that perfectly arrayed, dark-eyed young sultana looking on with curling lip, was more than Norah could summon courage to do, and she fled shamelessly, leaving the guests overwhelmed with mirth and curiosity.

Denis, discomfited by this hopeless outcome of his first resource, looking piteously at the radiant girl, who stood poised against the rail of the porch, ventured to say:

"If you will wait here a minute I will call Aunt Selina." Without delaying for the somewhat surprised assent, the lad ran into the room, and, catching sight of Aunt Selina, deeply engaged in the repair of a flannel garment, he cried in ungovernable excitement:

"O Aunt Selina, get the parlor-doors open quick; there is a most beautiful lady here to visit."

Now, it was the terror of the parlor not being immediately available that had embarrassed what the diplomates would call Denis's liberty of action when he arrived at the porch with the splendid visitors. The opening of the parlor he associated with a formulated plan: the removal of sundry sheets of paper from the communicating doors, the rolling up of the vestibule shades, and a final discreet touch of the duster upon the crystal floral shrines. Aunt Selina, perplexed by the announcement, doubted the discretion of a youth who suggested this family devotion so recklessly, and went herself to the door to verify the fact before the momentous command was given. Aunt Selina's confusion and penitence were the only satisfaction that Denis knew that disastrous day.

"Mrs. Marbury," said the young man, as Aunt Selina, quite prostrated, confronted the strangers, "we came over with the compliments of Colonel and Mrs. Warchester, who send you these." He handed the trembling lady a packet. "My mother begged me to say that we should be no trouble to you." Then, as if the identity of himself and sister might aid the puzzled old lady in understanding the situation better, he added, "You may remember me: I am Darcy Warchester, and this is my sister. We are going to accept your kind invitation through my father, and spend the day in your woods, if we can manage to get some one for a time to show us the fishing-places."

Aunt Selina was quite as fluttered before this bright-eyed, composed young fellow, standing hat in hand under the yellow sunshine, as she had been with his mother. She brought chairs to the porch in trembling discomfiture, not quite knowing what to do.

"Certainly, Mr. Darcy—Mr. Warchester. You shall have Denis to take you all over the meadows; he knows the places better than the Doctor himself." Then, going to the door precipitately, she called Norah to make the parlor ready.

"Oh, dear no, Mrs. Marbury, we can't think of going

in. We are come for a jaunt in the woods. My brother thinks that he can help Major Waffles's table by a stock of fish, and has promised me a prize if I will sit with him while he tries his green hand. Later in the evening papa is coming over, and then we hope to have a chance to make friends of our father's friends."

All the mother's grand air, without the mother's supercilious condescension, was in the girl's manner, which from one so young lent the deliberate phrases a certain charm that Aunt Selina yielded to with the ready credulity of old age, not much skilled in the physiognomy of features or character.

Darcy, though a little nettled, laughed good-humoredly. They were soon in the deep woods, Denis running fleetly in advance, and gallantly holding the young trees back while Mildred passed through laughing. He brought them to a mossy delve where the banks on one side sloped far up into a thicket of tangled briers covered with honeysuckle. The sunlight split into soft, arrowy lines upon the water as it gurgled into a wide, deep pool. Here Darcy adjusted his tackle and fell to fishing, while Mildred, enthroned on a green mound of moss, took out a book and pretended to read. Darcy's luck put his sister's prophecies to shame, for, thanks to the fat bait provided by Denis, the shy pickerel bit greedily, and were soon landed on the sward in a heap. At the beginning Darcy imposed silence on his sister, and Denis wouldn't presume to obtrude his prattle upon such grand people. He sat at a distance, admiring the gay hunting-jacket and the lovely girl reclining indolently upon the honeysuckles and dog-wood he had spread for her. The afternoon waned, and the fisherman, satisfied with his prowess, encouraged the boy to talk. Denis was ready enough, and soon had his guests shouting with laughter over his droll accounts of the city people that came out to fish and hunt.

It was long after the lad's supper hour, and Darcy had just proposed going, when Norah came bashfully into the little dell, saying that Aunt Selina bade them to supper. Darcy looked in admiring surprise at the girl as she stood blushing before him. She was the image of her dead mother. The same soft, mournful, tender gray eyes ; the same changing tints in the transparent cheeks ; the same delicate mold of limb and form—a living Murillo framed in the luxuriant foliage of the July wood. Darcy stood transfixed and Mildred opened her lustrous eyes in surprise. The girl, not comprehending the meaning of it, flamed crimson, and turned in an agony of shame to Denis. Mildred was the first to recover self-possession, and said sweetly :

" Ah, thank you, my good girl. Mrs. Marbury is too kind ; we couldn't think of disturbing her. We should worry mamma if we remained. Please tell your—tell Mrs. Marbury—"

" I say, Milly, if these people have made supper ready, we should go and eat. It wouldn't be manners to fly off in this unceremonious way. I vote to go, and they'll understand at the hotel that we've stayed to supper."

They talked as if the girl and boy before them—almost their own age—were some sort of wood-spirits, incapable of comprehending the rather disdainful estimate of the social exigency. Mildred allowed herself to be persuaded, and the group set off for the house, Denis carrying the basket of fish, which Darcy had at first vetoed indolently. He couldn't keep his eyes off the vision in a high-necked dress and simple linen cuffs and collar. Her movements were willowy and graceful, and the youth wondered if this could really be the draggled little reddish-haired child he had seen in the emigrant group in the packet so many years before. She fled swiftly and silently, never venturing to look at the brother and sister or address them a single word. Two or three times Darcy made a pretext to question her; but she glanced at him in startled wonder, surges of color covering her cheeks and neck, and looked appealingly to Denis to make answer, which that youth was very ready to do, the garrulity of his race being developed in him to the fullest measure.

They found the table laid out in Aunt Selina's snowiest linen, with the rare blue delf that came only when great occasions warranted its use. To the no small surprise of brother and sister, the boy and girl took their places at the table, for in those days the "help" were considered part of the family, even in the most pretentious country houses. Darcy was hungry, and delighted the hostess by asking ample "helpings" from the dainty muffins, the grilled fish, and the wild strawberries that the Doctor had, after infinite experiments, reared in his garden. Two or three times Darcy sent Norah from the table, under pretext of replenishing the silver tea-pot or the swiftly dwindling muffins, by glances that were more ardent than the poor child was accustomed to. After supper, which was soon over, as the guests did most of the talking, and found the effort a burden, the Doctor's two-seated wagon was driven to the gate, and the visitors, with profuse thanks, were carried away : Darcy remaining behind, as his sister was lifted into the vehicle, to catch a glimpse of Norah, who, with a large green-and-white-checked apron that masked her like a Quakeress, passed from the kitchen to the dairy with foaming pails of milk and piles of pans. Denis rode the pony, and prattled artlessly as they drove over the tranquil country roads, giving the history of every farm-house they passed, the number of its inmates, and the acres worked.

Milly listened, rather distraught, to these commonplace details, but Darcy encouraged the lad, rather, I suspect, to save himself the effort of talking than because the histories interested him, for he surprised Denis several times by asking the same question, and assenting gravely when he was expected to say "no."

CHAPTER VII.

A TALE FROM BOCCACCIO.

"Darcy, me dear, have ye been bewitched by the banshee?" asked Lady Molly one morning on the shaded veranda, as the lad stood carelessly on the steps below her, equipped, with gun and fishing-rod, for a jaunt in the Marbury woods. "Ye may as well tell me yer secret, me bye, for I know well it's not the fish in the Doctor's brooks, nor the birds on his branches, that coax a foine bye like you to forsake meself and the gurls here to pass yer mornings in the bush! Tell us now, ye young vilyain, is there a pretty colleen making soft eyes to ye beyant?" and Lady Molly lowered her voice and nodded over her shoulder toward the misty fringe of wood that outlined the Marbury farm.

Darcy laughed and blushed, and Lady Molly held up a warning finger:

"Remember, me lad, that madame has a princess in her oi for the son of the Warchesters, and ye'll do well to keep a hard heart under yer waistcoat."

"No, Lady Molly, it's the fish and the birds that make Marbury enticing. Do you think I could leave *you* if it

were a question of the heart?" and the young fellow
laughed good-humoredly as his gay monitress shook her
head incredulously.

"Ah, me dear, I know well what byes are! Sure,
wasn't I giving me own heart right and left when I was
your age? And where's the gurl could stand out ag'in
yer soft ways and yer wicked blue eyes? God bless
ye!"

Darcy took a step upward and lifted the soft, dimpled
hand to his lips, saying gallantly:

"I'm going to reserve all my wickedness until you're
a lovely widow, and then see what the eyes may be able
to do."

"Hah! as for that, patience isn't in the Warchester
blood, and I'd be old enough and gray enough if I put
trust in yer soft blarney," and she turned to salute her
lord, who came from the stables surrounded by a score of
yelping, frisking setters.

Darcy strode off, laughing softly. He liked Lady
Molly, and fell very readily into her willful banter: perhaps as much to tease his mother as anything else, for the
sum of the lady's original hatred to the Irish girl was increased by a suit the father had instituted against the
Warchester estate, which, if won, would clip the family
of its most valuable water privileges on the river-front.
But the Colonel's beseeching and Darcy's championship
could not bring concession from the intolerant patrician.
The law, and the law alone, should decide the contest,
though mutual friends had broadly hinted that Lord Poultney would intervene to adjust the feud if madame would
lower the scepter to Lady Molly. It had grown irksome
to Darcy to witness the forays in the two camps, and it
was perhaps to avoid taking a pronounced part in hostilities that of late he had passed much of his time in the

Marbury dales. Certainly, for a young fellow conceded high sway in all the gayeties of the court circles, the lad displayed a strange indifference to the allurements of Malvern; even the dance, where his tall figure glanced so graciously in the stately minuet and the Scotch reel, was no longer the delight to him it had been; and the girls, who had, in the early days of the season, counted on his strong arm, were piqued to note his persistent absence from the scene.

In those days early rising was part of the *régime* of watering-place life, and the young man hastened from the chattering groups at the breakfast-table without a care for the dawdlers who gathered on the sunny verandas to smoke and gossip. When he reached the brook, Denis could be seen or heard cheerily at work in the fields, and at such times Darcy assuaged his thirst at the dairy, or rested from the fatigue of his long jaunt in Aunt Selina's big rocking-chair. The awe at first felt by the family soon wore off, for he was very modest and simple, full of stories and boyish gayety, and seemed so thoroughly to enjoy the cool corner of the ingle nook, that the good housewife was thoroughly won. Even, Norah, in time, was brought to reply timidly to casual questions addressed her, without those mantling blushes that the youth thought so bewitching. He became very much interested in the dairy work, and very often in the early morning appeared on the cool, moss-grown steps with his gun on his shoulder, the dew glistening on his raiment like a hamadryad: at least Norah would have said hamadryad had she been the reader that Denis was, who had at his fingers' ends all the personages of mythic lore. He accommodated himself with good-natured ease to the cool stones as a seat, and watched the little maid as she deftly transferred the masses of yellow butter into little spheres for packing.

The churn, worked by a simple mechanism of Denis's fashioning, gave him endless concern. The cascade that turned the little wheel did not, he found, give it sufficient power, and in a little while, through his superior training in physics, the work was done with less friction, and the small water-power more equally distributed. Norah watched his labors with divided heart, but when, thanks to his mastery of engineering at the academy, he had perfected his hydraulic force, she owned that it was far more useful than Denis's crude planning. The Doctor himself pronounced it a discovery in mechanics, and sagely prophesied that its author would make a mark in the world.

So it soon came that the days that Darcy didn't appear at the farm seemed long and without event. He discussed politics and science with the Doctor, and was full of entertaining stories of the great city world with Aunt Selina. His ingenuity was equal to repairing a defect in the old lady's long-disused spectacles, and she soon found herself going to him as a resource in the complexities of the domestic *régime*. Now and then, under one pretext or another, he would send Denis to Malvern when it was time to go to the pasture for the cows, and he would meet Norah in the wooded lane as she came to let down the bars. Sometimes it was to give her a story-book, the gist of which he had already told her; sometimes to give her a simple trinket to put on her neck or arms. Once he slipped a pretty ring on her finger, and, as she raised her soft eyes in surprise and joy, he bent over and touched his mouth to her lips—pressing her to him in a glowing, passionate embrace. She stood trembling and astonished. He could not meet her eyes, full of perplexed questioning and trouble.

"Silly Norah, why shouldn't your true love kiss you?

All true lovers kiss their sweethearts," and he held the lovely little face up with the palm of his hand under the pink chin.

He tried to catch the liquid softness of the fascinating brogue—a sort of trill in voice, rather than the misplacing of vowel quantities—that lingered in the girl's tones, and laughed pleasantly as the flames of rose and pink came and went in her cheeks. But she was flushed, and shrank as she met his eye now, and darted away among the cows as they stopped to browse in the lush green of the corners of the rail-fence. He stood and laughed a low musical laugh, and followed her flying figure with admiring wonder. Her innocent coyness enchanted him. At West Point he had courted and caressed the belle of the "college widows" without scruple, for the little coquette had herself given the invitation to the combat, and he had borne her off from a score of rivals. But there was no joy in the pursuit such as this little Murillo maiden gave him. To him, as he expressed it, her "guilelessness and trust were epic." It was sweeter to look into the deep untroubled eyes, filled with wonder and love, than to listen to all the artful confessions of the "Point" widow. What his imprudence would lead to he never seriously asked himself. He was not of an age to think of consequences. The pursuit was an idyllic episode, that had at first lured him by its novelty and then swirled him onward by an impulse he never gave himself the trouble of analyzing. Norah was made to love, and, as he had nothing else to do, why should he not play Prince Charming to this dreamy damosel who transformed this pastoral scene into Virgilian romance?

At twenty we are not apt to think much of consequences. At that age there is no sharp monitor in the breast to warn us that what we do leads to other doing and other ends than the mere joy of the moment. There is no logical premonition in our madness. We think, if we think at all, that the rose may bloom, and become a bud again, to the end of the romance. Was not this the perennial teaching of the Nature about them? Under their very eyes, the purple doves were cooing and filling the alders with the soft twitter of their mating; and the primroses were nodding and nestling to each other; the robins shrilling in the soft complaint of fragile amours. But the girl's troubled flight had for the first time stirred the consciousness of the heedless boy with a vague sense of responsibility. A vision of the sorrowing mother, as he had once seen her wandering over the Holly Hills, came back to him, and he dimly associated this childish image with the sad figure. This made him pensive, and he wandered silently on, switching the caraway-tops with his riding-whip distractedly. When at last he looked for Norah she was not near him. He turned, and saw her coming after him, routing the cows as they lingered in the fence-corners. Her face was flushed, and her eyes glistened as she reached him. She had slipped over the fence near the brook, and brought him a nosegay of lilies of the valley. As she held them timidly to him, he took her two hands and drew her toward him, and again his hot lips met her mouth to stifle her protest while he held her in a dreamy, restful embrace. It was to be the last.

"Dear little Norah! what a sweet witch you are, do you know that?"

She fled from him again, startled by his rapturous movement, and turned her head away, burning with shyness and wonder. When they reached the gate to the farm-yard he stopped, and said tenderly:

"Good-by, Norah; I'm going to the city to-morrow, and I sha'n't see you again for I don't know how long."

She came quite close to him now, her eyes dilating with surprise and trouble.

"O Mr. Darcy, won't I see you again, at all, at all?"

"Why, of course you will, silly Norah; only I must be away perhaps a week, and you must be a good Norah, and have all your blushes and prettiness when I come back. You must read the "Paul and Virginia" I brought you, and the "Arabian Nights," and the verses of Mrs. Sigourney. Girls ought to read these, and Denny will explain them to you, instead of me. I will bring you some more books, perhaps, if you're very good. I will let you have the Byron that you read so much of in your poet Moore. It's not the right sort of reading for girls, my mother says, but I'll mark what you're to read and what to skip. Do you think you could be a wise girl and do as I bid you?"

"Ah yes, Mr. Darcy, indeed, indeed I shall. I would do anything in the world you bid me!"

"Well, then, you bewildering witch, come here under this hazel-bush, and bid me good-by. Put your arms about my neck and kiss me as if you were not afraid of me, and say, 'Dear Darcy, I love you!'"

Ah! Darcy was not as wise as Solomon; the ways of a man and a maid were not definable to him. A few minutes before he had snatched the last kiss from these demure lips. But he was true to the form of the word. What would you have? The spirit of the vow was broken by the girl! It was she who now held up the rose-leaf lips that were to close and be a bud again so soon as he had drunk the intoxicating purity of their bloom. He wound the supple, shapely arms about his neck, and stood under the branches looking down into those bewildering, appealing eyes—lip to lip

The cows had straggled into the barn-yard, and began to low plaintively for the milking-pails, and the girl started in mechanical response. Denny came out of the dairy with pail and stool, singing cheerily, and she, without a word, fled along the fence, sheltered by the gooseberry-hedge, to join him. Darcy turned, sauntered back along the lane reflectively, and, coming to the chestnut copse where his horse was cropping the rich grass, mounted, and rode away to Malvern, turning in the saddle to take a last glimpse of the pretty figure he could see moving among the cows. It was a final farewell he meant, and he sighed in the consciousness of a young St. Anthony flying temptation, and inaudibly asking his conscience to mark his heroic mold and stoic self-denial!

"Nody Pody, ye must have been with the fairies, yer step's so light and yer eyes so bright," said Denny, wonderingly, as he caught sight of his sister's flushed cheeks and sparkling eyes when she took a seat on a single-legged stool near him to milk the mottled heifer.

"O Denny, dear, I had to go to the far end of the beech-meadow to fetch the cows; they go farther and farther every day, though the grass is greener in the brook-field."

"I'll put up the bars in the beech-meadow, if you like. It's too far for ye to go in yer thin shoon," said the brother, considerately.

"O Denny, dear, not for the world; and Aunt Selina says it does me good, and I'm sure it does," cries the artless Chloe, bethinking her of some one that makes the beech-meadows all too short a jaunt.

Between themselves the boy and girl kept up the accent and form of the fatherland, an indulgence that brought shocked remonstrance from the Doctor and Aunt Selina, who saw nothing of the picturesque in this archaic

taste. Denis was a natural linguist, and at twelve, by
the Doctor's friendly though sadly limited aid, he had
mastered the elements of Latin, and read with some
readiness " Æsop's Fables," to the no small pride of
the family and wonder of his comrades. As for Norah,
she not only adored her brother with the deep adoration
of her race, she thought him the cleverest boy in all the
township—not even excepting the brilliant and dazzling
Darcy, who, though shining in conversation, was no
match for Denis in drollery and narrative faculty. Denis,
too, knew every plant in the fields, every bush in the wood,
down to the smallest blossom ; he could tell when the
flowers would peep out under the strawberry-leaves, when
the tadpoles would come in the green pond, when the
butterflies would leave their swathing in the spring, and
the turtle nest in the black currants. He was master of
many woodland lores that filled Norah's nights with delight, as the children sat together in the lavender-and-mint-
perfumed chamber under the attic, where they talked over
their simple lives, and wondered vaguely what the future
had in store for them. In these moonlight prattlings the
story always came to the same end. Denis was to earn
money and go to college. Then he was to become a
famous lawyer, like his uncle Phil Collamore, of Belfast ;
and then Norah was to be a fine lady, and marry the most
splendid young fellow in all the land ! Of late Norah had
brought the vaticinations to an end when her own part in
the fanciful play came, and, to the boy's surprise, kissed
him and went into her own room, sometimes even closing
the door when she thought he had fallen asleep.

That night she was especially distraught and irritating.
She forgot all the Æsop tales in the most shameless way.
She couldn't even remember the second declension, which,
after infinite pains, Denny had taught her. The mishaps

of the ass and the hay didn't move her to a smile; they had before thrown her into merriment repressed only to a pitch which should not reach the ears of the kind Doctor and Aunt Selina, who thought the conspirators asleep by nine o'clock, to be ready to rise with the sun. It was in vain that Denny displayed his most fascinating acquisition in the Latin tongue. Norah was listless and unheeding, and he got up and went to bed cross and aggrieved. He heard her place a chair at the window, and he knew she was sitting looking out over the moonlit orchard, and once or twice he heard her sigh softly. He was just dozing into a dream of sly foxes inveigling the credulous crows, when he heard the door closed! Perhaps she was saying her prayers, and he fell away into profound slumber, in which a dreadful vision came to him.

He saw Norah in the wood sleeping, a beautiful snake gliding toward her, its eyes emitting a lambent flame that hid the crawling folds as they wound along through the grass and leaves. He shouted in warning; but, as she opened her eyes languidly, there was no terror in them as the monster drew nearer and nearer, and coiled about her arm, darting its head toward her face. Then the snake was suddenly transformed into a youth, laughing and plucking flowers, looking boldly in Norah's eyes, and caressing her tenderly. Then the handsome youth was gone, and the snake lay coiled and menacing, and Denis found voice and movement. He shouted a troubled cry of fear and warning, and was awake, sitting up in his bed. There was a sudden crash in Norah's room, and leaping from the bed he flung open the door. The moonlight streamed in the windows, outlining every object in the room. Norah stood by the tall dresser, a candle lying at her feet, extinguished. He saw a gleaming object on her finger, and three or four books open in a line under the tilted mirror.

Her back was to the window, and he could not catch the expression of her face.

"O Norah, dear, what was it? I had such a fright. What are ye doing up till this time of night? And you wouldn't listen to Æsop—"

"It's nothing, Denny. I couldn't sleep, and I was reading the books." She was agitated and vexed; he could tell that by her voice.

"What books, Norah? What's that ye have on yer finger?"

"Never mind, Denny. I hear some one moving downstairs. We'll be scolded in the morning. Go to bed. I'm going myself. I'm very tired," and she gently pushed him into his own room, and closed the door again. There were no locks nor bolts on the Marbury doors. She moved a high-backed wooden chair softly against it, and, picking up the candle, reached her arm out of the window to strike the sulphur match on the brick outside, that it might not resound in the stillness of the chamber. The thick cotton wick spluttered feebly in the broken tallow, giving out a dismal glimmer in the transparent light of the moon. Then she took the books, one by one, wrapped them carefully in bits of waste linen, and put them in her little brown leather trunk. She lingered before the mirror, where the glitter of the ring might reflect itself in the dim old glass framed in pink dimity. There was none of the craning, posing vanity of her years or sex in the rapt gaze of her large deep eyes. On her own fair face she hardly cast a glance. It was upon the bit of gold—his gold; she let her eyes rest on these objects almost timidly.

He had touched it. It had been in his waistcoat-pocket, near his heart—the heart that she had felt beating against her own! She held the ring to her lips, kissing it softly.

But, because her face gave him pleasure, she looked at the profile which the sputtering light of the candle only enabled her to catch vaguely. Her tawny masses of hair flashed back limpid rills of gold in the wavering light; it fell over her bare shoulder and white neck: since he thought it was beautiful, she thought well of it too. But of personal vanity in its possession she felt none. Poor child! the æsthetic faculty was not hers in the sense of defining the thing she found beautiful. She had no basis of comparison, and, without a standard, Dante himself could not have painted the luster of Beatrice's beauty. But *he* had told her she must read, and make her mind as beautiful as her face. So she sat at the open window, the moonbeams illuminating the book, and gave her eyes to the pages of " Paul and Virginia," while her mind was far away in the beech-meadow, and a voice that was not Paul's whispered in her ear. The old cuckoo-clock in the "entry," as the vestibule was descriptively called in those days, struck one, and she started in affright. She would have scant rest if she didn't go to bed, for she never slept later than four in summer. She could keep the ring on her finger until morning, and then put it with her other treasures, and with the little circlet pressed to her lips she fell into a troubled sleep.

The birds interrupted her drowsy reveries three hours later, and it was time to be about at her work, while her eyes were heavy with the sleep she had not felt during the blissful solitude of the night. Two weeks passed; she saw nothing more of Darcy. She heard the Doctor say that the family had gone back to Warchester, and her little heart grew heavy; for now it was plain the beautiful vision would come no more. Denny wondered at her listlessness and preoccupation. Before this she was as clever in bird or bush lore as himself, or seemed to him to be, for her ready credulity and implicit belief in his oracular sayings were to him evidence that her assents were based on knowledge, just as the pundit in science holds the appreciative critic a man of parts and equal acquisition who does not take the trouble to contradict him. But she went no more with Denny now in the long twilight rovings she had loved, or, if she did, she was so distracted and heedless that he was vexed and ill-humored when they came back to the unlighted house. One day Doctor Marbury bade Norah get ready to go to the city with him next day.

Denny found a singular alteration in her that night. Her eyes sparkled as of old, and she sang so cheerily, as she flitted about the dairy, that he put off a tramp to the oak woods, where he was experimenting with a young brood of kingfishers. He watched her as she moved about, and for the first time it came into his mind that she was very pretty, almost as pretty, he thought, as the little girl toward whom he had vowed a boy's passionate chivalry.

"I say, Norah, why aren't you like this always?"

"Like what? Sure, I am always the same."

"No, you aren't; your face is as long as Black Dick's" (Black Dick was the Doctor's pet cob), "and you haven't enough spirit to say mud to a green turtle. I don't have any enjoyment with you lately at all. Come, now, tell me what it is. You're not going to be a 'Free Willer,' are you?"

A Free Willer was the name of a Baptist society just established in Marbury Center, and the congregation was derided a good deal by the Methodists and Quakers, who were in the majority in the township.

"Denny, dear, you're a silly little boy," said Norah, with a placid laugh, as she turned a great stream of milk into the shining tin pans. "You know very well I'm not

going to be a Free Willer to make myself a show in Marbury."

The two, when alone, were fond of reviving the forms
of speech and even the accent of their parents, as if an
instinct impelled them to cherish all that is left the Alien
among strangers not only antipathetic to their race, but
derisively alert to caricature the tokens of the lost *patrie*.
It was a pleasant sound to hear Norah dearing Denny in
the soft rich brogue she had kept better than the boy. It
was always a signal to him that his sister was in a merry
humor, and to-night she sang him "Kathleen, mavour-
neen" and "The Irish Jaunting-Car" until his eyes filled
with tears, and the tears were forgotten in Pegg's lyric
witchery. He was very happy when they went up-stairs,
and made sure that Norah would not shut the door as she
had of late done. But he was disappointed. She was gay
and talkative enough until she said she felt sleepy, but, so
soon as he was in bed, she shut the door; and, as he lay
awake, puzzling over the mystery, he saw a ray of light
under the door! Now, lights in the house in summer
were unknown outside the Doctor's study, and even there
they were rarely kept burning after ten o'clock.

What could Norah be doing with a light at such a time?
Reading? No, she couldn't be reading, because she always
let him read to her. She couldn't be getting ready for the
journey to the city, because her muslin gown he had seen
her take from the closet, and her silk mitts and hat from
the lavender-scented chest. He listened intently. He
was sure he could hear the rustle of stiffly starched skirts,
which were worn very voluminous in those days. Tor-
mented by the strange revolution in Norah's habits, the boy
sat up in bed and listened. He was sure Norah was moving about. He could hear the stiff fabric rustling against
the bureau-drawers as the brass handles were touched.

An ungovernable curiosity, mingled with wounded pride, filled his startled senses. How could Norah treat him so? He had never found a bird's-nest, nor an arbutus-bed, nor a fringed gentian, nor a tiger-lily, nor a Jack-in-the-pulpit (in those days these were rarities even to favored botanists in that part of the country, and could only be got by the most adventurous quest in such places as gave Denny deadly terror to approach, for they were the places where his mortal terror, the black snakes, most loved to coil themselves)—he had never, I say, denied her the bloom of these delights, and the spirit of fair play, sometimes keenest in a boy, revolted that she should deny him a share in her secrets or enjoyments. He slipped out of bed and tried to lift the latch, but it was fastened, and the door remained firm. This was a still more grievous mark of infidelity, and his eyes filled with tears of wounded love. He heard a furtive movement in the room, and then all was still.

"Norah," he whispered, for he knew the consequence of waking the old couple down-stairs, "Norah, let me in."

He could hear her moving to the door; he could even hear her starched skirts rustling, and he was in an agony of wonder. She didn't open the door to him, but whispered crossly through the thin panel:

"What do you want? I sha'n't let you in. Go to bed; you're a bad boy."

Stung by this reproach, and exasperated by his long vigil, Denny gave the door a loud knock, and began to work the latch violently.

"Wait a minute, and I will let you in," Norah said in a pleading, frightened voice. He heard her move swiftly away from the door and then come back. The peg over the latch was drawn out—Denny noted that it had been fashioned to fit the place—and the door opened, but the room was in darkness. He could distinguish Norah's form, and he saw that she was dressed as if to go out. The moon was at the full, and his eyes soon became enough accustomed to the dim light to see that she had on the cherished muslin gown which was only worn to church and town. The wick of the candle was still smoking.

"What are you doing, Norah? Why have you got your Sunday dress on? Why did you blow out the light?"

"I'm trying my clothes on for the morning. I never have time to look them over when I go to the city—I—"

"Why, Norah, what's that on your finger? And you've gold in your ears. Where did you get them?" and Denny took her hand, which she strove to wrench away.

"You're a silly bad boy, Denny, and I'll save no more doughnuts and ginger-cake for you, nor fill your dinner-pail; you sha'n't go to the surprise-party with me neither—"

But Denny, whose ungovernable curiosity was now more whetted by the discovery of the gimcracks, had found the matches and lighted the candle. Norah made as if to blow it out, but he said quite determinedly:

"If you do, miss, I shall stamp on the floor, and, when the Doctor asks what it is, I shall tell him, and he will come and see your goings on."

Norah turned her back on him and sank into a chair. She was dressed in her best, as Denny conjectured. In her ears she had put the two little golden drops Darcy had given her, and the ring was on her finger. She had evidently been admiring herself in the mirror; for it was lifted from the high bureau and set down on the chest. She sat under the boy's mute and wondering inspection quite rigid and silent. He walked all around her, and then set the candle down, wondering what it all meant, for he had never known her to care much for dress, and he was sure she couldn't have bought the trinkets.

"Are they gold, Norah?" he asked, pointing to the glittering things.

"I'll not tell you a word. I want to go to bed," and she arose and began to take the ring from her finger, and then the jewels from her ears. But she was careful not to let them out of her grasp. If Denny saw the ring he would read the letters cut inside, and then he would know all.

"You're a giddy, foolish girl, and I don't love you any more," said Denny, moving toward the door.

"I—I—O Denny! don't say that; we've been so close to each other this many a year. You never said anything cruel before. I—I can't bear it, Denny! It's like cruelty to the mother. O Denny! she wouldn't say that to me—" and Norah fell on the edge of the bed, disheveled and woe-begone.

"Well," Denny said haltingly, keeping his eyes resolutely from her, as he felt the hot tears betraying him, "when you sit up at night to keep secrets from me, and make a peg to fasten the door to keep me out, I think I ought to be angry with you, don't you?"

"Yes, but don't, Denny, for I can't bear it!"

"Well, then, tell me all about it."

"All about what?" and she looked up more composedly now, for she knew that when Denny was lulled into disputation all common grievances were forgotten.

"How silly you are, Norah. You know well enough—" But here Norah, in laying a garment on the dresser, managed to overturn the candle, which went out.

"But you don't feel angry, Denny, do you?"

"Yes, I do; that is—"

"Well, Denny, in the morning I shall have ever so

much to tell you; so be a good boy now and go to bed."
She fell on her knees, and Denny couldn't prolong the
contest, for prayer was a sacred rite to Kate's son.

He went out and closed the door. He sobbed himself
to sleep, cut to the heart that Norah had a secret from
him, and that she should seem to be indifferent whether he
loved her or not.

In the morning Norah was up long before Denis
awoke, and he peeped sadly into her room as he dressed
himself. The muslin gown, silk mantle edged with black
lace, and the ponderous scoop bonnet were carefully laid
out on the bed, ready to be put on when the morning
work should be done. He ran off down the dewy lane
with the cows, and when he got back from the meadow
the Doctor, with Norah by his side, was driving down the
Warchester road in the patriarchal gig-wagon. Norah's
cheeks bloomed like the wild roses in the fence-corners as
the wagon rolled cheerfully along over the road humid
with dew. The sun was just breaking through the green
fringe of the trees lining the hills to the eastward, and the
morning concert in the hedges filled the air with unstudied
symphonies that charmed the ear. The Doctor stopped a
dozen times to gossip with the farmers as they hailed him
from the wheat-fields, where the mowers were at work with
their great basket sickles, tumbling down wide swaths
of the yellow grain. Norah could hardly bide these delays
with patience, and her eyes brightened as they reached the
top of the hill, where the Doctor's neighborly amenities
were confined to a bow and cordial "good-day." When
they drove into the city it was still early morning: the
working-people were moving in crowds to the factories
and shops with dinner-pails and burdens; the stores were
just opening, and the main streets were otherwise quite
deserted. The horses were driven into the stables of the

Eagle tavern, and Norah was bestowed in the stiff parlor
to await the Doctor's return. She seated herself at the window and watched the bustling street. The Eagle was at
the junction of four streets, and she could see the main
traffic of the town. Others, like herself awaiting the movements of the "men-folks," presently made a considerable
company in the room, but she gave them no heed. She
was watching for a form she had been hungering to see for
weeks ; but she watched in vain.

At noon the Doctor came back, and took her into the
noisy dining-room, where the poor child tried to eat, but
could not. The Doctor remarked her want of appetite
and rallied her on her country tastes ; but a discussion
with a neighbor on a question of crops diverted him from
her abstemiousness, and she was relieved and glad, for she
felt that the tears were very near her eyes. After dinner
she resumed her post at the window. Her heart fluttered
when, toward the middle of the afternoon, she saw the
Doctor returning to the tavern in company with Colonel
Warchester. But they didn't come into the parlor. She
heard the Doctor's voice in the hallway and Warchester's
low responses. Presently the horses came around to the
door, and the Doctor bade her get into the vehicle. Colonel Warchester came out with the Doctor, who said, as he
took his place :

"I shall be at your house in less than an hour. I have
some shopping to do for the women folks."

Then Norah's eyes sparkled. She should see him, after
all! He would know that she was in the gig, and would
come out and speak to her. She loved to go into the
shops and look at the wonders displayed, but to-day she
could hardly help the Doctor in the simple purchases Aunt
Selina had written out so carefully. At length they were
finished, and the Doctor, with a sigh of relief, put her in the

6

seat and drove off to that enchanted court quarter of the town where the great houses stood far back from the street, with tall columns in front, like a colony of Grecian temples in an urban Arcady. Before the largest of these wonderful mansions, secluded behind a circular hedge, the Doctor halted, and getting out gave the lines to Norah.

Her heart beat as he disappeared through the high iron gates, bidding her await his return. She sat looking straight before her through a blinding mist of hot tears, which, as the time dragged wearily on, fell faster and grew more burning. She was sobbing bitterly, and the lines had fallen from her hands, when she was aroused by a great clatter in the street. Before she could seize the reins, a dreadful apparition arose a few yards in front coming toward her. There was a loud ringing of bells, shouting men and skurrying vehicles, as a ponderous fire-engine —a machine just introduced into the civic system of Warchester—came upon her sight. The country horses, terrified by the spectacle, backed and turned, tipping the awkward chariot, and before the frightened girl knew what was impending she was lying in the overturned cape of the gig, the horses struggling madly to get out of the street. Her head came violently in contact with a curbstone, and she knew no more. At the moment of the catastrophe a young gentleman, riding a large bay horse, and accompanied by a young girl on a pony, came cantering down the Warchester grounds. The Doctor, rushing out, shouted that his horses were running away; and the young man, leaving his companion, dashed into the street, and in an instant was almost abreast of the overturned vehicle, caught on the curb. Leaping from the horse, he caught the leader just as it turned and cleared the impediment, and relinquishing the rein to the stableman, who had run out, he extricated Norah from the

wreck. She was quite unconscious. Blood was streaming from her head, and for a moment he thought her dead.
The Doctor, coming up soon, decided that she was merely
stunned by the fright and concussion, and would be all
right after the application of restoratives.

"I will carry her into the house," said Darcy, for it
was he, "and the man will take care of the horses, while
you attend her."

He lifted her up tenderly, more agitated than the Doctor, and carried her easily up the bridle-path to the house.
The young lady leaped off the pony as he came up, and
asked him who it was.

"Dr. Marbury's ward, the girl you heard my mother
speaking about the other day," Darcy said, indifferently.
"She is badly hurt."

"Poor thing!" echoed the other, and they continued in
silence to the house. Darcy, in quaking terror lest Norah
should revive and recognize him in the presence of the
other, abruptly called for the housekeeper on entering the
hall, and ordered that Norah be taken up-stairs; but, as
there was some delay, he bade his companion wait while
he carried the victim to the housekeeper's room. His
burden was so slight that he leaped up-stairs and was
within the shelter of the room before any one else was
within hearing. Then, laying her gently on a couch, he
pressed a lingering kiss upon the white lips, murmuring:

"Norah, my own gentle girl!"

He could feel her reviving as she opened her eyes.
They were fixed upon him with a wondering joy, and
then closed. Before he could speak a word of caution,
the housekeeper's voice was heard at the door, and he
stood above the couch as she came in.

"O Mr. Darcy! is she dead?"

"No, Mrs. Ray, but she is badly hurt; the Doctor will

be here in a minute. I'll go, so that you may remove her clothes," and he walked hastily away. He met the Doctor on the stairs, and directed him where to go, and then rejoined his companion, who stood on the porch talking with Mrs. Warchester. The horses were brought up as he narrated the incident, and, bidding his mother attend the sufferer, he set out at a brisk canter, angry and ill at ease under the thoughtless banter of the young girl who dwelt unsuspiciously upon his heroic adventure.

"You were quite like the hero in the play, Darcy. I really must bring on a catastrophe to try your mettle; where your heart's engaged, do you think your presence of mind would be equal to that cavalier's readiness?"

She looked at him archly as he shot a little beyond her, his face concealed by the movement.

"Beauty in distress commands every man's heart, Agnes; don't put me to the test, where you doubt the result."

"But you didn't know there was beauty there—even rustic beauty."

"True hearts divine beauty when danger threatens. I'm for a canter—come!"

CHAPTER VIII.

YOUNG BARBARIANS AT PLAY.

On returning from his ride, two hours later, Darcy was just in time to meet the physician coming out with Dr. Marbury. He asked quietly after the invalid, and was told that her shoulder had been fractured, but that the injuries about the head were trifling. She could not bear removal for some days. There was, however, no cause for alarm. He breathed an inward sigh of devout relief, for he had been tortured by the fear that Norah would lie in the house in a fever, and in her delirium murmur his name in the horror-struck ears of the housekeeper or even his mother. He bade the Doctor good-by with relieved effusion, assuring him that the girl would be well cared for by his mother and family.

"I feel sure of that, Darcy. All that troubles me is the burden that poor Norah must be to you all until we can remove her," said the Doctor, pressing the young man's hand. "If it will be of any use I will send Denny to watch over his sister."

"Never think of such a thing, Doctor; we have plenty of people in the house, and the small attention Norah will need won't tax any of them," returned Darcy, heartily. He was immensely relieved, but he entered the supper-room musing and distracted. Madame Warchester sat in state at the head of the table, and, noticing her son's abstraction, said :

"Darcy, I have a message from Bucephalo, from sister Kate. They are going to have a great time there next week to commemorate the defeat of the British at Lundy's Lane. General Scott is to be their guest, and she wants us to come up and help her entertain the company. You must go, at any rate. I want you to know these eminent people. It is an opportunity for a young man."

"Are you all going?" he asked, his face brightening.

"I don't see how I can go with this young person in the house. By-the-way, do you know she is one of those Boynes—James Boyne's niece?"

"Is she?" he asked indifferently.

"Yes. The mother, it seems, is dead, and the family

has been scattered, as all these foreign folk do scatter. They seem to have no sense of family ties as we do."

"Perhaps, mother, it isn't so much a lack of our sense of family ties as the misfortune of incapacity to hold together in a new country, where, coming late in life, the parents do not understand how to manage. However, never mind that. I am delighted at the idea of the great doings at Bucephalo. Let Mrs. Ray take charge of the house, and we can all set off in the morning; for, unless you go, I shall decline the opportunity of meeting the commander-in-chief."

Perhaps, had the fond mother seen the processes of the filial mind she would not have smiled such complacent assent. He was thinking of the possible danger of the mother and Norah seeing too much of each other. The child's innocence might betray his past relations, and, while he was conscious of no wrong-doing, he knew his mother well enough to foresee the effect even such a harmless intimacy would produce upon her. The Bucephalo visit came like relief in a dark night, and he talked gayly of the fine times they would have with the great people assembled at his aunt's. So Norah saw no more of Darcy, though, in a day or two, when she recovered consciousness, she turned her eyes eagerly toward the door whenever any one entered. She was too timid to ask her nurse, whom at first she supposed to be Darcy's relative.

It was not for several days, and just as she was getting strong enough to sit up, that Denny, coming to see her, made known that the family were all away, and would not be back for some time. She sighed to be back in the Marbury home, as Denny prattled of the doings on the farm: how the mottled cow had come up to the dairy-door, for days after Norah's going, refusing at first to let any one milk her; how all the cows hid themselves in the deep wood of an evening, refusing to come to the bars until they were driven ; how the butter-pats were round and ugly under the manipulations of "Alameda," the neighbor's daughter, who came in to help Aunt Selina during Norah's absence.

The grandeur of this great house oppressed her. One day Mrs. Ray took her through all the chambers, to show her the state in which the family lived. She passed listlessly through Madame Warchester's fine boudoir, with high canopied windows and rich carpeting ; but when Mrs. Ray said, "This is Mr. Darcy's room," she grew instantly alert.

It was the room of a luxurious young man of the olden time, and would not be regarded as effeminate to-day. Double-barreled rifles were crossed over the mantel-piece, hunting-horns and Nimrod traps covered the walls. There were no French prints, such as young kinsmen of Darcy affect to-day, but in their place grim oil-paintings of the Puritan ancestry of the house, such as in old times adorned the apartments of the eldest sons of great houses. Darcy's tastes were evidently warlike, for, of recent works of art, he possessed turgid prints of the surrender at Yorktown ; General Gates, on a wondrously long-legged and prancing horse, pointing a ferocious sword at General Burgoyne on the hill of Saratoga ; another, in hues so varied that the spectator was for a time perplexed as to the manner of men portrayed, represented the then recent battle of Lundy's Lane, with the British army leaping over the Horseshoe Falls, pursued by long lines of very blue figures sheltered under canopies of red, white, and blue ! These artless works of patriotic genius did not impress Norah very much. She walked over to the wall, where the gun rested that she had seen often on the young man's arm, and laid her hand on the stock caressingly. It was the only familiar object in the room. It recalled the hours he had passed in the dairy, and his jocular assurances to her when she had at first avoided it with terror. She would have kissed the piece had Mrs. Ray not been in the room. As it was, with a gentle sigh she turned and followed her chaperone through the other solemn chambers, very distraught and, as the good woman thought, overawed by the unaccustomed grandeur. A few days after she was taken home, and sat, in the joyful state of a convalescent, in the happy corner where the broad hearth of bricks met the carpet she had long ago helped to fabricate.

It was peace and rest, and it was home. But somehow it was not the content she had once known. Everything was tender, cheerful, and devoted, but Norah felt, with a guilty pang, that she was not at rest as she used to be. Even when she was able to go out and welcome the lowing herd in the evening, the absurd gambols of the mottled cow " Penelope " failed to excite the joy she used to feel as she rubbed its shaggy nose and fed it the sweet apples from the harvest tree. What was still more grievous, she could never milk again. The dislocated shoulder had permanently injured the muscles of her arm, and Denny in future milked " Penelope," who refused to permit the stable-man to come near her.

By September, when Denny resumed school, after the long summer vacation, Norah had fallen into the old way of life, but her soul was full of a sad, tender yearning. Every shadow that fell on the dairy filled her with a tumultuous expectation, only to be disappointed. He never came. Even the Doctor, who occasionally went to town alone now, lost the habit of speaking of young Warchester. He had gone into the army, and was on the staff of the commander-in-chief. But his memory was embalmed in the little hair chest in Norah's room.

There, in the darkness, when the house was still, Norah would take out the books and trinkets and sit in the moonlight touching them, as a devotee fingers a rosary, repeating the caressing words he had said so long ago.

Denny, immersed in his school, was vaguely conscious that Norah had changed, but he was puzzled to say how. She was interested in all his activities as of yore; she never refused his invitations to the woodland mysteries : but somehow she didn't gibe him with her old humor, nor give such poetic guesses at the purposes of the occult sciences of flowers, plants, and insects, as in the old days. She was still proud of him, and went regularly of a Saturday afternoon to hear and applaud his declamations when the boys "spoke their pieces." He was secretly very proud and happy when he overheard the other boys descant on the beauty of "that Paddy's sister."

Marbury Center had become a considerable village. It was four miles from Warchester, and about this time the sedate community was scandalized by the opening of a tavern. Until this time the mill had been the rendezvous of the hamlet, where Seth Cook had entertained such stray guests as found bed and lodging needful. There was a good deal of traffic between Warchester and Bucephalo, and the enterprising Ritter had exchanged a town lot for the farm that jutted on the corner opposite the mill. Here he had installed his family, to build up a business and work the farm in the cherished German fashion. The older members of the community looked upon the invasion as a desecration of the township, and for a time the " Dutch rum-sellers" were avoided by their neighbors. But the young men found the simple dissipations of the place very agreeable. The estate had run down sadly, the mansion, which had been in the family of the previous owner for a quarter of a century, was a very imposing country residence. Its tall white pillars quite eclipsed anything nearer than War-chester. The whole of the front part of the building was made into a " bar," with white sanded floor and neat little tables. The broad spacious piazza was always cool, and here of an evening the young men began to find a pleasure in lounging after the work of the day, and watching the equi-pages from the city that began to make the place a " re-sort."

And when it was seen that Ritter's was not the "low groggery " that public rumor anticipated, and that the family was quiet, decent, laborious, and intelligent, Mar-bury recalled its fierce hostile purpose, and came to regard the new-comers as an acquisition. For the thrift, enter-prise, and assiduity with which the run-down acres were reclaimed were a revelation to the timid agriculture of the township. Such gardening had never been dreamed of in the careless methods of the country. The second year's crops paid the entire cost of the purchase, aside from the exchange, and the Ritters were accepted as people of "means," which in those days meant everything in the cautious estimation of our fathers. Mrs. Ritter no longer dispensed the beer in the pewter beakers that passed around among her clients. Wilhelmina and Oswald were the aptest students in the Marbury school, and Hans Ritter was, in the second year of his coming, elected trustee. Denny and Oswald were about the same age, and ardent rivals in their classes. These Alien interlopers were regarded with a good deal of jealousy and some scorn by the native youth. Oswald was nicknamed "young Dutchy " as Denny had been known from the first as "the Paddy." Beyond their scholastic rivalry the two boys were fairly good friends, and between them they were a match for the rest when covert enmity went beyond mere tantalizing. Denny was foremost in grammar, history, geography, spelling; while Oswald led the school in mathematics—with only one rival, Dilly Dane—who was a phenomenal pupil in algebra and geometry. Arthur Kennel, the ringleader in Denny's early persecutions, was still the tormentor-in-chief of the young tyrants, and, whenever he saw an opportunity, worked, with the malignant insight of a boy, all the petty oppression known to boyish ingenuity, against Denny. But harsh as were his young years, and burdensome as the routine of persecution grew, there were joys they could not lessen, rewards that they could not steep in tears. They could not depose him from the leadership of his classes, nor deprive him of the covert partiality of pretty Dilly Dane. In spite of persistent tricks, savage and relentless—in the face of such organized caricature and sarcasm as only boys can devise against the gentle and uncomplaining—the modest girl maintained her passive championship of the abhorred Alien.

There was always the loveliest little blush for him when he timidly laid the spoils of his wild-wood tours on her desk, and a responsive signal when, in the crisis of examination, he dextrously formed his lips into the answer that saved her pride from the mortification of displacement in the class. She accepted tacitly every meek sign of the timorous lad's devotion, and, in a sort of gentle bravado, shared the food in her ample basket with Denny when his inquisitors emptied or hid his own modest luncheon. Sometimes, too, she arose in stern wrath and put the leagued imps to shame when they became unbearably insolent in their small persecutions. Sometimes too—never-to-be-forgotten evenings, when the romping girls went berrying—Dilly walked sedately with her proud knight along the Marbury road to the parting of the ways, prattling

sweetly of the future, when her sweetheart should be a
great lawyer, and make speeches, like Governor Darcy, that
should set the jury in tears, and make the Warchester
"Watchman" speak of him as our "eminent and distinguished townsman."   In wanderings of this delightful
sort, she listened gravely to the boy's impulsive chatter
over the day's lessons, or sighed and blushed with delight
as he artlessly recounted, with the enthusiasm of an ama-
teur, his wondrous discoveries in the huckleberry swamps,
or listened sympathetically to his hair-breadth escapes in
the tall limbs of the chestnut- or walnut-trees as he gathered these dainty treasures for her.   Sometimes they
were set upon by jeering fellow-scholars in these homeward rambles; but Dilly had a mild dignity of her own
that disheartened all save the most audacious.

One day Denny fell into deep disgrace.   He was
worried into striking one of his tormentors, and there
was a prodigious agitation.   He had patiently endured
bent pins on his bench, had remained quiet when water
was poured down his back by means of an alder syringe ;
but, when a bench-mate daubed the pages of his new
grammar with maple sirup, Denny raised his arm and
gave the culprit a resounding smack that left a tell-tale
welt of red on the boy's face.

The teacher called Denny out, put a stiff sun-shade on
his head, lashed his bare palms with a birch ferule, and
forbade, for a week, his leaving the room at recess or the
long joyous nooning, when the boys and girls played
housekeeping under the laurels and odorous sassafras
bushes.   This was a severe penalty to Denny, for, besides
the pleasures of the noon hour, the punishment inflicted
was the last mark of disgrace.   Furthermore, the weather
was hot, and the boys always had a swim in the limpid
pond back of the mill.   Denny swam well, and loved to

lead the others in diving and what not. The first day he bore the punishment manfully, ignoring the taunts of the malignants as they rushed out joyously to the pond. It happened on the second day that the teacher was called away just before noon, and left a sister of Arthur Kennel's in charge. A few minutes after the boys had gone for the noon hour, Arthur came to Denny, who sat disconsolately trying to fasten his mind on his lesson, saying:

"I say, Paddy, Miss Kimball has been sent for to go to the city, and won't be back till Saturday. She will never know if you come out. Come on; we're going to play follow-the-leader, and Dave Walden has set up a high spring-board, and you dasent dive from it."

As Denny hesitated, the young tempter continued:

"Sue"—that was his sister—"has gone home to dinner, and she will never know, and I'll see that none of the fellows tell on you. Come on."

Denny looked around the vacant room, and thought of the long dismal hour to be passed, with the shouts of the others out at play, and yielded. The hour was a madly merry one. He "stumped" all of his fellows in diving, and when the bell rang he found himself alone at the farther side of the pond. When he reached the covert where he had laid his clothes, they were gone! He searched every nook by the waterside, but there was no sign of them. Then he realized his folly in listening to the tempter. He would be disgraced and expelled from school; and, worst of all, he was guilty!

Poor lad: it was his first lesson in the woful results of casuistry—that subtle law of consequence which follows transgression; but I doubt if Burr or Benedict Arnold suffered more accute agony in the cataclysm of transgression than the poor child, as he cowered in an agony of remorse under the trembling willows! For hours he writhed in an abandonment of grief on the sandy shore, helpless and despairing. There was no help. He couldn't call to any one. Shame restrained him. He must wait until his tormentors saw fit to bring his clothes. He heard the shouts of the boys at recess. Surely they would come to his relief? No; the half-hour passed, and no one appeared. At four he heard them come out. Surely he would be rescued now? The voices died out. The boys had gone. He rushed as far up the bank as he could without exposing his naked person to the tavern and the mill windows. No one was in sight. A swooning sensation of terror came on him. He was to be left all night. His voice was hoarse with hallooing, and he fell on the ground in a convulsion of impotent rage and anguish. He dared not present himself at the mill. He must wait for darkness, and then fly homeward across the fields. How long he sat in his misery he didn't know, but presently he heard:

"Hello, Denny, where be you?"

"He leaped with joy," and for a few moments could not answer as he made toward the sound. At the edge of the dam he saw the figure of a man in the twilight. He had a bundle in his hand, but Denny didn't recognize him.

"Be you there?" asked a voice in some doubt.

"Are you looking for me?" asked the lad despairingly, halting at the edge of the bushes in an agony of shame.

"Yaas, I'm looking for you. Where in creation be you? Oh, there you be! Here's some clothes Dilly Dane has sent you. You'd better put 'em on pretty quick, as the fox said to the cat when she found her claws," and chuckling at his jocose inconsequence, or the lad's shy approach, the man tossed the bundle toward him, and then began to fill his pipe.

"Mity lucky for yaou little Dilly heerd of yaour fix. Cute gurl that ere. Heerd young Art Kennel laffing over the joke he'd played yaou, and she jest sent these ere things. They won't fit yaou much, I guess, but they'll do better nor sheep-skin—ah, ha-ha!—till yaou git hum, eh? There's a hunk uv ginger-bread in the passle to keep yaou alive till yaou git hum. Found it, eh?" and the joker continued to explode at his own nimble wit.

"Oh, yes, thank you. Please thank Dilly, and tell her —tell her—"

"What, that yaou think she's just as sweet as peaches? Bless you, Irishy, she knows that. I suppose you mean fur me to tell her that yaou're obleeged, as the hen said when she found a china nest-egg. I reckon she knows yaou're obleeged. Most folks would be obleeged to have close brought 'em. Leastwise I don't remember no one but the 'postle John as enjoyed loafin' about in the bushes with no raiment nor nothin'. But in those days, yaou know, sonny, folks went naked for the most part; leastwise, from all I can make out, they didn't kiver thimselves any more'n they had to; but—"

"I think I will have to run home now," Denny said; "our folks will be very angry, and think I stayed away. Good-night."

"Well, that's a fact, though yaou might a spoke sooner," ejaculated the deliverer, as the figure of Denny fled over the rise in the road. Sereno Mapes was the Deacon's, Dilly Dane's father's, "hired man," and had been with the family since childhood. Dr. Marbury was just on the point of driving out of the lane when Denny came panting in. There was hot indignation in the household when the story was told, and the indignant Doctor declared that this odious persecution of his boy had gone far enough. He would himself go to the school the next day and teach that scamp Kennel a lesson. When Denny marched into school the next morning there was a subdued titter among the boys, and a good deal of wonder when the Doctor followed. He bowed grimly to the teacher, and said:

"I have come to say a word to you as the teacher of this school, and these boys as your pupils. Years ago I taught in this school myself. I know something of what boys are, but in all my experience I never heard of anything so cruel as the way certain boys here have set themselves on Denis Boyne." Then he rehearsed such of the lad's miseries as he had heard from Denny and gathered from the neighbors. "From the first day of his coming until now you have made his school-life a misery. You first tried to beat him, and, when you found he could take his own part, then you set to work to prejudice his teachers against him. You have laid plots to make him appear a thief; you have put lost articles in his desk; you have refused him equality in your games until his cleverness compelled you to let him share them. Now, this must stop. If the teacher is unable to make you act like decent and well-reared boys, I shall find means to do it."

When the Doctor stopped, the teacher said, in some embarrassment:

"Dr. Marbury, Denis has been expelled from this school. I have the letter here, which I meant to send you to-day with his books."

"Expelled, Miss Kimball! What do you mean?"

The teacher explained the scene in the school-room, and the penalty she had prescribed, and concluded: "I laid the case before Mr. Kennel, the President of the Trustees. He approved of the dismissal and signed it. Here it is."

The Doctor opened the envelope and read it through slowly.

"Very well, Miss Kimball. Denis, you will take your accustomed place, and remain until I come back."

With this, bowing in the most stately fashion to the astonished mistress, the Doctor put his spectacles in his pocket and strode out. He drove to the Kennel farm, a mile or more distant. The owner was in the field, and, following him thither, the Doctor found him cutting corn. The compliments of the day were passed with urbane' gravity on the Doctor's part, and with repressed wonder on that of Mr. Kennel, when the former said :

"I have come to tell you that I shall have to make out a warrant for your son Arthur."

"A warrant for Arthur! What has he done?"

"He stole the clothes of my adopted son last night."

"Ah! that was only a joke."

"But it is not a joke in law, I assure you. He will certainly be punished severely for it."

Kennel, who had never before seen Dr. Marbury in his *rôle* of Justice of the Peace, changed color at this, and cried out remonstratingly :

"Come, come, Doctor, you wouldn't act like that with a neighbor. You know very well that my boy only meant it as a joke. The clothes are at the school-house now, and I will have them sent back."

"But, if you thought it a joke, how could you make Denis's absence from school such a serious matter, and sign this order of expulsion?" and the Doctor held out the paper the teacher had given him.

Kennel took the paper, read it attentively, as if he had never seen it before, scratched his head in perplexity, and then said :

"Well, now, Doctor, I didn't think of that having anything to do with the other affair. Denis, you know, is a bad, vicious boy ; he has been the pest of the school, and is corrupting the other children by his ways."

"There, there, Kennel, that will do. I don't know where you learn all this, but, whoever your authority is, he or she is a liar and a sneak. Denis can't be at school any-thing else than he is at home—a high-spirited, tender, truthful, manly fellow—and, I may add, I don't know a child in this district that is his superior in any of the quali-'ties that mark a lovable, obedient child. But I'm not here to discuss the merits of the boy. This expulsion must be withdrawn, and an apology made to Denis before the whole school—now—this morning, or your son goes to the jail for malefactors."

Dr. Marbury's reputation was well known to Kennel, and, though the humiliation was bitter, he was forced to do it in the end. He got into the Doctor's gig, drove to the school, and, to the amazement of the open-mouthed scholars, said :

"I find that an injustice has been done to Denis Boyne. I signed an order for his expulsion, without knowing all the particulars. I revoke that expulsion, and I cordially assure Denis that his conduct merits praise instead of blame."

Here he paused, perspiring profusely, and, beckoning to his son Arthur, whose eyes had been fastened on his father in wonder, he resumed, as his hand rested on his son's shoulder :

"I hope the rest of the boys will take warning from the lesson my son is now learning. Arthur, go to Denis and ask his pardon. Go !"

The lad slunk down the aisle, amid the craning of necks and subdued titters, until he stood by Denny's side, who was blushing very red and looking very sheepish. Arthur

found his tongue tied, however, and Denny generously
held out his hand, accepting the stuttering monosyllables
of the other as the exacted apology. Thereafter, for a
time, Denny was suffered to go his way in silence. He
found no more dead snakes in his dinner-basket; no pins
on his seat; nor the leaves of his books glued together;
nor any of the malevolent pranks that boys play upon those
they hate and fear. He was let ceremoniously alone by
Arthur and his coterie, who pointedly refused to join in
games that included the Alien. He was excluded from
wintergreen picnics, and denied invitation to the Saturday
jaunts to the lake. But, on the other hand, the teacher
came to regard him as her best pupil. He stood at the
head of most of the classes, and it was conceded that he
was sure of the great prize to be awarded to the pupil taking the most merit-marks at the end of the term.

There was something unboyishly malignant in the pertinacity of Arthur's hatred of his rival. Though he had
ceased his former taunting and underhand trickery, he was
none the less intent on humiliating his enemy. After the
apology incident, he had set himself to work to breed hatred
between Oswald and Denny. Oswald was no longer called
" Dutchy." He was invited to all the select games led by
Arthur, and his mind filled with grievances against his
fellow-Alien. Oswald was very diligent in his mathematics,
and felt sure of gaining the prize in that branch. One
morning, just before the decisions were announced, the
teacher, on examining her books, found that they had been
tampered with. Each day it was her custom to enter the
marks against each name. She found that some one had
erased those against Oswald's and increased those before
Denny's. The attempt was a very stupid one, for, of
course, the increase for Denny could do him no good, nor
the erasure of Oswald's do him material harm, unless the

next highest number happened to be very nearly the same.

But, on examination, the next highest—Dilly Dane's—the score was found to have been increased by marks interlined. The obvious inference would be that Denis had tampered with the books. But, as the work had been done so bunglingly, he could not hope to benefit by the plot. When the school was dismissed for the day, the teacher called Denis to the desk and asked him to help her with some tallying. She read a long list of names, and directed him to make the marks such as she used in keeping the standings. When he had gone she examined the work, and compared the characters with those forged in her book. They were altogether unlike, and she was confirmed in her belief that the trick had been played by some one who wished Denis harm. During the last two weeks of the term, Oswald, confident in his lead, neglected his classes, and Dilly Dane carried all the marks. The teacher was uncertain as to the number Oswald had been falsely accredited, but, as well as she could judge, the girl's number was one or two more than the boy's. Hence, when the day came and she announced the awards, there was bitter disappointment when Denis Boyne and Cordelia Dane were declared the victors, the teacher explaining before the assembled parents and friends the forgeries she had found in her books. When school was dismissed, Arthur ran to Oswald, crying, in a voice that every one could hear:

"There, you see how that sneak has cheated you. He put those marks in the book, can't you see? I'd lick him if I were you."

Now, it so happened that all the family, including Dr. Marbury, Aunt Selina, Norah, and two relatives visiting at the house, had driven up to witness the last day's ceremonies. The vehicle could only hold this party, and Denny was to walk home. As he reached the green just beyond the tavern corner, he heard a shout behind him. Turning, he saw Arthur, Oswald, and half-a-dozen more of the boys coming after him. He turned and waited. It was the last day of the term, and the boys felt quite free to do as they pleased. So, when they reached Denny, Arthur said, tauntingly:

"Where's your stolen prize, Paddy? Oswald's going to thrash you for cheating him. You dasent fight him."

"You're a coward as well as a thief!" shouted Oswald, squaring up to Denny. Before Oswald could reach him, Denny sprang into the air, very much as he had seen the game-cock in the farm-yard at home, and planted his fist on the other's nose. Oswald reeled and turned, and the blood began to flow profusely. At this he set up a lugubrious howl, while the others whipped out their handkerchiefs and soothed him into quiet. Denis, turning on his heel, started to walk on, when he was grabbed by the rest of the boys, his head battered, and in the *mêlée* he was carried to the ground, Arthur Kennel's knees planted on his breast, and his fingers clenched in his hair.

"Now, you damned Irish sneak, you'll make me apologize, will you?"—whack, whack, whack—mingled kicks from the others on the sides of the prostrate victim. "I've a good notion to choke your dirty Irish breath out of you, you low-lived beggar bog-trotter. There, eat dirt, as you do in Paddyland!" and he held a handful of clay over Denny's lips!

"Let's put him in the pond!" suggested one of the imps. "He likes water."

"No, let's tie him on the snake-bushes; he likes animals," interposed another; and, picking the insensible boy up by the head, heels, and arms, they flung him over the rail

fence, and, dragging him by the heels, bore down toward
the edge of the upper dam, where the water-snakes were
often seen coiled in masses on the gnarled branches of
the willows. Denny was mercifully unconscious of his
surroundings, but his inquisitors declared he was "shamming." His head had been hammered so fiercely that he
was quite dazed. When he gained consciousness it was
quite dark. His limbs were stiff and sore, and, in the effort to move, excruciating pains shot through him. His
arms were pinioned, but the bonds broke so soon as he
could exert his muscles. His legs were also bound, but
with his arms free he reached down and broke the thongs
—slender willow boughs. He seemed to be lodged in a
clump of bushes. The darkness had no terror for him at
first. He could hear the low murmuring plash of water,
and thought for a moment he was in the apple-trees skirting the Marbury brook. But he could see no light.

He was too stiff and sore to move, and after an effort laid
his head against the branch to rest and collect himself.
His senses were dull, and he had no idea how long he had
rested, when he heard voices in the darkness behind him.
They were loud and unfamiliar. He turned and could
see lights gleaming in the strangest way through the
leaves. Where was he? He had lost all remembrance of
the evening attack. His head throbbed, and his eyes
ached. He strove to raise his voice; but he might as well
have been dumb, for he only made a hoarse clamor that
died away within a few feet of him. Then there was a
lull in the voices. He heard the bushes near him brushed
aside abruptly. He heard no voice, but some one seemed
breaking through the dark wall of foliage. He turned as
the stump beneath him shook. Four fiery eyes were
above him, glaring down at him. He choked, tried to
seize the limbs, but slid down—down ; a panic was upon

him, and the weak power remaining was not enough to brace his muscles against the fall, while his senses were frozen by the horrible apparition at his shoulder.

When the waters closed above him as he sank, there was a delightful sensation of safety and the luxury of absolute physical rest. He was hardly conscious that he was in water. He vaguely and deliciously felt that his tortured muscles were no longer strained, that his aching eyes no longer rested on the phantoms glaring at him ; but, as the water filled his lungs, and breathing became impossible, the actual situation darted into his jaded brain. He rose to the surface and cast an eager glance about him : Impenetrable darkness, save the distant glimmer of the mill. Then he realized his whereabout. He was in the snake swamp. A deadly terror smote him. Perhaps the snakes were clinging about him. He struck out with his arms. His hands came in contact with clammy, hideous things.

Were they the dreadful snakes he had often seen sunning themselves at noonday ? No, his woodcraft taught him better. Snakes do not remain in the open air at night. But perhaps water-snakes might. He had seen fishermen bring them up when eel-fishing in Devil's Lake. Then the horror of touching them overmastered the terror of sinking, and he became inert and sank limply into the dark, slimy water. But then a new terror awoke. A water-snake is more powerful the deeper it goes under the surface. He had often seen them in the Fern spring wind their coils about large stones and move them easily. This stirred him like an electric shock, and he struck out vigorously. All this time, however, he had been moving from the roots of the trees, and when he reached the surface he was far into the pond, carried along quite swiftly. But now he can struggle no longer; the interval below the surface has exhausted his already sorely tried powers, and, only conscious of his peril, he throws himself on his back and floats dreamily under the twinkling merry stars and the misty sky.   He is a good swimmer, and is insensible to the effort keeping him afloat.   He thinks he hears Norah calling him, and makes an effort to cry out.   He has lost his voice and can not utter a sound.   His ears are filled with a gentle murmur.   The stars blink in fantastic derision ; the dreamy cadence of some familiar harmony mingles with the confused noises in his ears.   Suddenly his head is pressed—crushed down—down—down —the stars disappear—he sees an unfathomable gulf—and he sees and hears no more—feels no more !

CHAPTER IX.

AN ELDRITCH COMEDY.

IF transmigration were scientifically established, I should venture the belief that the ferocious traits of the Comanches take possession of boys between the ages of ten and seventeen.   The helpless, the unoffending, the gentle, seem to make no appeal to the species between those years.   Torture for the sake of torment seems a pleasure to them.   I have seen mild-eyed cherubic urchins, models at home, of the discreet and well-behaved, who, in the company of their kind, were as fecund in cruelties to birds, beasts, and comrades as the myrmidons of Philip II, who sought court favor by the number and novelty of the forms by which the human body could be tortured without taking life at once.   The very lads who wrought Denny all his misery were ready to beseech his aid in their lessons, and ask his help in climbing the dizzy branches of

the tallest trees on the Marbury hills. Having secured
their victim in a place where his terror rather than the
improvised bonds would be certain to deprive him of his
faculties, Arthur and his companions quitted the edges of
the pond to concert the climax of their prank. It was
far from their purpose to put the prisoner's life in peril.

"But," suggested one, "what if the snakes really
should come out?"

"Pshaw!" interposed Arthur, contemptuously; "no
snake leaves his hole after sundown. Besides, snakes can't
see in the dark. I've often seen my dog Boone drag them
from under the barn at night, and when I called him off
they laid quite still, blind as bats."

So it was arranged that the boys should all go home to
supper, and come back just after dark supplied with sheets
and pumpkin lanterns to give Denny a final fright, and
then conduct him home in "Os" Ritter's "sulky," as the
hand-cart in which the Ritter garden-stuff was carried to
market was facetiously called by the natives. They
were all lads about Denny's age—Arthur, the eldest, passing eighteen. Boy-like, they never thought of a tragic ending to their joke. The detested Alien would be taught a
lesson, and in the future could be browbeaten by a mere
threat of repeating the jocularity. They knew his abject
terror of snakes, and they had with the inexplicable pene-
tration of boys remarked his extraordinary credulity in
the supernatural. He had been heard to allude, quite as
a matter of fact, to the "faeries" in the Wintergreen wood,
and in his lessons he had repeatedly shown his superstitious terror of ghosts. Now, having none of the horror of
snakes that Denny felt, they could not realize the serious
danger they were exposing their comrade to in fastening
him in the haunt of the coiling reptiles. None of the
boys particularly feared snakes. When other sports failed,

7

they often came down to the black willows to make tar-
gets of the lazy monsters knotted about the gnarled roots·
of the trees. Some adventurous spirits among them
aroused the admiring horror of the others by dexterously
catching the sluggish monsters by the neck and snapping
the ends of their tails off in a "crack of the whip," as the
pastime was called. To pranks of this sort Denny could
never be brought, and it was remarked that in games re-
quiring clasping hands he shrank back shuddering from
touching those that had been upon the snakes.

Hence, beside the fact that boys seem to lack the
reasoning faculty, or rather lack the apprehension of
corollary, or consequence of ideas, this group of merry-
makers saw nothing serious in subjecting such an im-
pressionable nature as Denny's to an ordeal which the
maturer mind could foresee would result in maniacy,
if not something more tragic. They scampered off homeward in the twilight, hilarious over the comedy to be
acted when they returned to the rendezvous. The pro-
curing of the pumpkins and candles, and the necessity
for slipping off unnoticed, delayed the gathering. It
was after nine o'clock when the band, recruited by
half a dozen more gathered from the thickly clustering
farm-houses, began to set the sylvan scene in order for
the elfin pranks they meditated. Some came prepared
with sheets, others with lanterns, others again with pumpkins with the interior scooped out, and so cut as to re-
semble the face of a human monster when a candle was
lighted inside. When these various devices were well
arranged, improvised lanterns were set on the limbs of
the trees, and the spectacle was ghostly enough to freeze
the blood of a less susceptible supernaturalist than poor
Denny.

Arthur and Oswald, their bodies covered with sheets,

and their heads decorated with the pumpkins, were then dispatched into the clump of willows, to unbind the victim and set him down in the center of this hideous circle. When, a few minutes later, Arthur, his mask gone, and the sheet streaming behind him, re-appeared with his face white, and his eyes staring in affright, the rest of the mummers thought it part of the play and began a mad dance.

"O boys, boys, he's drowned! he's drowned! O my God! O—" But his words froze on his lips. Just outside the circle he caught sight of a white figure with hair hanging down in wild disorder and two arms raised in a terror that seemed a weird invocation.

"Look—look! O my God, look there!" and Arthur sank cowering on the ground, covering his face with the sheet. The others rushed into a compact mass, dazed and uncomprehending. The few who were facing the figure fled toward the mill bridge, the others bent over Arthur, who lay writhing upon the ground.

"What in thunder's the matter, Art?"

"Are you making game of us now?"

They had stripped the sheet from his face, and, somewhat re-assured by the tones of his comrades, he ventured to turn his head; then, as his eye fell on the white figure, staring with wild eyes, but motionless, the rest followed his gaze.

"Good God! what is it?"

Then they all with one accord broke and fled.

"Ah, don't leave me—don't, don't!" and Arthur, half crawling, half running, fled with the terrified maskers. The fallen lantern went out, and the place was left in darkness. Then, as the boys ran, they heard a dreadful shriek —a cry so despairing and full of horror that some of them were arrested in their flight and would have hurried back if one of the elder boys hadn't shouted:

"It's Clara Roe's ghost!"

Clara Roe had been found drowned in the pond a few years before, and there was a legend that her ghost had been seen chasing fireflies on the mill meadow. None of the flying group missed Oswald, and Arthur was too much terrified to think of him. He did try to say something to his nearest companion, but his teeth chattered and he could not articulate. In a few minutes the pond road and the willow banks were silent and dark, and slowly the lights in the farm windows went out.

To make much of Denny's well-doing at school, Aunt Selina had invited company, and the table was spread for supper in great gala. Norah was very proud and happy when the visitors took up the theme of Denny's prodigies, prophesying great things for a boy who could eclipse such a smart school as the Marbury Academy. The good Doctor and Aunt Selina were as proud over the boy's conquest as if he had been flesh and blood of their own, and kept up the topic until the supper-table was surrounded. Denny's absence had not been remarked, as it was thought he had stopped for the last day's games and farewells the boys usually prolonged on these occasions. But when the feast was ended, and he had not come, there was a tone of offended affection in the Doctor's mild remonstrance. Norah had gone down the lane to the road and asked a neighbor passing schoolward to hurry the boy in case he was seen dawdling on the road.

At nine o'clock the company broke up, and the family began to feel real alarm. The Marbury homestead was as a rule closed and the lights put out by nine o'clock; but tonight there was no thought of bed. Denny had occasionally stopped to supper at the Danes's, but when he did his purpose was always known beforehand. Norah thought that perhaps he had been tempted to remain to-night, the

last of the term, and the family agreed with her that this
was the explanation of his absence. This, however, was
so unlike Denny that Norah soon set that hope aside and
grew restless. As the time passed, tears came into her
eyes, and she sat in the corner of the room by the window
to conceal her trouble. As it grew too dark to see as far
as the road, she went down the lane and watched the long,
straight line of highway westward, as it became more and
more indistinct in the falling darkness of the September
evening. When it was quite dark, she returned to her
post at the window, her eyes red and swollen with tears.
Even Aunt Selina grew fretful, and suggested that Jonas,
the man, be sent to Deacon Dane's to end the suspense.
The Doctor pooh-poohed this. Denis was a big boy. He
knew how to take care of himself. At any rate, they
might give him till ten o'clock; then, if he didn't come,
Barney could be hitched up and Jonas might drive up the
road to the tavern and inquire. Ten o'clock had now
come. Norah sat at the window, her head leaning on the
broad sill. She must have fallen into a doze, for she suddenly started up crying like one in sleep:

"Ah! he's sinking, he's sinking!"

The voice rang out in a piercing shriek, as she turned
imploringly to the startled group, the horror of conviction
and absolute certainty of seeing what she said in her face.

"Norah, child, what is it? Are you dreaming on your
feet?" asked the Doctor gently, putting his hand on her
shoulder.

She shuddered, looking at him in a dazed, perplexed
way, then turning and peering through the window into
the darkness; then at the floor in a mystified uncertainty.

"Ah! my God! I saw—I saw wather, black, black
wather, and bushes and slimy snakes, and I saw Denny
among them, and then I saw him sinking. Ah! for the

love of God come to him ; come, come!" She broke from the Doctor; darted through the doorway, out into the darkness, before the amazed group could arrest her. The horse had been harnessed, and stood at the gate. But she shot by, taking no heed. She was hid in the darkness when the Doctor reached the gate. He lost no time in getting into the vehicle, and, without waiting for Jonas, drove furiously down the lane. It was a dark but starry night. The broad road lay smooth before him, and he put the whip to Barney. Presently he caught a glimpse of a flying figure.

"Norah, Norah, my child, get in here with me. Norah, I say. It is I."

No answer. What could it mean? Had she gone insane? Had she the curious clairvoyance sometimes given the unsettled intellect? Why hadn't he waited for Jonas? It was too late to go back now. He would readily overtake her, for she would soon be exhausted. It was a full mile to the school. He had already traversed half the distance, but he seemed no nearer overtaking her. Or had she fallen by the way, and had he passed her? He halted the horse, agitated and in terror. He got out and listened. No sound! He bent down and put his ear to the ground. No sound! He took out his night-lantern—always in the gig—and waved it as a signal. No response! He got in again, and drove at the top of poor old Barney's speed. Once he thought he heard a hoarse shriek and stopped ; but there was no repetition, and he drove on. When he reached the tavern, lights streamed out of the windows. He halted and called out. Some one came to the door.

"Hello! What's wanted?" a voice shouted.

"Have you seen—" Here the poor Doctor stopped confusedly. It wouldn't do to ask for Norah. He didn't like to expose her strange freak to the gossip of the com-

munity. "Have you seen young Denis here this evening?"

"Denis Boyne, of Marburys?" asked the voice, as the
owner came forward to the gig. "No, I haven't seen the
boy since he passed this afternoon from school."

"He hasn't been home yet, and we became alarmed.
Where is Oswald? Perhaps he may know something about
him."

The Doctor had wholly lost patience when, after a
long delay, Ritter himself came to the door, saying, in
agitation:

"It is very strange, Doctor. Oswald isn't to be found.
He is always in bed at this time, but nobody has seen him
since supper. He must be at some of the neighbors, I—"

But, with an impatient exclamation, the Doctor drove
off, now thoroughly alarmed. Barney must have entertained curious reflections regarding his master that night.
Never, during the years of his faithful service, had his
stout back suffered the ignominy of a whip till to-night.
Do his best, he couldn't get over the ground fast enough,
and, when he drew up at the door of Kennel's house, he
was steaming and unhappy indeed. Kennel himself
opened the door, after a cautious parleying that sorely tried
the Doctor's patience. When he finally stood revealed, a
tallow candle in one hand and an old blunderbuss in the
other, the Doctor said, with a grim smile:

"Don't be afraid. I'm not going to rob you. I come
to ask Arthur what he has done with my boy, Denny."

"What he has done with your boy? Why, Doctor,
what do you mean?"

The facts were told, and the Doctor suggested sending
for Arthur. At this moment Mrs. Kennel appeared, and
said in a frightened tone:

"O Lemuel, Arthur hasn't come back. He went down

to the Denetts after supper to a 'snap' party, and I didn't like to tell you he wasn't come."

"Are you sure he was here at supper-time ?" asked the Doctor.

"Why, to be sure ; he didn't go away till all the chores were done ; about eight o'clock, I should say."

The Doctor turned and walked down the lane. He was at the end of his resources. That Arthur had something to do with Denny's disappearance he was sure. Barney gave a frightened whinny as the Doctor reached the hitching-post, and shied from him. At the same instant a figure staggered to the high-barred gate, and, instead of removing the wooden bolt, climbed over. In the darkness the Doctor couldn't distinguish it, but he was sure it was young Kennel.

"Arthur, is that you ?"

A husky voice, vibrating with terror answered :

"Yes, sir—I. I—"

The lantern in the Doctor's hand was thrust through the gate at the boy's side. Arthur turned his face to it, so white, so frightened, that the Doctor wouldn't have recognized him.

"What have you done with Denny ? Don't lie to me. I know—"

"O Doctor, I didn't ! He fell in himself. He—"

"Fell in what ?"

"In the pond by the snakes' pool."

Then, in a violent outburst of sobs which rose to groans as the Doctor's hold tightened, he related the story : How Denny, having thrashed Oswald, the boys had taken him, just for fun, to the water ; how they had bandaged his eyes and tied him on the willow notch ; and how they had meant to take him home in Oswald's cart, after the jack-o'lantern game. Then he broke down and fell upon his knees in terrified entreaty. It was only by the sternest threats he was forced to tell how, in climbing among the willows, Denny saw the jack-o'lanterns, and in his fright had fallen into the water, and how Oswald, trying to catch him, was pulled in with him. That he, Arthur, had hurried out to get the boys to fetch the boat, but was terrified by the ghost of Clara Roe, standing on the edge of the boys' ring, with snakes of fire in her hair, and clad in white.

"How long ago was this?" asked the Doctor in anguish.

"Twenty minutes; perhaps half an hour. I have run all the way from there."

"You heartless young ruffian, you have left the two boys to drown! Ah, well! there's no time for talk now. You must get into the gig with me and lead me to the spot."

The howl of terror that followed brought the parental Kennels to the doorway, and a voice asked:

"Who's there? What's the matter?"

"There's a murderer here, and you will do well to come and help undo, if it's not too late, his crime," said the Doctor, dragging the shrieking lad through the gateway. "I am going to the mill-pond, and you can follow. Your son will be with me until I deliver him to the lock-up."

In spite of his struggles, Arthur, limp and groaning, was lodged in the gig, and the Doctor drove off as the mother's shrieks for mercy came ringing down the lane. There were still lights in the Ritter tavern as the Doctor drove past, and some one came out and hallooed; but the Doctor drove straight down the pretty elm road, all dark and solemn. The water rippled over the dam, and the stars were reflected on the dark surface of the pool, as they shot over the bridge. Tying the horse near the road, the Doctor, with his clutch on Arthur's shoulder, bade him lead the way. The lantern cast a slender lance of light on the pathway as the boy tremblingly advanced. He pointed to the clump where Denny had been bound. The Doctor could not reach it, as there was marshy ground too soft for his heavy weight.

"Go in and see if there is any sign of them."

Shaking like a man in ague, the boy advanced, begging piteously that the light might be held up. He soon returned, and said, with chattering teeth :

"They are not there—they are drowned. O Doctor, shall I be hanged?"

"Where is the boat kept? Show me the boat."

The boy, whimpering and half dead with terror, pointed to the bend in the bank where the boat was kept. He went on in advance, the Doctor lighting the path from behind. As the two advanced, Arthur uttered a little gasp of mingled relief and terror. The gleam of the lantern on the thick grass fell upon a figure at full length. Arthur ran to it, but started back aghast.

"The ghost !" he cried, and fled past the Doctor like a shot. Even before the light fell fully upon the figure the Doctor felt that it was Norah. He set down the lantern and fell on his knees with a tender cry.

"Norah ! O Norah ! how could you leave in that cruel way? Didn't you know that I was as anxious about Denny as you could be ? You have given me a grievous fright by your wild conduct."

She had raised her head when he set the light down. She had not been insensible, but there was a dazed, lusterless look that warned the Doctor that she was not in her right mind. She raised her woful, haggard face to him quite calmly, and said, in a soft, reproachful voice :

"We let him die and never raised a hand ; I knew he

was in peril; I saw him in the wather; I saw the cruel black of the deeps, and I heard the gurgle in his throat. 'Twas a dream I often have—after Denny told me of the cruel things the boys did to him long ago. I think of nothing else ; when he's away—"

It was useless to attempt to re-assure such abandonment as this. The Doctor lifted her into the gig, and, hastening to the tavern, put her in the care of Mrs. Ritter. Then he got all the men about the place to turn out with lanterns to search the mill-pond. It was nearly midnight when a cap, recognized as Denny's, was found on the edge of the dam. The spot under the willows was dragged thoroughly, but there was no sign of the body. The uttermost that could be done had been done, and near daylight no trace of the lad could be found. The miller had been warned to keep the gates shut until the pond could be more systematically dragged. He assured the Doctor that this was useless, as the current in the pond came to the dam, and everything of any size was finally carried into the race and over the mill-wheel.

"Over the mill-wheel!" gasped the Doctor; "when was it at work last ? "

"Wal, let me see : I was a grindin' old man Warren's wheat until about nine last night— "

"Let me look at the wheel !" said the Doctor.

They entered the mill, descended through the trap, and entered the water-sluice in which the wheel turned. A thin veil of water fell with a tranquil plash on the open flanges of the great wheel, and sprinkled through the slats to the pebbly bed below. The Doctor looked up at the great flanges, and then, finding them impossible to climb, asked the miller to examine the broad fly which received the falling water. The miller climbed up, and as he looked down toward the hub uttered a loud shout:

"By the heavens, here's the body!"

Yes, there Denny lay, with his feet wedged into the hub of the wheel and his head resting on the outward edge, just as he had glided over the dam. Floating on his back when the shute came, he was unconscious that he was going with the current toward the dam, while his effort was to take himself near the shore. Hence, the body was in a reclining posture, though almost standing. Hope sprang into the Doctor's breast when he saw that. He could not have been lifeless when he was deposited there. The face and mouth were above the thin stream pouring into the wheel, and there was a chance of life yet. It was a very feeble chance, but the Doctor seized it. The cold body was soon well rubbed, and a thrill of the pulse, delicate as the expansion of a rose-leaf, told that life still lingered. Then remedies of the simple, old-fashioned sort, fortunately at hand, were administered, and, when the body was placed in Mrs. Ritter's room in the tavern, the Doctor was not without hope of rescuing the fleeting breath. Norah was told the event, and, under the sudden joy, quite as strange a transformation came to pass as grief had brought about. She became her old docile, shrinking self, asked submissively how she could be of use, and sat down patiently, following the Doctor's movements as he hovered over the life in peril. The Kennels, father and son, when the body was found, fled homeward. Arthur was packed off to Virginia within the hour, believing himself a murderer, and the family waited in terror the coming of the ministers of justice and vengeance.

In his anxiety for Denny the Doctor had quite lost sight of the missing Oswald. He made no inquiry, and perhaps it was just as well he didn't, for it would have made the anguish of the night of uncertainty more bitter had he learned that Oswald was in bed safe and sound before he reached the willows in search of Denny. Oswald, fresh and unterrified by the horrors that complicated Denny's disaster, found no difficulty in reaching the shore. Here, frightened by the disappearance of his comrades, he fled homeward, and slunk into the house unseen by any one save his mother.

Denny's hardy frame finally survived the maltreatment of that terrible night, and he was presently carried home in buoyant convalescence, where you may be sure there was a very happy and tender Norah to make him forget the hardships of the stranger.

When the winter term began Denny found the leader of his enemies gone. The school received him as a hero, and thenceforth he was not molested any further than it is the fortune of lads to undergo the pranks of comrades. Oswald could not forget the robust refutation Denny had made of the charge of cowardice, and the two lads maintained the wary neutrality that comes from a wholesome dread on one side and confident superiority on the other.

CHAPTER X.

VISIONS OF DELIGHT.

MERRY-MAKING in Marbury was given over to the young folks. Indeed, in country-places the custom has changed but little to this day. With marriage the gayety of youth suffers an eclipse. Balls and parties, as we know them, made no part of rural life. Young and old matrons set out for the day with a formidable baggage of knitting, sewing, or what not, to pass the hours of daylight at a distant neighbor's. The "men-folks" drove the visitor over

in the morning, in some carefully calculated interval when
the "team" was not in use, and in the evening the whole
family would drive over and take tea.   On rare occasions
a "quilting bee" would assemble all the matrons during
the day, and the "men-folks" in the evening.   Then the
affairs of the township were settled in shrill clamors of
revelation and hearsay.   Aunt Selina was not fond of this
"gadding," as she termed it, but was too sensible to set
herself up as a marplot by refusing to take her turn in vis-
itation.   It was a great day for Denny when the return
visit of the Danes brought his adored Dilly to pass the
day.   She came home with him from school, and even his
beloved blue jays flaunted their spreading plumage in the
purple alders in vain while his divinity walked demurely
by his side.   He was lost in astonishment at his own silence
—he who chattered incessantly as a hill brook at other
times.   The first visit had been during the summer Dilly
rescued him from his tormentors near the pond.   His
heart throbbed as he reached the brookside where he had
gathered the violets, and he longed to ask her to stop until
he could get a bunch.   But she walked on very soberly, carrying her dinner-basket primly by her side.   The sun glint-
ered from her heavy braids as she moved, and Denny kept
thinking of a story his mother had often murmured as they
sat in some flowering covert, where sunshine fell upon
the grass in lines of gold : how a lad that was faithful to
his mother had gone to church, and how his cloak being
too warm, he had innocently mistaken a ray of sunshine
for a golden cord and had flung the garment on the shining line, and how it rested there because the good God
had meant to show the congregation the lad's purity and
faith !

These shining braids Denny felt sure were made of
the sunbeams that boy had mistaken for a line.   He

wanted to tell her the story, wondering if she would believe it. He believed it firmly. When they came to the
gulch where the hills were cut by a solemn ravine, he
summoned courage to show her a swallow's hamlet in the
hard clay, and was in rapture when she opened her brown
eyes at the tameness of the young birds, as they put their
large beaks out of the nest to receive the crumbs which
Denny always saved from his dinner to feed them. The
old swallows hovered in scolding groups about the heads
of the two young people, and Denny said, apologetically:

"They are only pretending to be angry because I have
brought you." Then, turning to the birds with his hands
full of crumbs, he said, quite angrily, "You silly things!
don't you know Dilly? She won't hurt you; she never
kills birds."

But the little busy-bodies were not sure of that, and
they refused to come to his open hands as they had done
every day during the rearing of their broods; and Denny,
to punish this mark of incivility toward his deity, flung
the crumbs on the ground, where presently the crows began to dispute them vigorously with the faithless swallows.

"It's funny, isn't it, Dilly, birds aren't a bit afraid of
me after I know them a little while? I can bring nearly
all the birds at the barn to my hand when I have
crumbs."

"Perhaps they know you don't mean to hurt them,"
said Dilly, thoughtfully. "Birds like folks that don't hurt
them."

"So do I," said Denny, reflectively. "But I don't
hurt the fairies, and they never come to me now."

"Don't they?" said Dilly, eagerly. "How strange!"
and then she looked at him intently as the thought suddenly struck her, "but they never came to me at all."

"Oh, when mother and I lived in the woods," said Denny, confidently, "I used to see the fairies every night. They were so funny and small, and sometimes they had such odd dresses. They brought us good things to eat. They never came when mother was cross. She knew how to talk to them. They don't speak in our language, you know! If mother hadn't died I should have learned their speech. It was such a droll language, just like the birds when they stop singing in the bushes, and the old ones talk to the young ones! Mother always talked with the fairies, and they were glad to do her bidding. Once, when I was bad, she was going to give me to them, to stay forever. I was glad at first, but when they couldn't understand me at all, and hid under the bushes, and shook the dew on my bare neck, I got frightened and I ran away. Mother scolded the fairies, and they brought honey on, oh, such green leaves!"

"But you don't really believe, Denny, that they were fairies?"

"Oh, yes," said Denny, simply; "ask Norah."

That Denny did believe in them then, and all his life, I am quite sure. It is one of the articles of old-country belief that certain natures have command of the "little people," as the folk-lore of the land styles the fairies. No doubt in her half-demented misery poor Kate had seen and counseled with all Titania's elfin train, and the impression had been so vivid in Denny's mind that he never ceased to believe the fantasy a reality. Dilly was greatly interested in the boy's wondrous improvisations. She listened with gravity, thinking to herself all the while that it was no wonder the sharp-witted, hard-headed boys of the school badgered him so unmercifully if he betrayed these grotesque confidences to their cynical incredulity. Denny was a big boy in body. He would be called a "young gentleman " in the prematurity of to-day. However, in those days a lad of eighteen was regarded as a child, acted as a child, thought as a child, and was not expected to put away childish speech and thought until far beyond the time modern youth have taken all the virilities.

"Yes," continued Denny, quite soberly, "I should have lost mother lots of times if the fairies had not fetched me to her."

"But how did you understand them?"

"Oh, that's easy. When you believe in the fairies, they will always hear you when you think."

"Hear you when you think, Denny? I don't understand you."

"Why, don't you see, the fairies know who believe in them—who leave the yellow toadstools for them to sit upon. You know the yellow toadstools? They are always put in grassy places by the fairies, because they like to sit in the sun, and when they are there the snakes can't get near them! The fairies are afraid of the snakes. That's the reason the fairies are friendly to me. I saved the king of the fairies when he was asleep once from a snake. Oh, away, far off from here. Mother told me about it, because you know the fairies mustn't show themselves to little boys or girls alone, only to grown folks that have children! Then the folks have to take a vow over running waters, with a bit of witch-hazel burning in their hands. My mother used to take the vow every May-day, when we were in the fields. But it was at night, you know. Then the fire-flies came and made the place light, and I could hear the fairies singing!"

"Hear the fairies singing, Denny? How could they sing?"

"Oh, some chirped like a cricket, some like a whip-poor-will; oh, ever so many sounds. I couldn't tell you half of them."

"And you really believe it true, Denny?"

Denny stopped, and for the first time noticed her wondering look. Then he grew quite crimsom and silent. This was, as I said, the first summer of his abode in Marbury, and he never after that betrayed his childish faith. But Dilly's skepticism pained him for many a day. His talks with her after that were brief and embarrassing. He was in mortal terror of losing favor in her eyes; so beyond their studies, and such topics as came up in school, he never ventured to be communicative with her. Besides this he saw that her intimacy with him subjected her to tantalizing taunts from the girls, and coarse joking from the boys. He had cuffed some of the more outspoken mischief-makers for linking Dilly's name with his own, and though it was depriving himself of sunshine, he manfully resisted the impulse to show her his worship, by the devotions as natural to him as song to the bird, or fragrance to the flower. But he had a little ministry of his own that the little maid received with timid favor. He lent her his story-books, and wrote out her history and grammar lessons. He prompted her when he could, and kept her at the head of the classes, often missing questions purposely that she might stand first.

One famous night, when the Marbury school had challenged all the neighboring districts to a spelling-match, Denny, who had come off conqueror at two previous trials, drew down the teacher's wrath by trying to give Dilly the victory. All had been spelled down but Dilly, Denny, and the leader of the rival school. The teacher selected to put the words was from another district, and when the group was reduced to three he gave the word *entendre*. Denny on the instant spelled it as pronounced—*entender*.

" Next ! "

Now, Dilly was next, and couldn't conceive how the word should be spelled, if not as Denny had done. Suddenly Denny remembered that, in reading a history of Napoleon, he had seen the phrase *double entendre*, and he bent over, making a pretext to look for a seat, and whispered the correct spelling in Dilly's ear. She caught it and spelled it as he had told her. The teacher, in evident chagrin, continued ; but in the end Dilly's rival " beat " her. The Marbury teacher at once challenged the fairness of the contest, pointing out that *entendre* was a French word. This was admitted, but the rival party carried the day, as the Marbury school had not entered a protest against it. Now, Denny had been heard in his whisper by one of the girls, and when this was made known he was charged with the school's defeat in his desire to make Dilly Dean triumph. Poor Dilly was made to suffer bitterly for this indiscreet devotion of " Irishy." The matter was made the gossip of the neighborhood, and Dilly's family cautioned her against allowing such familiarity on the part of the Irish boy. The results went still further. Thereafter, when the Deacon's family came to spend the day with the Marburys, Dilly was escorted by her brother, to keep Denny at a distance.

At first the poor lad didn't comprehend it, but he soon discovered that the Deacon, who had formerly treated him with jocose condescension, now frowned sternly when he met him, and spoke very shortly the little he had to say. So, to spare Dilly from the jeering of her companions, Denny never spoke to her in school. Even that floral ministry which had been his delight he gave up with a heavy heart. He hurried homeward from school, too, as the other boys and girls made game of his simple gallantries in helping Dilly over the rough places, or gather-

ing the yellowest golden-rod and the purplest aster. His
school-days at this stage had grown somber indeed. It
had been such a joy to get to the stone portico first in the
morning and, slipping through the transom, adjust a fragrant nosegay on Dilly's desk. Now all this was given up.

Watchful eyes were upon him, and if he but raised his
trembling glance to the tender little maid there were buzz-
ing comments and tattling to the Deacon's family. Too
proud to complain, and too mindful of Dilly's comfort to
resent this, he never made known to her by word of
mouth the conduct he was pursuing. But he knew that
she understood it, for once, when the boys were formed in
two ranks and the girls had to "pass the gauntlet," as it
was called, she gave him an adorable smile as he fell out
of line and refused to claim his right to kiss her, as the
game provided. Poor Denny was so cowed by the persistent malevolence of his companions, boy and girl, that
he never supposed for a moment that Dilly had any other
feeling for him than pity. How could it be different?

How could she care for one whom all her associates
reviled? How could a native care for an alien—an Irish
alien at that? Wasn't the burden of it in his ears every
play-hour? If he were admitted to the boyish sports,
wasn't there always a sort of contemptuous toleration?
When the play-houses were made among the recesses of
the "huckleberry" swamp behind the school, where the
blackbirds kept up such a saucy protesting chatter, wasn't
he always excluded, after he had torn his flesh and frayed
his garments in climbing the birch-trees for the fragrant
limbs to adorn these sylvan bowers? None of the girls
would admit him as a member of the little households,
and he was left alone in the triumph of his elfin edifice.

Childish woes, you say! I doubt if the Napoleons felt
half as bitterly the refusal of the royal families to bestow

their daughters on the parvenu empire, as Denny when the Marbury boys and girls declined to take part with him in those youthful travesties of housekeeping. But persistent as this deconsideration was it didn't sour his temper. He was the merriest of the group. His wit was quick, his temper hot, his diligence untiring, his purpose unconquerable. He meant to lead all his classes, and he did it. He meant to lead in all games of skill, and he did. He was the swiftest runner in all the township. He could climb trees that made the other boys dizzy. In the water he was fearless as a duck—if there were no snakes about. Nature he read in all her varying pages by a sort of intuition. He knew where all manner of birds were to be found. He could point out the storehouses of half the squirrels that scampered over the Marbury fences. He could supply wild honey at an hour's notice for the school picnics. He wasn't fond of gunning or fishing, and was well hated by the others for that. Poor lad! he needed all these compensations to counterpoise the burdens of his daily life. He was a tall boy now in his last teens, but his mind was as simple as when he trudged over the hills with Kate.

Darcy Warchester was but a year or two older than Denny, but his mingling with the world, his repose and self-confidence, made him appear three or four years older. It was the last term Denny was to attend the Marbury school. There was nothing more for him to learn. Indeed, he had long ago exhausted the simple course of the curriculum, and this last winter, in return for desultory glimpses of French, he had relieved the teacher of all the elementary classes. Oswald, in return for hints in woodcraft, had lent him German text-books, and helped him in the acquirement of his soft Saxon pronunciation. The term, which ended in April, wound up with an even-

ing party at the school-house. The event was very gay.
All the families of the township came in cutters, for in
those days winter lingered in severity far into May.

There were to be games, and a modest feast was to be
set on the desks, which had been made into long tables
running through the middle of the school-house. The
windows were festooned with spruce-branches and holly-
berries, and the rostrum was turned into a fairy bower.
Some of the young men brought fiddles and a flute, and
there was an attempt at dancing, which was but feebly
supported, and collapsed with a very dispirited Virginia reel.
The diversions of the evening tended to games in which
there was a good deal of kissing. Norah and Denny sat in
the background, taking no part. They did not feel at all
neglected, for they had come to regard themselves very
much as the colored aliens of the South. They were set
apart by the crime of their birth, and were quite content
to be permitted to see the gayeties of their betters, without
being part of them. Once during the evening Dilly Dane,
who had been behind the green bushes on the rostrum,
found herself without a partner, or "beau," as it was the
simple fashion to call the masculine playmates in those
days. All the' rest of the girls were seated in rows,
with the indispensable "beau," and, as Dilly's name was
called, she came down to select her partner. But all were
taken. She looked about, and, seeing Denny, hesitated
and blushed.

"Oh, take Paddy, Dil; he'll do for the game, and I'll
do the kissing," said young Orlando Gates, a neighbor's
son.

A general titter followed this, and everybody looked
curiously at the blushing girl. She raised her head with
a flash of defiance in her kindly, serious eye, and, walking
down the aisle made by the boys and girls, stopped before

Denny and held out her hand. Denny was quaking like a leaf in a March wind. His head fairly reeled, and he sat quite immovable.

"Come, come, Paddy. It's bad manners to keep a lady waiting," called out one of the boys maliciously ; and then everybody tittered, the elders grinning discreetly.

"Go, Denny," whispered Norah.

He got up trembling and walked very much abashed to the vacant place reserved for the two, and never opened his lips to his partner. When the kissing came he turned his head away, and when the game was ended led Dilly back to her seat, under a merciless fusilade of jeers and cat-calls. The elders did not remain for the last of the frolics, and most of the young people were left in charge of neighbors who lived near the school. It was midnight when the lights were put out and the revelers packed themselves into the sleighs. Norah drove off with a neighbor from the farm-house next below the Doctor's, and Denny trudged off on foot. The night had suddenly grown warm. The roads were slushy and difficult, and he struck off across the fields. When he came to Bethesda Creek the waters had risen so high that he could not cross, and he made his way back to the high-road. As he neared it he heard shouting and laughing, and could distinguish the sleighs skimming fleetly down the hill toward the bridge. A half-dozen or more had passed, and he could see them like black dots to the eastward, when a great shout startled him. One of the sleighs had just crossed the light timber bridge and reached the ascent on the other side. There was a hoarse indistinguishable screech, and then a succession of screams, and a dull crash as of breaking timbers. He ran swiftly toward the bridge. On reaching it the screams and shouts were renewed. One of the sleighs in passing had struck the frail railing of the bridge, which had given way. The driver had whipped the horses up, but the right-hand runner had gone over the planks, and several of the people had been precipitated into the swollen stream below. How many, Denny couldn't guess, for the current ran so rapidly that the struggling figures could not be distinguished from the floating *débris*. Running along the edge, he could hear plaintive gurglings in the water a few feet from him. Fixing the object well in his eye, he plunged in, and, in spite of the ferocity of the current, was soon within reach of the victim. It was a girl, he could discern in an instant. He struggled with the body, but was likely to be borne down, as she clung in terror about his arms. Fortunately, a log passing offered a means of rescue ; he seized it with one hand and kept with the current, gently trending toward the bank as the stream curved. In a few moments he was safely on shore, and those from the bridge, who had followed down the field, were at hand to help him out.

"Who is it? Which have you got?" a voice, that he recognized as 'Tom Dane's, asked excitedly. Then, examining the drenched figure, he exclaimed :

"O my God! Boyne, Dilly is in the water yet ; she and Nell fell in."

Chilled to the bone, and nearly exhausted, Denny only waited to say :

"I will go down in the middle of the stream to the sand-shoal, and do you follow on the bank. Watch out, and tell me when you see anything." He ran down along the edge of the water and called. He could hear no sound, and then, dashing along the bank for fifty yards, watching the water, he struck out again. But there was no sign of the drowning girl. He gave up hope, and, crossing to the other side, when he remembered passing a sort of maelstrom a few feet back ; he returned, and leaped in again.

The place was full of whirling brush and the *débris* of the mill-pond. He felt sure that the body could not have passed down beyond him, and, with sickening dread, began to push about among the flying limbs. The waters covered the field, and near him one corner of the rail-fence was almost submerged. Excitement made him unconscious of the chill of the water, and, besides, he was used to exposure of the sort, often passing hours in the winter snow in the woods helping to draw out wood. But he was losing strength now, and, in attempting to move a heap of interlocked rails and limbs, he lost his foot-hold and was whirled into the fence corner before he could recover himself. As he grasped the rail to regain his feet his hand encountered cold, clammy fingers, apparently frozen to the rail. Bending down, he discerned a ghastly face staring upward at him, the head caught between two jutting rails. With a shriek of despair, he recognized Dilly. He was too exhausted to extricate her, but in a few minutes the rest of the party from the bridge were at his side, and the inanimate figure wrapped in warm robes. It was too far to take her home for restoration, and, resting in Denny's arms, she was hurried into the sleigh and driven to Ritter's tavern. Mrs. Ritter had lived on the Elbe, and encountered emergencies of the sort. She knew exactly what to do. The young men were sent to another room, and the cold body stripped, laid on the table, and vigorously rubbed. In half an hour the good wife pronounced her safe, just as Dr. Marbury, who had been sent for, appeared, startled and indignant, on the scene. When he had ministered to the convalescent, he came out into the general room, where the crowd still lingered. Denny was sitting far back in the corner unnoticed, waiting, with heavy heart, for tidings. Nobody spoke to him. Dilly's brother had gone home with his cousin Nelly, to warn the family of the cause of

8

the delay. The Doctor turned in wrath to the company, as he put his hand on Denny's wet shoulder.

"This poor boy risked his life for your two companions, and not one of you have heart enough to bring him near the stove, or give him a dry rag to warm his shivering body!"

"Why, I declare, Doctor," said one of the eldest of the group, "I never once thought of Denis. I—I—we thought he had gone home."

"And you would let him walk home, a mile, in this plight, while your horses, three of them, stand idle in the sheds? You're a Christian lot, indeed!"

But Denny was quite unmindful of himself. It was some one else he was thinking of, and, as the Doctor bent down to feel his pulse, he whispered in his ear:

"Is Dilly quite well and safe?"

"Yes, she's perfectly restored; no fear of her." Then, turning to the host, he added:

"Ritter, you must give this boy a bed here to-night. He mustn't venture out in his condition."

So Denny slept at Ritter's, and in the morning his clothes were dry, and he was up and about, none the worse for his exposure the night before. The house was full of Dilly's family. Her mother came into the breakfast-room, where Denny was eating, and, hearing Oswald call him by name, she laid down the dish she had in her hand, and, coming over behind him, pressed his head back and kissed him. The Deacon came in from the porch, and, as he caught sight of Denny, he coughed in embarrassment; then, coming over, he took his hand, saying, austerely:

"You have acted like a brave fellow, and we owe you a great deal. If we can ever do anything for you, don't forget we are your friends."

It was quite like his favorite fairy dialogues, where the

elves bade him command their magic methods in all his desires. How often he had repeated them! How often they had given him the realms of fancy to exploit, and the scepter and sword of these ample dominions! Alas! there was one fairy, whose gray eyes and golden pate he would rather have seen than to hear all this high and mighty tribute to his prowess. But he was not to see her. The Doctor came between. The invalid was not to be seen by anybody. Indeed, it would never have entered Denny's mind to ask such a bold thing as to see her. He went off home quite radiant, however, for now he might at least sometimes go to Deacon Dane's without the fear of bringing reproof upon Dilly for her partiality to the "Paddy." Indeed, the Saturday a fortnight after, when Dilly was quite brisk again, Mrs. Dane sent the wagon over, asking Denny and his sister to pass the day. None of his fairy friends, decked in the exuberant hues of his imagination, was ever such a picture as the sunny maid, standing on the trellised veranda to meet her young knight. Denny's timidity made the meeting very embarrassing, and it was the shy Norah who had to extricate them from it. She smiled softly to herself as the blushing girl led her visitors to the sitting-room, where her mother gave them a very cordial greeting.

"Dilly is to entertain you young folks, and we shall not disturb you. The men are tapping the maples, and perhaps you might like to go down and drink some fresh sap."

The young folks "allowed" that nothing could be more tempting, and went off awkwardly enough. The sun was warm, though the ground was not wholly clear of snow, and the little party had a merry time avoiding the wet places in the winding lane. Tom, who joined them at the barn, was full of praise of Denny's daring, and brought mantling waves of color to that small hero's cheeks as he dilated on Denny's resolute pertinacity in remaining in the creek, while he was freezing with cold. Dilly never alluded to the event, but she looked all that Denny felt the occasion called for. Just before the time set for the brother and sister's return, Dilly came out on the veranda, where Tom had carried the lad to show him some contrivance for catching squirrels, and had left him alone an instant; slipping a little packet into Denny's hand, she whispered, "Keep this for my sake"; then turned and ran back to the others. Denny thrust the parcel into his pocket, with a proud and delicious sense of confidential trust, and followed Tom's divagations with a most distracted mind. So soon as he and Norah had gone to their rooms at bed-time, he asked her to light the candle, and, taking out the little packet, opened the paper. It was an ebony locket with a tiny daguerreotype of Dilly, framed by a blue velvet border, and on white silk ribbon was the legend embroidered in crimson silk :

"To the best and bravest boy in the world."

Denny kissed it rapturously, and his eyes glistened. Norah was looking at him in wonder and terror. He caught sight of her startled face, and asked :

"What is it, Nody? Is there anything ye fear?"

"O Denny, I'm afeard ye're making a load to lay on yer own tender heart. Don't ye know, dear, it's not for the likes of you to love a proud man's daughter; don't ye know, Denny, he'd set the dogs on ye if he thought ye mad enough to think of his daughter?"

Denny sank down on the side of the bed, staring aghast at his sister. She came over, and, sitting beside him, caressed his hands and drew his head over on her bosom—as the mother was fond of doing—and then she poured out the little worldly wisdom that she had been taught by the hard experience of her alien life. When the boy arose to go to his own bed, he saw it all. He saw it a good deal more forcibly than poor Norah had been able to argue it. He lay awake hours revolving it in his mind. It was presumptuous to think of the high-born daughter of the Marbury magnate. It was only her gentle, sweet way that made her seem to care for him. Of course she didn't know the mad dreams he had been dreaming—his ambitions, his hopes, his confidence in the time when he should be a college graduate, a great lawyer, a law-maker—perhaps ruler of the State! Why not? Hadn't Dr. Marbury told him that aliens had reached all these distinctions? Why shouldn't he? And then— then why shouldn't Dilly Dane be his sweetheart? He flamed with the blood of guiltless shame as this bold thought came; but until all this should come to pass, how would he dare to let her know his mad vagaries? Would she for a moment listen to such wildness? Would she consent that her name should be joined to that of the contemned, the alien, the butt of the town ridicule, the Gibeonite of the social hierarchy? To let her know his love even would be an humiliation to her; to ask her to share it would be binding her to the moral torture of a social pillory. To seem to crave her love after the rescue would be as if he were making that act a claim upon her. No; Norah was right. He must shut himself out from the sunlight of this fair girl's smile; he must hear no more the gentle voice of her grateful joy. He must not be the one—he who loved her as life is loved only when it is in most peril—to make her heart heavy and her path hard.

For even to let her little world see that he adored her would be in some sort to reflect upon her, and he would bury the burning impulses of his shadowy dream before the shapes that seemed angels in his fancies should turn to specters to her peace of mind. The artless lad groaned and resolved, as many have done before, and as many will do to the end of time. But while the abnegation of the wisely conscientious is based upon the consideration of evil to follow, or temptation to be resisted, this poor lad, accepting a monstrous wrong as an implacable condition, came to his heart-breaking denial of self by processes whose interdependence few would have stopped to verify. Darcy had gone over this mental way of thorns. He, too, saw the face that made flame in his heart; he saw eyes in which he could divine unfathomable things ; and heard a voice that made such music as the inner chords alone transmit to the soul; he, too, halters, desire, but with a frail gyve. But his impulse involved no abnegation in the sense Denny's did. His love might be open as the day and crowned by a life of tranquil joy. But it involved the cutting out of pride, root and branch. Denny's involved nothing that need for a moment interrupt the serene current of his own or his sweetheart's life. But, deceived by the false conditions into which his troubled life had been passed, he thought the tribute of his love as compromising as the alliance of the Giaour to the Moslem. Darcy fled an animal impulse ; Denny confronted a spiritual crucifixion—all the more excruciating that it was intangible, vast, hydra-headed, menacing. Darcy, knowing his own world, fed his heart on desire until the soul of Norah caught the fragrant incense, and then he halted to weigh the consequences of further dallying. Denny, the victim of sordid prejudice and ignoble traditions, looked out into the radiant atmosphere of his beloved and refused to throw even a shadow on her path from his own dark destiny. Darcy, pinnacled in the world's high places, looked into the valley and debated whether he should withhold his hand or give the innocent —standing on the brink of the precipice—the impulse that must cast her into the abysm below !

CHAPTER XI.

A TEXT FROM LEVITICUS.

THOUGH Imperia was in Denny's youth, as it is now, the most populous State of the Union, rural life was as simple in plan as the pastoral pursuits of Jacob or Laban. Tilling the fields, and providing the needs of the seasons, brought the husbandman his distractions and delights, as well as his toils. Those educating and liberalizing diversions into flower-culture, vine-raising, vernal experimenting, which now lend such a gracious flavor to the hard lot of rural labor, were quite unknown. Great land-owners adorned the fields near their homesteads with English hedges of hawthorn, boxwood, prickly ash, and in rare cases rose-bushes ; but for the most part the "posy" beds and decorative shrubberies were left to the "women folks," as something outside the serious consideration of the men. About every farm-house door the air was sweet in summer with caraway-blossoms, bergamot-beds, four-o'clocks, sedulously framed in a network of sticks to keep the rapacious poultry from devouring the seeds. The greensward about the house was cut into long pebble- or shell-framed beds, wherein the housewife's hand reared, with tenderness and solicitude, "ragged robin," "sweet William," "pinks," "pansies," "marigolds," and "daffodils," that filled the summer air with color and fragrance.

Against the parlor windows morning-glory frames trained their rainbow-hued blossoms into the deep embrasures, and made the glories of Nature part of the furnishing of the modest rooms. The walk from the front gate was aflame in the season with the heavy heads of the crimson peony. At Marbury, Aunt Selina and Norah gave every available moment to this vernal decoration, and the porch and the green parterres before the veranda were a delightful sight to see, as the visitor penetrated the blossoming labyrinth until the door itself was reached under purple lilacs screening the front windows and shedding their soft perfume on the balmy air. The orchards, generally set out between the mansion and the roadway, gave an air of repose and even seclusion to the hard outlines of the red brick or rigid stone squares scattered over the billowy landscape. A farm of one hundred acres was a sign of affluence ; fifty acres were counted a prosperous domain. The Caribee Valley, stretching from the great lake Otranto to the Mingrelia Mountains, was famous in the mills of Kent and the looms of Manchester for its wheat and fleeces. With the opening of the great Canal, the butter from its fragrant meadows ruled the markets of New York, and was a luxurious delight as far as Boston and Baltimore. An enchanting simplicity of manners and desires welded the neighborhood groups in fraternal amity.

The socialism of the patriarchs ruled the communities, though the honest households would have been puzzled to define the relationship. Money, instead of being secreted in the stocking, or hoarded in mysterious recesses, was so soon as gained put into new buildings or enlarged individual acreage. Banks were almost unused. Interest was unknown. The only rivalry in rank was the possession of the best farm—the cultivation of the acres. The farmer who had planted the largest number of meadows in wheat, and rescued the crop intact, was the hierarchical person of the countryside. The squire, whose function comprised justice of the peace and legal adviser of the township, was often the least considered of the neighborhood magnates. Change of ownership was very rare. When the boys grew up and married, instead of sharing the family heritage, they were generally given an outfit, a small sum of money, and set out to make their fortunes in that unknown West which is now the center of population. A hundred years ago the face of the country was known only to the restless pioneer, the hunting-ground of the last of the Oneidas, Chippewas, and Onondagas.

On the banks of its crystal streams still towered forest trunks that had sheltered the fierce nomads, girdled with the scalps of the early settlers. The richest farmer rarely had enough ready money to afford the mechanical inventions without which his descendant of to-day would regard himself helpless in the tillage of his wheat-fields. In the roomy parlor such a thing as a piano was unknown. Beyond the Bible, the "Pilgrim's Progress," "Saint's Rest," and the "Book of Martyrs," the most pretentious household never dreamed. A family fortunate enough to have relations in the "city," as Warchester was known for an area of one hundred miles, might be favored with a well-thumbed copy of "Robinson Crusoe" and the "Arabian Nights." But these were regarded with a good deal of timid questioning by the sedate elders. One copy of Scott's works, possessed by Dr. Marbury, had for years excited strong aversion to that gentle sage as far as his name was known. A Quaker descendant of a member of the Continental Congress, who had come from the Valley of the Susquehanna, was discovered to have a copy of Tom Paine's "Age of Reason" among his simple household treasures, and for years he was regarded as a pagan.

Benjamin Franklin was, to the common mind, what Voltaire remains to this day to some minds which are not common. The most resolute democrat spoke in solemn deprecation when "Tom Jefferson's" creed was mentioned. He was the type of all that was godless and unbelieving.

Denny enjoyed the most advanced forms of the schooling of that day—simple enough, as we have seen. But Marbury was much in advance of the neighboring townships, where the school-houses were built of rough logs, and the seats made from the outside planks, the bark adhering for many a day, until successive dynasties of boys had pulled it off to kindle the morning fire in the great chest of iron that served as a stove. The seats were not calculated to effeminize the scholars, as the legs from below came up through the auger-holes, catching the students' garments, and sometimes, when the seats were crowded, crucifying the flesh. As the chill air became warm from the roaring iron stove, or perhaps from a great open fireplace taking up one side of the log academy, the smell of food stimulated the zealous pupils, as the bowls of apple-sauce and jelly made their odor felt in the unventilated room.

With this, the coriander and caraway seed, that Denny detested, permeated the close quarters, as the younger children surreptitiously anticipated the tardy noon hour. In the summer all the young people, boys and girls, went barefooted; but as the autumn frosts came, the children's joy was to watch the itinerant shoemaker, who went from house to house "shoeing" his clients, setting up his bench and passing a week, a fortnight, or perhaps longer, where many feet made the need. Many a time the shining new shoes, grown to such wondrous shape and beauty under their eyes, the children of those days put under their pillows before wearing, to bring good luck to their footsteps! All the clothing was made in the house, carded, woven, cut, and fashioned, and life was as complete, on a well-ordered farm, as it is now in a metropolis—so far as actual needs went.

I don't know that these limitations made our forefathers less perfect men. Indeed, when we open that enchanting romance—how the reader of fifty years ago would have stared to hear it so called—when, I say, we lose ourselves in the exuberance of Bunyan's exquisite images, and reflect on the constancy with which our ancestors read its tender fancies, it is impossible to think of them as uneducated. For the poet's fancies must have lingered in all their days of toil and nights of tranquil repose. It is the fancy that educates us, after all, and how could men be stolid in wit, or deficient in speech, who had the sayings of Christian, and the sophisms of Worldly-Wiseman to tinge the color of their daily thought and point the force of their simple maxims? It is only within a few years that the cast of thought and form of speech of the Puritan fathers has wholly disappeared from the first settled communities of the Eastern and Middle States. In the days I am writing about, the Bible was the best known book to old and young, for though there was not much of the expository in the teachings of the unlearned Levites that sat in the rural temples of a Sunday, they encouraged the retention of the text in the minds of the Sunday devotees.

It was no unusual thing to find boys and girls who could recite the chapters of the Galilean life with as much precision as a college man of to-day the stirring passages of the "Iliad" or the "Odyssey." This familiarity with The Word, devoid of doctrinal tone or dogmatic tendency, formed an ethic system rather sentimental than religious, rather humanitarian than devotional. Influences like these were bound to make individualities of even the prosaic personages of such communities. The ignoble rivalry of sectarian prejudices never disturbed the serene current of their eventless existences. They were born among Nature's smiling walks, and they lived with characteristics insensibly molded by the secret processes that environed them.

It is an intelligent, sympathetic perception of these conditions that makes Denny's boyhood and manhood comprehensible—I hope vivid even, with the charm of reality; for though the limitations of this Arcadian race made his young years miserable, the very credulities that bred those harsh conditions were a compensation, in the rounding of the boy's character and the fitting him for a sphere of wider activities.

Denny's school-days being at an end, his kind patron, Dr. Marbury, began seriously to ponder the ways and means of gratifying the boy's desire to round out his schooling in college. When the rumor of this reached the neighbors, the good Doctor was well abused for the evil example. What would become of the farmers if the youths taken by them came to expect such ridiculous indulgence? How could the great farms that made the Caribee Valley, even in those days, the garden of the land, be worked successfully if boys brought from the city to serve apprentisage got the notion that they were merely to give sign of love of learning to secure a college term from their weakly indulgent patrons? In those days, too, there was hardly a farm-house that didn't count among the members of the family an apprentice, whose indenture bound him to the service of his master until the age of twenty-one. In return for a home, clothes, and perfect equality with the family, the apprentice gave all the winter

and spring months to the jocund toils of the farm. He
was regarded as a son of the family, and generally the
farmer's name was added to his own. He sat at the same
table, shared the family chariot on Sunday, and grew up
knowing no other home or domestic relation than that of
his master's family. There was no helot line between the
lord of the land and his servitor. Jacob tilled the fields of
Laban, and shared his feasts and fasts with perfect equality.
The Marbury Jacob courted his master's daughter, and
when in the fullness of time he had won his apprentice-
ship, his hundred dollars, span of horses, and yoke of oxen,
he married his Rachel, and either settled down to work the
paternal acres "on shares," or struck out westward to
employ the secrets of husbandry, and the alchemy of
energy, upon the eager waste lands of the young West. Of
schooling he had but the barest rudiments, though in that,
little as it was, he, for the most part, possessed more
knowledge than his patron. College, even to the sons of
the most thrifty farmers, was a rare conclusion to the simple classes of the village or district school. The utmost
that was considered needful, even in the most ambitious
families, was a brief course at the Academy in Calao ; then,
as now, a prosperous sectarian institution of the Methodists. This famous academy received the sons and
daughters of all denominations, and its roomy halls were
filled every winter with pupils from every county in the
western part of Imperia. Accommodating itself to the
needs of the country, the Academy made its term coinci-
dent with the close of the autumn operations and the
beginning of spring work. In the last of October the
winter term began, and by the middle of May the classes
closed for the summer.

It was resolved that Denny should prepare himself for
college by a few terms at Calao. He had himself earned

the money for his outfit. The chestnuts of Marbury were a free preserve to the boys of the country-side, and Denny, up early in the frosty October mornings, had gathered great stores which he sold in Warchester. So that the kind Doctor's narrow means were not taxed for the lad's ordinary needs. He set out in the well-laden carry-all, late in October, with the Doctor and Norah, who was to "put his room to rights," and at the end of a twenty miles' drive came to the pretty village of Calao. The buildings were even then gray and venerable, and he crossed the academic threshold with a throb of delight. His room was far up under the gabled roof. It was bare and carpetless, and all Norah's devising, with the simple furnishing at hand, could not make it inviting. But I doubt if the most luxurious of the Sybarite quarters at Cambridge to-day ever gave their indulged tenants the tranquil joy that Denny felt, as he sat down and opened his "Anthon" to begin the first reading of that grandiose Latin tongue which was to make him kin of the Roman and Greek worthies. His bleak room was shared by a student quite unlikè Denny in his habits and aspirations. His parents had insisted on his "going through the 'Cadmy," and the lad was quite satisfied to humor them. He was rather abashed at first by his comrade's serious views of the duty of study, and the necessity of faithful application. After the first few days he found companions of congenial aspirations, and then Denny saw little of him. The second day of the term, when he entered the class-room, whom should he see smiling on the girl's side of the apartment but his demure divinity, Dilly ! When he got a chance to speak with her, he learned that she had entered for the course, and was living with a relative in the village. So, from that time forth he had a double stimulus in his ardent pursuit. His achievements were to be under the adored eyes of his idol. Often and often it was his felicity to help her baffled brain in the construction of the bewildering Latin, or the resolution of some mathematical enigma. Of a Sunday he was sometimes invited to her kinsman's to tea, and once a fortnight they met in the president's drawing-room at the Academic *soirées*. He was there many months before his alien antecedents found him out. But one bitter day, during a wrangle in some game on the play-ground, a surly contestant met his attempt at peace-making, by the taunt :

"Oh, you Paddy, keep your blarney for Dilly Dane; we don't want any of it here."

Denny paused, palpitating and trembling. He had begun to think that these precincts, sacred to learning, were a haven from the ills of his school-days—that the liberalizing atmosphere of classic erudition was free from the narrow prejudices and proscriptive arts that marred his childhood. He quitted the grounds without a word, and thereafter pushed on resolutely in his studies. This was a new and enchanting world to him. His mind expanding under the noble radiance of Grecian and Roman history, he took no count of the ignoble realities of his day and surroundings. Though he was thenceforth jocu-larly and satirically called "Paddy," even by those who had no purpose of bruising his spirit, he felt no sense of hurt. Above all, and it is to exhibit this that I dwell so long upon these details of his youthful hardships, the pro-scription of his fellows made no inroads on the wholesome fervor of his impulses. He was gay, light-hearted, and in-corrigibly hopeful. The faculty, for the most part clergy-men, marked the scholastic enthusiast, and were proud of his growing distinction. But, so deeply rooted was the native aversion to the alien race, that they insensibly fell into the habit of disparagement common to their pupils.

Without acknowledging such a thing to themselves, they resented the pre-eminence of this son of a despised nationality, possessing traits that were the prescriptive heritage of the children of the soil. One day the word *patrician* came up in the Latin class, and Denny, with gentle malice, traced the etymological history, ending in the patronymic, Patrick.

"Is that the reason the eldest son of Irish families take the given name, Patrick?" asked the professor suddenly, interrupting the recitation and addressing Denny.

"I don't know, sir," said Denny, blushing. "Patrick is the favorite name in Ireland, because the first Roman bishop, who was a very learned and good man, was named Patrick."

The boys tittered, and the girls tossed their heads. The professor smiled, and said nothing more. Thereafter Denny was called St. Paddy when his tormentors meant to be humorously satirical.

One day, when the class was on the story of Ovid's exile, the professor asked why the Roman State succeeded beyond its rivals. Various reasons were given, and, when it came to Denny's turn, he said:

"Because every man who deserved well was made a Roman citizen, no matter what land he was born in; and," he added, "even the Britons, who were the most despised of the barbarians, shared the highest rewards of the state."

But his proficiency in study did not lessen the enmity of his comrades, or gain the real regard of the faculty. While he won plaudits in the class-room, he was virtually shut out of that intimate *camaraderie* which makes the joy of youth and the most charming retrospect of manhood. There was one abiding consolation in all this adversity. In the class-room, the social assemblies, when whispered sarcasms and overt enmity were most trying, a gentle eye beamed on him kindly, and a tender voice whispered encouragement and sympathy. Dilly resolutely persisted in refusing to see inferiority or shame in Denny's Irish birth. She bore the raillery of her companions good-naturedly, and, while she entered into no conspicuous championship of the young man, she let it be seen that she admired and even liked him. In all their walks under the clustering maples of Calao, Denny never dreamed of love-making.

To touch her hand he would have regarded as presumption, if not desecration. For insidiously the estimate of his fellows in a subtle way ruled his self-esteem. He thought of himself as a species of intruder or pariah. It was the ineffable goodness of the girl that made her suffer him near her. It was her timid constraint that accepted his delighted help in her studies, where every boy in school would have been proud and glad to aid her. Humbly, tenderly, shrinkingly, he went on from week to week, month after month, forging the bonds that he himself alone was blind to. When the term was ended, one lovely May day, they set out together in the Marbury stage homeward. Denny had taken high rank. He stood first in all his classes, and, indeed, he might well do so, for, instead of learning the prescribed lessons from day to day, he had eagerly gone through his text-books, and could have entered higher, while his mates were dawdling in their first books. Nor did he remit his pursuit of learning in the long summer evenings at Marbury. When the next term-time came, Denny was qualified to enter college instead of going through the academic preliminaries. It then happened that, one of the professors falling ill, Denis was for the term intrusted with his classes, and was enabled to lay by earnings to defray the first expenses of his college career. But with this dizzy triumph he suffered a great blow. The gossip of Calao had reached as far as Mar-

bury, and Deacon Dane had withdrawn his daughter from
the Academy. It was not until the term was well under
way that Denny learned the cause, and the blow nearly
disheartened him. The story that came to him was that
the Deacon and his family believed that he had taken advantage of the girl to attempt to win her affections. The
rumor became common gossip in the Academy, and he
was looked upon with more hostility than ever. Then,
under pressure from the social forces of Calao, he was, in
the middle of the term, removed from his place, and an
inferior in every way promoted to the post. Discouraged
but not embittered by the blow, he quitted the Academy
and returned to Marbury, judging it useless to continue
in classes where there was nothing to be learned. This
step added to the scandal. It was an evidence that he
meant to follow up the girl, and the Danes became openly
hostile to the "upstart." He had barely arrived when
Norah told him that Dilly had been sent to Warchester to
finish her schooling at a fashionable seminary. One day,
while he was working in the field, Tom Dane, who had
some business with Dr. Marbury, tied his horse and followed Denny into the harvest-fields behind the red
barn.

"I hear you're going to college in Warchester in the
fall ?" Tom said, after a casual talk on another matter.

"Yes," said Denny ; "I hope to be able to take the junior and senior years. I have worked hard to get ready,
and feel pretty sure of my examinations."

"You know, of course, that Dilly is in the city ? "

"Yes ; I have heard she is in Miss Churchill's seminary," replied Denny, astonished.

Tom coughed, looked very much embarrassed, and
then blurted out :

"Of course you know, Denny, our folks don't like

to have you courting Dilly ; she—can't marry you, you know."

Denny held a cradle in his hand. He laid it down, and, looking fixedly at Tom, he said quite calmly :

" I never courted Dilly. I never thought of asking her to marry me. We have been good friends because she is the only one of my age who has been kind to me. I—I—'' But here he broke down, and the tears came to his eyes.

" Oh, well, Den, there ain't no use in boohooing about it. Dill's a soft sort of a piece, and she would be in love with you just to spite the other girls that poked fun at you. I think she rather pretended to be so much taken with you to tease the old man. He like to have a fit when Dill told him she would marry you."

" Did Dilly—did your sister say that ? "

" Oh, the old folks were teasing her, and she sort o' made believe to be very much smitten with you. I knew very well it was just out o' contrariness, and I told them so ; but they were sure you meant to elope with her, and all sorts of trash things. I thought I'd have a talk with you between ourselves. I'm glad to see that Dill was only shamming. You know our folks have set their hearts upon having Ed Kenneth for son-in-law. Their farm is next ours, and our pastures need their brook to make them yield all that's in them. It's no particular interest of mine, you understand. If Dill should marry you, I'd get the farm, for the old man would never leave her a red cent."

I doubt if Denny heard a word of all this homespun diplomacy, beyond the one overmastering assertion that Dilly had acknowledged her love for him. He swung the cradle with a giant's force and a dreamer's aberration for the next hour. He hardly noticed the astonished Tom, as that mystified youth sauntered away, leaving a broad swath of quivering wheat-tops behind him as he viciously whipped the golden stalks with his short, thick riding-whip.

Dilly loved him. This was the sentence that rang in Denny's ears. She was there before him in all her gentle, confiding loveliness. Her eyes were the azure blossoms that he rescued with every swath in the golden maize that tumbled from the sweeping knife. The soft murmur of the summer breeze, swaying the golden sheen before him, was the echo of the tenderness her voice had always assumed when she encouraged him to pay no heed to the taunts of his revilers. When Norah came out into the field with his luncheon, as she often did in harvest, his eyes were so bright that she said with placid *naïveté*:

"Denny, dear, one would say that you had been glozing all day with the little people, and that you had been given the blossom of good luck! Have you been finding a four-leaved clover, or have you turned up the pebble of the Wicklow sleepers?"

He threw down his cradle, and, taking her in his arms, kissed her fondly.

"O Nody, I'm very happy. The fairies have been with me the whole day, and ye'd never guess what they've been telling me."

"Where the seeds of the blue-bell cups hide on Hallowe'en?"

"No."

"Where the furze hides its gold?"

"No."

"Where the diamonds go in the bed of the brook?"

"No."

"Where the honey-birds go in winter?" (Norah called the humming-birds "honey-birds.")

" No ; you'd never guess, and I'm not going to tell you, because it's a secret, and I'd have bad luck if I told ye."

This explanation was taken quite soberly by Norah. The credulity of her race was stronger with her than it was with Denny, for he only preserved a tolerant belief in the traditions he had learned from his mother. To Norah they were awful verities, not to be lightly talked of nor dismissed with levity. She sat down on a level sheaf and spread the simple repast, regarding the favored of the fairies with something of awe, and waiting for him to impart whatever he thought wise in his character of goblin minister. But he did not refer to the subject again, and, when she went back with the empty basket, she was eagerly alert to catch the first token from the powers of the air that might indicate that she too was to be inducted into the mysterious band. She whispered to the wrens in the alderberry thicket, and made all manner of friendly advances ; but beyond a vehement scolding from a startled cat-bird, she could arouse no voice that seemed to convey any intelligible token to her anxious ear.

That night, when she bade Denny good-night, it was he who closed the door, and when, hours afterward, she peeped softly through into his room, she could see him, still dressed, leaning on the window-sill and gazing rapturously at the crystal spots in the sky that glimmered like a maze of tremulous diamonds in the dark-blue horizon. She sighed gently. She too had studied these same silent symbols of the night, in tears and anguish, in rapture and hope, in disappointment and woe. She wondered if the same poignant questionings were in his heart ; the same weary despairing ! She wondered if he too saw in the misty air a form he thought of by day and dreamed of by night, and waked to think of and dream again, sometimes in buoyant hope, sometimes in heart-breaking misery. No, the fairies had given him the sign, and he had a touchstone that could compel fidelity. Perhaps if she told him, he might bring the form she loved back, or teach her how to conjure it. Oh, no, she dare not name her secret! She must—wait! Alas, her secret! It was nearly two years now since the handsome sweetheart had stood under the bramble-bush and pressed his mouth to her lips.

He had forgotten her. He came no more to Malvern. She had gone over there with the Doctor during the summer, but among the great folks she saw no sign of her Endymion. She had begun to confuse the memory of him with the roseate fictions of Denny's telling. To-night she was so moved by the unreality of his ever having been, that it would have been easy for her to prattle the tale to Denny if he had but invited her confidence. But he, poor boy, was in that state of transport that comes to us when we discover that the miracle we had dreamed of—despaired of—is a reality, and that we have but to ask, that it may come to pass.

And so the brother and sister, knit by alien destiny into a tenderness and intimacy surpassing the love of lovers, were sundered by an impassable barrier from sharing the confidence that would, perhaps, have averted the fateful tragedy of one life and the cruel trials of another.

CHAPTER XII.

LADY MOLLY FALLS INTO BROGUE.

Autumn's touch was on the landscape. The vine that hugged the elm confessed it first, and the tint of bronze on the oak confirmed it. The long sweep of dusty road from Dr. Marbury's was alive with the gay equipages of the world at Malvern of an afternoon. The meadows were baked bare and glistening under the hot September sun. The wheat and hay had long since been garnered, and rose in green and golden pyramids under the sloping hills. The tasseled corn stood thick and shining in the back uplands, and the threshers were busy in the vast red barn to make the wheat ready for the mill. The voices of the men could be heard in joyous chorus echoing and re-echoing for a square mile. It was near tea-time, and Denny, standing at the well, between the house and lane, saw a grand carriage stop just before the gate at the road. The coachman got down and examined the leg of one of the horses, shook his head dubitably, and, as an elderly personage on the back seat leaned out, seemed to report to him. The latter got out slowly, and he too scrutinized the animal's foot. This done he turned and glanced toward the house. Ceremony is not part of country life, even to-day, and Denny, bred in the simple ways of the vicinage, ran down the lane to proffer his services if they were needed. The coachman had, however, opened the gate and met him half-way down the lane.

"My master, Lord Poultney, bids me ask if he can drive his horses into your stable, and borrow one from you to take his coach back to Malvern; one of our horses has gone lame and can't travel farther."

Denny had accompanied the man back to the road, and he said, as he reached Lord Poultney:

"Dr. Marbury has gone to the city, but if you will please come in and wait, perhaps some of the men at the barn can help your horse."

"Ah, it's Dr. Marbury that lives here, is it, my lad?" exclaimed a cheery voice, and Denny saw a kind, good-humored face smiling at him from the carriage.

"Yes'm; Dr. Marbury."

"Ah, well, me lord, we'll be welcome, and I'm glad to go in, for I've heerd a great deal of the Doctor's foine deery, and I'm dying to see the maids working the buther. Drive in, Mick; I'll walk with me lord," and, sure enough, down plumped the gay Lady Molly, to Denny's great delight, and taking her lord's arm, while she kept her eye on Denny, walked joyously up the apple-scented lane.

"Sure, it's the land o' Canaan ye have here, me lad. Oh, luk at the apples—like me sisther Rosie's cheeks for all th' world. And the sweet smells—by me soul, me lord, I'd like to live here, and, indeed, I would. The like of that hedge I never set eyes on since I left the ditches of Wicklow, God's glory to it! And the gooseberries! O me lord, did ye ever lay eyes on such berries? I must stop and ate wan"; and, stooping down, she picked a handful of the plumpest of the freckled fruit, smacking her lips with a relish that did Denny's heart good, as he afterward confided to Norah; and the honest woman held her amused lord in the lane until she had finished her feast.

"'Pon me honor, I envy the Doctor, and I'd like to live here the whole summer. And ye have th' threshing, me lad? And I see the hayricks in the fields beyant. Indeed, I'd like nothing bether than climbing them. Ye think I couldn't, me bye?" she interjected, as Denny's eyes measured her ample shape and stout figure. "Indeed, then, I could. Many's the time Phil Foley and meself played on the top of the ricks with the gurls and byes of Carlow?"

"I fancy, Molly, you'd find yourself too stout for games of that sort now," interrupted my lord, laughing.

"Fat is it? Then, indeed, I'm not. I'll wager I could retch that stile beyant before the young chap here.

Will ye give me the dar? Say it, now, give me the dar, if ye dar."

"Oh, indeed, no, Molly. I know you too well; you'd run a race with the Graces, if the two others were left on earth to contend with you." And the old lord, taking her plump hand, kissed it gallantly.

"No wonder I couldn't say *no* to ye, ye blarneying rogue!" and she gave the delighted old lover a hug, as simply unconscious of Denny as though she had been in the securest conjugal seclusion. Remarking Denny's admiring sympathy in this honest domestic outbreak, she quitted her husband's arm, and, putting her hand under the boy's chin, held back her voluminous skirts with the other, and said, with serio-comic jauntiness:

"Were ye ever in love, me lad? Ha, ha! ye're blushing like the Shannon wather when the redcoats crossed it. Very well, me lad. When ye marry, if ye're half the man to yer sweetheart mine is to me, ye wouldn't change places with the King of Kerry. And what are ye called? Ye're no Marbury, with your brown hair and gray een. I'll engage ye're a Mick, now, as they call us in Warchester."

"I'm called Denis Boyne, ma'am."

"To be sure it is. Denis Boyne, long life te ye. And, Denis Boyne, ye're a foine, well-turned lad, and keep the divil from yer eye when ye luk at the gurls, for there's none of them'll stop to plait their hair when ye give them that blushing luk, me boy!"

And with this Lady Molly broke into a merry laugh that quite set Denny into ecstasy. He could scarcely credit it. Here was a great lady—a countess—the wife of Lord Poultney—not only Irish, but proud of it, and lavishing her brogue as another would the French accent or the English drawl! The little comedy had been acted

9

near enough to be seen and heard in the dairy, where Norah was preparing her pans for the evening milk. She ran out to the gate, and caught sight of the fine lady in silks holding Denny's chin with the whitest and most bewitchingly dimpled hand that could be imagined. Norah was bareheaded, and the slanting sunbeams made her tresses a shining nodus for the sun-rays to sport with, framed in the soft rich tints of the hedge. Lady Molly stopped in surprise, then came quite up to the astonished maiden.

"Ye're his sister; I can see that. Ah, me gentle gurl, ye'll have God's cross and the divil's crown in that lovely face if ye're not wise every hour yer eyes are open. Ye're Denis's sister, aren't ye?"

"Yes, my lady"—for Norah had seen Lady Molly at Malvern.

"And we're coming to the deery to see you at th' buther."

"Oh, I'm afraid you'll get your fine gown spoiled; won't you please to sit in the parlor?" and Norah moved as if to go to prepare that tabernacle of the solemnities.

"Parlor indeed! with this musky air and th' green of the trees, like the wathers of Killarney, in bits above yer head. Divil o' wan o' me'll put foot on carpet while I can stand on this green grass."

"But, Molly, we must really apologize to Mrs. Marbury for this intrusion. My good girl, will you show us to your—your—to Mrs. Marbury?"

Aunt Selina at this moment came to the door. She was knitting a stocking, and quite unsuspicious of the presence of strangers. She was very short of sight, and at this moment her glasses were pushed up on her forehead, so that she could not distinguish anything more than the outline of the group. Lady Molly pushed through the open gate, and, as the good lady leaned against the door, plying her needles swiftly, she was at her side before Aunt Selina discovered that it was not Norah or the kitchen-maid.

"Mrs. Marbury, we make bold to come in on ye without ceremony, for a little while. Yer husband, Dr. Marbury, is a friend of my husband, Lord Poultney."

"Oh, Lady Poultney, why didn't the children bring you right in? Tea is going to be a little late, for we have the threshers; but I hope you won't mind."

"If ye'll be so kind, Mrs. Marbury. Pardon me, this is my husband, Lord Poultney—Mrs. Marbury. As I was saying," continued Lady Molly, caressing a cluster of woodbine that ran up by the doorway over a trellis, "we are only waiting for a horse. One of ours has given out, and your young man tells us that Dr. Marbury'll be back soon. If you will kindly let us look into your deery and barn, and browse around the garden and orchard, we shall be deeply obliged."

"Oh, but you must really come into the parlor and rest first," protested Aunt Selina, somewhat recovered from her confusion.

My lord resolutely favored this proposition. He was fatigued, he said, and as for his wife, she might divert herself in the fields if she liked. So off went Lady Molly, carrying Norah and Denny with her, quite as if she had known them both since the days she romped in the Vale of the Seven Sleepers in Wicklow. She uttered a cry of great delight as Denny helped her down the mossy steps into the "deery," and when she saw the cool slabs, the shining pans, the glistening delf jars, and the heaps of yellow butter-pats, she was quite transfigured with joy.

"Oh, many's the day I stud on the cowld clay flure and made th' buther at home. And have ye th' sprig o'

mint we always put in the linen to keep the buther fresh
and sweet? And the buther-milk? Ah, me dear, give
me a big bowl of it. That bates the Wicklow milk; sure
there's enough buther in it to make a pat!" and she
laughed like a delighted child as she held the big bowl in
her hand after a copious draught.

And then, having given her opinion of the dairy, and
held her white hand in the icy water of the spring until it
became rosy, she carried the two enraptured young people
out into the orchard, and bade Denny lead her to all his
favorite places. The lad wished nothing better, and there
was great laughter when Lady Molly stopped and asked
Norah for a pin to hold back "me gown," for not a
"toe" could she take that it didn't catch in the bram-
bles. She lifted and, folding the front widths, pinned
them back into a tail such as you may see when a good
housewife has company and gives a hand in the kitchen.

It was a very gay party then that set out over the fields.
Denny made straight for the dell by the brookside, to show
the cheery lady the oriole's nest, and the deep pool that
was said to have no bottom. During the ramble Lady
Molly beguiled the boy and girl into such garrulous prattling that when, two hours later, they returned to the house,
she knew the story of their sad lives; and once or twice
she turned, as the tale was told, and brushed something
from her eyes that was not a gnat nor the pestiferous
thistle-flies that pursued them. The Doctor had not returned when the party reached the house. Tea was set
in the parlor, and my lord sat down with relish to the
broiled lake-fish, crisp "biscuit," and countless country
rarities that Aunt Selina had the secret of improvising
from her ample stores. Lady Molly was all gayety, and
Lord Poultney was obviously interested in the homely
good-breeding of the hostess. For, after the first embar-

rassing moment, Aunt Selina was equal to the entertainment of a prince. Her speech was full of a serene good sense that held attention, and, when she was sure of her company, she was capable of a pleasant humor that greatly delighted Denis when she fell into it. Lady Molly's hearty enjoyment of the place, her extravagant declarations of immediately settling in the country, captivated Mrs. Marbury, and the two ladies entered into a discussion of the joys of such a life.

"But what should I do without a pretty maid like this to keep me deery?" asked Lady Molly, beaming on the crimson Norah. "Ah, me lass, there'll be many a call for yer blushes when ye'll need them more. Some fine bye'll be claiming all that rosiness for his own."

"In the country, girls don't have time to think of sweethearts," said Aunt Selina, making a diversion in Norah's favor. "Norah will be devoting herself to me for many a year. But here's Denis. He's full of ambition. He's going to leave us to get learning. He wants to be a lawyer, and go to Congress, and who knows what."

"Yes, the lad's been telling me his notions, and I hope he'll get on in them. He must be a very good bye, Mrs. Marbury."

"Oh, Denny *is* a very good boy, we think, and we're not afraid of spoiling him by telling it. When the Warchesters were here a year or two ago, they thought Denny as well learned as Mr. Darcy, who had been at West Point."

"And d'ye know the Warchesters?" asked Lady Molly with interest.

"My husband went to college with the Colonel, and they are very warm friends. We never met Madame Warchester but once. She was here with her family. I suppose you know them well?"

"Indeed, no. A drop of Irish blood is as bad to madame as pork to a Jew, or holly-berries to a banshee."

"I thought Mrs. Warchester a very proud woman," Aunt Selina answered simply, "but I didn't think her so wicked as that."

She was a good deal puzzled to say just how wicked, for she didn't know how obnoxious pork was to a Jew, nor the repugnance which a banshee might have for holly-berries—nor even what a banshee was. But, from her ladyship's tone, Aunt Selina imagined the banshee a sort of deity that had anathematized the holly as a sinister growth.

"Oh, it isn't wicked she is. It's crazy!" said Lady Molly judicially. "She's that set in her ways she'd make Peter open a side-wicket if she saw meself entering the gate of paradise with her! It gives her joy that the path to heaven is straight and narrow, that she may be sure of no doubtful person walking it with her," and Lady Molly laughed as she saw Denny grinning behind his cup.

"I'm surprised that none of the prejudice of the mother is evident in her son. He seemed to me a sensible, good-hearted young fellow," Aunt Selina said, not wishing to subject the wife of her husband's friend to a too exhaustive analysis before the young people.

"Is it Darcy? He's a fine lad! There's not a dishonest hair in his head, and I'll go bail he spakes his mind to the mother when she takes on before him. He's not spoiled yet, but there's no knowing when he will be. It broke his mother's heart that the father let him have his way about going into the army. It's my belief the bye chose it to get out of the mother's road sooner, for, if he had gone to college, he would have had her airs and graces in his porridge till he was married."

"He's too young for that this many a year," said my

lord, intending to draw his wife away from discussing the mother.

"He's twenty-two, coming January; a year or two older than Denis there, and at home b'yes often marry at eighteen or twenty."

But my lord, foreseeing the danger of going further into the domestic affairs of the Warchesters, rose from the table, and asked Denny to show him the way to the barn. It was now late twilight, and the Doctor had not yet come. Denny proposed, if his lordship were tired of waiting, to go to a neighbor's and borrow a horse, and, Lord Poultney assenting, he went to the stable and got a lamp. When he came to the house, Lady Molly scouted the idea.

"Sure, we're in no hurry, and we may as well be here as in the crowded hotel at Malvern. It isn't often we fall in with such pleasant company, and are made free of so many delightful things. It's all wan to us whether we're back now or at midnight. Anyway, we'll see the milk strained and panned, and then, if the Doctor isn't come, Denny may go and borrow a horse."

It was nine o'clock when Lady Molly finally appeared from the "deery" and assented to Denny's quest. He ran down the lane, and nearly dropped the lamp with fright as the glad whinny of the Doctor's horses saluted him. They were standing quietly at the gate, but when Denny, in amazement, called the Doctor, there was no response. He ran to the side and held his lantern over the vehicle. No sign of the Doctor! Opening the gate, he drove the horses into the front yard, and ran into the house. Perhaps the Doctor had gone up through the field, supposing the gate open. The horses often came up from the road by themselves. There were surprise and vague alarm when he entered, and, not finding the Doctor, told his story.

Aunt Selina was trembling and white. She could hardly speak as she bade Denny get into the vehicle and drive her back on the road toward Warchester.

"You don't fear any accident, do you?" asked Lady Molly, in quick sympathy with the overmastering anguish she saw in the wife's face. Aunt Selina was feverishly adjusting her bonnet, and, turning away with a moan, she said, brokenly:

"The Doctor is troubled with epileptic attacks, and may have fallen by the roadside. God grant that we may not be too late. I am sorry to leave you like this—"

"Oh, pray don't think of us. We shall stay all night if you will permit—that is, if we can be of service in your distress."

But Aunt Selina did not hear the kind proffer. She was hurrying after Denny, and a moment later they heard the wheels rolling down the lane. When the carriage reached the road, Denny, by Aunt Selina's direction, got out with the lantern and searched each side of the highway. The quest was continued perhaps a half mile, to the limit of the Marbury farm, when Denny, holding the light over his head to peer into the fence-corner, stumbled over something. It was the Doctor's body, lying just off the carriage-way. The face was downward, and, as Denny stooped over him, he noticed that the soft grassy soil was covered by perhaps two inches of water. He had probably been stricken suddenly by his malady, had pulled the lines unequally, the horses had shied from the road and thrown him out as the carriage leaned over the slight ridge. In a moment the stricken wife was at the side of the body. She wailed to the dead ears despairing calls; but the lips were forever silent. The two inches of water had been as fatal as the deeps of the ocean. He was stone dead. It took all Denny's and Aunt Selina's strength to lift the body into the carriage, and with bursting hearts they carried the dead body back to the desolated hearth. Lady Molly displayed another phase of her whimsically diverse character. It was she who became for the time head of the household. Her hearty voice fell into the soft measure of the plaintive group. She whisked her lord off, saying, as she pushed him outside the door:

"'Tis no place for the likes of you, me dear. When Death's in the house, the cabin and castle's kin. These poor childer"—Lady Molly referred sweepingly to Aunt Selina and the brother and sister in this general way—"these poor unfortunates'll need a frindly heart for a while. It's little good I do in the world, at all, at all ; so begone with ye, me darlin', and let me do as I'd have others do to me."

Lord Poultney looked with moist eyes into the troubled face of his wife, and with a conjugal embrace, as he reached the shelter of the lilacs, said tremulously :

"What a heart of gold you have, Molly! What a glad man I am that I had the sense to see the jewel that you are! Ah, Molly, Molly ! how much of my life was wasted in not meeting you in the days when I had something more than this worn old body to give in return for a heart so good and noble ! "

"Be away width ye," she said, looking up at him with swimming eyes. "Sure it's the tongue of blarney ye have, and ye're younger this minute than the bye beyant ! "

When she re-entered the house, Aunt Selina still hovered over the pale face—the body stretched on the bed. Molly gently forced her away. The dismal offices of preparing the grave-clothes were undertaken and carried on by the energetic Irishwoman, everybody coming to her for directions. She never quitted the scene of this uncongenial and self-imposed ministry until all the dreadful

work was at an end, and the simple chariots at the gate
to escort the body ·to the pretty green covert near the
maple-woods, where the Marburys slept in death—in
their own acres, as was the honest custom in the country in
those days.   Lady Molly's kindly vigor during the ordeal
sustained the family, who somehow conceived a less poignant sense of loss while she resolutely held the household
to the heart-breaking routine of daily duty, eating, drinking, and sleeping.   Her tact and faculty helped the bereaved to endure the first dreadful days of vague wonder
and insensible expectation of the Doctor's coming back.
But when she kissed them all good-by, even Denny, in
hearty affection, the humid eyes that looked after the kind
soul as she rode down the lane saw only the vision of a
saint, and cherished in their hearts for many a day the devotion of this genial Samaritan.   Death's sharpest wrench
is when it strikes unexpectedly.   There was not a soul in
the house that did not tenderly love the lost friend and
master.   Love was the law of his life, and gentleness its
ministry.   He was the father of the fatherless, the refuge
of the homeless, and—he was dead !—and dead in such a
cruel form that murder itself would have seemed less dire.
Dead! while those that loved him were making merry ;
dying ! while their mirth was perhaps at its full ; dying !
while the hearts that would have given their vital drops
to save him pain were light and without presentiment of
the coming woe.

Strangers came in, as was the kindly fashion in those
days, and relieved the family of all the aching offices of
the dead.   Strangers carried on the harsh realities of the
household life.   It was well that it was so, for Denny and
Norah wandered about the house with swollen eyes and
dead hearts.   Norah, with her apron over her face,
crouched beside the coffin, haggard, hollow-eyed, and de-

mented. When the last of him was taken away, it was Aunt Selina who comforted these two Alien adorers of her dead. It was her gentle voice that reminded them that Death had dealt them a cruel blow, for the homestead that had given them ease and shelter was no longer hers to shield them. I doubt if, when the cruel time came, when the farm and household treasures passed to the prodigal son, Byron, they felt the dim terror of the future half as keenly as the blank despair of the death they had witnessed. The Doctor's affairs were found to be in such a state as generous men are apt to leave their worldly possessions. He had literally given all he had to the poor. He had in many cases lent money on worthless securities, and when the settlement came his widow was not only penniless, but dependent on an almost alienated son for a home where she had lived thirty-five years as a mistress. Byron, her eldest born and only remaining child, came home, not as the prodigal, but in the spirit of the banished heir who had been held out of his own. Denny at once declared his purpose of seeking his fortune, and making a home for the dear mother and Norah; but Mrs. Marbury commanded him to wait and see how Byron and his wife meant to rule their kingdom. Perhaps things might go on as they had been, and the household need not be scattered.

CHAPTER XIII.

NEW MASTERS AT MARBURY.

THE hapless household, its dead buried, waited supine for the next vicissitude. Aunt Selina feared that the house would no longer be a fit home for Norah when her son

Byron fell into his old, dissolute ways. She was herself
sorely perplexed. She hated to quit her home, but she
could not live in the same house with her son's wife—
that she had long since found by trial. She had married
Dr. Marbury in the East, and all her kinsfolk were there.
She might find a refuge for Norah with them if she could
only go and see the situation of things for herself. But
how leave Norah? If she could only write, and have
a refuge ready for Norah before Byron took possession,
the flight wouldn't be so marked. In the eyes of the law
Byron had the same legal claim to guardianship that Dr.
Marbury had acquired in adopting Norah. For Denny
she had no fear. He was at a self-helping age, when
vicissitudes could make no permanent mark in his character.

But, wise and loyal as he was, he could not be intrusted with the care of Norah. Aunt Selina had trembled in fear many a day. Her very innocence was a snare
to her. Other girls of Norah's age might be committed
to the hazards of such a fate as confronted the homeless,
without much fear of destruction, but Norah's very guilelessness would invite the traps of the ungentle. Aunt Selina's only resource was a brother, a clergyman in Salem;
but, while his narrow means might suffice to give her shelter, he could not care for Norah. He wrote, so soon as the
calamity was made known to him, for the widow to come
on and share his home. She hesitated, hoping to secure
a refuge for the orphan. It was finally settled that Norah
should remain in the homestead until the future revealed
Byron's disposition and his wife's treatment of the aliens.

A few days after Aunt Selina's departure, Norah, at
work in the dairy, heard a horse coming up the lane.
Looking out through the trellis, she caught a glimpse of
the rider through the lilac-bushes. Her heart gave a great

bound, and she staggered against the wall. She heard a smart tramp on the flags of the front door and the reverberation of the brass knocker. There was no one in the house, and she hastened to answer. Yes, it was he—eager, bright, handsome, and, though not so gay, still with a smile on his charming face.

"O Mr. Darcy!" was all that Norah could say, and then she shrank back as he came toward her.

"Norah, how are you? I shouldn't have known you in this black gown." Then, looking into the room and seeing no one, he whispered, "You are lovelier in it than ever."

"Oh, don't, Mr. Darcy, don't. It wrongs this house to bring back old times now. It breaks my heart when I think of the evil days that have come—to think of the dear friends that have gone."

"Friends, Norah? What do you mean? Where is Aunt Selina?"

"Don't you know"—she looked at him with dazed wonder—"don't you know that we've lost the Doctor?"

"Yes, we just learned on our return from the East that the Doctor was dead, and my father has sent me to invite Mrs. Marbury to come and make our home hers until she settles on her future plans. Here's a letter for her."

"She isn't here. She's gone home to her brother's in Salem, far, far in the East by the ocean."

"Gone!" cried Darcy, sinking into the rocker that he had so often seen the good lady nodding in of an afternoon, while Norah tripped in and out of the pantry. Then he looked at the slender, graceful figure leaning at the door-post, clad in some black stuff, but which on her seemed to him gracious as the finest silk of Antwerp. "Gone!" he echoed again; "and you, Norah? Why are you here?"

"I'm keeping house until Amelia and Byron come from Bucephalo."

"And Denis, where is he?"

"He's at Ritter's this week, but comes down every night."

"And when Byron's family comes, what are you going to do?"

"Aunt Selina is looking out for something for me at Salem, in case we don't want to remain with Byron."

"Something? What do you mean by something?"

"A place to earn my bread."

"By George! Norah, you don't mean to say that they are going to let you turn servant?"

"That's all I ever was," she said, looking at him with large, gentle eyes, in which wonder and surprise struggled.

"But you were not a servant here. You were the adopted daughter of the Marburys. You ate at their table, and—and—" But here Darcy found himself puzzled to define the elements that constituted non-servitude. Then, as if the effort plagued him, he said, almost impatiently, "Do sit down, Norah; it makes me miserable to see you standing there. If it were anybody else, you would seem woe-begone; but you are so beautiful that you would be a vision if you were swathed in sackcloth."

She listened to him as if she didn't hear. He arose and walked about the room, examining the old mirror with its band of faded gold across the top, opened the tall clock in the vestibule and set the long pendulum in motion, examined the Doctor's books ranged on the shelves in the alcove, and then, as Norah remained immovable, following him with unquestioning glances, he came over to her and took her hands in his own. She made no resistance.

"Norah, did you think I'd never come back?"

She started and trembled; a great crimson tide surged

over her neck and face ; her eyes fell under his ardent glance.

"Yes, I knew you'd come back," she said, and then drew her hands gently from his caressing fingers.

"Then you're glad I've come back ? Oh, my darling, you're glad I'm here ? "

"O Mr. Darcy ! don't, don't. It's the house of the dead, and I daren't think of the old times now. Give me time. Wait till the good Doctor is covered by the lilies ; wait till the live-forever blooms on his grave. O Mr. Darcy ! I'd never have luck if I let me heart be light, or joy come in it, while the sod is red on his coffin."

He sank back in the chair. The hand of the dead still protected the helpless. He shuddered at himself. He could have welcomed hyssop as a less bitter draught than the cup this unsuspecting child held serenely to his lips. He had one moment of vague self-recognition. He saw dimly the hideous gulf he had for two years closed his eyes to, and he saw himself held back by the hand of the dead. He gave Norah the letter for Mrs. Marbury, and rode away, hardly bidding her good-by. And with him went sunshine and hope from the heart of the girl. She stole back with dry eyes to her work ; and when, that evening, Denny saw her sadder than usual, he thought it the brooding over the sorrows of the past. She told him of Darcy's coming, but there was no hint of the tender relations that made the visit a break in the monotony of her life.

In the simple conditions of the time of which I am writing, death, it seems to me, was a more desolating, a more serious event in a neighborhood than it is to-day. Though most of the farmers of the four townships had seemed to Denny to be present when the good Doctor's body was carried out under the great elm, and buried in the family acre, far back in the meadow, solemn embassies kept coming to condole with the widow and scrutinize the darkened parlors into which Norah was instructed to usher them. Denny's sense of the ludicrous struggled with his misery, as the artless envoys of curiosity ranged themselves in the stiff chairs, the hands of the women covered with streaky "mitts," the men uncomfortable in shining doeskin and stiff, shapeless bootwear. Their expressions of sympathy for the solace of the bereaved widow were a puzzling reflex of the orthodox, though ghostly, comforting of the meeting-house, rather than the spontaneous expression of individual feeling. The trial had become too much for the gentle spirit of Aunt Selina long before she set out for Salem. She gave up the attempt to meet the emissaries, and the entertainment of them fell upon Denny and Norah, who were asked such questions as made even Aunt Selina's patient spirit revolt when she was told of them.

But there came an end to this. There was a new head to the Marbury household. Byron Marbury, the Doctor's son, presently came with his wife and boy, and were installed in the old mansion. Byron had never since his early boyhood lived in accord with his father. He had wasted his opportunities at the township school, and ran riot when sent to the city academy. At nineteen, enamored of the sea, he had disappeared and shipped before the mast. At twenty-five he returned, resumed his place in the household, but led an irregular life, and was a sore trial to father and mother. In a tipsy frolic he had married the daughter of the neighborhood neer-do-weel, a carousing Jack-of-all-trades, who let his paternal acres melt away, from year to year, to pay his debts.

I think every country neighborhood has one such family, the object of the community's wonder and scorn. Amelia Crane brought none of the civilizing influences of woman to the reprobate Byron. She was a sharp-featured, energetic, shrill-toned little virago, and she signalized her first appearance in her husband's household by angry resentment of Aunt Selina's efforts to reclaim her son from his excesses. The attempt to domesticate the couple proved a heart-breaking failure. The Doctor had fitted up, with such simple adornment as seemed luxury in those days, the east wing of the old mansion, and set it apart for the pair. Byron was to help work the farm, and the two households were virtually independent. But Amelia could not endure the isolation of her own apartments.

She passed most of the time in Aunt Selina's sitting-room, fretfully complaining of Byron's shiftlessness, for the young man spent much of his time in the Marbury tavern. He was fond of hunting and fishing, and was forever commanding Denny's time and skill in preparing for these diversions. His work on the farm was neglected, and in time the Doctor relinquished all hope of reclaiming the reprobate. After the birth of Byron's first boy, Amelia became sour and more exacting than ever. She hated poor Norah, chiefly because Aunt Selina was fond of her and the motherless girl seemed to be the daughter of the house. Denny, too, she could not endure, and never vouchsafed to give him any other title than "Irish" or "Paddy." The aliens, to spare Aunt Selina's and the Doctor's feelings, concealed the more brutal evidences of Amelia's hostilities; enduring such passionate outbursts of temper as only the capricious hate of a termagant can exhibit.

The years of the couple's stay in the house were a heavy trial to the boy and girl. One day Byron, who was not unkind, discovered that Norah was a "devilish pretty little Paddy," and carelessly said it before his wife. After that the poor child was unbearably odious to the exasperated, energetically alert shrew. She watched the girl furtively, and began to drop insidious whispers into Aunt Selina's ears. Finally, one day, Byron, returning from the tavern half tipsy, encountered Norah at the well. He came upon her suddenly, seized her by the waist and kissed her, then rushed into the house laughing at the joke. The wife at her window had seen the incident. She fled to Aunt Selina, tears of rage in her snapping black eyes, and broke out:

"Now, mother-in-law, I ain't going to stand that Irish hussy any longer. If she don't get out of this house, I'm going—and I'm a-going right away too!"

"Why, Amelia, what has Norah done?" asked the elder lady, in agitation.

"What has she done? The brazen trull! What hasn't she done? Ever since I've been in this house she's acted more like the daughter than I have. She's been setting her cap for Byron, and she's just kissed him, there at the well, before my eyes. Ef that ain't enough to show you what she is, I don't mean to take any more trouble to learn you. She must leave this house this day, or I will; so there!"

With this, the outraged Amelia flung herself from the room, and in an instant Aunt Selina heard her shrill voice reproaching Byron. That good-natured culprit broke into peals of maudlin laughter, and then the wife's protests fell into tearful snatches of mingled fury and complaining. Norah, terrified and miserable, had hurried to the dairy, where she sat sobbing when Aunt Selina went to her a few minutes afterward. The windows were open, and she had heard the virago's monstrous calumny. It was not the first time she had hinted her jealousy to Norah, but she had never before broached it to the mother.

"My poor child," Aunt Selina said soothingly, taking

the golden head on her breast tenderly, "don't fear that I can be made to believe evil of you. Bear with Amelia's temper. She is very unhappy, because—because—she has been reared in the wrong way, and Byron is very trying." Here the poor mother broke down and the two women sat rocking in quiet grief. Dr. Marbury appeared in the door with a stern light in his kindly eye.

"Mother," he said, in a trembling voice, "you see yourself now that the house can not contain two families. I saw the thing that has just happened. It won't do to have Norah subjected to such trials. Byron means no harm, but such conduct must not be allowed by us."

"O father, father!" Aunt Selina was sobbing, "what have we ever done that this affliction should come to us? Byron was the kindest and best of children. He—he—" Then she quite broke down.

"Byron is under influences that we can not counteract. It is best that he should be in a house of his own. Amelia will be happier, and we shall be happier. As it is, we are in constant quarrels and disputes. The Elder house is empty. It is just far enough away to divide without separating us from them. It will make a comfortable home, and they must go to it. You and I are too old to keep up the sort of life we've been enduring. It is much better that Byron should be in a home of his own."

"Well, ef Byron isn't in his own home, I'd like to know who is!" Amelia stood in the doorway, her eyes flaming as she marked the attitude of Aunt Selina and Norah. "Ef we are to be kicked out for that Irish trollop, I want to know it. I guess we've got some rights in this place, and we'll see ef the law can't give them to us. Oh, I know very well that you always turned up your nose at my family, and just bore me here because you thought you'd have more hold on Byron. You've set him against

me fast enough, I can see that; and now you want to encourage him to make up to that brazen hussy. I won't
stand it. I will go to my father. I guess the Cranes are
as good as the Marburys, ef they don't pretend so much."

By this time the angry voice had grown loud and shrill,
the fierce denunciation mingling with little hysteric gasps.
The sound of the voice pierced the air like the sudden
burst of a steam-whistle. Byron heard the outbreak in
the house, and came staggering down to the dairy.

"Yes, it's time to come. You're going to be turned
out. This house is no home for you or yours so long as
this Irish shirk is here. They think more of her than
they do of you."

"What's the matter, eh? What's the matter?"

Byron looked in drunken dismay at the excited woman,
sobbing, and rubbing her eyes with the end of her green
gingham apron.

"Matter? Why, the matter is that I won't stay in this
house another day to be insulted by your family. They
take the part of this scheming beggar against you and me;
they say we must get out. That's what's the matter."

"Amelia!" Doctor Marbury turned and came out of
the dairy. "This is not the way to talk to us nor of us.
You are not in the right frame of mind to listen to me
now. We will talk the matter over some other time, and
I'm sure you will see that what I propose is for the best.
You and Byron are our children. We love you, and you
must let us be the judges of the way we think best to show
our love for you. Byron, come with me!"

"Byron sha'n't do any such thing. Whatever concerns him concerns me. I ain't going to have you talking
to him and setting him against his wife and baby. O
Byron, Byron! was it for this I gave up Pliny Hart? He
was rich, and would have given me a real home right

away. Oh, why—why did I listen to you—why—when father wanted me to marry Pliny?"

"Go to the devil, and take Pliny with you too, you fool! I—I—" But Doctor Marbury laid his hand on his son's arm, and with a wild shriek of baffled rage Amelia scudded into the house, and presently could be heard monologuing with baby, into whose astonished ears she was pouring a lurid tale of her griefs, not the least of which seemed to be that Pliny Hart was not baby's papa, "instead of the shiftless, good-for-nothing Byron Marbury!"

Father and son walked down the orchard-path toward the fields, away from the barn-yard, where the cows browsed of an evening, after they were milked. Byron made pretext of interest in his big Newfoundland, Sailor, that gamboled in unwieldy sportiveness by his side, emitting stertorous yelps as his master incited him to livelier pranks. The talk between father and son was watched by the wife, but what was said between them no one ever knew.

A few days later, Byron, whose tastes were nomadic, received a sum of money from the Doctor's savings, and bought a half interest in one of the packets running between Warchester and Bucephalo. Amelia refused to be placated. She turned a deaf ear to all of Aunt Selina's proffers in packing, and, when her effects were all laden in the great hay-wagon, she tripped out of the house turning her head aside, to avoid the kiss of reconciliation her husband's mother proffered. She declared that she would never put her foot inside the Marbury doors so long as Irish beggars were treated better than her husband's flesh and blood. This all happened soon after Denny's coming to Marbury. The exodus seemed to make the orphans dearer to the old couple, and Denny became really a son to the kind old Doctor, while Norah was the comfort of

Aunt Selina's lonely old age.   Once a fortnight, when the packet was due at Warchester, the Doctor drove to the city with kind messages and substantial testimonies of the parental love for the wayward children.   But Amelia was obdurate.   She refused to visit the house, and received the largess as no more than her due.   Byron came home occasionally with his father, but the tranquil hearth was uncongenial to him.   He liked the boisterous life of the canal.

He was captain of the boat, and became known all along the line as a merry, riotous, kindly spirit, likely to be his own ruin.   For a time he prospered in his calling, which in those days was not regarded as it came to be afterward.   Citizens of the first dignity in Warchester were packet-captains, and later in life rose to high civic and social state.   But his easy nature and facile disposition soon brought Byron to ruin.   He mortgaged his boat, drew on his father heavily, and shortly before the Doctor's death the venture came to a sudden collapse.   Byron in a tipsy debauch staked his interest on a game of cards, and lost.   Amelia went home, to " Father Crane's," as she called her home, and Byron skulked about Bucephalo, ashamed to show himself at home.

With the Doctor's death the conditions were again changed.   Byron inherited everything, his mother possessing only the right of dower in the homestead.   The husband and wife returned a fortnight after the funeral was over, and Amelia assumed the place of mistress.   Aunt Selina, who had returned from Salem disappointed, welcomed her with sad forebodings.   At first nothing was said about Denny and Norah, but the virago soon made it plain that the Aliens would find their lines unendurable.

Norah felt the first effects of the new *régime*.   She was, under one pretext and another, withheld from the coveted Sunday gathering in the school-house.   Her pretty gowns, which Aunt Selina fashioned with her own hands, were denied her; that is to say, when she needed a new gown, Amelia caused the poorest and coarsest stuff to be bought, and made up the material herself in the clumsiest and most unbecoming mode. So far as it was possible the brother and sister were denied their long walks and wild-wood saunterings. At night they were refused the poor tallow-dips, with which, as the evenings grew longer, the boy and girl were used to illuminate Norah's pretty chamber while they dreamed aloud and speculated on the wonderful future when Denny was to be a great lawyer like his uncle, whose picture, in his wig and gown, Norah had rescued from the wreck of her mother's treasures. Denny, too, came in for his share in the Draconian system that ruled the old home. He was no longer suffered to read in moments of leisure. Dr. Marbury's books were all sent off one day to the city to be sold, Amelia answering Aunt Selina's agitated questions by the remark :

"What earthly use is that truck here? It only gathers moths, and gives that lazy Irishman a chance to waste his time while he ought to be paying us for his living by work !"

Denny passed many a day in bitterness and pain when these old friends were gone. The tears welled up in his eyes as he rehearsed his loss to Norah. Even his " Robinson Crusoe," " Pilgrim's Progress," and " Plutarch," given him by the Doctor, were sent away with the rest.

"It's time you should learn your place, young man. You're old enough to do a man's work. You eat as much as a man, and we can't have any drones in this house !" Amelia said to the lad when he told her that many of the books were his own. " There's plenty for you to do of an evening. My brothers always made themselves of use in the house as well as out. There are apples to pare and cut for drying. The garret is full of rags that need cutting and sewing to get ready for the carpet-weavers. You can do that work very well, and help pay for the schooling we've given you."

The energetic little tyrant was as good as her word. Denny, so soon as the evening "chores" were done, was put to paring apples until late in the fall. Then came the carpet-rags, Denny sitting gravely on the floor tearing stuff into long shreds and then sewing them together. These in turn were made into balls, and, when enough were heaped on the attic floor, they were sent to the city to be woven into the many-colored fabrics known as rag-carpets. Amelia was a good housekeeper. Not a crumb was permitted to fall astray. The children were astonished at the exactness of the household calculations—an exactness that would have sent them both to bed hungry many a night if in summer Denny hadn't laid in stores of fruit and in winter nuts, and Aunt Selina, also, had not secreted "cookies" and "doughnuts." Amelia didn't mean to starve them. She was merely frugal, and made no allowance for the difference in appetite between age and growing youth. She was herself content with a bowl of Indian meal and milk for supper; why shouldn't the rest be?

The horror of the household ministry soon haunted Denny like a familiar phantom. He loathed the unchanging diet. Breakfast was a tolerable meal. Tea and coffee, since Amelia's arrival, had been denied the dependents, but milk was plenty, save in winter, when their mugs were filled with the skimmed remains of the day before. There were always fried pork cut very thin, potatoes, good bread dealt out very sparingly, and though fruit was abundant it was never seen on Amelia's table. Everything was sent to market. An egg or chicken was a rarity, where before both were always abundant. Amelia declared that such gluttony was sinful, and every staple that could find a market in Warchester was carefully guarded, and packed on Saturday to be sold. The resolute little manager directed all this herself; she held Byron to his work, by constant reminders of his luckless packet speculation, and doled out money to him with a niggard hand.

Now and then he broke loose and re-asserted his old humors. For days he secluded himself in the Ritter tavern, drinking and gaming with any reprobate at hand, and, when the fit had passed, returned tranquilly to his husbandry. Amelia never reproached him at the end of such escapades, but Denny dreaded them, for he was made to endure the pent-up wrath that would have been futilely spent upon the jovial profligate. The present was hard enough for Denny to bear; but, as he reflected over the new miseries that were come upon him, he saw the future more bleak, empty, and unlovely. If it were not for Norah, he would have fled from the hateful bonds. But she was helpless. She needed him. Once she would have been struck, in an outbreak of Amelia's wrath, if Aunt Selina had not intervened. How could he fly and leave her subject to such cruelty and iniquity? His heart was sore, and his spirit quite crushed. He could see no escape from the toils. Every day seemed to make his bondage more fixed and more unendurable. The birds and brooks seemed to sound in his ears in sadder strains. The woods were melancholy and strange to him now, when at rare intervals he found a stolen moment to revisit his sylvan haunts.

Dilly, too: she had gone to the city, and was still at the seminary. He saw her only rarely, as she drove past on her way to or from the school. The few joys that came into the lives of Denny and Norah were when, once

10

in a great while, Amelia with the little Byron drove off to pass the day with Father Crane. Then Aunt Selina seemed to grow young again, and the three rioted in a renewal of the pleasures of the past. The kind lady had, on a visit to the city, replaced the "Plutarch" and the "Arabian Nights," and these, guiltily secreted in the garret, were brought down and the dear old tales retold, the three laughing and wondering over the magic, miracle, and heroism that have filled so many millions with joy and hope and resolution. I fear that the good-natured Byron was privy to these conspiracies, for once, on going suddenly to the vestibule, Denny discovered the big husbandman leaning under the window, his eyes moist and kindling kindly, as if he, too, had the heart that helps the brain comprehend the things that are ennobling, inspiring, and softening in the deeds that men have done and dared and suffered, in reality as well as romance. He made a sign of amity and discretion to the dismayed culprit, and stalked away, laughing softly to himself.

CHAPTER XIV.

THE TELL-TALE TREASURE.

In youth sorrow is not long crowned by the remembrance of happier things. As time went on, the boy and girl made little of their burdens and much of such simple joys as were left them. Youth has a prodigious recuperative force. Imagination strips the harshest realities of their woes, and in time Norah's song and Denny's gayety resumed their old tone. Amelia, with the keen sagacity of the sordid shrew, soon discovered that as "help" the pair

were a fortune in the house, and, though the discovery
brought about no amelioration in her treatment, it lessened
the persistency of her brutality to them. She had at first
insisted that Norah should quit the house, but Byron,
though yielding and placable in everything else, came to
his mother's rescue, and declared that the Doctor's bequest
of a home to the children should be obeyed. Byron rarely
had his "say," as he reminded the indomitable little chief,
but, "when he did speak, he meant it." She made no
further attempt to carry out her purpose, and apparently
the girl's singular deftness in the household work reconciled the termagant to the fiat. But, under such conditions,
it was easy to foresee that the catastrophe was only postponed. One evening Byron, who had been to the city,
returned to tea in a tipsy, frolicsome humor. The little
woman at the head of the table pursed her thin lips, and
vented her virulence upon Norah whenever occasion presented itself. After a more cutting reprimand than usual,
the poor girl fled from the table in a convulsion of terror
and tears.

"Hey, hey, wat's this? Eh, Norah? Wat's matter?
Toothache? Hey, my girl, come back here and finish yer
supper."

"Just you never mind her; she don't need any supper.
It'll do her good to fast a little while," Amelia said, with
asperity.

"But, I say, by God, she shall have her supper!" and
Byron, not quite sobered, hurried after the fugitive. Norah
had fled to the dairy, where she sat sobbing when Byron
appeared.

"Come, Norah, girl, never mind Mele; she don't
mean anything. She's a darned fool. Just come right in
and eat your supper."

"Oh, thank you, Byron, I don't care for anything to

eat. Please go back, and let me go to my work. Indeed, indeed, I'm not hungry!"

"But I say you shall come to the table. I won't have you treated so. I guess I'll show who is master in this house. If Mcle don't like it she can lump it. Let her go to old Crane; he'll soon be glad enough to get rid of her. Norah"—he came quite close to the trembling girl, and put his arm around her waist—"Norah, I love you a thousand times more than I ever loved that sour-tempered screw; love her, ha!" and he laughed a mocking, bitter laugh that seemed to sober him; and then, by a mighty wrench, pressed the struggling girl to his breast, burning her averted face with his hot breath. "I love you," he panted; "you shall be mistress here. I swear it, by God, I—"

"O Byron—Mr. Marbury! in the name of your dead father, in the name of God, don't—don't say such dreadful things. Don't murder me by such doings. I shall die of shame. O my God! be merciful to me. Be your father's son! What would your mother—what would Amelia say? She is cruel to me, but I deserve it. Ah, yes, I deserve it, or you never would drag me in the dust of shame as you do by this cruel and wicked conduct! Oh, spare the motherless and fatherless—you who have an angel for the one and I a saint in heaven for the other." She panted and wrestled herself free, and stood before him with burning face.

"I tell you, Norah, I worship you. I have loved you since I first saw you. If I hadn't loved you I shouldn't be the good-for-nothing fool I've been for five years; I wouldn't have broken my father's heart." His voice was tremulous now with passion; his mighty arms were about her again; with one fierce wrench he pulled the slight form to him and planted a loathesome kiss on her lips.

Norah was powerless in the strong arms, but with a loud shriek she struggled desperately to free herself. A swift step was heard on the stone flags, and Byron relinquished her as Denny appeared in the doorway.

"What is it, Norah?" and he looked resolute and defiant. "What is it, Norah? Are you harmed? Are you in fear? Byron Marbury, what have you done to my sister? Surely you are a man and would scorn to persecute her as—as—" He stopped, not knowing, in his agitation, what to say.

"No, Denny, Norah hasn't a better friend in the world. I was only telling her that she shall suffer no more in this house while I'm master; and you may depend upon my word."

"If he does, he'll be the only person in this township that depends on it!" Amelia stood in the doorway behind Denny, sneering and calm. "So this is the way you teach my servants to act in my house, is it? I have to work and scrape to keep your poor shiftless bones from rotting in the gutter, and you are not contented with robbing me of my earnings, but you must go in the corners and put the servants up to make little of me! Denis, you go about your business and finish your work; while as for you, my lady, I'll teach you a lesson, or my name isn't Amelia Ann Crane! Come, come! Get out of here and go to your work; I'll give you something to whine for!"

She pushed resolutely past her husband, and, taking firm hold of Norah's shoulder, gave her a vicious push toward the door. The nails cut into the girl's delicate flesh, and she uttered a sharp cry. As the virago lifted her arm to repeat the push, Byron seized it, and with such vigor that she screamed.

"You she-devil, if you ever lay a hand on that girl again I'll brain you!"

His face was livid with passion. She gave one look in his blood-shot eye, and saw that he was in deadly earnest. Her eye quailed under this ferocious glare, and without a word she bent her head submissively and ran up the steps shuddering, as she had never in her life shuddered before, for she saw that in her husband's face which warned her that she had drawn the bow too far. He came with heavy step and muttered words into the pantry, where she had fled to evade him; he pushed the closed door back as though it had been paper, though her whole weight was against it. He forced her to face him as he said slowly, in a thick rush of repressed passion:

"Now, I've got just this to say to you: For ten years I've borne your deviltry; I may not be a good husband—I suppose I'm not. But bad as I may be, it is not in your family to find fault. If you had not been what you were, I would not have been what I have been. You entrapped me into marrying you—or your mother did; I'm not complaining about that. It was my own free work. I knew what I was doing. But if you had been half human you could have made the man of me that my father meant I should be, and that I know I could have been. You've been a clog and a curse to me. I've sworn a dozen times to turn over a new leaf; but, whenever I've tried, your cursed tongue and temper have driven me to the whisky-bottle—yes, your cursed tongue and temper. What you were when I married you, you know very well. What you've been since, I know only too well. But it's got to stop now. I won't have my mother turning and twisting in her own house to escape you. I won't have these children ill-treated, that my father loved as his own, and they were far more to him, God forgive me, than ever I was to him, though until I knew you I never was undutiful to him. You know your blood. It's damned bad blood. Your sister Becky drove her husband to the razor; but though you've driven me to the whisky-bottle, you're not going to push me till I cut my throat. No, by God, I'll cut yours first! I think that's all I have to say, and you know me well enough to know that I don't talk to hear myself talk. That girl and boy are in this house to stay, just as long as they please, and they must be treated as members of my father's family."

He opened the door, encountered his mother's terrified face, stopped an instant, stroked her hair, bent over her, and touched his lips to her forehead, and then stalked out of the house.

Norah, standing under the pantry window, had heard every word. He stopped when he saw her, then continued, saying, as he looked over his shoulder at her:

"I meant every word of it, and she knows it."

For days afterward the house suffered an indescribable change. Amelia never opened her lips to any one. When asked about the household affairs, she answered in monosyllables. She never came to the table, but, with little Byron, ate in the pantry. At the end of the week she took the boy and went off to Father Crane's. Byron never made any inquiry. He continued the common routine, was rather gayer at times, and, after supper of an evening, asked Denny to read from his "Plutarch" or "Arabian Nights." In the fields at work he rehearsed all the incidents narrated the evening before, asking the boy's judgment on the various events and the valorous deeds described. He softened wonderfully in his mother's presence, and for the first time since boyhood left her at night with a filial kiss. It was a tranquil time to all. Denny, however, was surprised at Norah's conduct. She never sat in the large room of an evening, as it had been her delight to do when he read. So soon as the evening work was done, she hurried to her own room, and there every night he found her with her sewing, if there was still light enough in the sky; gazing dreamily at the stars, if it were dark. She parried all his anxious queries as to the cause of this sudden change, and once, when he became impatient at her reticence, she burst into passionate tears.

At the end of a fortnight Amelia came back, and resumed her functions as if nothing had happened. She declared that she had been forced off to Bucephalo to attend a cousin's wedding, and the explanation was accepted without a question. She was markedly equable with Norah; never scolded her in the old fashion, but accepted her ministry without sign or token. She made much, in an uneasy, effusive way, of Aunt Selina, and rarely reminded Denny that he was Irish. Much of the sunshine of old days came back to Denny—a wintry sort of sunshine, perhaps, under the changed temper of the martinet. He even ventured to carry his beloved books into the field with him, and turn to his favorite pages when resting-spells came. Byron himself encouraged these systematic outbreaks of the boy's tendency, by lolling on the ground, his face covered by a big straw hat, and listening alertly, though pretending to doze. One day little Byron, toddling out into the harvest-field at noon, found his papa stretched under a spreading oak, while Denny read aloud. He, too, listened to the tale, and that evening innocently prattled of it on his father's knee. Amelia, sewing at the window, turned to Denny and asked sharply:

"Where did you get them books? Stole my money to buy them, I suppose."

"It's none of your business where he got them, and stealing isn't a habit in the Marbury family."

It was Byron who spoke, and his tone was quite easy and affable. Amelia turned scarlet, for the shot told. One of her brothers had come to shame before the whole county in a theft years before. She got up and left the room, and the rest could hear her sobbing all the evening. They didn't understand the sting in Byron's taunt, and were at a loss to account for the unwonted sensitiveness of the intrepid campaigner. Norah's curious abstention from the large sitting-room, so soon as her work was done, attracted Amelia's suspicions. She began to observe her closely, but could not comprehend the manœuver, as she made up her mind it was. On one pretext and another, she followed the girl, and found her in no forbidden employment.

One night, however, being awakened by little Byron toward midnight, she was startled, on going to the pantry, to see a gleaming trail of light reflected on the lilacs, and, putting her head out of the window, she saw that it came from Norah's room. What could Norah be doing up at such an hour? When Byron's needs had been satisfied, Amelia, in her stocking feet, stole softly up the stairs, through Denny's room to Norah's door, and listened. She could hear her moving about, and once, through a slit in the time-worn panel, she caught a glimpse of a figure in a silken sort of fabric, and the glitter of something like jewels in her ears. Trembling with anger, and her suspicions at once alert, Amelia gently tried the door.

It was fastened. For a moment she was madly minded to force the girl to open it, but, remembering Byron's anger, she resolved to bide her time. The next day Byron was going to the city, and Denny was in the fields. So soon as Norah was well at work in the dairy, Amelia went up to the girl's room, fastened Denny's door to secure herself from interruption, and began an examination of Norah's belongings. It was not the first time she had pried into the poor girl's treasures, but hitherto she had passed the little hair-covered box in the closet without scrutiny.

Now she dragged it from its *quasi* concealment, confident that the mystery of the night before was concealed in it. It was fastened with a hasp, and the key was not to be found in any of the drawers of the high dresser. Leaving the room for a few minutes, and assuring herself that she was alone in the house, Amelia returned with a hammer, and with a few blows the hasp was broken and the mystery disclosed.

We have seen the treasures that now startled the interloper. Amelia held Darcy's trinkets in her hand, her small eyes sparkling viciously. Now her vengeance was in her own hands. Byron would not be able to throw the burden of thieving on her family again, for here was the evidence that Norah was a thief! There was no other explanation of such things in the girl's possession. She never had money to buy such jewels; besides, if she had come by them lawfully, why secrete them and masquerade with them only at midnight? Amelia laughed a little cackling laugh of supreme enjoyment. Now the intruding beggar should be driven from the house in ignominy; even Aunt Selina wouldn't dare shield her in theft. She slipped the jewels into her pocket, put the box back into the closet, and resumed her work with an elastic step and a resumption of the old manner that struck Norah with dismay when she entered the kitchen a few minutes afterward. Amelia said nothing to her then. Her soul was in arms for the sort of fray the cruel love. To confront Norah, to put her guilt in bodily shape, leaving no loophole of pretext, prevarication, or shift—*that* was, to the ungenerous hate of Amelia, something of the mysterious joy of an inquisitor, when what was left of a heretic's body admitted the culpability of religious schism.

Byron was always noisily hilarious at the evening feast, and this evening he bantered Denny slyly on the re-appearance of Dilly, who had come home for the summer vacation. Even Norah was drawn into the merriment; but her laughing recreancy was swiftly avenged when she caught sight of the lurking malignity in Amelia's snapping eyes. When the kine had been cared for, and were wandering off back of the great peaceful barn, cropping the dewy grasses, Denny, returning to the house, wondered that Norah's voice was silent in the dairy. She always sang in the twilight as she busied herself in this scene of her own peculiar reign. He found her troubled and pensive, and she owned, falteringly, that she felt the shadow of coming sorrow in her heart. Denny ridiculed the foreboding, declaring that, with his stout arm and long head to ward between her and danger, she was a silly girl to look into the shadows for trouble when the realities were now all in her favor. A luminous twilight still bathed the western fields, and the windows, catching the lessening flashes of sunlight reflected from the clouds, threw a halo over Norah's golden tresses as she sat in the window. Byron was at ease on the homely, stiff-backed couch, while Denny sat close to Aunt Selina, holding his arms akimbo, supporting a "yarn cradle," from which the old lady slowly wound up a ball.

Amelia had waited for this moment, and suddenly going to her bedroom, she returned, and, standing in the middle of the room, she said, with sneering composure:

"Norah, where did you get these ear-drops and ring?"

Something in the voice, metallic, acrimonious, triumphant, shot like a dart to Denny's heart, and his eye sought his sister's face. She had turned to Amelia; her eyes were wide open, and a deadly terror shone from the soft depths. From her frightened face Denny gave one look at the gems in Amelia's hand, and his heart almost

ceased to beat. Byron raised himself on his elbow,
startled by the sudden change in the manner of the
children. Aunt Selina looked from one to the other,
petrified.

"Byron, you said that there were no thieves in this
house. Where did that girl get these ear-drops? *I* never
had any so costly! *I* never had a stone like this! And a
girl in *her* position never came honestly by them!"

She held the baubles up triumphantly, that all might
see them. Byron arose silently and took them from his
wife's hands. He examined them attentively, going to the
window and scrutinizing the letters inside the ring. At
this Norah seemed to regain her wits. Darting forward
she seized his hand, saying imploringly:

"Don't! don't look at that! These are mine—honestly mine! I have had them a long while! They are mine,
I say! Give them to me!" She snatched them passionately from Byron's hands and put them in her bosom,
then turned to leave the room.

"No, miss! You don't leave this room with your
plunder! We shall see whether they are yours or not.
People who will steal will lie. I shan't have a thief in this
house."

"There, there, Amelia! No such talk as that! You
know very well Norah's no thief!" and Byron, turning
from his wife to Norah, said, gently: "My girl, you had
better tell all there is to be told about the jewels. I know
you came by them honestly, but it would be better to
satisfy all hands, so that nothing can be said in future."

But Norah, with her back to the group, made no sign.
Byron waited, Denny watched with a sickening fear at his
heart, but she never opened her mouth. Aunt Selina
arose, and, going to the sobbing figure, laid her hand
gently on Norah's arm, saying soothingly:

"Dear child, it is best that you should explain. I know that you come by these things honestly, but every one doesn't know you as I do; every one doesn't know that you found money, time and again, in large sums, that the Doctor lost in the barn and the wood-house, and that you returned it faithfully. Some one gave you these trinkets as keepsakes. Who was it?"

She had pillowed the gentle head upon her breast by this time, and stroked the golden tangle that fell over the girl's shoulders; but Norah's sobs were all the answer that came to this kindly interrogation.

"Come, we will go to your chamber, and then you can tell me all about it," and the two passed from the room—Norah, as soon as the others were not in sight, flying up the staircase, leaving Aunt Selina far behind. When the latter reached the chamber she found Norah standing over the desecrated box, her mild eyes flashing with anger as she pointed to the evidences of Amelia's rape of her treasure.

"They are mine; they were given me. How dare she break my box open! How dare she—how dare she! Oh, what shall I do?"

"Norah, you must tell me, your mother, where these things came from. You know you are only a young girl to have such valuable ornaments, and though Amelia was wrong to break open your box, it is only natural that she should wonder where you got such things."

"It's nothing to her; they are mine! They were given me!" was all that Norah could be brought to say, as she turned from her perplexed friend, her hand on the treasures in the bosom of her gown. Aunt Selina waited, but there was no response to her tender pleading. Drawing the girl's head on her breast, she sat down on the edge of the bed, stroked her hair, and by gentle artifice

strove to make her talk. But Norah was sobbing hysterically, and after an hour's ineffectual urging the elder left
her sadly, puzzling over the mystery, but unshaken in her
belief in Norah's integrity. In the corridor she found
Denny sitting by the open window, his beloved volume
lying unopened on his knee, his elbows resting on the
wide window-ledge. The moon was streaming in, softening the outlines of the settee and chairs in the wide hallway in waves of soft, misty light. She sat down beside him
and asked :

"Do you know anything about these trinkets, Denny ?
Norah won't say where she got them. I thought at first
that perhaps they had been your mother's."

"No, I don't know at all where she got them. But
she has had them more than a year, for I saw them on her
the summer the Warchesters were at Malvern," Denny
replied, innocently unconscious of the obtruding clew that
Aunt Selina was equally too unsuspecting to follow. The
kind lady left the lad in the gathering darkness and went
sadly down-stairs.

"Norah came honestly by these jewels," she said to
Byron, who sat in the open doorway, the rising moon
lighting the square vestibule. "She is the soul of honesty.
Father"—Aunt Selina always spoke of the Doctor as
Father—"trusted her as he trusted me. He would as
soon have suspected me as either of the children."

"But where could she get such valuable things ? The
mother's relics were all sold long before her death !"
Amelia asked acridly from the gloom of the room. "Certainly she could not have saved the money to buy them ;
and, even supposing that some of the farmers' sons have
been courting her, they don't give presents like them ! I
tell you the minx has either stolen the money to buy
them, or she stole them from Mrs. Warchester when she

was in the house. It's been my opinion all along that she stole them then."

Aunt Selina uttered a cry of pain, and said, in an imploring tone:

"O Amelia, dont, don't! If you knew this girl as I know her, you would not do her such a cruel wrong. She came by these trinkets honestly, and it will be known some time. I beg that you will not let her think that you really suspect her of such misconduct."

"She knows my mind," cried Amelia, raising her voice; "she knows that I think her a thief, as I knew her to be deceitful and designing. And all I've got to say is, that if that brazen hussy stops in this house I shall quit it, and I don't put foot in it again until she is driven out!"

"Well, I reckon"—it was Byron who spoke, and he drawled his words out with careless deliberation—"if that's your notion, you might just as well move, for, so long as I am master of this house, Norah has a home here." He paused as if waiting for his wife to reply, and then, pushing back his chair, arose. "Is Norah in her room, mother?"

"Yes, she is there."

He strode to the stairway, mounted very deliberately, and, not noticing Denny in the gloom, passed into Norah's room without knocking. In the dim light he discerned her figure at the open window. She must have heard every one of Amelia's cruel words. Her head was bent over on the wide ledge and clasped in her hands. She did not move as Byron's heavy step resounded on the threshold, nor did she raise her head when he came close to her and said:

"Norah, you mustn't mind what my wife said about those jewels. I know you well enough to know that they are honestly yours. Whether you like to tell where you

got them or not, it is your own free will to say. I know
some one gave them to you. I don't ask you to tell me
who ; but, Norah, don't you know that it is dangerous for
a young girl like you to take such things from a young
man ? "

She lifted her head suddenly and looked at him. Even
in the dim half-moonlight, half-twilight, he could see panic
and wonder in her dilating eyes.

"Danger, Mr. Marbury! What do you mean ? "

He waited for her to go on, hoping that his speech
would provoke a betrayal of the unknown lover. But she
hesitated, staring at him mutely.

"Yes, Norah, young girls can not accept presents from
a man unless that man is a promised husband. Have you
promised any one to be his wife ? "

His voice trembled strangely, and he waited again. The
moon, rising higher, sent a strange weird shadow through
the room. Norah was very pale, and her soft eyes were
suffused with tears. With the adorable address of her
race, she answered the question, guilelessly but astutely:

"And who would ask the like of me to be his wife,
Mr. Marbury ? "

"If I were a free man, I'd ask you. O Norah, why
didn't I see you before—before— Norah "—Byron's voice
sank into a hoarse whisper—"Norah, if you like jewelry—
if you like silks—love me, and everything you want shall
be yours ! "

He had come within arm's reach while speaking, and in
an ungovernable paroxysm of passion clasped her head to
his bosom and kissed her again and again. With a loud
scream she broke from him and fled through the doorway.
As she reached the corridor, Denny was before her, coming to her aid.

"What is it, Norah? Is anybody harming you ? "

"No, no!" she gasped, flinging her arms about his neck and sinking down into the window-seat. "Don't leave me, Denny—don't, don't!"

"She's only nervous, Denny," said Byron, coming from the doorway. "She needs a sound night's rest. She's a little put out with me because I told her that I meant to find out the chap that gave her the jewels. She's afraid I'll make him walk Spanish; and, by hokey, I will!"

This was said in a tone of good-natured raillery, for Denny, but it fell like a menace on the ears of Norah, and she shivered as though stricken with a wintry blast in the protecting arms of her brother.

It was near midnight when Denny, after hours of pleading, went to bed baffled. He could get nothing from the resolute victim. Beyond the assertion that the suspected treasures were lawfully her own, she refused to say a word. Irritation, coaxing, threatening, could not push her beyond that.

CHAPTER XV.

FRIENDS AT THE BLUE JAY.

HAPLESS Norah! the very flawlessness of her innocence made her more easily the victim of the cruel suspicion leveled at her. She heard every word of Amelia's malevolent outbreak. She realized that, unless she confessed the jewels to be Darcy's gift, she must accept the suspicion of the household. But Darcy had charged her never to breathe the secret, and, with the superstitious fidelity of her race, she would have met the stake, silent and unshaken. Her trouble had been deep and wearying even before this dismal incident came to harass.   The declaration of Byron, his passionate embrace in the dairy, his furtive glances whenever she encountered his eyes, in the weeks intervening, filled her with a nameless terror no words can convey.

She dared not confide in Denny, lest there should be a quarrel and a rupture in the household.   If Denny were driven out, it would kill Aunt Selina, who loved him the more tenderly that he had been in every sense a son to the Doctor as well as a delight to herself.   Day after day the poor girl had made up her mind to fly.   The shadow of the sin that Byron's words conjured arose before her day and night, like a vengeance for some unknown fault of her own.   In her dreams the dead mother's face came before her, and the pale dead lips warned her to fly from the moral maelstrom in which the contaminating current was swirling her.   Fly?   She had asked herself, whither?   She knew no one.   Where could she hide herself that Byron's mad pursuit could not find her?   How explain to Denny?   How tell him the wicked passion that Byron had forced her to hear?   There would be bad blood.   Denny would be killed, for she knew Byron's ungovernable temper when crossed in his purposes.   Then, too, she dimly realized the relation of the orphan in the land of the stranger. "The *droits du seigneur*"—liege's-rights—still existed in this country.   The physical slavery of the South had its counterpart in the moral helotry of the North.   The handmaid of the patriarch was no more his chattel than the semifilial "help" of his descendant.   Guileless as she was, she had seen among the neighbors evidences that, while God-fearing men condemned laxities, few households were without specters of the sort that now arose before her terrified vision.

She had been in a turmoil of panic since that dreadful

day in the dairy when Byron avowed his unholy desires.
It was herself she blamed, poor child. She dimly reasoned
that it was a punishment for the presumption of loving
Darcy. That love was deep in her heart, and in the
silence of the night, as well as in the long hours of the day,
memory fed its lingering shadows. It had become her re-
ligion—silent, mystical, enduring. She never asked herself if the beautiful boy would come back to her. She
knew that his heart was full of her; that she had but to
raise her soft eyes to his, and his arms would be about her, his
lips to her own. She had his daguerreotype in her breast.

At first she secreted it in the little casket in her box,
where Amelia's prying eyes had discovered the jewels; but
she hungered to look at it so often through the day, that in
the end she had hung it as a talisman about her neck, near
her heart. Even before Amelia's discovery she had, after
nights of cruel anguish, made up her mind to fly. She
would go to the city. She would tell Darcy all, and ask
him to find her a hiding-place from Byron, where even
Denny should not for a time know of her whereabouts.
So, on this wretched night, with Amelia's savage words
burning in her brain, and Byron's still more hideous love
threatening her, she resolved to go far away and hide
from the danger she had no other means of escaping.

Yes, she must seek safety. After Denny had gone,
she sat down at the open window. The night without was
serenely tranquil. The mellow moonlight threw fairy
shadows on the greensward of the orchard, and the
friendly chirp of the crickets made the air melodious. She
got up resolutely, and, taking out her box, withdrew her
treasures. A few articles from her wardrobe were added,
and these tied up securely in a small shawl. This done,
she opened the door to Denny's room and listened. He
was sleeping peacefully, his quiet breathing sounding regu-

larly through the moonlit room. The clamor of the tall cuckoo-clock in the kitchen-hall startled her. She counted the strokes. Three o'clock ! She must wait a little longer.

Kneeling at the bedside, where she had said her simple prayers since childhood, she sobbed softly, her head buried in the clothing. Her sobs soothed her into a doze, for, when she started up, the moon had gone down, and the darkness of dawn was on the face of the land. She arose, trembling. The darkness and stillness frightened her. Even the crickets chirped their cheerful cries no longer. The world hung pulseless in the birth of day. The freshness of the air from the open window revived her benumbed energies. Stealing on tip-toe to Denny's bedside, she bent over and pressed her lips gently to his forehead. He murmured something, and moved. She sank down swiftly at the side of the bed, and knelt in a panic of hope and fear. If he awoke she could not go. Her heart beat with the hope that he would speak; but, with a sigh, he turned over, and his regular breathing told her that he slept. She went back, got her bundle, and, moving swiftly, descended the stairs, trembling in every limb, and her heart throbbing with such violence that she feared Amelia would hear it. But she reached the front door, let down the chain, and in an instant was cowering in the tall caraway-grass that grew quite up to the porch. With a swift glance about, she sank down on the dewy grass overcome.

The door had made a great noise in closing, and she expected to see some one appear. But the noise had seemed great only to her nerves at high tension. Five minutes passed, and, with a thrill of something like disappointment, she started to her feet and fled through the orchard. The cows were beginning to browse, and, as she passed near them, the mottled heifer uttered what seemed to her a reproachful cry. She stopped, climbed the fence, leaving her bundle on the other side, and, with a gasp of despair, flung her arms about the neck of the docile beast. As she stood there, the thick darkness suddenly grew transparent, then a great wave of purple rose along the hills to the eastward, and she knew the morning had come. There was something of a moan in the animal's cry as she kissed it on the forehead, and, climbing the fence again, fled swiftly through the orchard. She did not go in the highway, but kept on through the fields skirting it. The cocks were now crowing in the farm-yards, and she could hear the farmers' boys singing as they washed themselves at the watering-troughs.

So long as the route lay through farms, she hurried on rapidly and without concern; but, when she came to the straggling outskirts of Warchester, she grew frightened at the curious gaze of the people as they passed her. She had drawn a green veil over her eyes, and this precaution had much to do with the piquing, the curiosity, of those who saw a young and pretty girl tripping along with damp shoes and dripping skirts, telling plainly of a walk through the dewy grasses of the fields. But now she was in the city, and people began to notice her less. She had not formed any plan as to what she should do. Now she began to speculate confusedly. Without any distinct purpose, she had directed her steps to the Caribee tavern, where Dr. Marbury had always stabled his horses when he came to town. She had reached the alley behind the house, when she suddenly remembered that, if she were to go in, she could be easily traced, for the landlord knew her. He had seen her with the Doctor often. Her heart gave a great thump, and she turned hastily, fearing that, as it was, she might have been recognized. Remembering another inn further from the center of trade, she hurried thither. A young boy was singing cheerily at the door

while flinging a golden shower of corn to a clamorous
brood of geese and chickens. He was rosy-faced and
kind-looking, and Norah felt encouraged to speak to him.

"Do you take lodgers here?"

The boy suspended his ministry, and looked at her
good-humoredly.

"I reckon we do when we can git 'em. Want to board
with us?"

"Yes," Norah said faintly. "At least for a little while.
How much will you charge for a week?"

"Well, I don't know exactly, but walk right in. Father's gone to market, and mother's in the kitchen. She'll
tell you all about it. Sha'n't I take your bundle?"

The boy relieved her of her burden, and led the way
through a hallway scrupulously clean. It was papered
with variegated landscapes, bearing the relation to modern
designs that Japanese figures do to the artistic papers of
to-day. At the end of the long hallway the boy opened a
door, and ushered her into a pleasant room, with very low
ceilings and the same grotesque wall adornment. Leaving
her here, he hurried out and returned a moment later with
a jolly-faced matron, who fairly rolled into the room, she
was so fat. She surveyed Norah with a pair of merry
brown eyes, beginning the conversation abruptly.

"Be you from the country, miss?"

"Yes," Norah faltered, terrified lest she should be
asked to tell all that was on her troubled mind.

"Fur?"

"About seven miles."

"Got any friends in town?" She pronounced it
"taown."

Norah hesitated. She dared not speak of the Warchesters, for that would betray her to Byron. In the
crisis she suddenly thought of her uncle James.

"Yes, I have an uncle."

"Know where he lives?"

"No. I want to stay here until—until—"

"Jest so. You want to stay here until you can find him. Well, you seem to be a likely girl, and I guess you can stay until you find your uncle."

Norah was taken straightway to a small room up one flight of stairs, with a pretty dormer-window looking over the slanting roof into the street.

"Miss—ah, yes—what shall I call you?" The stout lady was puffing with the exertion of climbing the stairs, and sat down as Norah began to remove her bonnet and thin shawl.

"My name is Norah. You can call me Norah, please."

"Norah! That's a soft-sounding, pretty name. My husband's mother was called Norah. She was Irish— from the South of Ireland. Be you Irish?"

Norah's heart sank. Was she to be turned out now that the haven seemed to be gained? She answered, tremulously:

"Yes, I'm Irish." She waited in anguish to hear the response to this fatal admission.

"Well, I swan, I'd never have thought it! You look as nice, and your manners are as nice as—" But here the good lady's powers of comparison gave out, and she recollected that there might be a shade of ungraciousness in the reflective form her words had taken. She continued, with animation: "I see how it is. You have lived among folks, and you have nothing of the Irish about you! No one could ever tell, to hear you talk; why, you haven't a bit of brogue!"

Now, it is quite impossible to reproduce the humor of ﹍nis, as the shrill nasal and broad thin *as*, *es*, and *os* have no onomatopoetic equivalents that words or parts of words will reproduce. It was a cross between the flat vowels of Philadelphia and the prolonged sibilation of Connecticut of to-day, aggravated by the deliberation of the West. Norah fixed her gentle eyes on this jovial destiny, and waited the end.

"Jonas—that's my old man—rather favors the Irish. He don't own it in public, but he does really. He'll like you because you have his mother's name. There he is now! I hear him down-stairs. He'll help you to find your uncle. He knows every one from the lake to the last farm in Warchester County. Come down when you've fixed yourself, and we'll make you feel tu hum!"

When the kind lady waddled out, Norah sank on her knees and poured out a fervent prayer of thanksgiving and relief. The worst was over; she had shelter until she could look about her. Her little room was tidy and trim; the bed was fluffy and soft as her own at Marbury; the chintz vallance and the pink paper gave the place a cheerful air, and from her window she could see the misty column of spray that hung over the great cataract, whose roar, when the noise of the city died away, came over the house-tops quite plainly to her ear.

She had changed her wet shoes and stockings, and re-placed the draggled skirts when Mrs. Jonas re-appeared.

"I thought may be you'd feel kind o' shy 'bout comin' daown alone. I've asked Jonas 'bout yer uncle Boyne, an' he's got suthin' tu tell you." She looked pityingly at the girl as she said this, her kind voice faltering a little, and then added, cheerily, "But I don't believe you've had a mouthful tu eat, fur, ef you come in from so far, you must a' left hum before breakfast! I've set a little suthin' on the table, and you must come and eat while it is hot!"

"Oh, how good you are, Mrs.—Mrs.—"

"Blythe—that's our name. Jonas Blythe is my husband. Haven't you never heard of him? Why, he's as well known as Governor Darcy in this county! He's the best man livin', ef I du say it as shouldn't—just wait and see! Here we be, Jone!" she added, as she ushered Norah into a cozy, oblong dining-room with a table set in the middle.

"Jone" was engaged with a confused mass of cords, hooks, and pulleys, which he alluded to later on as "fishin'-tackle." He merely looked up as Mrs. "Jone" presented her *protégée*, and said, amicably:

"How d'ye do, miss?"

Norah was pushed into a chair at the table, and, under pretext of something to do in the kitchen, Mrs. Blythe left her guest, after heaping her plate and filling her cup.

"When did ye hear from yaour uncle Boyne last?" asked Jonas, without looking up, and as if he were continuing a conversation.

"Oh, ever so long ago—many years—I can't say how long, but not since I was a little girl."

"Jess so! jess so! I thought likely you hadn't. Didn't know much 'bout him, did yeou?"

"No, sir."

"Never saw him, may be?"

"I don't recollect seeing him, but we must have seen him, because we stopped at his house—a pretty brick cottage, with a long porch."

"Jess so! Waal, now, my girl, I'd as lief lose a summer's fishin' as tell yeou bad news, but the fact is—" Jonas halted in the awkward fumbling that had been going on among the "tackle," and added, looking resolutely away from Norah and out of the window at a mule the boys were teasing in the neighboring stable-yard, "Waal,

11

Norah—purty name that—" He hesitated again, looked furtively at Norah as she unsuspiciously sipped her coffee, and then added, desperately, "Uncle Boyne ain't here any more!"

"He isn't here?" Norah echoed, more in relief than surprise.

"No, he's gone."

"Ah, he's gone?"

"Yes, he's not in Warchester. But don't yeou feel bad. Cesty Jane's taken a powerful fancy to yeou, and ef yeou ain't got no home, why, jess set right down here and feel to hum!"

"Yes, Norah," Mrs. Blythe said, entering the room from behind the girl, "don't worry about yaour uncle. Ef it was tu find a hum with him yeou come to the city, don't fret, fur yeou can stay with us, and be our daughter."

The tears were in Norah's eyes, and her throat was choked. She could only rise and kiss the kind woman's hands, Jonas being much interested in the mule's antics, and resolutely refusing to witness "the 'tarnal foolin' o' them women folks," as he afterward averred.

Had she been the cleverest and most designing of her sex, as she was certainly the most artless and ingenuous, tempest-tossed Norah could not have allayed the surcharged storm more dexterously. Her very ignorance was a panoply. She had no sense of the incongruity of her conduct, the obvious contradiction between her assertions and her indifference to her surroundings. This quaint introduction to the Blythe household illustrates the homely pathos of her life at the time. The kind husband and wife thought they were sparing the poor child present grief by concealing the death of her kinsman, and she was tranquilly grateful that she had not been compelled to divulge anything likely to put Byron or Denny on her trail, and yet had brought it about without subterfuge or falsehood.

When Norah had gone from the room, Blythe looked up with a queer expression, and ejaculated :

"I say, Cesty,"—Mrs. Blythe's name was Alcestis—"I played that rather slick, don't yeou think?"

"But, Jone, how are we ever to tell her?"

"Oh, jess let her get to feelin' kind o' humlike. Set her to work doin' chores; that'll keep her mind from frettin', and then we'll kind o' let it come by jerks—as the eel said when he caught the hook."

"She's a mighty purty girl, ain't she, Jone? Favors my sister Melina, don't yeou think?"

"Waal, no, I hadn't thought on it. I'd like to know why she's alone. Father and mother dead, yeou say?"

"So she says. I know this is a proper girl, fur the fust thing she took out from her traps was a Bible; and she's got a sampler, worked real beautiful, with the words, 'Blessed are the meek, for they shall inherit the earth.' Reckon she's got good principles; perhaps she's a Methodist—shouldn't wonder if she was." And Mrs. Blythe stood reflectively, her arms akimbo, watching her husband as he sat, like an enormous spider in its web, with the fish lines and nets covering his limbs, while the more obdurate knots and kinks were unraveled or adjusted by his teeth.

It was James Boyne's death which the simple Samaritans had aimed to conceal from the friendless girl, and the artifice bound husband and wife in a conspiracy of kindliness and incuriousness which made Norah's condition very easy in the honest household. Released from the embarrassment of keeping up the comedy of seeking a relative that she by no means desired to see, Norah began to interest herself in the affairs of the household. Her trained skill soon made itself felt in the domestic *régime*. Her deft hands gave a new and home-like order to the hurried disorder of the house, for though Mrs. Blythe, like all the women of those days, knew how to manage, she had grown too stout to supervise details. Here the noiseless energy of Norah came into play.

Without ado, revolution, or obtrusion, the home-like rooms were given quite a new aspect; and when the silent minister set herself to the edibles, Jonas declared that such cooking couldn't be matched in the State, and he knew, he maintained, for he had broken bread in every tavern from the Hudson to the Ohio. The homely dining-room, with its gaudily bepictured paper, echoed to Jonas's vauntings over the rich, fluffy "Johnny-cake," the waffles, the biscuits, the pie, the doughnuts, the apple-fritters, the pot-pies and stews, that Norah produced with as little fuss as another in preparing the heavy and indigestible dishes that had before satisfied the "Blue Jays'" unexacting palate. Husband and wife agreed that a treasure had fallen into the house, and that they meant to keep it there if affection and domestic equality could bring it about.

But to all their urging Norah pleaded for seclusion. She could never be induced to sit on the veranda of an evening, when the boarders and neighbors joined in caucus to canvass the peccadilloes of the town. She shrank from meeting the curious females that came in to call on Mrs. Blythe, eager to see the new kinswoman who had come to live with the family, for the Blythes had carelessly "let on" that Norah was a relative, to the no small mystification of the son of the house, who had never heard of this "cousin" suddenly conferred on him. Manlius was the lad's name, abbreviated to "Manly," and he instantly lost his youthful heart to the pensive minister of such good things as small boys like. For, when she baked, Norah supplied Manly with divers delectables, dear to the hearts of small boys, and the fame of them went all over the neighborhood. For Manly, with a collection of preternatural pygmies, geese, manikins, dogs, elephants, and what not, turned out from Norah's dough-pans, invaded the play-houses of all the vicinage urchins, extolling the creator of them, and magnanimously sharing their dismembered limbs with his boy friends.

Of an evening, when the protecting twilight fell, Norah, with the proud Manlius for escort, wandered along the green banks of the Caribee, and sat silent and meditative on the secluded knoll overlooking the rushing cataract. The small Manlius was at first a good deal abashed by his responsible privilege, but the shyness soon wore off, and he entertained the maiden with such distorted fictions as his active mind retained from his associations and his meager store of books. But, when Norah revived the romances Denny had imparted to her—when she opened the fairy wonders of the "Arabian Nights," "Pilgrim's Progress," and "Robinson Crusoe," Manly secretly believed that she was the Princess Scheherezade herself, and the adoration which the sweets had aroused was transformed into a mystic devotion, more tenacious and adoring than was ever felt by a disciple of Apis. Sometimes, however, he wavered in this conviction. When he saw the dull, inanimate dough transformed by Norah's touch into the varied forms he loved, he was sure that she was Morgiana, or the household fairy, that a crony had told him of, who kept peace and plenty in families where fairies were loved. Of an evening, when she hovered over the shining pewter at the kitchen range, he expected to see the fairy chariot evolve itself from the vegetable hamper, and Norah turning into a beautiful thing of wings and shining raiment, endowed with aërial motion, sail up the roaring chimney-mouth, never to come back.

He was presently inspired with such a passion for reading that his astonished mother stood aghast when at bedtime he pleaded for another "spell." The father wagged his head owlishly.

"It is quite natural," he remarked, when the change came up for discussion. "The Blythes have always been great on book-larnin'. Grandfather Blythe was a chaplain in the army of General Sullivan, another Blythe was a school-teacher. Just as like as not Manly will be a learned and great man ; perhaps he may be a lawyer ! "

It was decided that the boy's bent should be encouraged : the glory of the house of Blythe might rest under his tow head. So some of the sorcery that Manly ascribed to the girl was believed by the parents, and Norah was treated as Naomi treated her new daughter. Relieved of the burden of her vague fears, she soon resumed her Celtic gayety, and Jonas loved, almost as well as his beloved fishing, to sit by the hour and cozen the unsuspecting sprite into merriment and repartee. Two or three times Norah had, as she sat at the window, recognized Darcy sauntering down the street. Once he dashed past on a beautiful horse, with a charming girl beside him—the girl she had seen the night of the disaster at the Warchesters' gate. After that she sat a good deal at the window, and Manly made it a duty to sit with her to have her help in his readings. He was much fonder of her exposition of the text than of reading it, and often wondered that she knew so much more than the books. One day she startled him with a little cry and a sudden withdrawal from the window. He looked out, but saw only a country vehicle with a large, good-natured man on the seat driving. The vehicle was well known to Norah. Many a time she had sat in it, and the man was to her the greatest terror that innocence can know—her lawless lover, Byron Marbury.

CHAPTER XVI.

A MYSTIC ROMAUNT.

AT Marbury Norah's cheerful voice was the first morning sound that mingled with the revels of the birds. Singing as she passed from the pantry to the dairy, the low notes of her song were a signal to Aunt Selina which for years had regulated the rising of the old folks. But when six o'clock came, the morning after Amelia's outbreak, and Norah's voice was unheard, Aunt Selina arose and, having dressed herself hurriedly, went to the girl's room. Denny was up and out, and the yellow sunlight was flooding the gay colors of the rag carpet. Norah's door was closed. Aunt Selina knocked, and, as there was no answer, she opened it and entered. The bed was undisturbed; the room was in perfect order; the candle was burned to the socket, but Norah was nowhere to be seen. The undisturbed bed startled Mrs. Marbury, and she sank into a chair, faint and frightened. Where could she be? Perhaps Denny knew. She heard his voice in the stable-yard placating the cows, lowing demonstratively to be relieved of their burden of milk. From the window she could watch his movements, and, as he led the horses up to the watering-trough near the garden-gate, she called to him. He nodded gayly, and, having taken the horses to the stable, he ran through the thick plantains, scattering swarms of thrifty bees pillaging their succulent stems. His face was aglow with his early morning work, and, as he came under the window, he looked up eagerly and asked :

"What is it, Aunt Selina ? Isn't Norah well ? "

"Come up here ; I want you."

But Denny was as mystified as she, and, at the end of an hour's search in the barn, the brook glen, and the orchard, the household was in an agony of alarm. Even Amelia looked cowed and frightened as Byron glared at her with stern questionings. She protested that she knew nothing of Norah ; that she hadn't seen her since the night before ; and, as Byron commented on this with an incredulous shake of the head, she fled to her room in tears. Byron questioned Denny as to the places where Norah would be apt to seek refuge. None but James Boyne's suggested itself, and thither, so soon as a hasty breakfast had been swallowed, the two hastened. But James had been dead a year ; his widow had gone to her family. Denny lingered about the place two or three days, hoping that Norah would come to inquire. But no one came. Byron made inquiries along all the highways leading from Marbury to Warchester ; but, as Norah had kept in the fields, he discovered no trace. One farmer had seen a young girl, that answered Norah's description, on the Bucephalo road, and this slender trace Byron followed twenty miles, only to return mystified and disheartened. He came for Denny on the third day, and, carrying him to the Caribee tavern, told him to remain there until he had searched the whole city : to take each street in turn, walk through from end to end, inquire, and keep his eyes open. As he got into the carriage to return to Marbury, he asked :

"Do you think Norah had a sweetheart ?"

"Of course not ! Norah is too bashful to look at a young man. Why, when she came with me to the school socials she wouldn't dance with any one, and the boys called her 'dummy.'"

Byron drove away, none the less convinced that his suspicions were well founded. Norah, he felt sure, had flown to some lover, and in her innocence had fallen into a trap craftily set for her. He ground his teeth with a ferocious execration as he returned home to give such comfort as he could to his mother. Denny began his miserable quest, and toiled day after day through the pretty umbrageous highways of the town. Strange, puzzling scenes from the past came back as he wandered in the net-work of leafy alleys surrounding the boys' asylum. He recalled vaguely the dreadful time when he sat at those cheerless, narrow windows, watching for the dear figure that represented all the love of life and the world to him. But his search was quite fruitless. When he made up his mind to this, he determined to return to Marbury and seek the lost through that neighborhood.

Until this he had borne up, stimulated by the work prescribed. Now, however, Norah's loss, at first a vague dread, took the shape of finality. He would see her no more! She was lost to him as the murdered mother, whose gentle life withered away under the cruel adversities of want and desertion. As he walked along the dusty highway, that glimmered in the hot afternoon sun, his memory was filled with mirage-like pictures. He saw his mother trudging wearily under the thick clustering branches, shunning the sight of her kind, or, terrified by jeers and menaces, humbly slipping under the high fences to escape pursuit. Then Norah appeared, as he saw her that happy day long ago at the Marbury doorsill, joy in her violet eyes, rapture in her voice.

"Ah, no. She is not gone! God could not be so cruel to the orphan. God could not take the last of his kin.

She is in the wood; she has seen the mother, and they are tramping the fields to do penance for some sin to the fairies."

Denny stopped in the path. He had reached the edge of the Marbury woods. He had spoken aloud, and the echoes of his voice came back from among the great aisles of oaks as though some one were answering him. All that was credulous in his nature was instantly receptive. Big boy as he was, he knelt down softly and laid his ear to the gnarled roots of the trees before him. The ground was covered with fluffy ferns and deep, cushiony moss. A bevy of birds in the branches above him broke into a symphony of elfin melody. Denny remained transfixed. The fibers of the tree vibrated to the concentrated pitch of the songsters, and the dissonance actually took on the awing musical hum that startles children when they put their ears to telegraph-poles. Denny's eyes glistened; the old childish yearnings were upon him. He closed his eyes and stretched himself out at full length. The monody spoke to him now intelligibly. He was sure that his mother's voice was coming to him. A lark in a neighboring meadow, in a lull, took up the refrain, sending gurgling, liquid notes of enchantment down from the silver rim of a passing cloud; then the choristers in the trees resumed:

"Dilly."

"Norah."

"Denny—Dilly—Denny—Norah."

The rapt listener heard these words as plainly as you who read see them. In an impulse of irresistible devotion he embraced the tree, crying:

"O fairy friends of my dead mother, comfort my heart, tell me where to seek Norah; tell me—tell—" His voice faltered and he looked about timidly and abashed.

Had some one heard him? He would be thought mad! His heart gave a great leap. Mad! Yes, his mother had gone mad when he was taken from her. Was he going mad now that Norah was lost to him? Oh, no! His mother had charged him that while he trusted in the "little people" they would befriend him! He did believe; yes, if they bade him hang his coat on the sunbeams, he would do it! But perhaps his one moment of skepticism, of insulting shame and disloyal doubt, had broken the spell, and his fairy kin would be as invisible to him as to the boisterous schoolmates who had laughed the story of their reality to scorn? He flung himself on the moss again, clasping the gnarled roots and sobbing piteously:

"I do believe! I do know! By my mother's grave, I believe. Tell me—tell me where is Norah!"

"Norah!"

The name was echoed and prolonged in a chorus of such diverse harmony that the confiding suppliant almost swooned with a joyous realization of penance accepted.

"Ah, I know! It is by running water the fairies give the sign to those they protect!"

He hurried far into the woods until he reached the brook that ran in limpid pools through glades and hollows into the Caribee miles below. In happy days he and Norah had often sat there of an afternoon and under the moonlight, the girl reciting the weird legends of her race and peopling the leafy coverts of the glen with "little people," to whom she spoke familarly—as is the childish custom in many parts of Ireland. He was in a vernal crypt, the perfection of such cunning construction as Nature alone can do. Seen through tender shades of green, gray lines of rock; so gray that their surface seemed atmosphere; so solemn that Denny whispered:

"Sentinels to guard the elves!"

But as he pushed on they seemed to mingle with the foliage, which took on a graceful movement of its own, to the cadence of soft music set loose by the breeze or the fluttering of restless birds.   Denny lies flat on the sward, and gazes with earnest, anxious questioning, Narcissus-like, into the pebbly deeps, for a sign.   He is perfectly sober in this dryad rite.   It would have seemed more curious to him not to believe than for you or me to watch him as he betrays in his mature youth the credulity of his childhood.   Where misery does not harden or pervert, it leaves the heart very soft and the soul very expansive. Denny's heart was very tender, and his intellect, though strong, tenacious of the mystic rubric of his race.

However, if you are tempted to discredit the realism of this spectacle, or weary yourself at the exhibition of this lad's childishness, let me remind you that the most cultivated races, the races from whom our arts and literature come, were for centuries the disciples of just the sort of superstition that held this boy's mind.   Turn to your Homer—turn to your classics—if you are tempted to become impatient with this dreamer.   Cæsar would not fight a battle until the auspices had presaged from the entrails of an animal !   Denny looked up from the water and searched the leafy covert.   A restful sense of the sanctity of the place stole over him, and he knelt bareheaded on the purple, coral-dotted moss.   He felt himself as absolutely a devotee as the Moor in the Mosque of Cordova, even though the priests of Islam no longer chant the word of the Koran.

In this tranquil world the rocks, the trees, the brook, were all friendly forms, and their music, though unheard, filled his soul like so many mystic ministers of the vernal academy, teaching a robuster philosophy than books or schools. He had always been at his happiest in the woods, and heard understandingly the language of its many nameless tribes, now consoling sprites to unlock the secret of his misery. Such visions as he had known in these secluded shades ! He always spoke of them with reluctance, except to Norah. Such joys, such revelations, such communings, should have a vehicle of expression far beyond the stale forms of our mortal tongue. Sometimes he read messages in the curves of the leaves, in the arabesques of the greensward, or the bending shapes of the twigs—precious secrets between himself and the demure deities of the sylvan temple.

And then the rocks—so grim, yet kindly ; so shapely, yet so deformed—they welcomed believers like Denny to mossy cushions, where their spreading bosoms were laid bare. Then the great fissures, where, Denny never made a doubt, awful conclaves were held by the secret black and grewsome forces that contended with the good spirits ! Denny has trodden every inch of the coral mosses, the arbutus-leaves, and wintergreen that carpet the rugged crests of these unterrifying monsters, and he turns to each familiar beauty now to appeal for the lost Norah— she that knew all these dumb friends, and worshiped far more sincerely at their altar than he. To tell the truth, the place had often filled the lad with an exquisite pain, a sweet unrest. His soul was so susceptible to the fantastic jocundity of idealities attached to the place that he never came without resolving to give up the grosser realities of daily endeavor, to think no more of books or a career, to turn his forces to bread-getting in the most primitive way, and his brain to feasting on these imperishable forms of loveliness. But now he scanned the glistening leaves for a sign that should lead him to the lost girl. As he sat, the air grew heavy and the sun was hidden under a cloud.

He was unconscious of the time that passed, but he heard
as if a whisper at his ear :

" Norah."

It was quite dusk now. He looked about eagerly. He
must have fallen into a doze, for the beams of the sun now
penetrated in slanting rays, and he could have fancied the
broad yellow splashes a pathway, through the glistening
green, to the clouds.

" Norah !" he called, " Norah ! where are you ? O
Norah, it's Denny. Come back—come back ! No one shall
harm you, no one shall mistrust you again ! O my God,
my God ! Must I give her up ! "

A cat-bird in the bush behind him piped gayly :

" No—rah, No—rah, No—rah ! "

It was one of a brood that his sister had rescued, and
the creature fed from her hand when she came from the
pool. Denny turned from the bird, his eyes swimming
with tears, and his glance fell on the water. Whether it
was a disturbed brain or whether he imagined it, he saw a
pretty bed with a blue chintz cover, and Norah kneeling
with her face raised in joy. He started, but the waters
rippled on. A large white lily lay on the surface, and he
bent down and plucked it.

" It is in the running water, and that was my mother's
sign. Norah is not hurt ! She is safe somewhere ! But
where ? "

He moved with buoyant alacrity now he had the
sign. Perhaps she was home ! He hastened to Marbury ;
but there were gloom and silence. Yes, it must be ! Why
hadn't he thought of it before ? Norah was with Dilly
Dane. He turned crimson as the thought shot into his
head. What more natural ! She had fled from Amelia's
torturing tongue, her vile suspicions, to the gentle Dilly.
It was supper-time when he came to this conclusion, and,

in spite of Deacon Dane's command, he set out afterward to try the last hope. It was just dark as he came in the back way, through the fields, which shortened the route from Marbury. He heard Tom singing in the barn, and his heart thumped so hard when he reached the porch that he did not hear a soft voice at the window chanting a lullaby. The jangling of the cow-bells in the barn-yard sounded loud and threatening in his ears. The frogs in the neighboring meadow ran the gamut of their musical madness as he stood irresolute on the white porch. There were no lights. Prudent wives circumvented the night insects by leaving the interior in darkness of a summer evening. The doors were all open, and now he heard the voice and the soft accents of the song. It was Dilly's, and his heart, it seemed to him, stood quite still. He made a noise with his feet, hoping to attract her attention ; but she gave no heed. He desperately stepped to the door-sill, and, as he raised his hand to knock on the post, Dilly said, without turning around :

"Is that you, Tom ? I thought you had gone for mother."

"It is I, Dilly—Denis."

"O Denny! I—I—I'm so glad to see you. I thought it was Tom. Won't you come in and sit down ? Or shall we sit in the darkness on the porch ?"

Denny remained quite dumb to all these queries, and the maiden drew a chair for him near the window; he sank into it murmuring he knew not what. There was no sign of Norah, and his temples throbbed under the contradictory and conflicting emotions: joy, at being near his darling ; guilt, that Norah's quest was now a secondary sentiment in his heart. Dilly didn't notice his agitation, and asked how the folks were at Marbury. This brought the guilty lad to a consciousness of his infidelity, and he

broke into sobs as he told of Norah's strange absence, and
the hope that he had of finding her with Dilly. The girl
was silent for a long time, and Denny had recovered his
presence of mind when she said :

"I don't think any harm can have come to her, Denny. I think I know her feeling. She is outraged at
Amelia's miserable suspicion, and she has gone from the
house to escape her persecution. She knows that if you
knew where she is Byron would watch you, or force you
to betray her, and she is keeping concealed for the present. You may be sure I am right. It is just what I
should do."

"O Dilly, what a relief this gives me ! I ought to have
thought of this myself, but I have been quite out of my
head since we missed her ; Byron has been so fierce and
overpowering that I have given way to him. You've
described exactly the way Norah would act. She is so
timid and distrustful that she would be capable of thinking that I would urge her to stay where she was not welcome. She is wrong. Whatever she thinks for the best
I would do, and do gladly. Indeed, Dilly, it was partly to
tell you of my resolution to leave Marbury that I came
over to-night."

"To leave Marbury, Denny!" she faltered. Even the
preoccupied lad could detect the tremor; his heart gave
a great throb of joyous recognition.

"I am, I know, doing wrong to talk of myself to you,
Dilly, for I as good as pledged myself to Tom never to
speak to you of myself or what I feel." He halted, stam-
mered, and rose to his feet. The moon was skirting the
dark wall of trees to the southward, where the rush of the
Caribee could be heard tumbling over the lower rapids.
The voices of the summer night stole in melodious and
tranquilizing. The dark shadows of playful bats shot

past the open window; the swallows under the eaves twittered as the marauding owls flapped their whirring wings on the boughs over them.

For the first time Denny realized that Dilly was alone in the house. The sense of isolation filled him with a guilty impulse to disregard his pledge, to make a compact with Dilly, to ask her love, and mutually help each other by the confession. But the instinct of honor, the intuition of faithfulness, held him back. He had been rejected even before the asking by Dilly's father, and it would be cruel to put her in the attitude of disregarding the father's wishes. He came again to her side. The moon now shone. Its light was clear and strong. The glow in Dilly's eyes told him that she was deeply moved. He would have sat silent in that delicious contiguity forever. All that Norah was to him, all that the memory of his mother taught him of the adorable in womanhood, Denny identified with Dilly. To the wondrous products of the processes of to-day Dilly would seem, I fear, a tame and undelighting personality. But all times have their manners and measures. To Denny she was to be sung and worshiped as the troubadours sang and worshiped the lovely damosels that bent out from high casements and wafted surreptitious signs of favor to the bannered steeds and plumed swains, secreted under the friendly shadow of my lord's ancestral forest.

Now, as a matter of fact, I suppose Dilly was the sort of girl you would see in any well-to-do country-side, sixty or seventy years ago, or, for that matter, to-day, though there are few farmsteads that are not better provided with the means of cultivation and the possibilities of refinement than were found in homes as well to do and even "genteel" as Deacon Dane's. There was none of the dynamic quality of inner motive or strong purpose in

Dilly's equable mind. She adored her father, she saw the practical teachings of generations of worldly wisdom illustrated in the thrift of her parent's acres, and the consideration in which the family name was held.

She saw that all these were good, and she would have gone uncomplainingly into the sordid mating of her unaspiring surroundings, I think, if destiny had not given her mind time to realize the difference between them and Denny's charm of mind and purity of heart. Her sentimental nature appealed to, Dilly was as devotedly and irrevocably true to the sanctified creed of love as the transcendentalist Denny himself. There were no heroic outbreaks in the processes that worked out the scheme of Dilly's heart history, or, for that matter, in any of the people whose simple vicissitudes I am reviving. There has always seemed to me something helpful as well as pathetic in a study of the incongruous conditions of the simply chivalric, ignobly prejudiced group; inevitable outcomes of enforced conditions, homely joys, and unmerited sorrows, that reveal the secret channels through which the current of every man's destiny runs.

At this time in their lives Dilly loved her timid lover with something of the dazed incomprehension of Elsa when the Swan Knight led her from the altar. Denny's robust frame, quick wit, and inextinguishable good-humor, contrasted with his feminine implicitness in accepting the mysterious marvels of fairy-land, wrought a sort of superstitious uncertainty in the more skeptic mind of Dilly; while, with a characteristic contradiction, she was the fonder and more entirely his own for it. I don't undertake to explain this perversity. Possibly you will comprehend it better as the tale is told.

. Meanwhile, Dilly had been thinking of Denny, and vaguely trying to identify him with his own heroes in the fairy-tales, before she confided what she had on her mind to say. She invited him nearer by a gesture, and said, with tender decision :

"I owe it to you, Denny, to tell you something. Knowing you as well as I do, I know that you would never take the matter in your own hands, for, as we of another race think, it is right for young people to act for themselves. I know what Tom told you, and I know what you promised." She slipped her hand into his. "But, Denny, it was by no wish of mine, and I told my father quite frankly that the life I owed your heroism should be yours if you asked it, as my heart had been yours long before I came to know I had a heart."

These last words were uttered in a smothered sob, as Denny, with a cry of rapture, drew the golden head down on his breast and pressed his lips to the white forehead.

"Ah, my darling, my darling ! "

"I have told father that I can never love any one else; that when—" she started. Tom's voice sounded under the window, and his tall form intercepted the silver sheen of moonlight.

"I say, Dill, don't you want to walk down to Kennel's with me for mother? The walk will do you good."

Dilly rose in a flutter. "Come in, Tom ; Denny is here."

The young men shook hands rather perfunctorily. Tom was much more embarrassed than the lover, for he felt the consciousness of treason in his heart. He had gone further than his text in the famous embassy to the forbidden suitor, and he felt that the lovers had detected his treason. The conversation was monosyllabic during the next few minutes, until Tom suddenly remembered his mother, and got up to go. The three walked down the turfy walk to the road, and as they reached it a heavy wagon was turning into the lane.

"There is father!" exclaimed Tom, and hurried forward to relieve him of the horses. The old gentleman came up to his daughter and Denny, evidently aware of the latter's presence, for he said, in loud, even tones, wholly devoid of surprise or ill intent :

"You are there, are you, Denis, my lad? Glad to see you!"

He gave the young man a hard, expressionless hand, and passed up the walk without another word.

"I must go and get father a little supper, and we must say good-by," Dilly said, her hand in Denny's.

"I am very happy, Dilly. I have the courage of an army now. I ask no more than you have given me. God bless and keep you."

The long walk over the fields was filled with a world of fantastic creations as Denny stalked along in the clear light, his mind in a whirl of delicious perplexities. It was not until he sat in Norah's empty room, and the woe of her loss came back, that he returned to reality. And, as he knelt beside her empty bed, there was strange inconsequence in the sobbing prayer that went up from his agitated heart.

CHAPTER XVII.

DARCY GAINS A VICTORY.

BYRON marked Denny's manner the next day with surprise and suspicion. He instantly came to the conclusion that the brother knew the sister's whereabouts, and

was in the plot to keep the secret from him. He knew
Denny too well to imagine that threat or menace would
shake his determination, and he instantly set himself to
devise a stratagem which should betray the secret. His
wits were not swift, though when once at work they were
what is called sharp in unschooled societies. He suggested, later in the day, that Denny should return to Warchester, and "keep an eye on the farmers coming to and
going from town, as it was market-day, and if Norah had
joined another family she would be likely to go to market,
as she was good at disposing of the pretty pats of butter
she took such pride in making."

Denny, nothing loath, set off, and entered the city near
the Warchester lane. As he passed down the wide avenue
whereon the porticoes of the Warchester mansion glistened
from end to end, a light cabriolet came in front of him at
the street-crossing. Looking up abstractedly, he recognized Darcy with Lady Molly, who was driving. He
took off his cap and stood bareheaded, bowing, with the
first gleam of comfort he had known since Norah's disappearance. Lady Molly recognized him, pulled up the
horses, and held out her hand.

"And how are ye, my foine lad, and the good folks of
Marbury? How are they all?"

Denny, shaking the hand cordially held out by Darcy,
told with suppressed sobs the new trouble that had come
upon the country home.

"Dear, O dear, poor child! poor child! Get in here,
my dear bye, and come home with us for a bit of dinner.
Take comfort, Denny, boy, take comfort! We'll leave
no stone unturned to find that pretty girl. She's not for
such a world as this, at all, at all."

Denny got into the vehicle, and, as it whirled along,
he related all the painful incidents leading to the flight.

Darcy's face was averted after the first start and change
of color on the mention of the jewels. Absorbed in the
pitiful tale, Lady Molly had not remarked Darcy's agitation.
Denny, who did notice it, felt his heart warming to the
kind young fellow at his very evident sympathy for Norah's
misfortunes. Darcy was relieved when the harrowing tale
was finished, and saw no cause for alarm so far as his own
handiwork was involved. Norah was probably at some
neighboring farm-house. "She would," he said decisively,
"be discovered so soon as a systematic search was set on
foot." Under the impulse of this re-assurance, Denny's
heart grew light, and Lady Molly, turning to Darcy, said
soberly :

"Norah's a wise lass, Denny, me dear, and ye need
have no fear of her. I'll go bail it's to get beyond the
sharp tongue of Mrs. Byron the child's made off. She's
not gone that far, ye may believe, that, if anything befell
Denny or her Aunt Selina, the child couldn't come te
them as quick as Dick Maginnis to the coort when the
judge gav' sintence of death to his sweetheart for murther-
ing him."

"I suppose the lady-love broke his heart. That's
murder in Irish, isn't it, Lady Molly?" Darcy asked,
naïvely.

"Ye'd make a jest, ye villian, if ye were up till yer
neck in the bog of Arran," cries my lady, laughing; then
adds, smiling at Denny, who was plainly high in her whimsical good graces, "Do you know, me lad, this boy Denis
has a sister that would make a saint pass the open door of
paradise, and a sinner like you commit murther?"

"Wouldn't that depend somewhat on the paradise?
Not Lady Poultney's, for example, or the murder of her
peace of mind!" Darcy said, with affected temerity at a
homage so outspoken.

"Begone, ye blarneyin' Rap! Is it for an ould married woman like me to hear such talk? I'm ashamed of ye, so I am. I'm old enough to be your mother."

"Well, since you can't be my mother-in-law, I must be satisfied with that."

Lady Molly tossed her head, by no means displeased with the ardent though melancholy glance of the handsome flatterer, and turned to Denny.

"'Twas heavy on me soul this many a day that I didn't take Norah away from that house whin the poor Docther died. And I had it in my mind to do it, too, so I did, but off we wint to New York, and I'm only back now. But we'll find her, and she shall never leave us, me bye, mark that!"

"When we carry off beauty it must be on the heart, not the mind, my lady!" interposed Darcy. "For example, when you were carried off it took mind and heart; but then you are a law to others and lawless to yourself."

"Ye wicked, honey-tongued rogue, let me lord hear yer impudence, and it's a wake, not a wedding, that yer muther'll have on her mind! Hould yer tongue till I have me say out to Denny here!"

"If you don't have your say it won't be for the want of letting, as my lord can attest!" retorts the incorrigible railer, and Lady Molly shuts him out of the conversation with her sunshade.

Denny recited the events which had come to pass since the melancholy day of the Poultneys's visit.

"And the poor child was there all alone in that dreadful house of death! Oh, what a wicked villian I am! She sha'n't stay there another day when she's found. Who's to hinder me from taking her meself? I will do it the very minute Poultney comes back, so I will. She shall live with me and be my adopted daughter."

"Then you'll have to put a label on yourself when you're together, so that people will know which is the mother and which the daughter!" cries Darcy behind the sunshade.

"Hold yer tongue, impudence. Now, Denis, come home and have dinner with us. The minute ye find Norah I'll come to her meself!" and the honest soul, delighted with her own decisive measures, lowered the silken rampart, and invoked Master Darcy's shafts to their full extent.

"I was going to call at your house, Mr. Darcy, to see you. I made so bold as to believe that you would not think me intruding to ask you to recommend me for something to do," Denny said.

"Of course he will. What is the beggar good for if he can't get something for a fine likely b'y as yourself to do? It's as good as settled. Here we are at the steps, and never a man with the decency to hand me down from me carriage," and, before either of the abashed youths could offer a hand, she was out and laughing at their discomfiture.

Denny had never been in a grand house before, and he was quite dazed by the solemn grandeur, which his taste had not been educated as yet to detect as ugly and pretentious. The walls were a dead white, the moldings gilt, and the furniture a dull mahogany. The carpets were in staring patterns, prodigious flowers, and fantastic borders, that gave the large rooms the appearance of flower-beds in which gigantic blossoms had been crushed, leaving only their outlines on the fiery groundwork. The servants were in livery; Denny thought they were soldiers at first, and shrank abashed when one of them came forward to take his hat. He was shown up a broad staircase to a large room overlooking vast gardens; and Darcy, who was in an adjoining room, came to the door and, knocking, entered without waiting for a response.

"I have been thinking over your matter, Denny, and I will see my father when I get home. I am sure something can be done."

"I shall be most grateful. You know the Doctor's death has been a blow to my prospects as well as a sadness. I was to have entered college this fall."

"Were you, indeed? Where did you prepare?"

"At Calao and at home. I'm ready for the junior year."

"'Pon my soul, you're ahead of me, for I couldn't stand an exam. for fresh."

"Yes, but you've been graduated from West Point."

"Ah, that was merely a technical cram. By the way, I think that a good idea of Lady Molly's for your sister. She's an impulsive, kind-hearted woman, and, though she's forgetful, she'll do all she says. You mustn't let her forget her proposal."

"Ah, it's too good to be true! She never saw Norah but once, and doesn't know what a noble, sweet girl she is. If she did, I should feel more certain of her keeping her word."

"You need have no fear. I'll keep her in mind of it."

"Will you? How good you are! God bless you!" and Denny seized Darcy's hand.

"Pshaw, my boy, you make too much of trifles; why shouldn't any one who had seen N—your sister speak for her; I'm sure I thought her a very well-bred, fine girl!" He turned away as he said this. Somehow the honest adoration in Denny's eyes brought the dead face of Dr. Marbury before him as Lady Molly had described it, when the poor widow brought the body home.

12

At the dinner Denny's wonder grew. He had never seen wine on the table, and was greatly embarrassed when the silent menial in buttons poured the red Burgundy out into the glistening crystal. He would have been more embarrassed if Darcy, remembering Denny's home ways, hadn't said, "Denis, you don't drink wine in your virtuous country home. For that matter, only the godless in town drink it at dinner. There are not a dozen houses in the city where it's set on the tables. Lady Molly will not be offended if you stick to home ways and neglect your wine."

Denny gave him a grateful glance, and the wine stood untasted. He was surprised at his own self-possession under circumstances so wholly outside of his experience. For, though a well-bred family, Dr. Marbury's honest table gave him no opportunity to learn how subsidiary a part of the feast the eating is. Lady Molly's kindliness made up for the lack of that graceful tact with which women of the world know how to invest the scene when company is *bizarre* or not homogeneous. Denny forgot the grandeur of the two great folks, and his droll comments and modest essays, in answer to the covert banter of Darcy, set the merry mistress of the feast into peals of infectious laughter. When she dismissed the young men at the end of the dinner, Darcy accompanied Denny some way on his homeward route.

"I think you are very lucky to have gained Lady Molly's good-will—both you and your sister. She will be a most kind friend to Norah, who is far too pretty a girl to be left among country bumpkins." Then, suddenly bethinking himself that it was imprudent to admit that he had noticed the girl, he added, "I mean a girl who had the advantage of such guardianship as Dr. and Mrs. Marbury's."

"Yes," Denny answered, eagerly, "Norah is a very good girl."

"As for yourself," said Darcy, looking at the other admiringly, "you ought to make something of yourself. I will do my best to open the way for you."

"You sha'n't have cause to be sorry for it, you may be sure," replied Denny, gratefully.

Darcy was about to say something more, but halting, as they came to the street crossing the Rialto bridge, he held out his hand, bade the other good-night, and sauntered in the direction of his home.

It was still early twilight, and Darcy lingered pensively under the shadows, watching the arrowy shafts of vermilion breaking in great waves over the western sky. He came presently to the Blue Jay, whose pretty veranda was thronged with the neighborhood gossips. Their gayety arrested his attention, and he let his glance wander down to them. As he slackened his step, a lad's voice behind him asked, in that suppressed, awed tone children employ when their imagination is at play :

"But how can the fairies tell whether we are good or not? They live in the woods, and they can't see us while we are in the cellar or pantry?"

"Oh, yes, Manly, the fairies are given power to read our consciences as we read books. Our consciences always put down what we do that is not right, and then the fairies keep the record and punish us in the ways that are hardest for each one of us to bear."

All the blood in Darcy's body seemed to rush to his head. He came to a full stop as the boy and his companion passed him slowly on the foot-path. He knew the voice in an instant ; even in the darkness he recognized the supple, graceful figure and the timid, gliding step. He followed, not knowing whether to make himself known or not. His mind was very busy now with a problem that tortured him a great deal.

Plainly Providence had intervened. He had shunned temptation. He had resolutely kept from the edge of the precipice ; but here, though his steps were far from the fatal brink, destiny had turned its course, and planted the gulf before him for his feet to walk over. Should he hurry after her and inform her of Denny's anguish and fruitless search ? Perhaps that might take the temptation from his trembling steps. Yes, he would speak to her, and chide her for not making known her distress to him.

But, as he lingered in his uncertainty, the two figures had faded far ahead of him in the gloom. He hurried his pace ; but at the corner was a band of young people romping, and he could not make out whether Norah was one of them or not. He waited to catch her voice, but he waited in vain. When the merry-makers dispersed, there was no sign of the fugitive. He raised his eyes to a dormer-window jutting above a trellised porch, and his heart leaped wildly. A fair outline in the window he was sure he recognized. His heart throbbed in a tumult of guilty recognition. Yes, it was Norah ! He couldn't be mistaken !

But she had disappeared. He continued up the street and then came back ; but the curtain was drawn. He passed the house a dozen times, until a light twinkled behind the muslin curtain ; but Norah's face did not re-appear. He was sure that it was she. He understood the situation at a glance. Norah was waiting in this refuge until she could secure a home elsewhere. Why had she come to the city ? She loved the country : the birds and fields were the joys of her life ! He couldn't imagine her outside of these pastoral surroundings, and he felt with an indescribable pang that it was his madness, his thoughtlessness, that had driven her from the life she loved.

His foolish gifts had brought the suspicion of the shrew upon her, and she was too proud and too pure to endure the shame of a charge of theft. But he would find a means of convincing the Marburys, without betraying his part in the domestic tragedy; for, of course, Denny, knowing nothing of the real cause of Norah's panic and flight, ascribed it to Amelia's cruel charge. Darcy had no suspicion of Byron's odious part in the complicated causes of Nora'hs act. He wandered up and down the shadowy, silent street until the noisy group on the veranda separated and the light behind the curtain went out, then took his way, glowing and restless, to his own luxurious room. He tried to read: but a rosy face was before him; pouting lips were near his own; gentle, pleading eyes were gazing into his soul; and he started up with a bitter cry of love and despair.

"No!" he said. "I shall be tempted no more. I shall go at once in the morning and tell Denny, and have Norah sent back. I shall never see her again. I should be a villain if I did."

The resolution gave him great comfort. He disrobed himself tranquilly, with a little throb of self-admiration at his constancy. "No, it should never be said that a Warchester had brought sorrow to the humblest. He could look all mankind in the face." And to prove it he stood before the diamond rift made by the muslin curtains drawn over the mirror, and surveyed his sparkling eyes, his handsome features, caressed the budding down on his upper lip, and smiled until the glistening, irregular teeth shone in the flattered glass. Serenely content with what he saw, he sat down, pulled off one stocking, then, manlike, fell to thinking; being so far in his disrobing, the operation at this stage seemed to invite reflection. He sat with his garments half off: his mind went back to the

sylvan tryst under the apple-tree; the thrill of the last
embrace in the dairy; the tender beseeching of the soft,
sweet eyes; the inexpressible yielding of that elfin embrace, when in his heart he had sworn that life held nothing so precious; that social allurements were cheats; fame,
an echo; and love, enough. When, a half hour later, he
found the stocking still suspended from his foot, he hurriedly disrobed, but he turned in dread from the mirror
as he extinguished the candle; he dared not confront
himself in the glass now, for his resolution had oozed into
an equivocation.

CHAPTER XVIII.

THE HANDMAID OF BOAZ.

HAD she dared communicate with Denny, or relieve
Aunt Selina's suspense, Norah would have found her new
life not only supportable but perhaps happy. She had
racked her brain in agonies of indecision; at one moment
she resolved to write to Denny and Aunt Selina, and tell
them where she was. But, if she did, she would have to
reveal the horror of Byron's hideous passion. Then, too,
she feared that, if her whereabouts were known to others
of the household, Byron would watch and wrest the secret
from them. If she remained hidden long enough, he
would forget his fever and be ashamed of his Tarquin purpose. Of Darcy she thought, and thought, until her gentle
heart grew heavy. She knew she was near him. She
could have summoned him at a moment's notice.

But, though too pure and guileless to dream the danger
their intimacy involved, she was protected, by the instinct

that Heaven implants, from that fatal peril which is held
in almost superstitious horror by women of Irish blood.
I don't know whether she ever thought of the obstacles
which lay between her and Darcy, that is, the impossibility
of a scion of a family so pretentious taking her in marriage.

Darcy had once called her his "witch wife," and she
had blushed rosily, and dreamed of a woodland ritual and
a Queen Mab *cortége* at the ceremonial which gave her this
beautiful husband. But it was all vague [and unreal to
her. She only thought of Darcy as she thought of the
birds and flowers that she roved among, listening to the
song of the birds, inhaling the fragrance of the blossoms,
taking no thought of the future. But her purpose of giving the jewels back had changed. Why should she wound
him by returning them? Why pain him by the story of
the woe they had brought upon her? Then, too, he was
so proud and determined; he would have gone straight to
Amelia and told her outright that it was he who had given
these emblems of love. And then Denny would know
that she had kept a secret from him, and Aunt Selina's
reproachful eyes would grow dim over the treason. Ah,
no! It was better, now she had faced the cruelty of separation, that she should wait until Aunt Selina and Denny
could be told without danger of bringing Byron near
her.

One evening, about a fortnight after she had become
domesticated in the Blythe household, as she sat embroid-
ering in the sitting-room, a stranger came in with Manly,
and the boy in great glee brought him over to Norah,
saying:

"This is our new cousin, Mab." It was by this name
that Norah was called altogether in the household, owing
to the fairy lore she dealt out so profusely to the lad.

"Mab has deserted her dells for the hearth, has she?" said the stranger good-humoredly, as Norah raised her eyes. But, when he caught sight of her face, he started. Norah replied, blushing:

"Yes, Mab was fond of the chimney-corner when the frost fell, and sometimes in summer."

Mrs. Blythe entered the room, and, catching sight of her visitor, bustled forward in great delight.

"Why, Mr. Dunn, I didn't know you had come back! Do take a seat. Manly, I wonder that you don't give folks a chair when they come in; you are losing all your manners! How are all the folks in Bucephalo?"

"Oh, I've just come in," said Dunn, shaking hands cordially, as Mrs. Blythe placed a seat for him; "and it is not Manly's fault that I didn't have a seat sooner. I was paying court to Queen Mab."

"Eh? Oh, yes; that's Manly's silly nonsense."

"No, mother, it's not nonsense. My book says that Mab lives in the flowers and can talk with them, and so does cousin Norah."

"Very well reasoned out, Manly, boy; Kris Kringle shall know of your fidelity to his tribe when Christmas comes," and Manly, with glowing eyes, planted himself on Dunn's broad knees, who meanwhile kept his eyes on the downcast face of Norah, as she plied her needle swiftly in the cloth before her. Mrs. Blythe was waddling about the room, movement having been recommended to her by the new homœopathic doctor as a certain means of reducing portliness that began to hang heavy on her spirits as well as on her frame.

So it happened often after this that Marcus Dunn remained after tea to talk with Norah in the mellow evening light. Marcus had changed but little since we saw him thirteen or fourteen years before. He was still slender, shapely, and student-like in deportment. His gray eyes were softer and kindlier ; his voice rich, harmonious, and re-assuring. He was the despair of Warchester mammas and maids, who had pronounced him the best "catch" in town for years. But, engrossed in his profession and fond of books, he had resisted the guiles of the man-ensnaring and the seductions of beauty, and now, at thirty-five or forty, he was still ranked among the "beaus" of the upper social ranks. For years he had made the hospitable table of the Blythes his family circle, and was considered as one of the family. His rooms were in his law building. There he reigned in a domain of such æsthetic luxury as few of the most pretentious Warchesters could hope to equal. Statuary and painting were not then the vogue in the pushing and complacent circles that considered themselves "first" ; but Marcus had brought home many precious evidences of the taste that reigned in older societies beyond the sea.

Such groups of young men as were permitted to come to Dunn's quarters on rare occasions, when he gave small parties to the Pundit Club, an organization of which he was president and founder, were looked upon as singularly favored ; for, though comparatively a young man, Marcus chose his companions among the elders of the bar and the faculty of the college. His practice was very large, and his cases took him all over the State. It was during one of these absences that Norah became an inmate of the Blue Jay and a settled member of the family when he returned. Norah had said nothing to the Blythes about keeping her strange advent secret, but, with the delicacy that is often found in the least sensitive or unschooled, they repulsed all gossip, and simply represented the girl as a kinswoman fallen to their care.

The sight of Norah that first evening had aroused

strange memories in Marcus Dunn. He recalled that
summer voyage on the canal long ago, when his heart had
been solemnly stirred by the Madonna loveliness of the
emigrant mother ; of the piteous tragedy, and the lonely
grave. Mab was the image of that dolorous mother, with
something of her melancholy splendor of face and form.
But the melancholy was not sadness in Norah's case.
The wit of her race bubbled from her heart so soon as
her girlish shyness wore off. Presently nothing but the
assemblage of the "Pundits" could lure the studious
jurisconsult from his simple *tête-à-tête* with the demure
maiden.

He was greatly puzzled by her presence in the family,
but made no inquiry. He had casually led the conversation to the past, occasionally, in order to discover the
girl's antecedents ; but, as she became silent and pensive,
he forebore. At her old home Norah was called Marbury
almost exclusively, and it was as Norah Marbury that
Marcus knew her. He had no suspicion, at first, even
though reminding him of the sad mother, that she was the
Murillo's daughter. He brought books of more varied
range than poor Denny's limited treasures afforded, and
he found her an apt and diligent student. She treated
him with the sincerity and open frankness of a sister, and
he was careful to preserve a fraternal tone in all his
goings and comings. Even the household saw nothing to
comment on. The friendship was quite natural.

Norah amused and distracted the overworked student ;
what more natural than that he should sit by the window,
while the gossips chatted outside, and address an occasional
word to the young girl reading or sewing in the room ?
He could see in Norah's voice, movement, and manner,
that she had been gently bred. She had none of the
blemishes that come from superficial or unlettered sur-

roundings. She might have been the daughter of a War-chester or a Darcy so far as her bearing and conversation told the story.

It was not long before Marcus Dunn took himself to task anent this new motive that began to manifest itself in his life. Was he in love? he asked himself, walking distractedly where the roar of the cataract drowned the sound of his voice. Was this creature of rose-leaves, pomegranate, and gentleness the vestal of the altar he had so long shunned? What, a middle-aged man, who had dedicated his years to a noble profession, was he subject to the torments whose incipience he had felt as a boy, so many years before, when to love was guilt—dishonor—misery!

What a strange, tranquilizing sweetness hovered about her! How the world and its waywardness, its pomps and ignoble rewards, faded into thin air as he listened to the rich, soft voice, and with gentle craft encouraged the artless prattler! But how could he hope to win the peri? How proffer the sober years and sedate yearnings of his so long obdurate heart to this creature of love and tenderness? Often, in the lonely luxury of his rooms, he let his fancy picture the pretty figure of Norah flitting about, a thing of rarer beauty than his Canova marbles, his Van Dyck replicas. What a crown she would be to his tranquil life? How the folly of ambition would evaporate before that delicious reality! But he would wait. There was no hurry. She was so shy that he must give her a chance to know him.

Her reluctance to go out at first puzzled, but finally pleased him. He often strolled with her of an evening now, when Manly escorted her to the rushing waters of the Caribee, to hear for the hundredth time the fascinating fables she invented of the nymphs of the stream and the dryads of the grove. He let the boy do all the talking, and thus made himself welcome to that exacting tyrant, who would have whisked Mab away had the elder cavalier monopolized his adored necromancer. Days and weeks of joy unspeakable these to the silent, rapt worshiper, who fed on his own uncertainty; for he did not know whether to dare and lose, or to be silent and enjoy.

Once he asked her to let him have a miniature painted by an artist friend visiting him from New York. She consented with roseate delight on her dimpled face; but, when the painter saw her, and started, in glowing rapture, Marcus's heart sank, and he regretted in days and nights of anguish that he had run the risk. For the painter was a gay young fellow, and prattled amorously of the Cinderella kept by her wicked kinsfolk in the demure corner of the little inn. A second miniature that Marcus had contemplated was not ordered from this too susceptible master. When Norah's was finished, he was promptly paid, that he might take himself elsewhere. But the pertinacious artist informed his patron that he was enchanted with Warchester, and that he should remain and sketch there for some time. And he did. He set up a studio, and on the walls were studies of Norah in scores of ideal attitudes, the very mention of which drove Marcus into a frenzy of jealous madness. Worse than all, the young scamp became one of the Blue Jay's family circle, and lost no opportunity of ingratiating himself with the household.

Meanwhile Darcy had met with a mishap! He had met with a mishap we all experience some time in our lives. He had, as we have seen, summoned the powers of mind and conscience in grand debate. Mind had routed conscience! He had faced his handsome self in the mirror before the decision, and resolved that he would fly temptation ; that he would not see Norah ; that he would write to Denny and tell him where the fugitive was to be found. But, later, the forces of mind had overcome this resolve, and he had compromised with conscience. He would see her just once, and then summon the powers of virtue—her shield and defender, Denny.

But, alas ! humiliation was added to self-reproach when, after an hour's sauntering before the cottage where he had seen Norah, he discovered that he had been deceived—that, though the girl resembled her, it was not she. He brooded bitterly over his inanity now. Why hadn't he boldly spoken to her when she was by his side in the street? Why had he stupidly let her be lost to him in the group of merry-makers? What a dolt he was not to know that the gentle Norah would not linger in the street to join such hoyden pranks. But he was not to be baffled now. He would find her; he would caress that lithe form ; he would press those rosebud lips and look deep, deep into those limpid eyes, in which he knew his image lingered—knew— Great God ! he knew that, sleeping and waking, he was in her thoughts.

He knew she was in Warchester because he was there ! He knew that on a nod from him she would put a dagger into her gentle heart ! It was the knowledge of all this that had restrained him so long. But, maddened now, the self-accusing voice of conscience upbraiding him for his compromise, he recklessly resolved to hunt from street to street, and house to house, until he found her. Had no obstacle been placed in his way—had he really found Norah in the cottage that morning—who knows but the better angel might have had the last word? When his young blood had been tamed by denial; when his purpose had been strengthened by doubt ! When Darcy came in to the luncheon-table his usually gay face was gloomy.

His mother, sensitive to his humors as mercury to temperature, asked in dismay :

"Why, Darcy, what can have happened! Is your horse lame ?"

"No, not that I know; I'm a little knocked up. I read late last night and didn't sleep well."

"You look as if you had met a creditor," said the Colonel, tossing off a glass of wine. "Try a glass of Bordeaux, and you'll be all right."

Darcy sat down and made a pretense of eating ; his mother tempting him with tid-bits she knew his fondness for. The Colonel was engaged with a newspaper, and broke out presently :

"Mr. Soldier, you may polish up your sword ; there is no longer any doubt that the politicians mean that we shall fight the Mexicans. All the news from Washington looks warlike."

Darcy's eyes glistened.

"Yes, the fellows were full of it last night at the Chancellor's, and we're going to raise a company to march with Taylor, and I'm to be captain. West Point has done me that much service ! " and Darcy smiled at his mother.

"If West Point had done nothing else, Darcy, it gave you the tone of a gentleman. That is a good deal in our country, in such society as we have to endure, where lawyers, doctors, and all sorts of tradespeople are admitted as the equals of old families like ours, the Vanes, the Kents, the Thurstons, the Darcys—"

"And the Poultneys," interjected Darcy with a grin.

"Faugh! Don't, I beg of you, Darcy, mention that odious vulgarian to me. I have commanded Mrs. Vane to keep Agnes from associating with that ill-bred person !"

"She'll miss great fun if she doesn't, I assure you. Lady Molly is the cleverest woman in Warchester. Of course," added the young rogue archly, "always excepting Madame Warchester!"

"She may do for silly boys like you to intrigue with; but I warn you, my son, now that you are nearly ready to settle in life, you must think of your own standing and your wife's."

"But, mother, what's the use of being a Warchester, if one can't do as one pleases? I always supposed that rank gave one a right to do as one likes. Else not, ''twould be as gay to be a plowman,'" Darcy said solemnly.

"It is in the fact that you are a Warchester that you must be careful what you do. It is the mission of families like ours to set an example, and, if our son is seen mingling on terms of equality with such personages as the one we have named, all distinctive marks are lost. *Noblesse oblige*, my son!—*Noblesse oblige*."

Mrs. Warchester was very proud of a limited knowledge of the French tongue, which she had learned in a very select school in New York, presided over by a French countess, a cousin of the famous Lafayette. This lady's portrait adorned the hall of the Warchester mansion, with a faded paper tied to one corner, upon which was written the most charming little note in the French tongue to "Mademoiselle Vane," with the most distinguished consideration and profound amities "of her *vieille amie*, Euphrasie de Cottin." Darcy's French was the fragmentary West Point phrases, that imperil the venturous person infatuated enough to use it, and it broke his mother's heart that he sensibly refrained, in spite of her frequent incursions into that tongue.

"*Noblesse oblige*—that may be! but the king cures evil by touching it! Why is not vulgarity made the mode when a Warchester gives it countenance?" and Darcy, with pretended gravity, met his mother's indignant glance.

"Tush, Darcy! If we were in a land where our rank held its precedence without assertion, it would be a different thing. Here anybody that you speak to civilly presumes upon it to invite you to his house, and expects to be invited to yours."

At this point Darcy willingly dropped the discussion, for it was by no means a new one between mother and son. She was very earnest in this harmless dogmatism. It was not unknown to Darcy that his mother's sentiments were the mingled amusement and reverence of the town, for she was consistent in enforcing them. The heterodox son would not have escaped, however, so easily if the door had not opened to admit a vision so radiant that even the question of caste vanished from the Warchester mind as a young girl, majestic in movement, imperial in manner, sailed into the room.

"Aunt Warchester, won't you give me some lunch? Papa is entertaining the judge, and I ran away!" she exclaimed, kissing the mother, courtesying to the Colonel, and holding out her hand to the son.

"My dear, you shall have something to eat and you shall hear the news. Darcy's going to the wars, and you shall be a general's wife, perhaps."

"Going to the wars? What wars? Where? When?"

Then mamma narrates the rumors, and the girl laughs gayly.

"Is that all? I thought that perhaps the English had declared war against us. There's not much chance for glory in Mexico. There's no one there to fight but half-breeds and Indians."

"Your knowledge of contemporary history does discredit to Mrs. Fitz-Hughes's seminary, Agnes, if that's all you know of Mexico," and Darcy smiled in a mildly superior way at the incredulous beauty.

"I must leave you at your history-lessons, young people, and set the house in order betimes, if we are going to have war," said the Colonel, rising from the table.

"That means you must go to the bank and wrangle with those vulgar directors, I suppose," Mrs. Warchester said, rising and leaving the room with her husband.

"It was charming in you to come in this morning," Darcy said as the door closed. "I have been out of sorts, and now we can take a jaunt. What do you say to a dash Malvernward? Do you feel equal to such a pull?"

"Really, I feel equal to scolding you."

"Scolding, Agnes! Why, what have I done?"

"It's for what you've left undone."

"But there's grace still in me."

"No. But it's lucky for you there's grace in *me!*"

"But the undone : what is it? 'Pon my honor—"

"Never mind your honor, faithless. I won't say any more. If your conscience doesn't prick you, nothing I can say will arouse its still, small voice."

"Angels and ministers of grace, defend us!"

"It would take all those and more to make successful defense of your sins."

"Shall I, pining in despair, mourn because a maid is fair? Tell, oh, tell!"

"No, I sha'n't!"

"Ah, I have it! The musicale last night! But, Agnes, you know I said I *might* come ; I didn't say I *would* come. I should have gone had it not been—"

"Had it not been for what?"

"On my honor—"

"Oh, no, something tangible ; something admitted."

"Well, on my soul—"

"Um! still doubtful."

"On my love for the fairest being that ever—"

"Who is she?"

"Agnes, can you ask? Look in my eyes, and you will
see her glorious image. Look in my heart, and you will
see it filled with her— Look—"

"No, I'm not armed with a scalpel, and I can't examine your heart."

"But the eyes!" He was near her, looking into her
own dark luminous eyes, tenderly pleading. She bent
over suddenly, their lips met, and the quarrel was
ended.

An hour later, Agnes, in a Diana-like robe that almost
trailed to the ground from her horse, side by side with
Darcy, emerged into the river road from the sparse city
dwellings. As they trotted slowly along, Agnes, pointing
to the roadside, said:

"What a pretty girl that is! She looks like a wood-
nymph."

Darcy's eyes fell upon two figures bending over a cluster of purple asters. He started, and gave the rein such a
pull that the horse came to a halt. Agnes, startled, turned
to see if he had fallen. But his eyes were fastened upon
Norah, who, diverted by the sudden hoof-beats, had turned.
Her eyes met Darcy's, and she made an eager motion as
if to rush forward and speak; but her eye, wandering
from Darcy's flushed face, rested upon the staring figure
of his companion. She shrank back; the two horses shot
past and onward, without a sign from the lover. Some
evil spirit seized Darcy's horse at this juncture, or perhaps
the muttered execrations of the young man had startled
the beast, for he tore on quite wildly for a mile or more,
effectually preventing conversation. When a tranquil pace
was again resumed, Agnes, turning in the saddle, said inquiringly:

"You know her?"

"Yes, it is Dr. Marbury's ward—the young girl that was ill in our house last year."

"She's wonderfully pretty. What's her name?"

"Norah Marbury."

"Norah? A soft, pretty name. But what is she doing up here? Marbury is four miles from this."

"I believe she lives in the city now. There's a magnificent tiger-lily by the water yonder. Wouldn't you like it?" and Darcy, leaping from the saddle, cut the lustrous flower from its stalk.

The young girl placed it at her girdle, and they rode on over the hills, Darcy torn by an inward debate, in which conscience was doing some desperate comminatory dialoguing with no faculty or weighty force to reply in behalf of Darcy's impulse.

CHAPTER XIX.

COWARD CONSCIENCE.

A WEED, set in a hot-house, rivals in delicacy of color, fragrance, and beauty the untended plants of the garden. The rarest blossoms that decorate the bosom of beauty are only the survivals of the hardiest shoots of the wild wood. I remember well when the daisy, the primrose, and ragged robin were looked upon as weeds, fitted only for the brookside or the field. In my young days the aster and golden-rod had no place in the flora of the parlor. Poets had long sung the purple pansy, the merry buttercup, the royal clover, before these modest blossoms found place in the parterres of the garden. Social and natural evolution work, if not by the same processes, in

much the same ways. The sunflower of to-day is the same
rugged stalk of the kitchen garden that it was a half century ago, but it is now not only a decoration of the æsthetic
illuminati, but a spiritual type.

Reared from the tenderest years among the ideals and
symbols of a conceded caste, Agnes Vane was as completely identified in external characteristics with her later
conditions as the Roman slave who had become part of
the optimate ranks in the time of Cicero. She was put to
school with the daughters of the house, and she surpassed
her high-born mates in seizing the sense of all that was
taught her infant understanding. The Vanes were proud
of an ancestry that held Sir Harry Vane, Cromwell's lieutenant and Charles's *bête noire*, among the glories of its history. Mansfield Vane had settled upon a Continental
grant on the banks of the Caribee, long before the site of
Warchester was selected as the preordained spot for a
town. His son Percy had grown rich by simply holding
his paternal acres until the city borders reached them, and
the family mansion, which had been in the country, was,
by the growth of the city, made hardly suburban. Playing under the stately Vane elms one day, Agnes had attracted Mrs. Vane's attention, first by her infant terror of
a formidable mastiff, and then by a childish beauty that
recalled the stately lady's own kin. James Boyne was only
too glad to yield all claim to the orphan, and thorcefor-
ward the little Agnes Boyne became part in the blood and
ambition of the patrician caste. Her mind was strong and
subtle, as the North Irish intellect generally is. The hard-
ness that tinges it, however, in the dynamic northern cli-
mate, lost the sharpness of its tone in the milder amenities
of the girl's new surroundings.

Partly for the girl's sake, partly for policy, her relationship to James Boyne was sedulously concealed, so soon

as Percy Vane saw that the uncle really had no interest in his brother's child. James Boyne had on a memorable occasion rescued Vane from an awful death in the mill machinery. The patrician had never ceased to bear the grim bread-winner in the kindest remembrance. He had given him the lots upon which his substantial house stood, and he never let a chance slip, as the years rolled by, to evince the liveliness of his gratitude. It was through this sentimental relation that Agnes came to the notice of the Vanes, and it was on learning the hostility of James Boyne's wife to the orphan's presence that the idea of adoption was first suggested. When Agnes Boyne became Agnes Vane, James Boyne made no doubt that he was her lawful guardian—as her mother had been two years before laid in the Potter's corner of God's acre. Hugh Boyne was dead by circumstantial report, and the little waif was legally given over to her new and munificent destiny.

Every year her beauty grew more enchanting. She might have been of Andalusian blood, so dark her eyes, so clearly olive her complexion, so ebon and massy her lustrous coils of hair. With the languorous beauty of the South, she developed the vigorous mental faculties of the North, and at school was the pride and wonder of her preceptors. Of her origin she had but the vaguest recollection. Under her Uncle James's guardianship, a little lass of four or five years, she was told that the large-eyed, wandering woman who haunted her, was mad and fancied herself the child's mother. The Vane children, her brothers and sisters, were too young to understand the status of their new sister, and she was never in any way reminded of her past, her parentage, or her adoptive relationship. As the years went by the family itself lost sight of the unconsanguineal relationship, and when, during the ravages of the great epidemic of 1840, the girls of the household were carried off, Agnes became more preciously the darling of the house. In Warchester, though it was known to the friends of the family that Agnes was only a daughter by adoption, her origin was not suspected, for just at the time she entered the family, Percy Vane was sent abroad on a diplomatic mission, and, remaining away six years, the girl's appearance among his household excited no comment. She was the joy of the desolated family, smitten by the loss of its own children. She was a prime favorite with Mrs. Warchester, who knew that she was an adopted child, but did not know the details, nor the lowliness of her origin. She knew that she was heiress of half the princely Vane possessions, and very early began to point her out to Darcy as a fit mate for his future. The alliance, she reminded him, would join the lands of Warchester and Vane, and give the possessor an estate equal to a ducal principality. The Vanes were nothing loath to mate the girl to the handsome dreamer, and in the end the match was rather understood than ostensibly arranged.

Darcy fell into the plan listlessly. He was not madly in love with the tantalizing beauty—save when she seemed indifferent to his good looks, fine manners, and conquering graces. A courtship that might have been suggested by Beatrice and Benedick's went on for years, and though both felt that in the end it would result in marriage, neither was quite sure. It was only in moments of jealous wrath that Darcy reminded the coquette of her destiny, and it was only when Darcy seemed smitten with other eyes that Agnes implied assent, by actions rather than words.

Now, something of the odds against that persistent prime minister Darcy's conscience may be understood. In his moments of pride he glowed in the thought of this magnificent creature of physical splendor and mental pre-eminence as his very own. In moments of reverie a still small voice pleaded the softer, subtler charms of the gentle Norah. With the one love was a combat and the conquest dubitative; with the other love was a rest, a dream, a fulfillment. The one would be a voyage of feverish struggle over billowy seas; the other a delicious, soothing journey over bubbling waters, with bird-note echoes and sensuous blossoms. With one he would share a realm—with the other he would be lord over all.

With Norah it was enough that she loved him. Therein Agnes held the vantage; for the man has yet to be born that is faithful to fidelity of the sort Norah's love implied. If she had been coy, if she could have pretended doubt, if she could have held him in fear of her absolute surrender, the scale would have held the measure firmly. On the other hand, the difficulties unexpectedly put in his way tipped the scale in Norah's favor. Darcy was piqued that he should be robbed of the chance to be magnanimous. He had determined that Norah should be warned that she must not love him, that he could never marry her, and that she must fall in love with some one else.

But fate had intervened, and his heroic resolve had come too late. There is nothing so maddening to a certain state of self-sophistication as good intention wasted. Put upon honor, men in the condition of Darcy would respond nobly; rebuffed by circumstances that mock the good resolutions by proving them unneeded, a self-denial more stoical than Darcy's must waver! So, as he rode along under the mulberry trees, that arched quite over the tranquil highway, he fell into a moody and not amiable humor. Agnes, piqued by his sudden change, said nothing. When they came to the Marbury lane, Darcy turned his horse's head to the gate.

"I want to see a friend in here a moment; will you wait for me?—I sha'n't be a moment."

He got down, swung the gate back, and, leading his horse, went up the well-known way. There was no one at the house, apparently, for he was suffered to tie the horse, and had nearly reached the door when Amelia met him, coming from the dairy. She looked at him with surprised, vague recognition, but waited until he spoke.

"I beg your pardon. This is Mrs. Marbury, is it not? I am looking for Denis. Is he near the house?"

"Denis is over in the brook-meadow with my husband. Just come in and sit down, and I will blow the horn, for him."

"Ah, thank you kindly. I won't go in; I must keep an eye on the horse. If you will give me the horn I will sound it and meet Denis as he comes."

She took the horn from the nail inside the kitchen door, saying, "Two blasts for Denny—I suppose you know?"

He laughed. "Yes, I know the signals pretty well." He blew with some difficulty two strident notes, and heard a distant responsive halloo from the fields. Presently through the green alders he saw some one in shirt-sleeves coming toward the house. He set off to meet him half way, and, as Denny recognized the visitor, he hastened his pace. The lad's eyes brightened as he came near, and Darcy gave him his hand.

"Denny, I've been as good as my word. You are to go into Uncle Darcy's law-office, and, while you are studying, you shall earn enough to keep you by teaching in the academy, when there is a tutorship vacant."

"O Mr. Warchester, how good you are! What shall I say? How can I show you what I feel?" and Denny's eyes moistened as he turned his head away.

"Fudge! you must not take things so seriously. I dare say you will put me to shame before many years by the progress you make. But I'm not envious. I shall rejoice in your success—mind that! Ah, yes; I've more good news. I've seen Norah."

"Seen Norah! when?"

Darcy told the two encounters, and continued:

"Now, if I might advise you, I would say nothing to the people here—not even to Aunt Selina."

"Ah, Mr. Warchester, Aunt Selina has gone to Salem. She couldn't get along with Amelia—she—she—Amelia persists in calling Norah—a thief!"

"Good God, Denis, she didn't say that of Norah! Surely she can't know what a tender, modest, shy child your sister is." Darcy grew pale, and his eyes moistened. He turned and brushed his forehead furtively. "It can't be, Denis! there must be some motive for Mrs. Marbury's cruel persecution! I will make Lady Molly come out to Marbury to stop this dreadful little woman's cruelty. Dr. Marbury was my father's oldest and closest school-fellow, and, as the Doctor often told us, he loved Norah better than any child of his own. We—I owe it to the kind Doctor's memory, to see that his ward is not wronged or maltreated."

Denny looked at him in bewilderment, and Darcy recollected his *rôle* in time to add: "Any one who could be so cruel to a defenseless girl must have a good deal of the Satanic in her nature!"

"But you don't know where Norah is?" Denny asked, recurring to the point that interested him most.

"No, but I feel sure she is happy and safe, for she wouldn't be gathering flowers if she were in trouble."

Denny assented, dreamily: "She never loved the fields except when she was peaceful and happy. Ah,

13

thank God, she is safe, and thank you for being so kind to strangers. You know we Irish have a saying about friends in need."

"No—what is it?" asked Darcy, his heart smiting him sharply.

"A friend in need is the hand of God," said Denny, solemnly. "For him we would go through fire and water; for him we would burn our flesh, break our bones, deny our kin, and abjure all but faith in God."

"It is too serious a creed, Denny, my boy, and reminds me of the Arab tradition: 'Don't count friends until you've proved them.'" And, with this bit of wisdom, dictated by conscience pricking him sorely at the moment, Darcy moved toward the gate. "When will you come?"

"I will tell Byron, and go at once—perhaps in a day or two."

"Very well; you can come right to our house, and we will hunt up quarters for you when you come." He leaped lightly on his horse. Denny secretly thought him an Antinous of grace, and trotted beside him down the lane, to close the gate. Darcy looked about in surprise. There was no sign of Agnes. But Denis caught sight of her in the clover-field beyond, and pointed her out to Darcy. He hallooed, and she made a sign that she heard him, touched her horse, and made toward the road, and, to the surprise of the young men, cleared the four rails like a Centaur. Then, with a signal to Darcy to catch her, set off homeward like an arrow. Denny watched the figures as they disappeared. His heart was very light, for it was buoyed with an overmastering grateful love, and he blessed the brave young rider as his fine form was lost to sight. When he got back to the house, Amelia came out as he was passing the door.

" That was young Warchester, wa'n't it ? "

" Yes, that's Mr. Darcy, the Colonel's son."

" Hello, what's the trouble ? " Byron came hurrying up as Denny spoke. " Who was that gal I saw leap the fence ? By Jemmie, she did it like a pigeon. I never saw anything cleverer."

" I don't know the young lady," said Denny ; " the gentleman was Mr. Warchester."

" What did he want—who does he know here ? " Byron asked, in surprise.

" Oh, he used to come here when your father was alive. He knew Aunt Selina," Denny answered, evasively. He shrank from telling Darcy's mission before Amelia. She detected something of his reserve in his manner, and, glancing significantly at Byron as Denny hurried away, said :

" I think he didn't come to see Aunt Selina. I saw him in the dairy with that bold hussy, Norah, a few days after we came ! "

Byron started and flushed. His suspicions were at once alert. He heard Amelia's story, and made up his mind that he had the mystery of the jewels and the disappearance. When the two returned to the field, Byron led the conversation to Darcy, and Denny prattled artlessly and ardently of the princely young paragon ; of his condescension in strolling through the woods, and the visits he made the summer of his stay at Malvern to the Doctor and Aunt Selina. When the tale was told, Denny falteringly imparted the secret of Darcy's mission. Byron threw down his scythe—he was mowing—and stared at the lad.

" But you can't leave us ; you were bound to my father. I have the papers."

" Bound until my eighteenth year. I was eighteen last

year; besides, the plan to study law was Dr. Marbury's. He meant that I should begin at college long ago."

Denny suffered a cruel ordeal before the final parting. Byron gloomily charged him with ingratitude, and prophesied that he would come to no good. Amelia tossed her head and sniffed when the departure was announced to her.

"I ain't a bit surprised. It's just Irish all over. You pick them out of the gutter, and, as soon as you've made folks of them, they just ride right over you. But I want you to know, young man, that, once you've stepped over that doorsill with your pack, you need never come back here again when your fine city friends get tired of you. The poor-house won't be far away. You were there once, and you can find it easy again."

So, penniless as he had come, but, ah! so light of heart, so radiant in hope, the lad of nineteen left the kindly walls that had been shelter and joy since, an urchin of seven or eight, he had entered its sacred portals. His heart was light, but there were tears, hot and half sad, as he turned on the green hill-side and saw the red walls gleaming through the apple-trees. Long sweeps of dusty road, hemmed with tender green, lay before him, and he trudged on, boy-like, casting the past behind and wondering where his new destiny was to carry him. But it was as well that he could not see far into the future, for I doubt whether the buoyancy of youth or the ardor of hope would have upheld his purpose to penetrate into the night that began to descend upon him.

Within a week he was installed as mathematical instructor in the Fitzhugh Academy, and one of the first pupils that entered his room was Dilly Dane! I am afraid the girls thought this new teacher a very abstracted and embarrassed young man that day, for he made the most preposterous definitions and deductions, and fairly shook the faith of the advanced minds in the exactness of the science of equations. Before many days Dilly found means of giving her old playmate a rendezvous, and then the two had much to tell. The girl had grown in city graces, but she was still the same faithful, tender, constant friend, and looked calmly into Denny's eyes with a fervor that a lad less timid would have understood. But to Denny there was a gulf—the more impassable that it was intangible—which in his wildest dreams he never thought of passing. That the adorable creature should think him worthy of friendship and confidence was a bliss so unmerited, so unhoped, that he lived in the joy of its realization as one more adventurous would have lived in the certainty of the fulfillment of love's hope.

Life opened before him now with all the roseate lamps, youth and hope hang in the horizon. His alien race was no longer made a reproach. Kindness and consideration met him among his associates in the academy, where the patronage of the Warchesters was potential. He had one reminder of other and bitterer days, however. He was in the college library one day, when he recognized a familiar face. It was Oswald Ritter. He was, he informed Denny proudly, in his senior year, and would graduate class orator in a few months. His father was now rich. He had applied a new principle to brewing, and was at the head of a great corporation exploiting the patent. Denny returned to the book-shelves, and a few minutes later he heard some one asking Oswald who the studious-looking person was.

"Oh, he's an Irishman that used to live out at Marbury. He's a teacher, or tutor, or something of the sort in Madam Fitz's."

Thereafter, whenever he appeared in the campus, library, or chapel, he could see that the tale had been told, and, where before he had been regarded with respectful curiosity, he now met insolent stares and suppressed sneers. But these things had no present terror for him. He met liberal toleration from some of the faculty, to whom Darcy had spoken in his behalf, and, with the purposes animating him, no evidence of social disparagement could shake his determination or long cloud his happiness.

Lady Molly, too, was persistently gracious to him. She insisted on his calling and dining. Even my lord took a languid interest in him, and affably discussed French history over the sherry and walnuts. My lord had commanded a squadron of cavalry at Walcheren, and, when he found any one so well posted on the career of Napoleon as Denny, he made himself happy by the hour fighting his battles over again. He was severely shocked at Denny's glorification of the emperor and his poor opinion of Wellington's generalship, and set himself, with an ardor never before known in him, to prove "the duke's" superiority to "Bonaparte." He insisted on calling Napoleon "Bonaparte," as the fashion was after the restoration of the Bourbons, and was quite helpless with astonishment when Denny slyly interpolated, each time reference was made to "the duke," "What duke?"

"Why, Wellington, of course. That is the title he is known by from Moscow to Naples, and that is the title he will be known by in history. It is only necessary to say 'the duke' anywhere in Europe, and every one will know whom you mean."

"Sure, you ought to loike th' juke, Denny, me lad; he was Irish, like ourselves—God bless him!" Lady Molly cried out, as Lord Poultney gathered breath for a fresh flight.

"Yes, Denis, Lord Wellington's family was Irish,

and some of his majesty's best troops came from Ireland."

"Ye can't make th' Americans believe that then," cries Lady Molly, laughing wickedly. "They think we're all bogtrotters and Rapparees, bedad!" She was fond of her most piquant Hibernicisms when talking at her own table, and my lord encouraged her with roars of laughter, for it was one of the merry dame's charms to mimic her rural countrymen.

"Yes, my Lady Poultney," said Denny quite soberly. "Why is it that Americans so mislike us, look down upon us, and revile us; why are we from our mere birth placed a degraded, a disclassed—if I may use the word—race? Ireland has produced men of letters equal to the best that wrote in the English tongue : statesmen; soldiers; students. I could understand it if we were like the Saxons that William conquered, or the Gauls that withstood Cæsar, or the Italians that held their necks for Spanish, French, and Austrian heels; but a people that has produced a Swift, a Spencer, a Moore, a, Sheridan, a Burke, an O'Connell—I can't understand it."

"It's simple enough, Denny," Lord Poultney rejoined, briskly. "This slice of country was settled by the Puritans. Their descendants are the majority in all this part of the States. When the Puritans quit England—I mean those who fled during the reigns of Charles II and James—the Irish were hated and dreaded by the English people, as the Indians in the West are by the pioneers. The colonies planted in Ireland by Cromwell were engaged in constant warfare with the Irish ; neither side gave quarter. The Irish, dispossessed of their lands, and pillaged by Strongbow's troopers, were not scrupulous in reprisal. The stories of these atrocities reached England, and the Irish name became synonymous with ignorance, barbarity, and rapine. To make it worse, King James attempted to make himself absolute in England by the use of Irish soldiers, and was driven from his throne. When the English in the Americans has been worn out, the prejudice against the Irish will vanish. It is because the Irish have been for generations a robbed and wronged people that the English hate and despise them. We never hate any one so much as the men we have wronged!"

Lord Poultney leaned back in his chair after this astonishing manifesto, and Lady Molly took up the tale :

"Ye're surprised to hear me Lord Poultney talking like this, Denny, dear? The Poultneys are true Irish blood. They are a clane house, and stud with the patriots in 'ninety-eight.' But don't trouble yerself about what the Americans think of ye; sure it's pure ignorance. Whin ye go to Naples, the besotted beggars there look down on Americans as Americans look down on the Mexicans. Indeed, there isn't a country in Europe where Americans aren't thought a cross betune a Camanche and a Nagur." And Lady Molly appealed to her lord, as being more traveled, to expatiate on the point.

Denny carried a good deal of comfort away from these discussions, and found himself fortified against the covert sarcasms that from time to time met him on account of his nationality, or his origin rather, for he was very proud of being a citizen of the Republic, and a worshiper of Jefferson—whom he had studied with great diligence, led thereto by Dr. Marbury, who pronounced that great man the stoutest friend of humanity since Voltaire.

CHAPTER XX.

BETWEEN TWO LOVES.

BENT upon finding Norah, now that the Fates seemed to make a mock of his resolution, Darcy gave himself up to long evening walks and loiterings in the churches. Often in the twilight he encountered a trim figure among the evening companies, that he felt sure was hers, but so soon as he caught the tones of the voice he turned away in disgust. He paid his court to Agnes meanwhile in the most perfunctory and unloverlike fashion. Indeed, there was something so much like estrangement that Madame Warchester felt called upon to intervene.

" You must really show yourself more devoted to your *fiancée*, my son, or she will give her heart to some one else, and you know she won't have to wait for a choice."

"What more can she ask? I am to be her husband— isn't that enough? As for giving her heart to some one else—I don't think you need fear. She is the last girl in the world to let her heart be at the mercy of a passing encounter. You wouldn't have me writing sonnets to her and sighing at her feet all the time ! "

" Monstrous, Darcy ! Monstrous ! I never heard a lover talk in this cynical fashion. When I was young, the colonel rode over every day—ten miles or more—to 'take my commands,' as he called it. Any other gallant that paid me court had to wait for a chance, while you leave Agnes to go where she will, with whom she will, and I really believe you don't care a rush."

" I can't say that I do—for these things. If Agnes enjoys other gallants, she will hold me in good part for letting her enjoy herself. By-and-by, when we are Darby and

Joan, she can't indulge these gallantries, and I think it magnanimous in me to leave her free now," and Darcy retired precipitately from an encounter in which he felt he was not armed adequately. He sauntered pensively through the busy streets to the most thriving quarter of the town, with an idle fancy that he would look in on Denny in Uncle Darcy's law office. As he ascended the stairs his eye encountered the name "Frederic Darwin, Artist." He had met the young man some time before and had promised him a sitting. He might as well give it now as any time, he resolved suddenly, and on the impulse he entered the studio. Darwin was at work on an allegorical group, and after shaking hands with his visitor continued the sketch.

"Just amuse yourself looking at the traps and sketches. I will give you my 'art and 'and in a minute or two."

Darcy was too much engrossed in a fanciful head in crayon to note the pun. He recognized the original in an instant. It was an idealized portrait of Norah, standing on a Queen Mab car surrounded by elfin figures.

"A charming head, that," he said carelessly, over his shoulder, to the artist. "She seems to be a favorite with you. I see you have her face in most of your sketches."

"Yes, that is the most perfect Madonna model I ever saw. She is incomparably finer than anything I can do with her in colors. You can have no idea of her beauty without seeing her."

"You saw her abroad, I suppose? We don't have mild, angelic beauties of that type in these wild-wood towns."

"Oh, dear, no! I met her in this city. She lives in the 'Blue Jay,' and, 'pon my soul, she's such a delight that I've cast my lines here simply for the purpose of studying her."

So, at last, he had found her, when she seemed to be

completely lost to him. He burned with impatience to quit the studio and fly to her. But he restrained his eagerness, gave a sitting, and presently he was at the "Blue Jay." He entered the homely, old-fashioned "office," very unlike the elaborate "bureaus" of to-day, and, sitting down near the window, asked to be served a bottle of ale. He knew Blythe passingly, and the loquacious host, in the interval of his "chores," often discussed politics in a friendly bout with him.

"I suppose, Mr. Darcy, you'll be off to the wars in the spring if the President calls for volunteers?"

"Yes, I shall take a company; but I'm afraid the Mexicans won't give us the chance. It looks as if Santa Anna meant to back down. The Texas people seem to have been too much for him."

"I've got a brother in New Orleans, and he writes that there's bound to be fun. So you may just as well make up your mind to hear the music of the drum for a spell, or I'll miss my guess."

"I'm sure I hope you're a prophet, Blythe. I'm tired of this quiet life; I should like to see some excitement," Darcy said, a little distraught.

"Yes, it might be a trifle dull here for a young fellow, unless he is fond of fishing. Naow, if you took to fishin'—darn that boy! he's gone and mixed up my hooks to that pass that I sha'n't know which is trout and which pickerel," and, disconcerted by this mishap, the fisherman forgot the thread of his talk, muttering mild imprecations on the head of the urchin.

"That boy never was wuth a cent, but he's just no 'count at all sence Norah began to fill his head with them 'tarnal stories."

"I didn't know you had a daughter, Blythe," said Darcy, seeing a chance to ask a question.

"Oh, Norah ain't our daughter; she's our cousin, you know—kinder adoptive, but cousin all the same. Darn that boy! here's my sinkers all gone. Manly, Manly, you derned little cuss, I say, come right here!"

But no Manly coming, the indignant parent arose and sallied out in search of the delinquent. As he passed into the hall, the door of the modest reception-room opened, and Norah, putting her head in, said:

"Manly's gone to the river."

"Norah!"

"Ah, Mr. Darcy!"

In an instant he was at her side, pressing her fondly to him. She broke away, retreating toward the other room. He closed the door softly, and, as she turned piteous, entreating, he whispered passionately:

"My darling! my darling! you shall never hide from me again! Why didn't you come to me when that wretch accused you? Why didn't you let me know? If you knew how your flight has worried me, to say nothing of Denny, you could not have been so cruel."

His questions were so rapid, his embrace so close, that she could hardly get her breath to answer:

"O Mr. Darcy! it's a great misfortune that you have found me. It isn't well for us to meet. It will be your disgrace to be known as the friend of the likes of me."

"Disgrace, you witch! It is my pride, my joy. I will declare from whom the jewels came. I will prove that you are the purest angel breathing."

"Mr. Darcy, don't stay here. Some one will come, and what sort of a bold girl will they think me to be talking like this with a strange young man? Ah, go! go!"

"Yes, my darling, I will go, but you must meet me when the twilight comes in the grove by our park-gates. Bring the little boy with you, and then you can remain unnoticed and tell me all; and I will tell you about Denny."

Frightened and rapturous, she clung to him in a parting embrace—she was still rosy and palpitating when Jonas's heavy tread resounded on the sanded floor. He looked about the room in perplexity when he saw Darcy's seat vacant, and, with renewed objurgations against Manly, set about re-adjusting his "tackle."

When twilight came, Norah, with Manly disporting himself gayly, set out falteringly for the tryst. Darcy was waiting. As the two came up, he said, ingratiatingly:

"Well, Manly, what's become of your squirrel?"

Now Manly had been caught in the Warchester hickories trapping squirrels. The gardener had haled the culprit before the Colonel, but Darcy had good-naturedly intervened and presented him with the booty. Manly had never divulged this experience at home. He therefore hung back awkwardly, abashed when confronted by his benefactor. Darcy stroked the boy's shaggy hair good-naturedly, and said, encouragingly:

"Come into the park; I will show you where the owls hold their concerts. This is your cousin Norah, is it? She shall come too?"

Darcy's acquaintance with Norah did not strike the lad as at all curious. He supposed that everybody knew Norah. They lingered in the park, and as the moon arose walked down to the water's edge, where a pretty boathouse stood on the shelving bank. Darcy took the key from his pocket and opened the door. It was more like a pavilion than a boat-house. There were three rooms, handsomely furnished, one of them a sort of studio where Darcy had employed his taste in decoration. The walls were lined with prints, and small statuettes of heroes,

graces, and goddesses rested on fragile brackets between
the other works of art. Darcy slipped one of the boats
from the rest, and the three getting in, the little shallop
was soon gliding over the moonlit waters. Presently they
returned and sat on the little balcony overhanging the
plashing water. Manly, however, found this irksome after
the joy of the boat, and begged to be permitted to paddle
out in the little cove. Darcy assented with alacrity, for
while the boy hovered near he had no opportunity of
talking with Norah. She explained her purpose in quit-
ting Marbury without touching Byron's part of the business. Then Darcy told her of Denny's translation. She
was greatly perplexed now. She was hungering to see
Denny, but feared that if she discovered her whereabouts
to him that Byron would get track of her. He could compel her return to Marbury, and rather than go back she
would fly to the ends of the earth. Darcy couldn't understand her horror of returning, but it was delicious to have
her so near; he made no urgent plea that she should
either summon Denny or return. The bells were ringing
for nine o'clock when Norah was reminded of the lateness
of the hour, and called to Manly.

"You will come again to-morrow night, Norah?"

"No; I think it will be better not. I will come
some time, perhaps, but I won't say. Don't ask me! Oh,
don't!"

"Foolish Norah! You will come, I know you will.
You wouldn't be at rest if you knew I was unhappy, and
you know very well I should be miserable here sitting with
my heart aching and thinking every sound was the echo
of your footfall!"

But Norah wouldn't promise, and hastened away with
the delighted Manly, to whom Darcy had whispered a
caution to say nothing at home of where he had been or

whom he had seen. The gossips had separated when the pair reached the Blue Jay. Marcus Dunn was sitting with Mrs. Blythe, and looked up questioningly as Norah, flushed and breathless, sat down where the dim lights of the candles threw her discomposed visage into friendly obscurity. Darcy waited in the park the next and many nights thereafter, but Norah did not come. He raged like a young Narcissus denied the mirror of his beauty. What! Norah suddenly transformed into a wiseacre— into a prude! His sweet wood-nymph, that had no duty but beauty, that had no thought but of pleasing him, suddenly turned coy, and, like the children of Lamech, grown into the knowledge of Death! As well might a flower refuse to open its petals because the wind blew, and the chill of autumn inevitably must come to scatter its leaves with its fragrance. Ah, the tree of knowledge had bloomed in Norah's path since he had known her in her Arcady, where all was innocence, and love was her ministry! He wouldn't endure it! What, he who had fought the fight and conquered himself, to be made the object of an unreasoning terror!

He flamed with indignant protest. He, who would have served as the tree-imprisoned god, a sacrifice to spotlessness—he shunned by the sprite! He swore a dreadful oath that he would not be so put upon. He wandered down to the leafy square near the " Blue Jay," where the voices of the gossips on the veranda angered him. He listened for the one voice, the lightest cadence of which he could have recognized in a clash of matter, but its music did not mingle with the shrill clamor. He passed close to the porch and looked in. Yes, there she was, and near her, holding the skein of her worsted, sat Marcus Dunn! Darcy could hardly resist the impulse to enter and denounce the faithless siren. But no! how could he contain himself before that impassive old prig, Marcus? He should only make matters worse.

He wandered home moodily, and slunk away from the gayety of the drawing-room, where his mother was entertaining her own circle, and his father was playing his evening rubber with the bishop. What could possess the girl? At Marbury she seemed to divine his coming, and her eyes, if not her tongue, pleaded with him for the woodland tryst. Now that he had determined to teach her gradually that their paths in future must be divided; now that he had made up his mind to show her that their relations must be purely Platonic, that she must look on him as she did on Denny; she fled from him with cruel distrust! A father-confessor could not have asked her to the rendezvous with more saintly tenderness than had actuated him!

It was unendurable; just when he had armed himself for self-conquest to be stripped of his heroic panoply by this insulting doubt. And all the time—concurrent with this specious, delusive sophistry—the quenchless yearning to hold the lovely form in his arms, to look into the clear eyes and read the idolatry of the beating heart! Wild resolves to carry Norah far away, make her his bride, and live in the forest, alternated with Spartan determination to see her no more, to erase this tantalizing image from his heart and follow the path traced by his mother. Oh, yes, if the path had not been of that other's tracing, it would have been so easy to follow. If he had won Agnes through his own initiative, the charm of conquest would have been there; but now! ah! now he had been entrapped into a yoke. Now, for a young Hercules, shapely and well favored, this was a reflection that cut most poignantly.

Adonis may be courted, but Adonis can't endure being made a market. Why shouldn't he be free to choose the mate of his heart? The dullest clown in the country was free to love where he pleased. Where had Norah learned this repulsive lesson of distrust? Surely there must be evil influences about her! Could it be that Marcus had instilled the poison of suspicion into her guileless heart? Of herself, Norah knew no more of the possibilities of evil than of its form or appearance! At Marbury she had naïvely worshiped him as a naiad might a wood-god. Now she fled from him as Diana from Actæon.

You observe in his introspection Darcy's similes and illustrations were all classical. In those days the youth of his degree were classicists, and all the stores of knowledge were based upon the conceits of the schools. Chapman's Homer and Pope's verses were then the final expression of poetic form. Wordsworth and Coleridge were little known, or, if known, regarded as the encyclopedists regarded Shakespeare or Spenser—creators of beauties without form or coherence.

Darcy faced himself in the mirror to prove to himself that he was a St. Anthony successful from the ordeal. His lustrous eyes were wide open and clear, there was no furtive dodging in them. His round, sensuous, well-chiseled lips were firm and truthful. His brown, curling locks framed a physiognomy in every line of which truth, manliness, and sincerity were outlined. Why should any human being doubt that open page? He had no doubt; and after all, if one can believe in one's self—most rigorous of judges—how can any one else have doubts? Darcy snuffed the candles and lay down, feeling himself a deeply injured person, and in his dreams he sat by Norah, and he read in her eyes the confession that she had deeply wronged him.

The meditations of the night brought no soothings or rest to his perturbations. He resolved to see Norah, even if it must be in the presence of the Blue Jay gossips. He wrote a note and, taking it himself to the tap-room, waited a chance to slip it into her hands. But the chance did not come, and he was finally compelled to slip it into Manly's hand as that youth lingered fondly about him. He asked Manly why he didn't come of an evening to the boat-house, and the boy aggrievedly confided to him that Mr. Dunn had told his mother that it was improper for a young girl to be in the streets so late without a grown person for escort. That he had offered to walk with Norah, but that she had not cared to go out since the evening they has been on the water.

So, he reflected, as he strode away, it is that prig, Marcus, that has interfered ! What could it mean ? Was he fond of Norah ? Was he winning her love ? The thought amused him. No, Norah's love was his, but all the same Dunn had put notions into her head that changed her from the paradisaic innocence he had first loved in her. She, who had never dreamed of such a thing as propriety or impropriety ! Oh, it was damnable to destroy the perfect child of Marbury, and he raged over the sinful handiwork of his kinsman as the companions of Cain when they found he had brought death into the conditions of life.

The small Manly, with the letter and a shilling alternately in his pocket and his mouth, retired to the stable to enjoy the sense of confidential minister, which was growing upon him. He had long known Darcy, as small boys know young men of their vicinage. He had admired the young prince darting down the winding roadways in the paternal park, and had stood aside with awe as the young patrician passed him on the street. Everybody knew Darcy, and the young boys admired his free hand on the fourth of July, and the wonderful pyrotechnical exhibitions which he made from the Warchester façade on those jubilee occasions.

When, therefore, Darcy's whispered confidences at the boat-house had made Manly a sort of comrade, that small conspirator had much the feeling of an acolyte called into the mysteries of the Delphic oracle. The letter would confirm this mystic bond. Perhaps it would bring the delights of the boat-house and the row on the river. Manly debated with the colt in the stable the best way of reaching Norah unseen by all eyes. It would not do to call her away from his mother, for that kindly soul was curious in all that went on. It would not do to wait until Norah went to her room, for then it would be too late to go to the boat-house. Manly thought of various devices to bring Norah to him. At first he meditated cutting his finger and setting up a great shout, for, whenever he met with the misfortunes that seem to come to small boys impartially, Norah was always the first to fly to him. But he wisely concluded that, if he cut his finger, he could not paddle in Darcy's boat, and that was a sacrifice he could not summon resolution to make until all other expedients failed.

While he stood staring reflectively into the wide-opened eyes of the colt, as it nibbled at the hayseed clinging to his garments, he heard his mother's voice calling to him. Thrusting the letter into his pocket, he hurried out. His mother was on the back porch with her bonnet on, ready to go out. She commanded her son to accompany her to the market—it was market-day—and pointed to a basket he was to carry. Manly looked ruefully into the kitchen —Norah was nowhere about—and, with sad misgivings that he shouldn't enjoy Darcy's boat that evening, he trudged off with his mother. At the market Mrs. Blythe fell in with a farmer whose store of butter was too tempting to let go, and she directed her son to get into the vehicle and show the man where to take it. Manly's eyes glistened. This was just the chance to get Norah alone, and see what the letter meant.

"Tell Norah to get the money out of my drawer to pay for the butter," Mrs. Blythe said as the boy climbed up into the wagon beside the driver. Manly noticed the man start as his mother spoke, and wondered why he looked so fixedly at her. Manly remarked that the man was not a farmerlike-looking person ; that he was much better dressed than the farmers who came to town, and that, unlike most of them, he had no beard. When they had driven a little way, the man turned to the boy and said :

"Norah is your sister?"

"No, she's our cousin," Manly said, vaguely conscious of misleading the pensive stranger, but not liking to admit that there was no tie between such close friends.

"Ah !"

The wagon was driven into the stable and the butter lifted out, Manly meanwhile flying into the house to give Norah the precious letter. She was alone in the tap-room, arranging the curtains. Manly delivered the letter first, and then his mother's message. She opened the envelope, read it with glistening eyes and smiling lips, Manly watching her eagerly. As she finished, a man's voice at the kitchen-door said :

"I say, my boy, the butter's in ; who's to pay me ?"

Norah turned white, trembled, and reeled against the table, the note falling from her hand. A heavy step sounded on the hall floor, and, with a low cry, she fled through the front door to the stairway, and never stopped until she was in her room and the door locked. Manly, amazed and terrified, followed, and begged to be let in.

She opened the door, and the child burst into a passion of sobs at her white face and trembling limbs.

"Ah! Manly, Manly, don't let that man see me! Don't let him know I am here! O my God! my God! what shall I do?"

"Why, Norah, it's only the farmer with the butter. Mother sent him up for you to pay him."

She gave the boy the key of the money-drawer and bade him find out the price or wait for his mother to pay. Byron, meanwhile—for it was he who had entered the tap-room—heard Manly's step on the stairs, and thought, quite naturally, that he was going to tell the person charged with the business to get the money. As he sank into a chair his eye spied the open note lying on the floor. Glancing a second time, he saw the name "Norah." There was no sound in the lower part of the house. He picked the paper up and read:

"MY DARLING NORAH: You are not the sweet girl you were at Marbury, or you would never treat me so coldly. What have I done that you can no longer see me? Has some one else won your love? Unless you come to me this evening at the boat-house, I shall believe this, and I shall always be your heart-broken

"DARCY."

Byron thrust the note into his wallet as Manly's noisy step was heard upon the stair. He took the money the boy handed him and drove away. When he was gone, Norah, hurrying down, found only the envelope of Darcy's note, which she thrust into her bosom; too deeply agitated to miss the inclosure, she returned to her household work. Poor Norah was cruelly perplexed. It was fear of herself and fear for Darcy that disturbed her. Byron had breathed his suspicion to her that it was Darcy's love that filled her heart. He had sworn an awful oath that the young man should feel his vengeance if he trifled with her, and she felt that Byron was capable of all that he threatened. The voice in which he had told Amelia that he would cut her throat sounded in poor Norah's ears whenever she recalled his fierce protest of his wicked love for her.

She trembled at every strange step she heard on the veranda, and couldn't get rid of the paralyzing fear that Byron knew her whereabouts and that his eye was watching her. When Marcus came in the evening she was silent and distressed, starting at every sound. He was reading "Ivanhoe" to her, and she confusedly thought of Byron whenever the wicked Templar came on the scene to distress Rebecca. Darcy had given her the book to read long before, and it was Rebecca's melancholy fate that had given her a dismal and abiding premonition that it prefigured what her own fate might be. For wasn't Darcy a knight more splendid than Ivanhoe, and wasn't she the sad daughter of a ruined family, more alien to his proud kin than the hapless Hebrew maid? Yes, his love for her could only drag Darcy down, and she would wear her poor heart out rather than let woe come to that godlike being.

Marcus meanwhile had been startled anew by the artist. That dashing youth came often of an evening and made merry in the homely group, and Norah welcomed him with a glad smile that tortured the elderly lover. Darwin had established himself on the most friendly footing in the house, and was, to Dunn's dismay, called "Mr. Fred" by Manly and his mother. Norah prattled as artlessly and innocently with the gay young fellow as if he had been a member of the family, and the unhappy Marcus saw that his younger rival was winning an intimacy that Norah seemed tacitly to deny him, her old friend. So that evening, when the chance came, and he was alone with the maiden, he said:

"I'm going to row on the river to-morrow; won't you come with me?"

"Oh, yes," she said, simply; "Manly is very fond of the boats, and he will be very glad of the chance."

He had not bargained on Manly's being of the party, but she said it so guilelessly that he could not suspect that she had any motive. Nor had she. Manly's going seemed as natural to her as her own, and she spoke of it only because the thought of his pleasure was the first that came into her head. As he walked to his room Marcus devised with himself measures to get rid of the small boy, making no doubt but he could bring that to pass.

Sitting at her window, Norah watched the moon as she had often sat watching it at Marbury. Her heart was sore and heavy. She was giving Darcy pain. She could never explain to him that it was his good she had at heart in denying his prayer; that, as they could never mate, it would be better they should never meet. Ah, there was the thought that burned—that embittered—the blessed victory over self. Conscience, that pleaded with a still, small voice to Darcy, stood with rod and branding-iron in the mind of Norah. The spasmodic resolution, that gave Darcy such complacent satisfaction, brought sharp pain and the vista of unsatisfied yearning to Norah. It was a conquest of the demon with Darcy, it was the thorns and the cross to Norah.

CHAPTER XXI.

BRISEIS.

THE little Manly, very exuberant and impatient, meeting Darcy the next morning, confided to that mercurial lover the great event of the afternoon. How Norah and Marcus were to row on the river as far as Verulam Pond to gather lilies; how they were to picnic in the grove, and how they were to take him, Manly! Darcy heard the tale with outward composure and inward raging. Marcus, as a kinsman of the Warchesters, kept a small boat in the water-pavilion, but he rarely used it. When, in the early afternoon, the three set out, Darcy, hidden among the laurel bushes, watched Norah and her elderly adorer. He chafed angrily at her oblivious gayety. She looked wistfully at the curtained window of the jutting alcove where he had welcomed her, but did not enter the place.

Marcus was not outwardly perturbed, but he was strangely reticent and capricious in using the oars. Norah laughed immoderately at these landsmen tricks, sitting at the tiller as the skiff wobbled among the cat-tails on leaving the shore.

It was a sultry afternoon in early September; the faint glow of autumn was just distinguishable among the maples of the low hills. Manly usurped most of the noisy pleasure of the jaunt. Marcus found no pretext for disposing of the urchin, though he would have been grateful to the boy had he gone turtle-hunting, as he had hinted his purpose to do. At sundown they spread a cloth on the moss, and shared the edibles provided for the sylvan supper. Manly became more adventurous, but Norah kept him near her. They returned to the boat in the soft, transparent twilight, and while the western sky was still aglow reached the pavilion.

Manly insisted on a furlough to gather cat-tails, and he was allowed to remain in the boat, while Norah and Marcus sat on the veranda watching him as he cut the slender stems. They sat some time in pondering silence. The stars came out, and the water plashed tranquilly below them. Manly was at a safe distance, and Marcus, with a deep tremor in his voice, said :

" Norah, do you know why I asked you to come out on the river with me to-night ? "

She looked at his grave face in a startled doubt, as if her mind had been far away, sighing softly at her thought, rather than the suggestion of his words, then answered falteringly, " Oh yes, Mr. Marcus, because you were very kind, and knew it would give Manly and me pleasure."

" Yes, Norah, it was partly that, but it was a selfish kindness, for I wanted the chance for a greater pleasure than I can give you ; Norah, my child, I asked you here to tell you I love you, that I want you to be my wife. You are so innocent, so unlike the girls of the world, that you have had no suspicion of the feelings that have been growing in me since the happy day I saw you in your present home. Any other girl but you would have known the meaning of my—my devotion to you these many months ! I haven't known whether to be happy or sad over your unsuspecting behavior. Sometimes I have thought you knew and shared my feelings, but I fear that what I am saying is a surprise to you—is it ? "

" O Mr. Dunn, it is a very great surprise ! "

" But, Norah, dear Norah, it is not, I hope, a very disagreeable surprise, is it ? " He took her unresisting hand eagerly. " I am not a young fellow ; I am not, I know, as attractive to a girl like you as many of the young men

14

you see, but I know I can make you very happy if you will give me the right to care for your happiness."

She sat painfully still, her eyes fixed on the rippling waves, that now began to take the tinge of the broad line of yellow light falling, as it seemed, from the vast fringe of forest crowning the Holly Hills, where they touched the horizon. She trembled a little as he slipped his arm timidly, gently, about her waist, and whispered:

"One word, my darling Norah, just one word."

"O Mr. Dunn, the curse is on me; the curse is on me; I'm no wife for you; God forgive me! The curse is on me, my love is lost, my love is a curse!"

Her voice grew quite hoarse, and she trembled violently.

"O Mr. Dunn, misfortune comes to all that have to do with me; the sins of my kin are on my head. I can be no man's wife. My love is a curse! My heart is lost to me!"

"Trust me, Norah, I will find it. I know something of the burden of your sad life. I, Norah, knew your mother, and, my darling, it was my precious privilege to be a friend to her when she needed a friend; but," he added hastily, "I do not say this to win your consent. You must give me freely what I ask, or it would be more miserable for both of us. I want your love; surely, Norah, you could give me that!"

"It's my mother's curse that's on me—don't touch me —don't look at me! I'm not fit to be your love!"

"Hush, Norah, such talk is wild and wicked. A spotless girl like you should not cherish the superstitions of your race; trust me, love me, believe me and be my wife!"

"I can not love you; how could I be your wife?"

Marcus arose to his feet, and in the moonlight his face

was solemn and questioning, drawn into lines of patient
pain.

"Do you love some one else, Norah?"

"Every drop of blood in my veins, every breath that I
draw, every thought that comes into my head—God forgive me. I think my soul is another's!"

"Young Darwin, Norah?"

She looked at him helplessly, in a sort of dazed uncertainty, shook her head, and, breathing heavily, said
faintly:

"No, no; not him."

At this moment a crash was heard in the reeds, and a
sharp, frightened cry from Manly.

"Ah! Mr. Dunn, the child has fallen into the water!
He'll be drowned, and the guilt will be on my head."

Arising swiftly, Norah started as if to leap into the
water. Marcus pushed her gently back to the bench, saying quietly:

"Have no fear. The water is not deep, and Manly's
a good swimmer. Beyond a drenching, he'll come to no
harm."

He lifted one of the light boats, slipped it down the
grooved way into the water, and shot among the tall cat-
tails that obscured the surface of the stream. The current ran strong, and Manly's shouts grew fainter and
fainter. Norah stood at the rail, peering in eager apprehension into the silvery gloom. She started with a scream
and palsied limbs as a hand suddenly clutched her arm,
and the voice of Byron, husky and decisive, said, in mingled appeal and menace:

"Norah, you must come with me. Your home is under
my roof; you were left to me with Marbury; you are
mine. It was my father's will, and it is mine."

She sank on her knees—cowering, panic-stricken for a

moment, dumb—then raised her hands supplicatingly, her lips refusing to articulate the frantic prayer on her tongue.

"You must come with me, my girl—my love, my own love! Did you think that you could hide from me? By law you are mine. You are the daughter of my house; my father's will says it, and the law will uphold me in possessing you."

"Ah! no, no. Denny! Darcy! Oh, what shall I do, what shall I do? Father of the fatherless, help me, save me!"

"Do? Come at once, before that old fool gets back! The wagon is in the grove, a step from here. Come at once, for come you must, if I have to take you by force. If you resist, I will take you all the same."

"Oh, no, no!" She tried to raise her voice, but it broke, thin and gasping, as she called in agony, "Mr. Dunn! Mr. Dunn! save me!"

Byron bent down. With a giant wrench he tore her hands from the railing, to which she clung with piteous helplessness, and lifted her in the air. Then she found voice, and shrieked hoarsely. He put his hand over her mouth; then, supporting her against the rail, said determinedly:

"All your calls will do no good, even if Dunn were here. I am your guardian, and the law gives me a right to hold you until you are a wife. Furthermore, I am a magistrate, and I have a warrant for your arrest for theft."

That dreadful sentence did swift work. Had it been a bullet, the effect could not have been more decisive. Further threats were not needed. Norah fell limp and helpless into his arms. But, as he bent forward to support her, a strong hand seized him by the shoulder and flung him against the railings, and a passionate voice said:

"You miserable coward, how dare you impose on an innocent girl like that! How dare you lay your vile hands upon her! You ought to have every bone in your villainous body broken!" and, stooping over Norah, Darcy lifted her tenderly.

Byron, stunned by the shock, did not at first recognize Darcy, but in a moment he recalled the shapely figure, the imperious gesture, the high-bred face, in the moonlight. As Darcy bent to raise Norah, Byron made a savage spring, and, catching the slender, graceful stripling by the body, lifted the light, struggling form clear from the floor. He carried him to the edge of the balcony, and, with a mighty wrench, got the body on a line with the balustrade. But Darcy, regaining his wits, caught the rail, and held it so pertinaciously that Byron was forced to release his hold. Then, with his clenched fist, he dealt the young man a deadly blow square in the face. Darcy reeled like one shot. He was, in fact, lifted from his feet; as he fell, his head struck the sharp edge of the open door, where he lay supine and helpless. Byron, however, had another antagonist at the same instant. Marcus had fished Manly out of the water, and heard the confused noise of struggle. As Darcy fell, he confronted Byron on the porch.

"What does this mean? Who are you?"

"I am that girl's guardian, and I'm going to take her home."

Dunn's eyes fell upon Norah lying upon the floor. He bent over her in cruel despair, and lifted her up.

"Open the door, Manly," he said to the child, pointing to the pavilion.

He carried Norah in, and poured some spirits into her mouth through the compressed lips. She opened her eyes dreamily. A candle had been lighted, and she looked about her in perplexity.

"I reckon she's ready to go now," Byron said, and pushed nearer to Norah.

"My man, I don't know who you are, but, I assure you, Norah does not go with you without her free consent. Norah, do you wish to go with this person?"

She shuddered, "Oh, no. No! Never, never! O Mr. Marcus! don't let him take me. He—he—" She covered her face, and broke into convulsive sobs.

"Have no fear, Norah; you shall not be molested further. Sir, you must withdraw from here; the poor girl needs repose. This is private property; it is the Warchester estate. You are trespassing, and liable to arrest."

Before Byron could answer, Manly, who had been on the outside, tugged at Marcus's coat, and whispered in a frightened tone:

"Mr. Darcy is out there, and I think he's dead!"

Marcus darted out. Darcy was lying where Byron had flung him. In an instant he was lifted up and carried into the light. His head was bleeding profusely, and blood covered his face. The movement aroused Norah. Recognizing the form, she arose with a prolonged, gasping, heart-rending cry.

"Didn't I tell you the curse was on me?" she cried hysterically. "It has brought him to his death! It has murdered him! Oh, my love, my love! let me die with you!"

She flung herself on the limp body, and Darcy, conscious of her presence, lifted his arm feebly to embrace her. She kissed the blood-stained lips, holding, with tender caressing, the head in her arms. Inexpressibly shocked, Marcus gently pushed her aside, bathed the bloody face, Norah hovering by, tearless and silent. Presently, when Darcy was able to recline on the chintz-covered couch, Marcus turned sternly to Byron:

"Sir, this is no place for you. This house is the property of this young man you have attempted to murder. You must be gone; the law will deal with you in good time."

"I will be gone," retorted Byron undauntedly, "when my ward is ready to go with me. Come, Norah, if you won't come peaceably, I will take you on a warrant."

"On a warrant upon what grounds?" cried Marcus.

"For theft!"

"Theft! What do you mean?" and Marcus turned to Byron as if for the first time free to inform himself of the sort of person the interloper was—whether malefactor or madman.

"She is in possession of jewels which she can give no explanation of," Byron said, in confident eagerness.

"I can give an explanation of them," and Darcy confronted Marcus. "I gave Norah the jewels a year or more ago, when my family visited Dr. Marbury."

Marcus started. His heart sank. Now he understood Norah's reticence. He would rather have had her admit the theft, for it would have been less misery to her in the end. Byron was in no wise surprised. He had suspected from the first. He said insolently to Marcus:

"I suppose, now that you find the sort of person she is, you will have no objection to my taking her home, where her folly will be buried in silence."

"I don't know what you may choose to mean by that, sir, but Norah is with friends, and shall remain with them until due process of law pronounces otherwise. You must leave this place. It is private property, and, if you are a magistrate, you must recognize that you are a trespasser."

"Very well, sir. I will go; but the law shall compel what you refuse," and Byron stalked out of the room with

an appealing glance at Norah, who never saw him at all,
nor was hardly conscious of his presence, since her fear
had fled while Darcy lay helpless beside her. The single
candle burned dimly in the pretty room, throwing out the
artistic *bric-à-brac* in grotesque relief, as the figures of
Marcus and Manly moved about, succoring the victims of
Byron's fierce wrath.

"This is no place for you, Norah. I will take you
home and return to Darcy. He will need care during the
night, and I will give it to him."

She looked from Darcy to Marcus in dumb, tearless
woe. Her glance pleaded to be allowed to stay, but Marcus
firmly lifted her up, and, with a sign to Darcy, he led her
from the room. It was a silent walk home; even Manly,
who rather enjoyed his dripping garments, trotted along
silently, deeply puzzled by the uncanny doings of the
tryst.

"Little boy," said Marcus, slipping something in Manly's hand, "it will be a great trouble to Norah if anything
that you've seen or heard to-night is spoken of at home.
You will be a little man, and not speak of it?" and, with
many profuse promises, Manly, proud of the atmosphere
of mystery into which he had been introduced, resolved
that bears and dragons should not frighten him into a dis-
closure.

"Be of good cheer, Norah; all will be well. I know
you and trust you, and whatever is for your good shall
be done."

She turned toward him with a wild light in her eyes,
seized his hand, and kissed it passionately, sacredly. He
withdrew it trembling, abashed, and hurried away to the
boat-house. Darcy still remained on the cot where they
had left him. He blushed guiltily when he met Dunn's
grave face, but let the elder speak first. He was weak

still, but the wound in his head was no longer bleeding. Dunn made him comfortable, and then asked :

"Wouldn't it be better for you to remain here than venture home? In your present plight you would only alarm your mother, and bring about questions that I fancy it would embarrass you to answer."

"Yes, by all means, I shall stay here, and to-morrow all signs of the fracas will be gone. What a beast it was ! "

Marcus for a moment did not reply. He got up and walked the floor in deep agitation. Darcy watched him, dreading the inevitable question that he felt sure was coming. At length, Marcus, as if having settled something in his own mind, drew a chair over to the couch, and said, in a repressed monotone, as if hardly daring to trust himself :

"Darcy, you have been a boy—a child—to me so long that I can hardly realize that you are a man. But you are a man, and I must talk to you as man to man. How long have you known Norah ? "

"Since the first summer we spent at Malvern—two years or more."

"That was before you were engaged to Agnes ? "

"Yes."

"And you loved Norah from the first ? "

"I loved Norah the first moment I saw her. I let myself love her as men love saints all that summer. Afterward I fought with myself and saw her no more for a year. Since then I have only seen her twice. I should never have seen her again if I hadn't heard this monstrous charge against her. Knowing that it was my fault, I have done all I could to find Norah, and let her know that I could safely for her and myself clear her from the charge. On my word of honor, I have never attempted to win her love otherwise. I asked her for a meeting to tell her of my plight to Agnes. She has avoided me. I knew she was coming here to-night with you, and I meant to take leave of her in your presence."

Marcus kept his troubled eyes on the culprit. When his confession ended, a glad light shone in them.

"Thank God, Darcy, I knew, I felt that the boy I had caressed, frank and honest, could never have been guilty in such a monstrous thing as the deluding of this sweet child! That you were imprudent, I can see; but that you have been guilty of willful deceit I can not believe. I love the child—in fact, no one that comes near her can escape loving. My heart, which was very heavy, is almost light now, for since you confess your wrong, though it may wrench the child's heart, it will not break it. Now that things are as they are, I must tell her that you are the promised husband of another, and strive thereafter with patience and devotion to win her to a new love. You, Darcy, can help me by refusing to see or communicate with her in any way. That, my poor boy, is the only amends you can make for the disaster you have brought upon a life that has never known much peace or joy!"

Darcy had covered his eyes with a movement of impatience; as the other waited, he murmured:

"I will do as you say, but, O Mark, I don't want her to hate me. I don't want her to be humiliated by having this from any other lips than mine! I will tell her in my way—on my word of honor—I will tell her, and I will quit her forever."

Marcus started and paced the floor. The disheartening truth flashed upon him that Darcy's love was real love; that, put to the test, he could not quit Norah as he glibly promised. There was a tremor in the young man's voice that told of a depth of attachment that he himself but dimly understood. Face to face with Norah, and on the verge of the ordeal of separation, a nature like Darcy's was capable of throwing prudence to the Fates, capable of daring family wrath or personal dishonor.

No, it would never do ! Darcy must not see Norah until a stronger head and an unshakable will stood between the lovers. He soothed the young man and dropped the subject, bidding him sleep to gather strength for the morrow. Presently the little room was quiet, Darcy breathing softly, and Marcus sitting by the window, his mind full of hope that in the end all would be well.

But Darcy was not asleep. A curious resolution had been brought about by the climax of the evening. He resented with peevish, resentful wrath, the interposition of Marcus in the drama of his love. How dared he, a chilly-blooded man of middle age, presume to judge the sacred sentiment of the heart of youth ? How dared a passionless prig like this grave mentor conclude that he, Darcy, was not capable of the magnaminity of standing before the world with Norah ? And to insult him by the suspicion that he had not been scrupulously heedful of Norah's reputation ! He, who had fled from the pleasant haunts of Marbury lest injustice might befall Norah ! He, who had remained in the dull circles of Malvern rather than add to Norah's miseries ! He who, in fine, promised his heart to another, that Norah might be spared doubt or compromising ! And this was the summing up of all his sacrifice !

He had wronged her ? he, who would have spilled his blood to save her a pang ! Oh, it was monstrous, and she was to hear the story of his betrothal from this love-sick old heart of ice ! Never ; if he had to see Norah before the whole world, he would himself tell her his struggle, point to his torn heart-strings, show her his remorse, part from her with the benediction of a forgiving kiss.

But why should they part ? Agnes was his promised

wife only because the families had set their hearts on the match! Why should he assent to be a mere thing of merchandise? What was it to him whether the Vane estates the Warchester's acres ever joined?

Faugh! all such Old World notions and caste traditions were disgusting in this republican country! He would do as Lord Poultney had done: he would defy public opinion; he would marry the girl of his heart. After all, he was his own master, and it was his own future that was at stake. And while Marcus's eye followed the broad moonlit path across the water to where it was lost in the dim shadows of the field of the dead, Darcy's heart buoyant with the delicious, torturing thought of love's fulfillment, his inner eyes saw Norah pillowed on his own bosom, and the felicity of true love for the reward of his constancy.

CHAPTER XXII.

THE CURSE OF THE ALIEN.

DARCY kept his room at home the next day, and his mother, who came anxiously to discover his ailment, saw with alarm the signs of the night's encounter. But he protested that it was nothing serious—merely the result of a bruise in falling; he was simply unwell, but needed no physician. Late in the day the servant came up to say that Denis Boyne implored a moment's speech. Darcy bade him come up, and as the lad entered the room Darcy's heart misgave him, for Denny's eyes were swollen, and he was trembling as if in an ague.

"Heavens! Denny, what is it? Norah—nothing has happened to her?"

"Ah, no. It's not Norah! It's worse than that, Mr. Darcy; I am disgraced and ruined."

"What is it, my lad? take heart." Darcy was so relieved by the assurance that Denny's misery was not on Norah's account that he was prepared to hear anything else with complacency.

"The brother that I've never seen since I was a child is in the 'Black Hawk' jail." Denny stopped—his sobs stifled him. He could utter no more. Darcy rose from the couch and put his hand on the youth's bowed head.

"Well, Denny, if he is in prison, we must get him out, that's all."

"He'll never leave prison. Ah! my God—my God! He's a murderer."

Darcy recoiled. "What! explain. It can't be possible. Tell me the facts."

Denny then related with choking sobs how, the day before, the town had been startled by a tragedy at Thebia, a small village on the river below Warchester. In a quarrel over some petty grievance, a young fellow had shot an overseer of the transportation line. When arrested, he had at first given one name, but, after a few hours in his cell, he had divulged the fact that his name was Lawrence Boyne; that he had a brother teaching in the city, and that he desired him to be sent for. Denis was summoned from the class-room and this dreadful story told him. He had visited the wretched criminal, and learned the circumstances of the tragedy. The murdered man had taken a malicious delight in provoking Larry, who was none too peaceable at best.

The two had known each other in Canada, where Larry had gone years before and served his term as a silversmith. The murdered man—Graham by name—had been in the same shop. A theft was discovered one day,

and Graham had ingeniously trained the circumstance to
bear upon Larry, who was guiltless. He afterward found
that Graham had himself done the theft. Larry had
vowed revenge, and, on meeting Graham, had thrashed
him mercilessly. Graham had in the presence of several
people threatened to "maim the Paddy" for life. The
two, after years of separation, were brought together in
the transportation office at Thebia, where Larry held a
responsible post in the accountant's department. In a
drunken frolic, Graham climbed into Larry's sleeping-room
window in the dead of night, and, taking him for a robber,
Larry had leaped from his bed and struck him with an
iron bar, fracturing his skull. Public sympathy, except
in Larry's office, was with the victim, who was a native,
and Larry only an "Irish immigrant." Graham had never
been able to speak after the blow, and Larry had promptly
been indicted for murder.

"If these facts can be substantiated, the worst that
can be made of the affair is manslaughter. I can't say to
you that there is no cause for grief—that would be untrue.
The stigma of the crime will attach to you among people
of narrow prejudices. But all that I can do, and all that
my family can do, shall be done to lighten the penalty of
your brother's madness. Go at once to my cousin Marcus Dunn. He is one of the foremost lawyers in the
city. He is Norah's friend." Darcy suddenly recollected
that Denny knew nothing of her whereabouts, and having
explained about her, and the motive for keeping him in
the dark, continued:

"Mark will take up Larry's case, and what clear brains
and a kind heart can do, you may be sure he will do."

He wrote to his cousin and hurried Denny away; then
sank back on the couch with a low cry of anguish. Larry's crime had in an instant dashed the airy towers, the

roseate pinnacles of his dreams. His mother, perhaps, might have been brought to consent to an alliance with obscurity, but even the happiness of her first-born would never weigh an instant when criminal notoriety was added to low birth.

Great was Manly's amazement during that eventful day to see a tall young man enter the Blue Jay, walk past the "tap" straight to the kitchen, whither, following him in wonder, he found Norah clasped in the young fellow's stout arms, and the two weeping and smiling together. Catching sight of Manly's startled face, Norah cried out eagerly:

"Manly, dear, this is brother Denny, and you must love him as you love me."

Manly was uncertain as to that; he couldn't bring his small mind to receive in amity a stranger who seemed to be free to rumple Norah's soft tresses, and kiss her as no one in the Blue Jay but he, Manly, had ever been permitted to do. It was asking a good deal to concede this to a stranger, but he would give the interloper a chance. However, so soon as Norah had whispered in his ear that it was Denny who had conjured all her fairy stories, and had told them to her, Manly made up his mind to the sacrifice unmurmuringly. Adversity should have some sweet uses, was the summing up of his thoughts, though he was far from formulating it so precisely.

Denny had resolved to keep the story of Larry's crime from Norah. There was no likelihood that she would ever hear of it, if the household could be cautioned, and that Marcus had not only suggested but promised to charge himself with. So Denny assumed a gayety he was far from feeling, even in the gladness and relief of Norah's restoration, as he called it. They sat for hours in Norah's pretty room, the green hills beyond the river recalling

Marbury, and the story of the long separation was told on each side.

Norah blushed and wept over Darcy's goodness to Denny, but said nothing to reveal any other sentiment than gratitude. And so Dilly was in his academy? She must go at once and see her. It would be quite like old Marbury days. But Denny did not respond to this suggestion. He knew that Larry's crime would drive him from the school, even if he had wished to remain. But he didn't. He had already arranged the terms in which he was to give up the place he had held with such pride.

He returned to the school late in the afternoon, and requested an interview with the principal. That austere dame had made a trying concession to her conscience in admitting an alien of the Irish race into the sacred precincts of her academy. But he came supported by such potent names that she had waived her scruples. She listened in dismay to Denny's brief summary of the situation, and heard, with a sigh of manifest relief, his conclusion that he must withdraw at once from the school. She dismissed him with frigid dignity, and mentally went through a spiritual ablution when the door closed behind the quondam instructor. Denny's most agonizing ordeal was yet before him. He must tell Dilly, before she heard it from strangers' lips, the cause of his leaving, and the miserable story of Larry's misdeed.

She came presently down the pleasant, shaded walk, and, espying Denny, left her companions to speak with him.

"Why weren't you at the lessons to-day, Master Professor? Everybody wondered, and you have been rated a very black mark, with punishment based upon the goodness of your excuses." She stopped suddenly as she caught his eye. "O Denny! forgive me, you have heard bad news! Norah? Something has happened to Norah?"

"No. On the contrary, Norah is safe, and I have seen her. Ah! Dilly, it is much worse than anything you can imagine. It is the loss of all I love, the flight of all my ambitions."

"Ah! Denis, don't talk in that way; you really frighten me. One would think you had committed a crime."

He turned deadly pale. "I have not committed a crime, Dilly, but my brother has. He is in the jail yonder, for striking a man dead."

"Your brother, Denny?" she faltered, stopping quite still, and supporting herself against a spreading elm. "I didn't know you had a brother."

"And I had forgotten it almost," echoed the poor fellow sadly. Then he recounted such glimpses of his youth as he remembered, ending with the circumstances of Larry's crime. They had reached the river-bank, where the thick laurels grew in sheltering groups. Dilly faced him when he ended, and said, with tears gleaming in her eyes:

"O Denis! must you always be a victim of caste and crime and misfortune not of your own doing?"

"Yes, Dilly. I have the alien's curse of social servitude upon me. I can not evade it. I am resigned to it now. What matter? The kinsman of a malefactor need excite no pity. If I were reviled simply because the sea rolls between this land and the land of my birth, what will be my fate now, pointed out as a felon's brother?"

"Only the ignorant will do that, Denis. Those who know you will love you all the same"—she colored, and her eyes glistened. "I—I shall, at least," and, with an adorable blush, she took his hand and pressed it confidingly. Denny looked in her eyes with a wild, despairing glance, tried vainly to utter something; then, falling on the bench beside her, with her two willing hands in his own, he broke out:

"It can't be true! Do you know, Dilly, what you say? Even when the future was a world of equality for me, I trembled to hint my love for you; and now—now, that all men will turn their back on me, you do not; you give me courage—you, O—O Dilly! If the unfortunate have the ear of Heaven, as the legends say, may they hear my blessings invoked on you and yours. You are not angry at my love! You are not ashamed to love me! O God! that hears us, as man flies from us, rain blessings on this sweet head, joy on this true heart! I may love you! I may love you!"

Dilly was smiling sweetly. "I think it is only right that you should love me a little, since I have loved you so long, and without a word from you that it was welcome."

The ineffable archness and tender modesty of this little speech restored the woeful lover. His sudden joy displaced his grief, and he fairly smiled as he pressed his lips unchecked to the brow of his beloved. Then he monologued excitedly about the angelic qualities his adored had exhibited. In short, Denis in love was much as men have been, are, and ever will be until the story which is never threadbare shall become a myth and take its place in the necrology of the gods. Then he broke into startling outbursts of wonder that he, of all the unworthy sons of the children of men, should have won this amazing boon; and he looked with such intensity at the merry eyes before him that Dilly broke into a tantalizing laugh—mocking him saucily:

"Really, Denny, all this seems as unreal as the fantastic stories you used to tell me as we walked home at Marbury. When I think of you, it is always as some sort of kinsman to the will-o'-the-wisps, banshees, and what not, that play the enchanting parts in your stories. Who knows, perhaps if I had really believed you were flesh and blood, as other boys were, I should never have been won by your sorrows or interested in your tales."

"But, Dilly! O Dilly! I do love you. If you should turn on me now, I won't say I should break my heart, for I should have none to break, but the sky would be without stars at night and sun by day, the waters would be bitterness to my mouth, and all that makes earth a refuge would be the misery of a bondage to me. Ah, Dilly, I love to see you merry, but don't deny your love!"

"What a silly fellow you are, Denny! There wasn't a boy at Marbury school that could have been blind so long as you were. Don't you know that with your breezy blarney you could win a queen's love? You don't mean it for blarney, I know," she said repentingly, as Denny raised a reproachful eye, "but don't you know, to sober people like us, all your charming conceits about fairies, elves, flower-goblins, and water-sprites are like the legends of Bible people? That tale you told me about the sunbeams was enough to win a girl's heart. That, however, is neither here nor there. Now, listen to the dark side. My worldly father can not be brought to consent to our marriage—" she blushed in the most charming manner— "so you are to say nothing of our vows until I give you leave. You must win a name of your own, and then I shall find it easier to bring father to see you as I see you. Tom likes you and mother likes you, but father has an Englishman's blood in some remote degree, and he hates the name of an Irishman. But he won't when he knows what a fine heart you have, how loyal you are, how modest, and how brave—"

"There won't be much modesty left, I fear, if you go on in this way. I feel now like a knight, accoutered in the saddle."

"But it is in the saddle the knight is in the greatest

danger. He may fall on his head if his arms are too heavy."

"Not if his heart is light and his conscience clear," whispered the sly rogue, and, blushing divinely, she assents with kisses—and—and— But there—I protest this love-making adds no light or shade, no character perspective to the story, and if not, why risk the sharp pen-thrusts of the critics over the maunderings of this pair? For, of course, stories are written, as carpenters make boxes, by rule and plane! No wise carpenter leaves the twigs, be they ever so fragrant, on his timbers, nor employs the graceful curve of the branches in completing his polygon! It was only Portia's caskets that bore tales on the sides as well as within. Still, it may be well to remember that the eminent critic Shylock missed the moral of his story by refusing to take in the details. He wanted the flesh, but hadn't patience to think of the blood, and the heart, and all the small accessories, without which the pound of flesh made murder!

So, let us look benignantly on Denny's love-lapses; they are not so moving as Darcy's, for in those warring impulses we read between the good and evil of human purpose; we confront the mysterious problem of right and wrong, a problem which, like truth, has many aspects, and is resolved helpfully or hurtfully for good or ill, by the qualities that are brought to bear on the relation. This Darcy was beginning dimly to see. He waited feverishly for Denny's report on the tragedy—but there was little balm for his eager and wounded spirit. Larry would suffer the penalty for manslaughter, and Norah would be a felon's sister. Now, how plain and pitiable his past conduct seemed to him! If he had manfully taken Norah by the hand and led her to his mother, before this shadow had come upon her life, the proud woman might have relented for the sake of her boy's love. Was the retaliation on his cowardice the outcome of the slow movement of moral retribution? Was leaden-heeled justice clinching its iron hand for another blow?

Darcy cursed himself with bitter curses. He felt that morally he was a blacker sinner than the malefactor in the jail yonder, for he had struck in passion, but he, Darcy, had breasted the passion that was holiest, and struck in cowardly, in cold blood! And Norah—what was to become of her? Would the fastidious Marcus now share his irreproachable life, his stainless name, with the sister of misfortune and crime!

CHAPTER XXIII.

A WOMAN'S REASON.

WARCHESTER, whose doings are now chronicled in a dozen journals, daily and weekly, by a trained phalanx of reporters, had, in the period of which I am writing, but one rudely printed sheet, appearing once a week, and singularly enough rarely devoted a line to events happening in or near the city. "Social news," the life of the modern journal, was, in those days, relegated to the tea-parties and tap-rooms. The editor of the "Columbian" was a New World Walpole who, for many years, filled a conspicuous place in the public eye. The great mind of this publicist was given exclusively to the making of governors, presidents, and senators, and within the scope of his vision such trivial incidents as the life and movements of a locality never halted long enough to take form. It thus happened that Larry's crime and incarceration were not known outside of the headquarters of the gossipers, and as the topic was not of a sort to divert the tea-tables, the higher circles of the town barely knew that some vulgar ruffian had murdered some other vulgar ruffian, and, with a languid regret that both had not suffered from the same blow, refined society dismissed the event.

Criminal trials were held in the distant town of Canderauga, whither the culprit was removed so soon as the Grand Jury had acted on the indictment. Denny was thus spared the ordeal of his shame being the town topic, and all else concerned were spared the knowledge of the fact of the trial itself. The Vanes, with Agnes, had been in Bucephalo a fortnight covering the preceding events, and Darcy was spared perhaps the bitterest pangs of his self-wrought wretchedness. One day Mrs. Blythe, prattling in the dining-room with Norah, was surprised by a visit from the Warchester housekeeper, who came with madam's compliments to ask if Mrs. Blythe would permit Norah to go to the great house to help in the preparation of a banquet, to be given a distinguished party of foreigners, making a tour of the country. Mrs. Warchester's cook had fallen ill, and as the fame of the Blue Jay had spread since Norah's coming, Madame Warchester made bold to ask Mrs. Blythe if she would spare the young woman to direct the Warchester maids in the preparation of such things as she did best. Norah, of course, was willing, and was installed in the great house, applying her cunning recipes for the dainties Mrs. Warchester coveted. That lady received Norah very graciously, recalled her sojourn under the Warchester roof at the time of her accident, and in every way showed herself sensible of Norah's handiwork.

Wide verandas, shaded by swinging veils of Virginia creepers, syringa, and clematis, ran quite around the

Warchester house to the kitchen doors. This apartment was like an ancient baronial hall, in amplitude of dimensions—quite unlike the kitchens of to-day, even in fine mansions—nor was the mistress of the house, no matter how pretentious or exclusive, the rare visitor in this odorous domain she is to-day. Our grandmothers were proud of their aptitudes in the kitchen, and the ministers at the altar of the palate were more friends than domestics in the family circle. The second day of Norah's lieutenancy she left the kitchen and sat down with some trifling work near the dining-room window, hidden under a mass of fragrant creepers. By turning her head she could see far into the drawing-room. Mrs. Warchester was engaged in replacing some tapestry near the buffet, when Norah heard a domestic saying :

"He is a country-looking person, ma'am, and I think may be for his pay."

"Ah, very well; show him in here !"

Norah went on with her work, until the tone of a voice she knew, a voice that made her heart stop beating, sounded distinctly :

"I crave your pardon, Madame Warchester ; I would not have disturbed you, but duty compels me." There was a rustle of skirts and the noise of a chair placed against the wainscot. The voice continued : "I called at the bank to see the Colonel, but they told me that he was in New York and would be there for some time. I don't know, after all, but it is best that you should hear what I have to tell ; as a mother has more influence over a son than a father. Yes, madam," Byron continued—for it was his voice that froze Norah's blood, and fixed her to the fatal spot as firmly as if she had been nailed there or mesmerized—"your son has deprived our family of a daughter. I don't mean that he has carried her off, but he has been

the cause of her leaving her home and coming to this city."
Thence Byron continued, ingeniously bringing into the
circumstantial chain all that he knew or conjectured,
winding up with an account of his discovery of Norah at
the boat-house with Darcy.

"Now, of course, your son can't mean marriage with
our poor girl, for if all else were out of the way, I understand he is engaged to be married to Miss Vane. I have
come to you to ask your help in persuading this poor
deluded girl to return to her home. As it is, your son
threatens to resist by law, and we have no money to throw
away in that luxury."

Before Mrs. Warchester could make response, while
the words were still on Byron's lips, Norah heard a quick
step on the threshold, then an imperious voice: "You
low-bred scoundrel; what are you doing in this house?
—I beg your pardon, mother, but no other treatment is due
this ruffian : he tried to murder me in the dark.—Leave
this house instantly, or the servants shall fling you out;
go—"

"As I have finished the business that brings me here,
sir, I shall go," and, with a reverent inclination to Mrs.
Warchester, Byron retired, keeping a wary eye on Darcy,
who, however, turned his back on his foe.

"Ah, Darcy—my son—my son ! Can this horrible story
be true? Oh, it can't be ! No son of mine would so de-
grade himself—say it isn't true."

"Say what isn't true? What has that skulking sneak
told you? If it be anything to my discredit, it is a lie; if
it be that I love an honest, sweet girl—fit to be a king's
wife—it is true. The scoundrel told you the story, did
he? Well, I was going to tell you myself. I can tell it
now, and you can see how far his malice goes. I met
Norah the summer we were at Malvern. Her gentleness,

modesty, and amazing innocence enchanted me. Before I thought of myself I was so wrapt up in her that I could do nothing, go nowhere, that her image didn't come before me. I gave up the summer to walks and talks with her. Then I recalled your ambitions and the purpose you had, and, as you have been the best mother that son ever had, I fled from the temptation of my heart.

" I never saw or wrote to Norah for more than eighteen months. I should never, probably, have seen her had the wife of this wretch—young Marbury—not accused Norah of stealing the jewels I gave her—trifling things for a keepsake. Her brother came to me in his trouble, and I promised to aid him in discovering the fugitive. She was living in the city—in the next square—at the Blue Jay. She is there now—and—ah, mother, she is an angel ; she is in every sense above her condition. She is a finer lady than any we see in Warchester. She is well read, has fine manners, and—and—I love her."

He dropped on his knees and buried his head on his mother's lap. She stroked his hair soothingly. She began in a low, agitated voice, that gradually deepened into a tremulous pathos :

" My son, you have been grievously tempted, and you have acted like a Warchester—what that means from me, you know. But now—you have lost your poise. You love this poor girl, you say—you have told Agnes that you love her— Stay ! let me speak, and then I will listen. You have, therefore, done a great wrong to Agnes, in winning her love under false pretenses. Now, having done this wrong, is it better to make it worse by throwing your life away on a low-born ? Ah, I make no reflection, mind ! Is it like a Warchester to lie—to steal ? for you do both in deserting Agnes. But, of that part of the matter I will say no more. You love this girl ; you

15

would marry her. Why? Because, being a simple child, who had never, probably, seen a young man woo her, she gave her heart to you. It came lightly, Darcy! it will go as lightly. Ah, trust me. I know. But, admitting that you have a moral obligation to her, you are dispensed in the eye of man and God, for within a week her brother is to stand his trial for murder. Even Agnes herself, if in the same relationship, wouldn't expect you to fulfill a pledge given. No law demands it, social or religious.

"No, Darcy, you must do your duty, as the Vanes and the Warchesters have always done their duty. You must purge yourself of this low-born passion. It would be the death of your father; it would be to me an inexpressible shame; I should never lift my head again in the ranks of my equals. No, Darcy, if you feel that you owe me anything as your mother and best friend, now is the time to prove it, by acting at once in such a manner as will show this unfortunate girl that your condescension to her was only such as a superior may show an inferior."

At this he broke into something like an imprecation. He had arisen, and was facing his mother—now perfectly mistress of the field, and herself; she regarded him steadily, kindly, the overweening pride of race softened by the immeasurable love for her first-born.

Darcy had expected a violent outbreak, indignant reproaches, and scornful references to his low-born love. He had not counted on his mother's far-sighted calmness, her placative and direct reasoning. He could have met denunciation, and the charge of unfilial conduct; he could have taken with savage joy the burden of an ingrate; but against this impenetrable array of reason and fact he felt disarmed, helpless. Knowing his mother's pride, the almost mystic reverence for gentility in the social accidence of life, her haughty intolerance of the unequal in the world's advantages, he had prepared himself for anger, scorn, upbraiding, command. He was impotent before an argument based on solidity itself, calm, kindly, addressed to his heart as well as his head.

He had anticipated that Agnes would be used as the strong rock of his mother's position, and he had prepared to meet the indictment of infidelity, treachery, by the plain fact that his pledge to the girl was not of his own initiative and impulse, though voluntarily given; that the love-making had been perfunctory, the courtship formal. That there was no reality in the love between them. That Agnes would release him with a light and untouched heart. But the mother had astutely evaded this. She had arrayed reasons that, in spite of his anger, his desperate purpose, shook him in the whirl of doubt. Denny in his place, we may be sure, would have found wits and words to expose the sophistry of the mother's argument. But Darcy was not a free agent in the combat. He had given hostages to cowardice—to the enemy of his hope. He was conscious of ulterior compacts, of moral infirmities in the integrity of his desires, that left him morally crippled before the worldly craft of his parent.

We fashion our own shackles. We sin and we suffer in this world, but we suffer often almost as much when we sin least. The forces that make us strong are the instruments of our own self-torture. Our sighs and sorrows are as often for the sin undone as the sin committed. It is a mere whim that turns a paradox into an axiom; a mere point of view that transforms wrong into right, selfishness into magnanimity. The cast from the dead face of vice is as comely as the lines left by virtue in the plastic mold. Caprice rules with as sure a hand as constancy, for it has new life for its forces, while constancy wields but one set of faculties. However, these formulas were only dim and vague to Darcy. He lived before the cult of sweetness and light had become a craft in the hands of the sophisticated, and he confronted his dilemma as inadequate in arms as the red men who combated Cortez or Pizarro. He found voice to say, desperately:

"And you think, mother, that I am nothing to—to Norah? That I have done no wrong in encouraging her love, that I shall do no wrong in denying her now?"

"How absurd you are, Darcy! She must be sensible enough to know that the gallantries of a high-born young man like you have no meaning. She is not an adventuress, nor an evil-minded young person. I think she would be the first to tell you that she was mad or criminal if she counted on the wreck of your life to satisfy her vanity. Agnes will be back to-morrow; pass your time with her. In her wit and gayety you will soon forget the silly charms of this wild-wood Phyllis, and by-and-by the army will give your mind new pleasures to occupy it."

She arose and drew the handsome head to her bosom, kissed the averted cheeks, and passed from the room. Left alone, Darcy walked the floor in agitation. He couldn't even think. The place grew stifling; he passed out of the window to the veranda, and paced backward and forward in the mellow sunlight. A noisy cat-bird, chattering in the vines of the farther window, distracted him, and he walked pensively toward it. He started in anguish. There, lying prone on the leaf-strewn floor, Norah was before him, pulseless and still. Her face was down, and her right arm was doubled under her. She was quite cold when he lifted her head. He pressed her wildly to his bosom, imploring her to speak, to open her eyes. He shouted for aid. In a moment his mother came hurriedly through the dining-room. She realized the situation at a glance.

"Carry her to my room," she said gently. "She has fainted."

So soon as the girl had been placed on the couch, the mother said :

"Go and send Reed to me. And Darcy, of course, it won't do for you to be in the room when the girl recovers, and the servants are here."

Darcy, hardly hearing this admonition, flew to the housekeeper's room, told her the exigency, and then, recollecting his mother's injunction, put on his hat and stalked out on the lawn. A new link in the chain of consequences had been forged. Norah had suffered the bitterness of death. Now he could pursue the advice of worldliness and prudence. Before, he had dreaded the revelation to her. Ah ! that ordeal was now passed. She had evidently heard all ; she would see that it was not his fault ; that he had been willing to sacrifice all, and that his mother's irresistible reasoning had prevailed. If there could be such a thing as hate in her gentle breast, she could not feel it for him, for he had given no sign that he would not keep the tacit pledges of his long courtship. An image of himself free, untrammeled, the center of the social adulation that had made his father's life a patrician dream, arose before him.

Loveless, in the delicious sense that he associated with Norah, very likely he would be. But, after all, love becomes a small thing as men settle down to the business of life and the rearing of families. Then this image grew hateful to him. He shuddered at its complacent smirk, its shallow semblance of manliness, its mock abnegation of all that distinguishes heroism from sham. But the end was bewilderment, and when, as the dusk fell, he entered his mother's room, he was in the crisis of revolt. She knew it in an instant, and warily placated his rising protest. Norah was restored and tranquil. She would be perfectly well before the night ended. The physician was with her, Mrs. Blythe, and Denis. But she must not be agitated by anything that would recall the cause of her attack. She, Mrs. Warchester, had withdrawn so soon as consciousness was restored, and Darcy must under no circumstances be seen by the invalid. Why not run up to Bucephalo for a few days? It would be the very best thing for everybody concerned. It would avert gossip, and perhaps scandal, and it would give him time to meet Agnes in a more tranquil frame of mind. This last dexterous stroke was enough. The very thought of meeting Agnes, with the hideous results of his treachery before his eyes, fairly maddened him. His portmanteau was ready in a few minutes, and he was in the Red Jacket as it drew out from the Rialto as the yellow sunbeams threw lingering shadows over the peaceful streets.

CHAPTER XXIV.

SWEET BELLS JANGLED OUT OF TUNE.

WHEN Norah was able to leave Warchester Manor, as madam was fond of hearing the great mansion called, it was not to return to the Blue Jay, though Manly's paroxysms of despair would have moved her soft heart had she witnessed his rage and grief when he learned that the brother was to take his fairy queen to a cottage of her own.

Marcus, who had conceived a deep affection for Denny, had compared notes with the boy, and pointed out the necessity of removing Norah from the vicissitudes of the life she had been leading. Among Marcus's possessions was a pretty villa on the banks of the Caribee, which he had fitted up for a maiden aunt, who had occupied it but a few months when death broke up the domestic union.

Denny was given a place as clerk in Marcus's office, and, with the pay from this and some tutoring his patron procured, he would be able to support the small expense of this little home. It was to this tranquil retreat, nestling at the edge of the Holly Hills, that Norah came with a little train, of which Manly was the most demonstrative and disconsolate. But when Norah kissed his freckled cheek, and showed him a little chamber under the peaked gable that was to be his own nook to play in or sleep in, he became reconciled in a measure ; and thereafter Manly was a member of the small household, where of an afternoon Mrs. Blythe came with her sewing, to keep track of the wayward truant, and counsel Norah in her new responsibilities. To crown all, the skill and eloquence of Marcus Dunn had snatched Larry from the perils that threatened. The case was much more favorable to the young man when the scattered witnesses, at first inaccessible, had been heard. The jury, after very short deliberation, returned a verdict of justifiable homicide, and Larry, a transformed if not redeemed man, joined Denny in maintaining the home for their sister. It was a modest frame cottage, embowered in foliage, where the sweep of the river could be seen from all the southern windows, and an air of repose gave it the charm Denny loved.

In this retreat Norah was mistress, but only in name, for she was quite unconscious of her surroundings. Her mind had suffered a curious eclipse. She knew Denny and Marcus, Manly and the Blythes, but she looked in vague alarm at Larry when he came into the room. The past was completely obliterated, so far as she gave any sign. Her strength was all her own again, and she was the same tender, confiding playfellow for Manly; but of the past she never spoke, and, if it were alluded to, she looked distraught and troubled.

Watching her sometimes of an evening, as he pored over his law-books, Denny trembled as the resemblance to his mother came back, recalled by Norah's fanciful speeches or inconsistent actions. She was never tired of retelling stories to Manly, and the boy was a more regular inmate of the cottage than of the Blue Jay.

Marcus alone conjectured the cause of Norah's mental aberration—though this is too strong a term to describe it. Only those who knew her intimately saw anything indicating mania in her listless conduct. Larry, who had never seen her since her childhood, had no suspicion that she was in any sense different from the rest of the family. She had a natural gift for music, and when Marcus sent a piano to the cottage, she passed hours in evoking the tender melodies she had not heard since childhood. Her tones were rich and soft, and there was no joy so great for Marcus as to sit in Denny's little study and listen to the soft strains stealing from the cozy parlor, where Norah, quite oblivious of his quality of guest, played on for hours without addressing him a word. She received him precisely on the same footing as Larry, whose constant presence in the house seemed at first to puzzle her, until she saw that Denny treated him with yearning tenderness.

It was Denny's purpose to wean his brother from his old ways and tippling habits. The furnace of his late trial had burned all that was vicious out of the prodigal. He came to adore Denny, and his softest remonstrance was an inexorable command to the duller understanding of the elder. He resumed his trade, and was regarded with great satisfaction by his employers. To this tranquil domesticity Dilly often came of an evening to take tea and revive the memories of Marbury with Norah. But, though the latter listened with evident understanding, she never mentioned the beloved places or the ancient scenes of childhood. Marcus had with kindly tact hinted enough to put Dilly on her guard, and she soon dropped the dangerous theme. She helped Norah with her music, but she soon saw that what was not naturally in Norah's possession she learned with difficulty. She could "play by ear" almost anything she had once heard, but the science or its application bewildered her. And so the winter passed, and the soft airs of a mild April coaxed the buds and blossoms into bewildering beauty in the leafy lanes about the Holly Hills.

Norah drank new life in the arousal of Nature, and her eyes grew strangely bright in her rambles among the hills. One day of delicious balminess, when the arrogant robins chattered defiance from the starry branches, she wandered with little Manly to the river's vernal brim, gathering forget-me-nots and twining them with arbutus. She sat on a mossy bank, winding them about her hair, until Manly cried out in rapture at the sight :

"O Nody, you're just like Mab in the picture-book. I will get the car and we will play fairy."

He scampered off to get the car, and presently she heard his step behind her.

"Come, Oberon, harness your shoulders with this line of arbutus, and we will fly through the air !"

But Manly did not move. She turned petulantly to upbraid him. Standing behind her, his eyes dilated and incredulous, stood Darcy, all the blood gone from his face. She did not cry out. She did not even look surprised. She rose demurely, and, walking to him, said archly :

"I saw you coming over the hills—flying—flying. I saw you when the banshee made you sign the black-book,

but I knew you wouldn't break your oath.   I sang all the
days to distract the banshees, and I prayed all night that
your heart might be strong."

She put up her two arms, wound them around his
neck as he had taught her to do at Marbury, and, pressing
his head down, thrilled him to the marrow with the old,
lingering kiss.   It was said and done with a movement so
simple, so natural, so seductive, that it was only at the
meeting of the lips—a meeting that makes a man saint or
devil, according to the fiber of him—that Darcy realized
the situation.   He had gone to Bucephalo while she lay
under his mother's roof.   From Bucephalo, tortured and
unequal to the part before him at home, he had joined a
party of exploring engineers in the Marquette Peninsula,
and was only a few days home.   Of Norah, all he had
heard was that she was living contentedly with her brothers.   But it was not said where.   The meeting, therefore,
was as unsought as it was unexpected.   His first thought
was that she had wandered from a careless keeper, and
that it was necessary to humor her mad whim.   But there
was more than passive yielding in the feverish embrace in
which he held her willowy form.   She caught the garland
of arbutus hanging on her neck, and, twining the ends together, threw them over his head, then gently led him to
the mossy knoll where she had been sitting, and enthroned
him gravely, as though the act had been a prearranged
ceremonial.   Then, in a soft, crooning chant, to a fantastic-
ally capricious measure, she sang in soft, clear notes, evidently improvisations from the ballads she had heard her
mother sing long ago :

> " *Winter's wraith is fled afield,*
> *And bids false love beware !*
> *Spring is come with balm and shield,*
> *And bids true love to dare !* "

With an indescribable swaying unison of body and intent she repeated the lines, arranging the flowers in her lap at the same time :

> " *On the lea the crocus nods,*
> *Breaking through the frosty sods,*
> *As love that's fettered wrests its gyves,*
> *And in its cruel hardship thrives.*
> *Shamrocks tremble in the winds,*
> *Hope fulfills to him that finds.*"

She took from her bosom a four-leaved clover, pressed it to her lips, and with a capricious gesture laid it in the palm of Darcy's hand, closing her own over his with the talisman in it :

> " *By the pool the goblins stray,*
> *Prank by night and hide by day ;*
> *Under furzes midges sleep,*
> *Waiting May-day's breath to peep ;*
> *Under brambles fairies roam,*
> *Pining till the flowers be come.*
> *In bosky dells the Elf-men hide,*
> *Till Ariel comes to claim his bride !*"

She stopped suddenly. Her voice had grown softer and the accentuation was recitative. Then she sat down near Darcy and looked solemnly at him, as if in wonder that he didn't join her melodious memoir of her past love. As he sat quite still, fairly panic-stricken by the spectacle of the unstrung fibers of her mind, she began again, now scattering the shining arbutus leaves in a sort of Druid ceremonial :

> " *Through the hedges bluebells ring*
> *Welcome to the voice of spring,*
> *Mab weaves her robe of moss and thyme,*
> *While maidens put the tale in rhyme,*
> *To sing to love that's leal and true ;*
> *Faithless love they deck with rue.*"

How long she could have continued these fantastic rhythmic reminiscences, Darcy was not destined to learn, for at this point the astonished Manly obtruded himself. He had been standing unseen by Norah for some moments, but, as he saw that she was growing strangely unlike herself, he became frightened and touched her hand. She looked at him composedly, smiled at Darcy, and said :

"It's a child the little people are fond of. He carries the light for the fire-flies." She patted Manly on the shoulder caressingly, and seemed quite unconscious that Darcy hadn't opened his lips.

"We must go now, you know!" She looked at Darcy, then at Manly. "Come, we must not be in the dark until the fire-flies come. The evil eye will look into our hearts and pick out our love's secrets. Come!"

Chanting as she walked with her arm about Darcy, and looking confidingly in his eyes she sang :

> " *Sweetheart, mine by every token,*
> *By fairy laws that ne'er were broken ;*
> *By holy troth, in faith to keep ;*
> *Mine in waking, mine in sleep,*
> *Mine by Nature's sweet decree,*
> *Mine in wedlock's destiny.*
> *Lip to lip, heart to heart,*
> *Ours the link no fate can part.*

Darcy looked in perplexity from Manly to Norah. She grew coaxingly caressing. She seized his hand, kissed it, stroked it, and then—winding the broken shreds of the arbutus garland about his neck—playfully led him through the thickets along the river path to the cottage. Manly trudged on ahead and Darcy dared not ask him a question. He was as much mystified when she led him into the trim little villa, and quite soberly said :

"It has been all ready for you this many a day. The fairies did it. They bid you come when you were far away." She sank into a seat as she looked at Darcy ; slowly her gaze changed to a stare. Then she rose, walked confusedly to the door, turned and looked at Darcy again, and, without a word, disappeared.

Manly explained, so far as he knew, the situation. Ever since the attack, Norah had been out of her head ; didn't know people that she had known well, and seemed to know others that she had never seen. Darcy left the house with a heavy, heavy heart. All the old forces in his soul began the combats anew. Here was his handiwork. God ! how lovely she was, how pure, how like the seraph faces of the masters ! Could the ideal of an angel be fairer or lovelier ! Even with unbalanced mind, whom had he ever seen that compared with her elfin beauty ?

He met Denny as he emerged into the park road and told him that he had seen Norah—alluding even to her curious delusion—thinking that perhaps it was better to prepare the brother for anything Norah might divulge. The freak did not surprise Denny. Her treatment of Larry showed that she had no realization of the personality of the people about her. But on reaching home he found Norah's manner inexplicably altered. She looked at him in a questioning surprise, and when, later, Larry came home, she fled from the room, as though he had been a stranger. Late in the night, as she did not reappear, Denny went to her room. Her mirror was garlanded with the laurel leaves, arbutus, and untimely blossoms lured into bloom by the May warmth of April. She had decked herself in the pretty gown Denny had discovered her in that memorable night long before at Marbury. The jewels sparkled in her ears, and she held up her hand, with her finger to her lips, on which the ring glittered.

"I sang the fairy song, and he came back to me, Denny dear. Did you see him with the love-light in his eye? He came when I sang:

> " *Violets blue for lovers true,*
> *Marigold for lovers bold,*
> *Garlands sweet for lovers mete,*
> *Kisses blithe*
> *True love's tithe.*
> *We will wed now, willy nilly,*
> *Nosegays fine of daffodilly—*
> *Daffodilly—daffodilly—*"

Her voice rose soft and clear with unutterable joy in it. She followed the words with slow mimic dance movement, and at the end stood before her brother palpitating, radiant!

He was greatly disturbed. Her mania had never before defined itself so openly. He feared to leave her alone, and without her knowledge brought a couch and slept within sound of her voice during the night.

Marcus had been called East on a professional mission, and Denny had no one to consult with save the physician who had attended her in the first illness. He sent for the doctor, who listened to the new symptoms, and having examined Norah carefully, charged Denny to encourage the invalid's delusion, to let her see all that was possible of the person who had changed the current of her thought. That he felt sure this was the beginning of a complete restoration, for, said the medical man, she associated him with scenes that have a powerful influence on the memory preceding her mental collapse, and if he be prudent and will consent to humor her for a few days, the heart will restore the missing link, and she will be herself again.

Denny told Darcy this later. He did not notice the

frightened look in the young man's eyes, as Darcy said constrainedly:

"I shall be very glad, indeed, to try the experiment, though I think it dangerous to trifle with the poor child's delusion."

He came to the cottage that day and many days thereafter. She was expecting him, and the scenes of the first meeting were renewed. One day, however, Darcy failed to come. Norah wandered off by herself, and, as she flitted about in the budding grasses, she came suddenly before Darcy, who was gathering primroses by a little stream of running water. Agnes was with him, and their horses browsed on the young shrubs. Agnes started in surprise as Norah, with dilated eyes and heaving breast, stood with a trailing train of green leaves wreathed with gentians falling from her wrist.

"What dryad priestess is this? I declare, she has an unreal look—unsubstantial as Spenser's mythic maids," and Agnes shuddered.

"Ah, it is Norah—you remember—the pretty ward of Dr. Marbury," and Darcy made a significant gesture. The brook was between him and Norah. It ran limpid and gurgling over white pebbles and soft, velvety reefs of rich moss, flecked by coral buds, that gleamed like lurid eyes in the transparent green of the moss. She came quite to the edge of the stream, threw the wreaths from her body into the cove, and looked fixedly into Darcy's eyes. She held out her hand archly. Darcy, smiling at Agnes, placed his own within Norah's across the little channel. She hesitated a moment, then, gazing into the clear water fixedly, she murmured in a whisper that Darcy alone distinctly heard:

" In the book of hearts 'tis writ,
List' true love, give heed to it.

> *By the running water's edge*
> *Fairies seal the lover's pledge:*
> *If he breaks, a life he takes."*

Startled and trembling, Darcy drew his hand away and recoiled. She leaned forward, her lips parted, and a strange light slowly filled her wide-open eyes.

"Really, Darcy, if this is a little comedy you have invented, I must congratulate you. Nothing could be more romantic than this sylvan setting, and the *dramatis personæ* are as moving as a certain scene in the ' Midsummer Night's Dream.' Only the ass's ears have been forgotten." And, drawing up the flowing skirts of her riding habit, Agnes turned her back, and, walking haughtily to her horse, neighing a loud welcome, she fell to caressing its glossy neck. Darcy followed her, whispering :

"Don't you see the poor girl's insane ? She has been suffering delusion since last autumn, when she received a dreadful shock."

"Indeed ! " and Agnes turned to look at her rival with more curiosity than sympathy. "Why don't her people keep her under guard ? It must be embarrassing for the young men, if she constrains them all into her mystic rites in this preposterous fashion, or does she confine her mad devotion to you ? "

"I'm surprised at you, Agnes ! " And, shocked by the girl's heartlessness, Darcy turned to see what had become of Norah. She was standing motionless, rooted, dumb, on the mossy pedestal on the brink of the brook, the wild light faded from her eye, an expression of doubt and terror replacing it. She did not stir as Darcy came back ; nor did she answer when he said caressingly :

"Go home, Norah. I will come soon ! "

She was in the same attitude when they rode away, and when, two hours later, Darcy hurried to the cottage, she had not returned. Filled with vague apprehensions, he scoured the leafy coverts of the Holly Hills, but there was no trace of her. As a last hope, he set out for the brook, which was far from the cottage. The air had grown chilly, as it was late in the afternoon. He came suddenly upon her as she sat on the same spot, dropping the coral blossoms of the moss into the water, and muttering something like an incantation as the dainty petals were whirled buoyantly on the bosom of the dancing stream. The picture was so pretty, her attitude so graceful, and the smile reflected back from the water so tranquil and happy, that Darcy couldn't bear to break in on the tryst. He stole softly to her side and bent over her to see what she was watching so intently. In an instant his face was mirrored beside her own in the limpid wave.

She caught sight of it, and started with a little cry. He caught her, or she would have sunk in the stream. She turned her face upward, and, recognizing him, paled to a deathly pallor, gasped something he could not understand, and her head fell backward. She had lost consciousness, he could see at once. It was useless to call for help. He picked her up and carried her as best he could back to the cottage. The physician was summoned. He declared that she would recover with reason restored, or become a hopelessly mad woman. For three days she wandered deliriously, and on the fourth she aroused early in the morning, got up and dressed herself calmly—looking with a puzzled air at the room as though it was strange to her.

The nurse who occupied a cot in the chamber said :

" What is it, Norah—do you need anything ? "

" O Betty, are you there ? Why am I here ? In your room, isn't it ? "

" Well, yes, but why do you rise so early ? It's hardly daylight."

"I ought to have been down much earlier. Mrs. Blythe has a great deal to do to-day. The Convocation is to be held, and the house will be full."

The nurse hastened out of the room, leaving Norah, who looked in amazement at her surroundings. Denny was soon with her, and explained that she had been ill, and that she was now her own mistress, and head of the little home. It was a long time before she could bring her mind to comprehend the change. Nothing was said about the time she had been ill, but when she looked out and saw the soft spring colors, she said: "Why, Denny, I've been ill since October! It's spring now."

"Yes, dear, you've been ill a long time. It's now the last week in May. The winter was very open, and the spring is very early." He passed all the morning with her: led her through all the pretty shrubbery, which seemed quite new to her; and when, near noon, he set out for his office, Norah was in a flutter of delight. When Darcy came, after noon, she was in the garden, and, when she saw him, welcomed him with a look of shy delight, resuming exactly the old manner at Marbury, where her timid joy in his presence had first won his heart.

She had no suspicion of the recent past, and showed him about the little home with a girlish enjoyment that gave her new beauty in Darcy's eyes. Later in the day they wandered through the pretty copses near the river, and went as far as the boat-house. She recalled that, but looked upon her late haunts with wondering eyes. Never had her strange beauty shone out so enchantingly. It was as if a spirit had clothed itself just so far in flesh as to bear resemblance to mortal, with hardly any of the imperfections of the body.

Wretched Darcy! He had fought and fled; and here he was anew on the brink of the maelstrom, with less and less power of resistance. Day after day he came, resolving every day that he would come no more. Weeks passed. His mother had long before settled the marriage day, and before the end of June he was to take his bride to Europe. His meetings with Norah were, toward the end, stolen moments of transport, for Marcus had returned, and the cottage was no longer accessible under that stern eye. He invented pretexts for her to go to the boat-house, and there she came artlessly, with the small Manly, who became a very expert boatman during the trysts of the lovers in the pretty pavilion. In May the company for the war had been raised. It was to join General Scott at Vera Cruz. Unknown to his family, Darcy accepted the captaincy, and when the lieutenant marched off for New York, Darcy gave his word that he would be with them before they sailed. He told Norah that he was going to the wars, and that she must wait patiently for him. He would be back in six months at the farthest; she must be brave. To his mother's angry reproaches he remained silent, saying, doggedly:

"It was yours and my father's wish that I should go into the war. I signed the roll long ago. The call is come, and I must go." So the preparations for the wedding were stopped. Agnes laughed gayly when it was told her, and said, lightly:

"A soldier fresh from the wars will make a more ardent lover. It will do Darcy no harm to wait."

When Denny heard of Darcy's going, he went straight to Marcus. "Darcy Warchester goes in command of the city company. I owe him a great debt of gratitude. I owe the country my services. I am going to join the army."

Marcus did not approve, but he did not remonstrate. He undertook to watch over the inmates of the cottage.

He was to collect Denny's pay as a private soldier, and expend it for the maintenance of the little household. This, with Larry's earnings, would keep them comfortably. Norah heard Denny's resolution with mingled joy and sorrow. He would be near Darcy, and protect him in the hour of danger. Darcy, too, would be Denny's friend. She bade him God speed, with a strange light in her eye, and a look so wistful and intent that Denny carried the sadness of it in his heart for many a day afterward.

CHAPTER XXV.

AN ARMY WITH BANNERS.

To the generation actively or passively part of the stupendous Iliad whose movements filled this continent from 1861 until 1865, the incursion into Mexico in 1846 lingers in the memory as a mere episode. But, though millions did not march to battle, and the nation's destiny was not staked on the issue, our fathers watched the contest with clouded hopes and beating hearts. The war, which had at first seemed the impulse of one group of States, gradually fired the patriotism of all; and from the gloomy pine lands of Maine, and the sterile quarries of Massachusetts, volunteers poured forth, as eager and resolute as the bands that leaped first to arms from the tropic prairies of Texas and Louisiana. And, though there was no telegraph then to keep the country informed within a few minutes of every blow struck and march made, news-letters were passed from hand to hand in the public marts, apprising anxious kinsmen of the intrepid deeds of their distant darlings. The glorious tidings of Scott's master-stroke at Jalapa, April 18, 1847, were ringing through the North, when Darcy's company reached New York in June. A few days later Denny joined him as the troups were embarking for Vera Cruz.

Darcy welcomed him with a peculiar expression of countenance, which puzzled the eager recruit. But he was very kind to him, though Denny did not presume upon his relation to the friend to escape the formal allegiance of the soldier. Darcy's contingent was assigned to a regular regiment, which he found at Puebla after a month's voyage. The army had just moved out from the town, the general-in-chief having decided on that brilliant and daring move which ended in the seizure of the Mexican capital.

Darcy had shown a strange reluctance to Denny's serving under him, and it was with grief rather than surprise the young soldier learned that, on the recommendation of his captain, he was assigned to headquarters duty. With bursting heart he hurried to the captain's tent, and, with very unsoldierly tears streaming from his eyes, faltered :

"Captain Darcy, what have I done? How have I offended you, that you won't let me serve in your company ? "

"Done, Denny? Good God, done ! It is I who should be serving and you commanding. I gave your name to the adjutant-general when he asked for clerical aids, because I knew that you would win his notice and secure promotion. That was my motive, Denny. God knows, I owe you much—how much I can not say. With your education and tastes, the place of private must be unendurable. It was that you may escape it that I seized the chance for you."

Denny's eyes were not dry, but they glistened with pride and joy.

"I should not have felt so badly, only—only I got the notion somehow that you didn't want me near you. You have seemed different in a sense from what you used to be, and I feared that I had provoked or offended you."

Darcy's head was bent down. He never met the lad's eyes now when he talked with him, and it was this curious change that had chilled Denny, for hitherto Darcy's eyes had met his gaze tranquilly and fearlessly. He arose and walked the little space in the tent, keeping his face away from his subordinate, and at length said huskily:

"Denny, I am a miserable, unhappy fellow. If death comes to me in this campaign, it will be the happiest end of my troubles, and perhaps—" He hesitated. "Never mind me, Denny; I am as I always was to you. Don't forget that—" he looked at him wistfully—"don't forget that." Then, recurring to the original subject, he said: "The company is in need of a sergeant, and I shall appoint you to-morrow. That will release you from the heavy manual labor of police and guard duty. You need not hesitate. It is not favoritism. You have been recommended by the lieutenant already, who bears testimony to your efficiency in drill and company manœuvres."

That evening at parade Denny's name was read off as sergeant, and thereafter he found his lines less laborious. He was not routed at daylight to clear the company "streets," make the fires, or, unless he chose, do any manual labor, save caring for his gun and accouterments. A few days later he was chosen to be color-sergeant, and thenceforward he saw little of Darcy, as the color-sergeants' tents are in a group, and for the time being are detached from their respective companies.

Having swung the army from its base, by a movement like McClellan's in 1862, General Scott pushed rapidly toward the plateau of Mexico. The march was a prodigy of precision and audacity. The sun by day beat down like the breath of invisible furnaces. The soil rose up like an impenetrable wall of sand. The horizon was lost in a glittering mirage, and the soldiers seemed gaunt specters of an army, pursuing thin air. Food was scarce and foraging fatal, for the guerrillas hovered on the compact flanks in energetic watchfulness. Water so brackish, alkaline, and astringent that it maddened the vitals without allaying thirst, was all that could be got. Sickness and the scourge fell upon the wan and ghastly companies.

Darcy was stricken with a noisome malady, and, when it came to Denny's ears, he found him bundled in an ambulance, deserted and maniacal. For days the lad hovered over him, marching by the wagon, and cooling his parched lips with water painfully got, boiled and strained. Skilled in the lore of herbs, he made a decoction from the moist plaintain leaves found under the rocky bowlders, and, in the end, Darcy mended slowly. Others, not so desperately seized, died, and the regimental surgeon declared that Captain Warchester owed his life to the devotion of Sergeant Boyne. Darcy heard the verdict with an expression of such ghastly emotion that the kind surgeon drew a very poor conclusion of the young officer's bravery, for he ascribed the look to terror of death.

Denny resumed his place with the colors, very proud and happy. He watched Darcy, so splendid and handsome on his fine steed, for the young officer was now of the staff, and he secretly exulted in the chance that had enabled him to do his adored friend a service. He watched the pensive rider, as, of an evening, when the columns were separated, the vigilant *arrieros* came swooping down from the thick *chaparral* to stampede the cattle, and his heart swelled with the pride of a father as he saw his hero whip out his sabre, throw his stately shoulders back, and

dash to the point of danger. All this he wrote home, and
Marcus was careful that the fond mother should regularly
get sight of the letters, for Darcy wrote seldom, and then
only a brief line to say that all was well. But patriot
homes were not the agitated groups of 1861–'65. Tender
hearts were not torn by the deadly panic of the civil war.
The absent soldier-boy was missed, but the tales of death
were so slow in coming northward that it was not until the
war was ended that the pillage of death was fully known.
It was mostly the petty miseries or amusements of the
camp, the march, and the stirring movements in the chase
that filled the home mind.

It was only the adventurous who had marched to conquest; the few that left the quiet villages of the land
made no gap in the social or industrial activities. Such
seasons of agonized doubts and despair as filled those dire
July days, when the whispers of Bull Run flew North,
were never known. Seasons of sickening dread and pray-
erful protest, such as held the country's heart in terror,
during those awful hours when the race was not to the
swift nor the battle to the strong—Gaines's Mill, Seven
Pines, Malvern—had no part in the brief but decisive
promenade in the Mexican jungles. Hearts that hung in
trembling hope on the bulletins that told the bloody tale,
from Antietam and Gettysburg to Atlanta and Five Forks,
which bore the swift alternation of mortal death and immortal deed, as the dreadful battle-play changed from defeat and disaster to victory and conquest, found little play
in the spectacular drama of the Mexican campaign.

It was a wonderful *epos* notwithstanding. It was real
war so long as it lasted, and its conduct was another illus-
tration of the indomitable, aggressive, sustained pertinacity of the Saxon race. The history of it, read centuries
hence, will strike our descendants as the incursions of

Hannibal or Attila sounded to the degenerate Romans of the Eastern Empire. There were no official correspondents in those days to embalm the minutest details as well as the grand manœuvres in ten thousand home prints. Official bulletins gave all the news, and they were rare.

A paragraph in the county paper contained the result of a battle, and the lists of the lost were only known months after the killed and wounded had been sleeping under the Southern sands. But our gentle Dilly was not restricted to the cold and perfunctory reports of the staff. She had a Xenophon in the column, who kept her apprised of the army's movements with a copiousness and point of view that would have astonished General Scott or his observant aids. In this Anabasis Dilly recognized the vigorous insight of Cæsar and the precision of Thucydides. Under his imaginative glance the tame details of camp life, the hurry of the march, the terrors of the encounter, took a perfervid tone of romance that recalled the tragedy of the Spanish invasion, and the poetry of the religious pageant that signalized the Castilian conquest.

He had, in order to fit himself for the double part of soldier and historian, taken Spanish text-books with him, and at the end of three months was able to talk in broken phrases with the prisoners, or gossip with the few natives that remained on the line of march. His mastery of Latin made the latter easy, and he was regarded with much awe by his indolent comrades in the ranks, and with great favor by his superiors, who were often compelled to make use of his acquisitions in questioning the free lances brought in by the pickets. In September Dilly received a long letter resuming the operations since the famous movement from Vera Cruz :

"For six weeks," he wrote, "we have been marching day and night; fighting, skirmishing, flanking, and pushing

16

Santa Anna nearer and nearer Mexico—where we hope
our labors end. Our course has taken us over the same
arid wastes and burning sands, under the same glistening pinnacles of rock that Cortez and his men looked
upon two centuries ago. The land is in air, verdure,
color, and everything that makes a country — everything, I mean, that impresses the eye and the sense—so
different from our sober Northern climes, that I can
hardly hope to make you see what has now become so familiar to me that it seems, if not quite natural, in keeping
with this picturesque campaign. Houses, in one sense,
there are none.

"Sometimes in high hopes we come to a village announced long before by some enchanting Spanish name,
and, when we get to it, there is nothing but a cross with a
Madonna and child in an alcove, a lighted taper, and perhaps two or three ruined mud cabins, called 'adobes.'
By day the soil is a glare of burning particles; the air is
filled with needles of light, that penetrate, irritate, and
madden the palate and lungs. But when there is no
movement of the army, the illuminated miles of cloud are
the haven of the argosies of all that I can conceive as
beautiful. It is the mirage, and the fantastic tricks that
it plays were never dreamed in Dante's vision, or in the
Hadean wastes that Milton painted. The men are for
the most part gay and uncomplaining, though the food is
something that surprises Northern digestion. If I could
send you a heap of the wonderful blossoms that fill the
air with their odors, you would dream of Arcady for a
year. To-day we came to a leafy pinnacle in the winding
road; we stood on the very rock where Cortez received the
emissaries of Montezuma.

"There is a cross and column with an inscription glori-
fying Ferdinand and Isabella, and never a word of the re-

morseless hero who added this country to the Spanish crown. We are a hundred miles from Mexico ; but the signal-men declared that, through the transparent air, the great plateau on which the city stands was discernible. I took the glass, but I couldn't see it ! The eye needs training for this just as other faculties do for other work. We could see Santa Anna's cavalry glittering in the distant sunlight like a moving forest of color. We expect to have a great battle shortly, as we shall be near the city within three days. The soldiers are confident. They adore General Scott, who is the most magnificent cavalier ever seen in saddle. When he rides along the ranks, however tired the soldiers may be, they leap up and salute him with joyful shouts. He has done wonders with this army.

"He has, all told, not over ten thousand effective troops, while Santa Anna has forty thousand. But Scott manages so skillfully that when we come before the intrenched positions, prepared by the Mexicans, only a thin wall of men is kept before the fortifications, while others who have been sent by the flank—a way roundabout—come behind the Mexicans, and the fortifications are of no use. We are kept so constantly moving that the time doesn't hang heavy on our hands now as it did when we were in camp. There is not a watch in the regiment outside of the general and staff officers. So the days come and go, and we only guess from the sun the hours as they fly past, like the blurred landscape from a swift packet. I couldn't keep track of the days of the month or the month itself, if it were not for an occasional general order.

"It is a week since I wrote the foregoing. Since then we have fought three severe battles at the time-worn towns of Contreras, San Antonio, and Churubusco. These were really towns, and the Mexicans fought valiantly to keep us out of them. Captain Darcy distin-

guished himself, and has been promoted to a majority.
His company waited upon him the day after the battle
and congratulated him on his bravery and good fortune.
There is an armistice now for two weeks, and the rumor is
loud that peace has been proposed. But our generals
don't seem to expect it, for we are cutting through rocks
and building roads for the artillery by day and night.

"Perhaps you will rejoice to know that I was made lieutenant in the Warchester company on the recommendation
of all my brother non-commissioned officers—for doing
well in the night fights, and saving the flag when a squadron of the enemy's cavalry had cut us off. Darcy came
to my tent to congratulate me, and the kind fellow insisted
on giving me his sword, as he had a second. Chapultepec
(the hill of locusts) used to be the vice-regal residence of
the Spanish governors. It is on the top of a mighty hill,
and from a distance the walls seem part of the clouds. It
was defended bravely. When we got in I saw some of
the soldiers. They were most of them young men, the
flower of the Mexican race, and cadets of the National
Military School—the Mexican West Point. We have
already thirty-seven hundred prisoners, thirteen generals,
and three statesmen who have been presidents of the
Republic. Our men have singled out their favorites
among the officers who lead us. Most of them are very
young men, and, though they come from West Point, they
are not at all martinetish. Our great engineer is a young
man with sandy hair and brown eyes, who resembles
Darcy, but is not so tall, nor so graceful—Captain George
McClellan. It was he who cut a road through a valley
of rocks that Santa Anna left unguarded as so inaccessible that no army could master it. If we should ever have
another war, the men prophesy great things for a dashing
young staff officer who seems to glory in danger—'Phil'

Kearney—a bright fellow who is always riding out among the enemy. At Molino del Rey—the King's Mill—Major Sumner, with a single regiment of cavalry, fought an entire army in order to give General Scott time to concentrate a large force on the enemy's main line. But, dear me, these details can't interest you, only as in some degree part of the life I am living. Old soldiers tell me that no war ever offered the rank and file such opportunities for seeing and learning. The country is so broken up that often a division or brigade taking part in an action can see the whole combat, just as one might sit in a Roman amphitheatre and watch all the combatants in the arena. These last fights have compelled the evacuation of the City of Mexico, and we are to march in to-morrow. This letter leaves by courier, and I don't know when another will set out."

With that picturesque movement which threw the intrepid hosts of Scott from the sea-base of Vera Cruz to the crater-like plateaus of the city of Mexico, this history has nothing to do ; but Denny's personal narrative to Dilly made but passing mention of an episode which bore directly and sinisterly upon the fortunes of the Aliens. Early in August the advance columns came to a land where the caprices of Nature defied all ordinary means of advance. The worn granite of the mountains seemed to have been, in a moment of liquid fusion, poured down in vast fluxions over the sandy plains, where, suddenly cooling, the mass was left in broad flanges of jagged needle-like cones, impassable crevices, defiles and spurs, that made an impenetrable wall to the advance of footmen as well as horses and artillery. Brought to a halt in this lava land, the staff decided that the most accessible straight line must be followed, and a road cut through the iron wall. A company of volunteers was called for ; they were not tardy in responding. Major Darcy was second in command, and under a burning sun they set out to explore a line of march that the army might follow. The little band pushed on, creating the road for the legions.

They were kept on the *qui vive* day and night by the swarming *arrieros* of the enemy, but at the end of a week's march, turned about to meet the main army with a circuitous but feasible line of march secured. A day's tramp from the outposts, Major Darcy was left with a company of fifty men to hold a narrow defile, vital to the security of the troops. It was a wildly magnificent gap, flanked by precipitous cliffs, on which the *chaparral* glistened like petrified waves of a summer sea. The little camp was well intrenched, patrols set, and a vigilant watch kept.

The alert guerrillas watched the departure of half of the company, and kept up an incessant fire on the little picket, from the craggy sides of the frowning rocks. During the night this fire increased, and one or two men were struck in their tents. Darcy thought it wiser to dislodge these adventurous spirits, and sent out a squad to rout them. This seemed to have been the very end they were manœuvring for. So soon as the little force had become involved in the rocks, a preconcerted signal sounded on all sides, and the cañon was alive with Mexicans. The Americans were drawn behind the rocky walls, thrown up from the loose stones and bowlders, and fought with desperation. But toward night their ammunition gave out. The moon rose and filled the cavern-like gap with floods of clear, transparent light, revealing the little fort and its resolute defenders almost as clearly as sunshine.

The enemy, secreted in the rocks, were invisible, save when the flashes of their carbines revealed their whereabouts. The last shot was fired, and Darcy ordered bayonets. If they could hold out a few hours, rescue would be at hand. He had sent messengers to warn the van-guard. As the sun rose, shots could be heard far to the rear, and the Americans grasped their guns with re-newed determination. But the sounds of relief had in-spired the enemy also. Closing in from all sides, they swarmed over the rocky breastwork, and in a few mo-ments, by mere force of numbers, the garrison was over-come. The killed and wounded were left in the bloody shambles, stripped and pillaged, the rest were tied in pairs and marched off hurriedly into the gloomy fastnesses of the hills.

An hour later the cavalry advance of the army was at the spot. Several of the wounded were able to tell the story, and the cavalry hastened on with but faint hopes of catching the marauders. Denny was on duty at the head-quarters of the advance brigade, and heard the news within a few hours. He knew of Darcy's presence in the little post, and set out at once to question the survivors. All that they could tell was that Warchester had fought with a musket, that he had been struck on the head just before the "Greasers" had swarmed in, and that he had been carried off. Denny readily obtained permission for a day's scouting and hastened to the fatal fort. The Mexicans had thrown some of their own garments on the ground, and put on those pillaged from the Americans. Covering himself in a suit of the enemy's, Denny pushed into the hills in the direction Darcy's captors were said to have taken. He followed the trail easily enough, for there were red spots of blood on the rocks for a long distance, and from time to time other signs of a halt. It was quite dark when, despairing of coming upon the captors, Denny sat down on a moss-covered rock, and began to consider the wisdom of going further on his wild chase. If he could get track of the main body, and find the disposition made of the prisoners, he would be able to arrange for an exchange. In many cases the Mexicans killed prisoners outright, but swift retaliation on the part of General Scott had to some extent stopped that practice. Prisoners were, however, still maltreated in a manner that made death preferable, and it was the hideous prospect of the gently nurtured Darcy undergoing harsh calamities of this sort that moved Denny to seek him and aid him. If he were wounded, he would need a friendly hand.

The wild hill-sides were still, as Nature alone can be at intervals. Even the insects were at rest, and the desolation of his situation fell upon the lad for the first time. The hateful crackling shots, that had made part of the last three months' noises, would now have fallen on his ears as a friendly sound. Presently, in the stillness, the gentle trickle of water, tumbling over rocks near him, drew his attention. He had some hard biscuits with him, and, soaking one in the little stream, began to eat. As he sat there, his eye, wandering over the jagged outline of the rocks, and growing accustomed to the dim light, caught a peculiar change in the shadows just above and in front of him. The whole face of the rock seemed to rise and melt in the clouds. What could it be? He crept up toward the singular apparition, and in a few moments heard voices. He fell on his hands and knees, and crawled toward the sound. It took him perhaps twenty minutes to reach the place whence the voices sounded, and then he discovered that it was a column of smoke rising in the air that had confused him. He was on a line with and looking over a low wall of jagged rocks upon a level plateau, standing out like a platform from the mountain side.

The fires were made of dry twigs, and over them hung camp-kettles—the very same that had formed part of the accouterment of the American camp. A score of figures, clad in American uniforms, were grouped about at a distance from the low fire. A faint hum of sound, more like singing than conversation, fell on Denny's ear. It was the soft patois of the Spanish tongue, now and then distinguishable as some one demanded hearing for his contribution to the discussion. Another group, at some distance from the Mexicans and nearer the edge of the plateau, arrested Denny's attention. These were apparently naked men huddled together, and guarded by two tall fellows with drawn sabers and carbines slung over their shoulders. From his point of observation Denny was farthest removed from these—prisoners, he concluded. Retreating softly the same way he came, Denny made a circuit wide enough to avoid attracting the attention of the guard by any untimely misstep ; and, when he thought himself abreast of the spot near the prisoners, he again crawled up the rocks.

Yes, they were the prisoners. He could even distinguish Darcy, as the flame under the kettles flared up now and then, and his heart leaped with joy. Darcy was alive, suffering indignity, but alive. How best secure his safety now ? The advance guard was miles away in another direction. To go back for a rescue would perhaps lose all, for the band would be *en route* before the soldiers could reach this spot, difficult of access, and easily defensible against a regiment for hours. No, Darcy must be snatched from peril now, at any risk.

Presently the steaming pots were lifted from the long poles, and the savory contents dished out. When the captors had finished, the cooks ladled out a supply which was handed the prisoners. All, save Darcy, ate greedily. He drank from a large tin cup some steaming beverage which Denny couldn't guess, as the Mexicans had no coffee. He could see that the prisoners were tied leg to leg, but their arms were free. The night was very sultry, and presently, when the supper was over, each guerrilla betook himself to a blanket spread on the ground, and the camp was silent.

Four guards kept a perfunctory watch, for the place itself was a natural defense. Toward midnight the moon passed behind a high peak of the rocks, and left the plateau in deep shadow. Now was Denny's opportunity. Climbing to the edge of the plateau, with his clothes in a bundle, he crawled over the intervening ground, which was fortunately covered by deep herbage, until he was among the prisoners. They were all sleeping soundly. The guards were seated on the ground at some distance from them, and, had they been alert, they could not have distinguished Denny from the rest. Darcy was stretched on a blanket nearest the guard. To reach him, Denny must crawl over his sleeping comrades, sprawling in a confused huddle. If he awaked them, the guard would be aroused, and he held his breath as this perilous manœuvre was executed. He touched Darcy when he reached him, but the young man did not stir. Then, fastening his lips to the sleeper's ear, he breathed, "Darcy, it's Denny."

"Eh? What?"

Denny's blood congealed as Darcy was startled into speaking aloud. The guard rose and came toward them, and Denny, now breathless and trembling with dread, crouched down among the sleepers. The guard came a few steps and asked:

"*Qué tiene usted? Tiene usted algo?*"

Receiving no response, he scrutinized the group, and went back muttering that the Americans were dreaming of their sweethearts. The assurance gave Denny new courage. Darcy was now awake and alert. Denny whispered:

"Put on these clothes, then crawl straight backward to the edge of the plateau, push straight before you, and by daylight you will be somewhere near our outposts. You can then send a party to rescue us. But, in any event, you will be safe."

"Ah! Denny, is it you? How did you get here?"

"Never mind me; you have but a short time. Hurry!"

"I could never stand the journey, Denny; my head is badly cut, and I can scarcely see. I couldn't go a mile if I were given free passport. No, it is useless. Leave me here. My misery will soon be ended; and it is better that it should be so, as you will say yourself some day."

"In God's name, Mr. Darcy, don't talk like this! Besides, I shall be considered a deserter, if you don't go back to speak for me, for I had only permission to be gone until sunset."

"Good God, Denny! must I always be the curse of you and yours? What devil put it into your head to come to me? I am quite content to die and be forgot."

"Don't you see, Mr. Darcy, this is wasting time!" Denny thought that the young man's wounds, and the frightful march over the rocks, had affected his brain. "I had intended to take your place here, so that you might not be missed; but it is as you say—you could not hold out alone, nor find the way. Follow me, and we will go together."

"Since I have got you into this scrape, I will do as you say; but when the time comes, I want you to remember that I was resigned to my fortunes, and that I did not fear the death that appalled the others!"

He followed exactly Denny's sinuous tracks as he crawled backward, keeping his eyes on the guard. In a few minutes they were both over the edge of the plateau, and among the broken rocks and thick bushes. Here

Denny made a division of the clothing, Darcy taking the trousers and jacket, while Denny wrapped the blanket around himself. He led the way as well as he could remember over the same ground that he had come. By daylight they were far from the plateau, with shining walls of lava behind them, and dense thickets of tropic pines, palms, and cactus on all sides. They made but slow progress, as Darcy's wound broke out afresh, and it required all Denny's skill to invent effective means to stanch the blood. From the ready ingredients of vegetable nature he did, however, succeed in the end, but there was a narcotic as well as coagulative quality in the herbs, and the young man slept for hours, watched by the agitated physician. It was night again when they resumed their journey, directed by the moon. Denny had to carry his friend over some of the rougher places, and when, on the second day, they heard the booming of cannon, both were at the end of endurance. By the greatest good fortune another of General Scott's wide flanking operations was going on, and, as the two wanderers, halting in despair on the brow of a hill, gave up the attempt to push farther, bands of horsemen passed near and beneath them, and, though their voices were too weak to attract attention, a white handkerchief swung on a stick was seen, and an hour later they were taken among friends.

CHAPTER XXVI.

THE END OF THE DREAM.

NORAH's new life filled Marcus Dunn with a sweet, solemn, almost paternal repose. All trace of her tempo-

rary alienation had passed away. The tranquil domesticity of the home in which she found herself gave her mind
a new direction. Larry was a constant wonder and delight. He was so strong, so cheery and devoted, that she
could hardly realize that they had been sundered since
childhood. When Marcus came to the cottage of an evening, Larry betook himself to his tool-house, where he surprised Norah by the fashioning of all manner of fantastic
household conceits. Indeed, it was in this pleasant labo-
ratory that Marcus often found the girl singing in a low
voice, while Larry turned his lathe or fabricated the *bric-
à-brac* that adorned the pretty chambers. Denny's room
had been equipped with an elaborate writing-desk, with
cunning drawers running down each side, and an overhanging cabinet in which all the legal memoranda of a
life-time might be stored. Nor was Marcus forgotten.
From the purple cherry on the Marbury hills, Larry's cunning had fashioned the lawyer a desk as beautiful as
Denny's, with a little silver plate recording it as the gift of
Norah and Larry Boyne. For this rare object Norah had
worked a cover of quaint colors and complicated pattern,
such as delighted the fancy and engaged the minds and
hands of the women of those days.

Sometimes Dilly came and read Denny's letters, but
this was rare, for her school-days were done, and she had
gone back to Marbury. The correspondence with Denny
was known only to her mother, and, as a consequence, she
was obliged to come to the cottage for her letters. The
memory of Marcus's wooing had gone from Norah's mind,
when she came back to her normal state, and he dared
not recur to the subject until time enough had elapsed to
assure him that she was capable of understanding herself
and him. So the weeks and months passed. It was August. Denny and Darcy had gone in May, and their first

letters had only begun to come. Norah listened wistfully as Dilly read Denny's meager allusions to Darcy—and such emotion as Norah showed, Dilly thought naturally enough was for the absent brother. But Marcus, observing her keenly on such occasions, was tortured by a suspicion that became a certainty when one day, happening on the river with the small Manly, that indiscreet confidant made casual allusion to Darcy's visit at the cottage, and Norah's rendezvous at the water-pavilion.

If Norah were to be spared cruel heart-ache, Marcus made up his mind that it were better to have Darcy's engagement with Agnes publicly announced, in order that any secret hopes Norah might still cherish would be definitely put to flight. Madame Warchester was the half-sister of Marcus's mother. The two families had not been on the best of terms, as the union of a Vane with a Dunn had been looked upon as a great stepping down for a daughter of that princely brood. Orphaned early, Marcus had pushed his own career, with but small concern for the wishes of his dominating kinswoman. But he was on good terms in the great house, and was always expected on occasions of state. He resolved to speak to "Aunt Elizabeth" about Darcy's attachment for Norah, and his fear that the thoughtless boy was still encouraging the poor child to look forward to what could never be. Mrs. Warchester had been made very miserable by her son's conduct. He had quit the city with the coldest adieux to Agnes, and since his departure had never written her a line. When Marcus, after an embarrassing preliminary talk, finally said :

"Aunt Betty, I must say something to you that I fear will pain you very much, but I say it in order that you may be saved a greater pain—"

As Marcus paused, the great lady suspended the rocking motion of her chair, and looked up eagerly from the work she had been busying her hands with.

"Why, Mark, what do you mean? what can it be? You have not been getting into any imprudent entanglement—you—?"

The embassador smiled. His aunt's foibles were well known to him, but he couldn't resist a small feeling of malice, in all his distress, as the self-contained arrogance of his kinswoman's nature asserted itself. Tainting the Warchester blood, lowering the banner of its pretense— these were the evils in her shallow sphere of action that seemed to her the most direful, the most unendurable.

"Oh, Aunt Betty, as for me, when I get ready to give myself up, I shall not involve any of you. I shall drop out of the ken of prying kin. No, the apprehension I have is for Darcy." She started, as a towering swan encountering a squawking duckling might. "I think you knew something of Darcy's romantic attachment for that pretty Norah, Dr. Marbury's ward?" She leaned back, as Elizabeth may have thrown her haughty shoulders back when my Lord Cecil gently began to insinuate the story of my Lord Essex's misbehaving. She listened as a sovereign lady might, bound to give ear to whatsoever concerned her subjects, but personally incredulous that eyes which had rested on royalty could wander to vulgar clay. She waved him to go on, with a dry, disdainful gesture, very significant of what he must be prepared to endure, should he fail to make his impeachment good. Marcus continued : "Something of Darcy's unfortunate weakness you already know. It was, I think, your own intervention in the affair that turned Norah's brain last year !"

" Surely, Mark, my son has not seen, or had to do with this person, since that wretched incident ?"

"Yes, and I don't know that he should be condemned

for that, for it was the meeting him that restored the poor girl's lost intellect, and—"

"She was very well without her intellect, I think. Darcy should have been kept from her sight."

"Surely, Aunt Betty, you would not condemn the poor girl for the accidental meeting, nor for the revulsion which broke the bondage in which her wits were held?"

"I don't see that people of that class need intellects. I thought her very well as she was; but what is the end of the story? There is something else, isn't there?"

A little angered, Marcus, all pity for the motherless girl, continued, mercilessly: "Yes, there is something else. Norah, wandering on the Holly Hills, again met Darcy— Agnes was with him. She seemed to have no memory of the sad scene in this house, and began to talk to him as they had talked before the shock. Darcy left her weaving garlands by the lily brook. He wandered back an hour later, and she was still there. He felt pity for her state, for the evening was fallen, and the air very chill. He led her home, and her joy was so evident that he remained a time. Thereafter he returned day after day, and the poor brain, picking up the links of memory under the charm of his presence, failed to seize the cause of its overthrow. I have found out, quite by accident, that Darcy was with Norah daily; that her recovered mind retains no memory of the cause that brought on the shock, and I fear that Darcy, in his madness and weakness, has gone, leaving the poor girl confident of his love and his return."

Still maintaining an almost judicial visage, and the manner of incredulity with which the conversation began, madam plied the envoy with questions that gave her the situation from points of view that Marcus had sedulously screened. Her steely gray eyes brightened as the secret of Marcus's interest stood revealed to her, but she affably ignored the discovery, and pushed the subject to its last recesses. During the long narrative, that was bitter to her as hyssop, for it revealed a taint in the family blood that was death to her pride, she sat with a steady—at times resentful—eye on the embarrassed envoy. When he told, with sympathetic tenderness, the idyl of the sylvan courtship, the dark gulf of insanity, the reappearance of Darcy, and the dawn of recovered reason, she smiled a stern smile of tolerant, contemptuous scorn. As the story came to an end, Mrs. Warchester's face became quite rigid. She knew that Marcus was the most cautious and unimpressionable of men. She knew that he would never have spoken if there had not been justification.

She sat silent a long time, unmoved by this new menace. She trusted her son so implicitly; deceit in him she couldn't understand; but was it deceit? Hadn't he shown conspicuously his indifference to Agnes? Hadn't he, by his hasty departure, prevented all discussion of the marriage? Were not his brief letters corroborative testimony of Marcus's averring that the old spell was upon him, that the old danger confronted the fortunes of the family!

"Let me think the matter over, Mark; I am so startled, so shocked, that I can not reflect now. Come over to-morrow—I shall want your advice."

When Marcus had gone, the hard look quit her face. She fled to her chamber, and the cold light melted from her eyes. She took a letter-packet from the drawer of the tall mahogany dresser, and, seating herself by the open window, untied the blue ribbon that held it. There were a few yellow sheets—the ink faded; there were others where the ink was clear and fresh; at the bottom there was an ivory miniature of a lovely boy, blue-eyed and frank, with tangled masses of yellow curls covering a shapely brow. Tears came to her eyes as she sat with those bright eyes laughing up into her own. She pressed the miniature to her lips, and then she began at the yellow sheets and read. They were Darcy's letters from school. Boyish prattle of dogs and toys and prizes and small heart-burnings. Then came the West Point epistles, breathing high purpose and renown. Then the brief lines from Mexico. These were cold, uncharacteristic, almost per-functory. She read them now with a key that translated the unspoken thought. She sighed wearily as each gave confirmation to Marcus's wretched surmises. Yes, Darcy —her first-born, the head of the house—was abdicating. He was preparing for that recreancy which would be her humiliation and shame.

What had she done that this cross should come to her.? There was another thought more poignant. Colonel Warchester had involved himself perilously in the enter-prises of Lord Poultney and Myrickson. His estate was deeply mortgaged. Darcy's union with Agnes had been looked forward to as a means of rescue. If that were not carried out, the Warchesters would be painfully crippled, perhaps forced to surrender the estate. The war had disturbed values and suspended the business of the bank. For a time it had been a question whether it could keep its doors open. The Vanes had come forward generous-ly and given Colonel Warchester the use of their name— but that was only a temporary reprieve. She knew all this, and dwelt upon it more seriously than the easy-natured husband, whose mind was serene so long as he could en-joy his rubber of whist and the good cheer of life.

There was only one thing to be done. She must write to Darcy—write at once—and recall him to his senses. She could not believe that he seriously meant to break his plight to Agnes. He was a boy and had been bewildered by this lightly won love. She wrote in a strain of tender affection and confidence—sympathizing in his chivalrous loyalty to the unfortunate girl, but reminding him of the hearts that his obstinacy would break, if he persisted in dallying with his duty. She hinted vaguely at the family entanglements, the ruin of Milly's prospects, and the family's loss of caste and future, if the heir of the house refused to maintain its interests. It was a masterful piece of maternal pleading—all the more eloquent that it admitted the young man's blamelessness, without reproaching Norah, or impeaching her ingenuousness.

The letter was dispatched that night, and the miserable mother resigned herself impatiently to the long delay before she could get her boy's answer. In the mean while she artfully pushed Agnes into writing her indifferent lover, representing his coldness as the natural waywardness of spoiled boys, immersed in the excitement of war. She induced Colonel Warchester to write, exposing his embarrassments and the vital urgency of Darcy's immediate marriage. When all this was set in force, she made a pilgrimage to Marbury and adroitly gathered from Byron the status of Norah. It was with a grim sense of relief that she learned that he, as head of the Marbury family, still held, and would, until Norah was married, parental control of her destinies. Through Marcus she kept track of Denny's bulletins from the field, and assured herself that her son was not in correspondence with Norah.

Late in October a letter came from Denny, telling of the capture and long illness, the march to the City of Mexico, and Darcy's renewed illness and his nursing into health. Then the information that Major Warchester had been sent to join the army of occupation on the Rio Grande, and the probability that neither of them would reach home before the middle of the next year.

The mother said nothing, but waited feverishly for the answer to her letter. Early in November it came. She locked herself in the room, and opened the large envelope with trembling hands. She read the first tender, dutiful phrases with bounding exultation. Her own Darcy—her high-minded boy. How base she had been to doubt his loyalty—his obedience! He covered three pages before touching the burning subject :

" I have shrunk from the pain I must give you, dearest mother ! I have reflected, until death seemed to me far the easier way of ending the evil I have wound myself in. But life has clung to me, and I must face the consequences of my own doing ! All that you say or can say, I know. All that you have written I have pondered, and I see no way out of my miserable folly, consistent with manhood. Whether I am to blame for loving Norah and winning her love, it is idle to discuss. I have won her love. I do love her. That is enough. There is no escape from it. In the sight of God she is my wife. So soon as I get home I shall make her my wife in the sight of the world. Even if her image were not always in my heart, and if I did not associate her with all my happiness in the future, it is no longer in my power to deny her.

" My life is hers. Her brother Denny has twice held me out of a closing grave. How could I ever raise my head among men if I brought this misery upon a heart that has shown such devotion to me ! Dismiss me from your plans of life. I will remain in the army, and with Norah will end my life tranquilly in the dull routine of a soldier's career. Milly is beautiful, accomplished, and when she returns from abroad, will bring about, by a great marriage, all and more than you could ever have hoped from your profligate first-born. Tell Agnes all, for I can't bring myself to write to her. I don't think she will care much; her pride may be a little wounded, but such feelings as she had for me will soon be forgotten. I have said nothing to Norah, nor do I mean to, until my return. I know your nature too well to hope that you could ever be brought to receive her as a daughter of our house, but you would give me great comfort if you could force yourself to show her some kindness for my sake. She needs it, poor innocent child, for I have been a coward and villain! I should have written this to you long ago, before you wrote me, had I not expected to be home before now. I shall get a furlough this month, and go home to marry Norah."

The pages dropped from the trembling hands. She drew her chair nearer, with a shiver, to the bright crackling wood-fire, and sank deeper into the cushions. The sheets of the letter lay unnoticed at her side. For a time she was too stunned to think. What did the letter mean? He had promised the low-born girl marriage! "He, a Vane, a Warchester, had given his word to two women! One of them a madwoman! Ah!—mad—mad"—the word burned into her brain. It thrilled her with a wild, fierce joy. "Mad? yes! this low-born obstacle, this low-born destroyer of the family pride was mad. Is mad!" she whispered. "She is mad! My son shall never marry a madwoman! The law would protect us against that."

It was late in the afternoon, and the day was raw and threatening. She called for the carriage, and drove straight to the law-office of Governor Darcy. She stated a case bearing on the story, without mentioning names. The Governor's answer made her heart bound. Such a union would be null. It could be prevented by a writ of lunacy. But the better way would be to remove the girl for a time. She drove home, her terror lessened, her grief assuaged. Yes, she must save her rash, soft-hearted boy from himself. She must prevent this sacrifice of himself and family. Agnes! Yes, he would be the first to recognize his mother's wisdom when the glamour of this low love was gone. She would save Marcus, too, from the meshes of this siren; for the barriers once thrown down, when would these odious mismatings end? Colonel Warchester had spoken a day or two before of a legal contest in Bucephalo. Marcus must be secured to argue it, and while he was gone, Norah could be managed. To this the Colonel readily assented, as it would spare him a journey he dreaded. The same day she drove out to Marbury, and bade Byron be ready to receive his ward in the evening. Byron was mystified as to the means of inducing her to come, but the resolute mother simply said:

"My son is headstrong and ungovernable. He thinks himself bound to this girl. It is my belief that she is mad, and you can test the question by keeping her well guarded here!"

The astute simplicity and naturalness of the stroke flashed upon Byron in an instant. The mother's pride and the son's folly were in alliance to bring about what he had in vain attempted. He laughed a little laugh of knowingness, and the lady added, in a coldly indifferent tone:

"Until the poor girl is quite restored, of course it will be wise to keep her presence here as secret as possible."

"Ah, that is easily managed. If we are troubled by busybodies, we can send her over to the spring farm, just now untenanted. There's more ways of killing a rabbit than breaking its bones."

She looked at him fixedly, then said, with the slightest shade of stateliness:

"It is as Norah's best friends, you understand, that we

take this step, otherwise I should have her sent to a public institution. She must be treated with the tenderest consideration, and denied nothing, except liberty. The law is really her guardian now, and in the end "—she added, significantly—" we shall have to render an account of your stewardship of the fortunes of your ward. Sooner or later her brother will be back, and, of course, she will be traced here."

"To her legal guardian."

"Exactly, and her legal guardian must be able to show that he has acted in her interests—not his own."

The chilly November air had for some time stopped Norah's rambles on the Holly Hills. This day was bleak and wintry, and she sat in the pretty parlor, moving her fingers lightly over the keys of the piano. Manly would be with her presently, when released from school, and she glanced from the window from time to time to catch a glimpse of his tow-head and shining school-boy face, trudging over the fallen leaves and frisking over the bare ground. A bright wood-fire gleamed and sputtered in the shining grate, and the air of comfort and even refinement made a congenial frame for the lonely mistress of this tranquil interior. A book, "Kenilworth," lay open on the little table near an arm-chair; evidences of the reader's tears were on the pages of Amy Robsart's sorrowful taking off. A bit of embroidery, with the needles in it and the threads strung out like a web of pea-blossoms, hung on the head of a low couch.

But Norah could not keep her mind on the book or her hands to the work. Even as she sat at the piano her eyes gazed far off absently before her, and she fell into soft, timorous sighs as the random chords floated into the melancholy strains of long-forgotten airs. Though there was no chill in the genial air of the room, she had a dainty worsted shawl over her shoulders, fastened at the throat by the little brooch, the object of her furtive joy at Marbury so long ago, but now worn openly, for there was none to question or wonder at her wearing it. The clouds outside grew denser, and presently large flakes of snow whirled among the bare limbs and vanished as they reached the ground. Manly would hardly come now. He could not resist this first fall of the snow, and she turned with a little sigh to her embroidery. Suddenly, in the still air she heard the clatter of horses drawing near, and hurried to the window. She caught a glimpse of a carriage as it passed, and returned to her seat on the couch. Presently a low knock startled her. That was a sound rarely heard, for the visitors to the cottage were intimates who rarely made use of the knocker. She was alone in the house, and, drawing the shawl about her with care, she hurried to the door. In the dim light she did not at first recognize the visitor.

"You don't know me, Norah? It is Mrs. Warchester."

"Oh yes; won't you come in? I am alone, and I was a bit startled," and she stepped aside to give the grand lady space to pass in the narrow hallway.

"Alone, are you? Well, I want to speak with you just a moment; it's quite as well that you are alone." This was said with just the shade of change from the first insinuating tone, a sort of suppressed triumph that Norah's sensitive ear instantly distinguished. She drew the shawl still more closely around her, and, pointing the way, followed the visitor to the little parlor. She placed a chair near the grate and shrank back to the couch, where the light was dim and herself in shadow.

Mrs. Warchester did not offer to remove her cloak, and poor Norah was too much overwhelmed by the apparition to think of suggesting it. The great lady glanced scrutinizingly about the trim apartment, her eye lingering with well-bred wonder on the handsome piano, and the few admirable engravings decorating the modest walls. The books in the little racks, and the open volume, arrested her eye, and her well-curved lips were a trifle compressed as she said in a tone meant to be engagingly sympathetic :

"Why, Norah, you have a charming little home here; you ought to be a very happy girl."

Norah, grown more and more disturbed as she watched the visitor, could make no answer beyond bending her head and moving the worsted work, as though it were in some sort an offense to the æsthetic harmony of the details of the interior.

"Your brothers are very good to you, Norah; you owe them a great deal; no lady in Warchester is more tastefully housed than you are."

"Yes, Madame Warchester, Denny and Larry are very kind brothers; they are very good to me."

"It would be hard not to be good to you, Norah, for, from all I have heard, you deserve it."

Mrs. Warchester pushed her chair from the glowing fire, but, as she moved it, she managed to get nearer the couch, where she could see the girl's face more distinctly. The movement and the words were perfectly natural, but they produced a sinister impression on Norah. She shrank farther back in shadow and said tremulously :

"Everybody is friendlier to me than I'm deserving of. My brother Denny has always been like a father to me."

"Yes," with effusion, "Denny is a noble fellow. In my letters from my son, his conduct is spoken of with praise and affection." She watched the girl as this was said. Even in the obscure light she could detect a heightening of color and a quickened breathing. "Yes,"

17

she resumed, "Denny twice saved my son from deadly peril, and he shall never lack friends in our house." She waited; Norah's reticence was beginning to puzzle her. Could it be artifice? it wasn't timidity. Her purpose was to lead Norah into some expression that would make the topic she had come to treat a natural sequence. But the girl's non-committal responses promised to drag the interview interminably. She made a last attempt to evoke a decisive answer.

"I suppose you hear regularly from—your brother?"

"Yes, ma'am! Denis writes whenever he can."

"And you have heard of his goodness to my son?"

"Yes, ma'am; Denis wrote about it to Dilly Dane, but he said only a word of it to me. If Dilly hadn't read me her letters, I shouldn't have known much about it; for Denny is very little given to talking about matters that concern others."

Here, at least, was an admission. Darcy was evidently not in correspondence with Norah, and the measures she had resolved upon were not endangered in that direction.

"Have you Denny's letters, Norah? My son is so busy that he writes me very sparingly, and I am very eager to learn all I can about the poor boy."

"Yes." The cherished packet was at hand, and Norah eagerly got them out and handed them to the mother. She went to the window and stood with her back to Norah as she ran through them. Not a line indicated any confidence between Denis and Darcy—nor any hint that the brother suspected the relation between his sister and his friend. Indeed, Norah's readiness to show them re-assured her before she had looked at them. They breathed admiration and love for Darcy, but without a syllable that Norah was intimate with the young man, or more than the most distant acquaintance. There was a triumphant gleam in the mother's eye; the room was too warm, and she slipped her fur cloak off and laid it on the table. Resuming her chair, drawn still closer to Norah, she said gently:

"Norah, your brother is a real friend to my son; do you think you could be as good a friend—as self-sacrificing—if it came to you to be?"

Norah was shrinking far back in the corner of the couch. Her breath came and went in little gasps. I believe that she dimly foresaw what was coming; that living so much in the realm of dreams, and construing actualities from her fanciful prepossessions, she had the clairvoyant sense, sometimes seen in children and dreamers given to commune with nature. Her silence did not disconcert the mother, who now saw her way clear.

"Yes, Norah, I have come to ask you to do your duty like a Christian girl. My son in boyish thoughtlessness gave you his heart. I don't blame you that you gave him yours. It was quite natural, deprived as you were of a mother's counsel, and the safeguards that protect young girls in their own home. My son is of a race that never did dishonor. Had he been of any other sort, such relations as yours would have put you in deadly peril—would have left you a ruined life. But having innocently and, I have no doubt, undesignedly won your love, he has felt it a duty to sacrifice himself and his family by—by—" Here the smooth tone grew hard, and only a dry gasping sound came from the throat. "You may not know—he has been for two years the promised husband of a sweet girl in his own rank in life. His own and his family's fortune depend upon that union; for I may tell you in confidence that my husband's business is badly involved, and it is only by my son's marriage with—with the lady he long ago chose, and his family desires, that he and we

can be saved the greatest distress. I know that this would
be enough to decide you in the matter ; but I will confide
still farther in your discretion. My son will return shortly,
and the marriage will follow immediately. I know him,
however, so well, that I fear, unless you give him a release,
he will hesitate as to his duty. He will feel that Denny
has put a burden upon him, and that, though his heart is
another's, he must remain unmarried, as long as you do
not bid him keep his pledge to his sweetheart, and his
duty to his parents ! "—a pause—

"You are listening to me, Norah ? "—for the mute figure now crouched far in the corner, the head down on the
cushion, and no audible sound heard.

"You would not be happy if you consented to my
son's sacrifice, for he would be giving himself up to pay
the debt due your brother. No self-respecting girl would
consent to put a man in such bondage ; no right-feeling
girl would consent to accept a sacrifice that would make
the man she loved miserable ! I know you to be a good
girl, and if you love this unhappy boy with half the love
of his mother, you will take this load from all our hearts,
by giving me the power to write him that he is free."

She had moved to the couch as she spoke, and lifted
Norah's head. The girl started convulsively, and moved
from her in a panic of terror, holding up her hands in
piteous entreaty, as the mother attempted to support her.

"Ah ! my God ! my God ! What can I say ? What
can I do ? "

"Say what I ask of you, my poor child ! God will give
you strength and the peace that comes of right doing."

Suddenly, clasping her head with both hands, Norah
turned in the firelight and panted hoarsely :

"Does—Dar—does *he* bid me do this—does he ask
it ? "

The mother, desperate, believing that in Darcy's behalf all things were justified, didn't flinch from this final wrench of conscience.

"Yes, Norah, Darcy, conscious of his duty, and to spare other hearts, asks this sacrifice of you. He—"

But, as this cruel blow came, the strength that had supported the sorely-tried heart gave way. She reeled as from the impact of a blow, and slid limply from the soft cushion to the floor. Before applying a restorative, Mrs. Warchester hurried to the hall door, and called lightly. She had barely stooped over Norah's inanimate form, when Byron was at her side. He lifted the helpless body and laid it on the couch. Byron's arms were filled with warm wraps. Mrs. Warchester lifted the girl's shoulders and slipped a thick shawl under her. But as she was adjusting it, she became rigid, uttered a little stifled cry, and sat quite still, staring helplessly at the lifeless form in her arm. When she rose, she moved in a dazed, frightened way, and gasped hoarsely:

"You must see to her; I—I can not touch her. She is your ward. Take her."

"I reckon she ain't poison, madam; it can't soil any one to touch her, can it?"

Mrs. Warchester shuddered, as she hastily fastened her cloak with trembling hands, and moved to the door. Byron carried Norah out and placed her in the carriage, and remarked with angry impatience that Mrs. Warchester, in the carriage, shrank as far from the body as she could.

He got upon the box and drove off. When near the Warchester gates he was directed to stop. Mrs. Warchester got out, closed the door carefully, and handed him a small leather bag.

"There are salts and brandy in this. When you get out a short distance, you had better revive her. It may be dangerous to drive all the way to Marbury before attending to her. And "—she said this with curious significance—"be very careful to have the physician for her at once."

"Then you're not going home with us, ma'am?" Byron asked in surprise. "What shall I do with the team?"

"Send them to the Cataract Stables, where my coachman will come for them; and let me know how you succeed with—with the person." She hurried away hastily, as if fearing dissent, and disappeared in the darkness.

"Well, she's about the chilliest bit of human natur' I've struck. She's got about as much heart as an acorn in plowin' time," and, with a vicious lash on the halting horses, Byron set off down the Marbury road, never stopping until the horses drew up at the lane gate.

CHAPTER XXVII.

A NEW LOVE.

An hour later Larry entered the cottage. He had been down to the new station to meet Aunt Selina, who, on Denny's urgent invitation, was to make her future home under his roof. She had not arrived, and Larry, who was keeping her coming as a surprise for Norah, ran up to the room prepared for Aunt Selina's reception, without looking for his sister. He slipped down the stairs presently, and went to his workshop, where he was giving the finishing touches to a pretty cabinet to be set in Aunt Selina's room. He noticed that the tea-table was not laid as usual, but the fact did not rest on his mind with any significance.

It was seven o'clock almost when he bethought himself of supper. On re-entering the house, there was still no sign of Norah. He called, but there was no answer. He was a good deal surprised but not alarmed, for sometimes Norah, visiting Mrs. Blythe, lost track of time, and came home late with little Manly.

She had never, however, left him supperless, and he set about preparing the meal to surprise her when she came. But he was hungry, and, long after the tall clock in the hall had struck eight, he poured out the tea and ate in discontent. It was near ten o'clock when he resolved to set out for the "Blue Jay" to fetch the truant home. Manly was alone in the tap-room, apostrophizing a much-beruffled owl that blinked vaguely under the straggling beams of a tallow candle.

When Larry appeared, Manly gave him a nod, and, as if continuing the conversation, went on:

"Now, Minerva won't hoot any more in the night than she does in the day. Norah said if I kept her in the dark she'd say, tu-whoo, tu-he-he, but she don't say a blamed thing. I don't believe she's got the least bit of a voice!"

Larry laughed. He was given to sympathizing with the small Manly's troubles, and had made the lad sleds and traps of such wondrous beauty that he was the envy of all the school-boys in Warchester.

"You must put Minerva in the dark, the light frightens her. Keep her in the barn, and she'll hoot fast enough. Where's Norah?"

"Home, I reckon."

"No, I've just come from home; she hasn't been there since six o'clock. She wasn't there when I got home to supper," and Larry's voice now had a shade of tremor that impressed Manly.

"O Larry, she can't have gone out of her head again! Did you look in the copse-in the hills?"

Larry sank into the long settle by the wall, and his heart began to beat.

"And she hasn't been here at all?"

"No, I've been sliding since I came from school right by the house, but I haven't seen her, and she always plays with me when she comes. But I'll ask mother."

He came back almost immediately with Mrs. Blythe, and that good soul made no disguise of her alarm. Larry was provided with a lantern, and with Manly set out to scour Norah's haunts in the hazel copses. But there was, of course, no sign. A night of piteous anxiety passed, and a score of people made search the next day. Late at night a scarf that Manly recognized as Norah's was found among the rocks at the edge of the cataract, and the stream below the falls was searched. When, two or three days later, Marcus returned, systematic effort was renewed, but, beyond remnants of woman's apparel, faded and in shreds, there was nothing found to confirm the general belief that the poor girl had been carried over the cataract. It was not until the last hope was gone that Marcus wrote the awful story to Denny, his own anguish keener than the brother could feel. It had never occurred to him that there might be an unknown cause for Norah's disappearance. He had driven out to Marbury, but Byron was not at home, and Amelia made no allusion to the tragedy, which had been briefly related in the county paper. When Marcus called on his aunt she was ill, and so the subject was never mentioned afterward.

Agnes had returned from a visit to Bucephalo, and, after a short stay in Warchester, had gone to spend the winter in Washington, where the Vanes had a kinsman a

Cabinet Minister. The young girl delighted in the ceremonial of capital life, and was greatly courted by the stately young men of the republican court. One among them, the son of an eminent Southern statesman, became so markedly assiduous in his devotion that rumors of an engagement penetrated to Warchester. But the mother's fears were presently allayed on receiving tidings from Darcy that he was on his way to the capital, with dispatches for the War Department. He would meet Agnes, she foresaw, and the court paid her by rivals would spur him into holding his own.

Sure enough, Agnes, one day, sharing the homage of the great with the lady of the White House, met her lover under the ordeal of a hundred eyes. Both were surprised, but the girl bore the shock more composedly than the recreant lover. In fact, for a few minutes, Darcy was dumfounded. He did not know on what terms to meet her. If his mother had made known his determination, Agnes must regard him with hatred and loathing. But she met him gayly, even with tenderness. He was distraught and silent, till presently an opportunity came to walk with her in the wide hall leading to the conservatory. She took his arm with the old familiarity, and bent her head in the old seductive way. He was explaining his coming to Washington, and his ignorance of her being there, when a dashing young fellow, coming from the rear entrance of the reception-room, made up to them, exclaiming:

"Well, Miss Vane, is this the way you keep faith? You were to have joined General Marline and me for a turn in the greenhouse Fie on such fickleness!"

Darcy looked from the smiling face of the intruder to the blushes of Agnes in surprise. She disengaged herself gayly, and with a bewitching gesture said :

"Mr. Brinton, this is my nearest friend and neighbor, Major Darcy Warchester."

The young man frankly extended his hand in the impulsive Southern way, and said good-humoredly :

"Ah, that excuses your faithlessness ! An old friend always takes the claim from a new one. I know of Major Warchester very well ; my cousin Colonel Ewell has written of your doings at Molino del Rey. Are you to be in town long, Major?"

"No, I think not ; I believe I return at once to join my regiment on the Rio Grande."

Lionel Brinton was at the moment the heir-apparent of a political personage in Washington. His father was openly proclaimed the prospective successor of the present Executive at the next election. The family was one of the conceded potentialities of Virginia, and the young man was the caressed darling of every social activity. Darcy watched him as Agnes, bidding the young man join them, rattled on in the high spirits natural to her race. Brinton's florid compliments and subdued manners were at first puzzling to Darcy, but he made up his mind that the youth held a place in Agnes's heart. When he quitted them, Brinton bowed him off quite as if he was in some sort the young girl's protector.

Darcy was confounded ! He hurried off through the dreary unkempt grounds of the White House to his lodgings, anxious for seclusion to give him a chance to think. It must be, of course, that his mother had told Agnes the story of his love for Norah ! She had, as he foresaw, accepted the release from him rather as a relief, and was probably pledged to the confident young cavalier. Yes—that must be it. But then, surely, she would have given some sign of pique on meeting him ; she wouldn't have called him "Darcy." She wouldn't have fallen into the tender undertone she had begun in if the memory of his miserable trifling had been in her heart. But perhaps it was to show him that his treason had not wounded her. He was perplexed, and saw no way of solving the mystery. In the evening he called on his kinsmen the Vanes, and as he arose to leave his uncle followed him to the street.

"You say you return to the Rio Grande, Darcy, my boy. Your mother expected you here when we left home, and the marriage robes are in order, and waiting. I tell you what it is, my dear fellow, you mustn't trust too much to your fine eyes and your Apollo form! Agnes is besieged on all sides, and, unless you bind her fast, you don't know when some enterprising chap may make off with her. We can't keep the song-bird caged forever, you know!"

It was well for Darcy that the obscurity of the miserably lighted street stood his friend. He paled and flushed as this jocose reproach fell on his ear; his kinsman was far from suspecting the revelation he was making.

"Ah, love must wait till the laurels bloom," he retorted, with an effort at gayety, and, pressing the other's hand, he strode away. Washington was then a hamlet with a single lighted street, and he was in no humor to risk the mud in his pensive ramble. He returned to his dismal room in the noisy hotel, and walked its narrow circumference until far into the morning hours. It was plain to him that his mother had not given Agnes his message, and he must do it himself. But how tell the girl, radiant in the recognition of her beauty, adored by all with whom she came in contact, that he was a craven, that he had courted her by command, and gave her up to save himself the stigma of dastard and ingrate! Then, too, the time was to be so short in the city that he could not let events reconcile her gradually to his defection, so that, when the declaration came, she would be prepared.

Perhaps she would herself relieve him if he gave her time and pretext.

This young fellow Brinton—surely his manner told of more than merely perfunctory devotion. But then, the Southron was much given to exaggeration and hyperbolic expression to women. Darcy would at least find out for himself. Brinton might mean much, he might mean nothing. Fate was his pronounced friend the next morning, for what should he find but a note from Brinton, inviting him to luncheon!

The young fellow met Darcy with the effusive cordiality of his clime, and in ten minutes was divulging his most cherished confidences. It was not necessary for Darcy to intrigue for the topic he had at heart. In a burst of irrestrainable impulse Brinton burst out:

"Do you know, Major, your relative, Miss Vane, is a peerless beauty? There isn't such a princess in all Virginia!" He leaned back with the wine-glass held as a sort of shield before his face, possibly to conceal the emotion that his words but partly revealed. Darcy nodded vaguely, not so much struck by Agnes's superiority to the Virginia princesses as the amorous eulogist thought he would be. Brinton took the silence for encouragement, and added, in a tone of mingled entreaty and assurance:

"Do you think my suit would be acceptable to her? You know our family is the best in Virginia! We were noble when the Lees, Custises, and Washingtons were poor tobacco-planters!"

Darcy couldn't resist a smile, and answered, very blandly:

"Such claims as you have to present, Mr. Brinton, no young lady of any sensibility could treat other than seriously."

"Do you really think so, sir, and—do you know—are you at liberty to tell me—ah, that is—" his brown cheeks grew quite red, and his eyes a little humid—"do you think that Miss Vane is heart-free, fancy-free, as we say in Virginia?"—he called it "Vaginiya."

"Ah, as to that, Mr. Brinton, who can tell about these beauties? Heart-breaking, I am told, is their by-play. You know the adage, 'Faint heart never won fair lady.'"

"Yes, I know, but your Northern girls are so different from Virginia girls"—he always spoke of Virginia as if it were another country, merely identified with the other States of the Union by the amenities of international usage. "In Virginia a girl prides herself on the number of hearts she breaks, and engages herself to the fellow that cuts cover with the most to-do!"

So my Lord Warchester sallied out a free man. He knew in his heart that Agnes was smitten with the tall *caballero ;* that his wicked black eyes had flashed a soft story into her empty heart, that, for the moment at least, filled it with the divine symphony his own had never echoed there. But what a confusing code the law of love is!

With the assurance that her heart was in another's keeping, he began to feel the gnawing of a jealous tooth. And this is a phase of this melancholy comedy passing before you, that has always made me scout the astuteness that the gossips of Warchester ascribed to Madame Warchester, Darcy's fond mamma. If she had been as clever as she was resolute and ambitious, I am convinced that she would have fired her son with jealousy, instead of making way with Norah after the manner of the old-school novels. She never knew how nearly the work that she undertook came to being done by the dark-eyed young Virginian. His brag and complacency did more in ten minutes to shake Darcy's constancy to Norah than all the plotting of the anxious mamma. Mars and Bellona were plainly at work, however, against the peace of the Warchester family. On calling at the War Office, Major Darcy received orders hurrying him at once to the Rio Grande again, where he must report with vital dispatches within a time so limited that he would be forced to ride Southward day and night.

When his traps were packed and everything in readiness, he hastened to bid Agnes adieu. When he gave his name and asked for her, the domestic looked a little uncertain, but requested him to wait a moment. Almost at the same instant Darcy caught the sound of Agnes's voice quite near, and, recurring to old ways, he pushed open a door at the side of the vestibule. Yes, Agnes was there, and before her, on his knees, the Virginian knight ! His back was toward Darcy, and he did not for a moment notice the blush and start by which Agnes signalized the apparition of her old sweetheart.

"You will be queen of my heart, and princess of our little realm ! You shall have minions to obey your slightest beck ! The glories of the house of Brinton shall be revived to do honor to your regal beauty. Ah, Agnes—"

But at this point Darcy coughed, and regained gravity and composure to say :

"Pardon me, Agnes, I supposed you were alone. I—"

The swain paused deliberately, still resting on one knee, and turned his head, not at all disconcerted. Agnes was blushing, unable to speak, whether from a realization of the ludicrousness of the scene or embarrassment, Darcy couldn't guess. The heir of the Brintons, concluding to make use of his feet, arose and said with comic gravity :

"I am not sorry that you have come, Major Warchester. It is right that you should know that I have paid my addresses to your incomparable kinswoman, and that she deigns to accept them ! "

" I have only time to add my felicitations to my adieus. I am ordered to the army on the instant, and I took the right of an old friend and relative to run in and say good-by ! "

He eyed Agnes a little disdainfully as he said this, and waited for her to speak. But she stood immovable and silent, with high color and glistening eyes. He advanced and held out his hand, Brinton turning to the window.

" I hope you will be very happy, Agnes. It is better after all that you have chosen as you have. I—I—have no right to complain."

" No, Darcy, you certainly have no right to complain ! "

"Well—I wish you every happiness ! " He raised her hand to his lips, turned, and was gone !

She remained standing where Darcy had left her so long that Brinton, buried in the embrasure of the window, fancied that both must have left the room. He emerged from the heavy draperies, astonished and scared.

" Has your cousin gone, Agnes ? "

She aroused herself and sank into a chair.

" Yes, he is gone."

" Why, how abrupt ! He is very much cut up, isn't he, at his marching orders ? "

" Yes, he is very much put out."

The ardent prattle of the Virginian soon restored the temperature of love, and an hour later I doubt whether there was in the girl's heart a thought of the man upon whom she had looked for years as the companion of her life. But as he cantered toward Annapolis, Darcy saw all the past with torturing vividness. He didn't know whether this was a release or a punishment. He was certainly free ; free beyond the possibility of a reproach from his mother, for Agnes had herself broken the bond.

Meanwhile, the tidings of Darcy's coming to Washington had suffused Mrs. Warchester's cheeks with a tinge of higher color than usually adorned that unimpressionable face. Had Darcy learned of Norah's disappearance? What would the effect be? Wouldn't he suspect some outside handiwork, and wouldn't he in his boyish wrath undo all that had been done? Would he come from Washington to Warchester? He would meet Agnes. She surley would employ all her arts to hold her sweetheart?

If she dared write to the girl and warn her! But how word a letter that would not at the same time excite strange doubts on the score of her lover's loyalty? If she had already begun to resent Darcy's indifference— and it had long been plain that she did—she would be exasperated beyond soothing by the strange story of the Norah episode.

But it was plain that Darcy must be made aware of his freedom from even a shadow of an obligation. The mother's decision was promptly taken. She was on the road within forty-eight hours of the intelligence of Darcy's mission to the capital, and early one morning, as the Vane family were sitting at the breakfast table, she was announced. When Agnes submitted her charming cheek for Madam's effusive kiss, she was blushing furiously, and the lady marked it with an inward throb of joy. If she was thus strongly moved by the mother's embrace, what would the conquering Darcy's welcome be! To spare the maternal feelings for the moment, nothing was said of Darcy's sudden departure. He had been gone twelve hours when the mother entered her brother's door. The news was told her by Mrs. Vane, when the two ladies had retired to Mrs. Warchester's apartment. She withstood the shock with a firmness that quite awed her timid kinswoman.

"And Darcy was in town only two days?"

"He came Wednesday evening and went Friday noon."

"Did you see much of him? Did he spend much time with you—with Agnes?"

"Yes, he was here to dine, and to breakfast, and he was at a reception with Agnes, given by the President's lady." Mrs. Vane was ill at ease, and did her best to turn the subject to other channels, but the resolute querist kept her on the rack until, finding it futile to push the attempt, dropped it, resolved to put Agnes in the inquisition so soon as she could get her ear privately. But Agnes, with admirable adroitness, evaded the chances engineered by Mrs. Warchester, who, however, felt quite re-assured that Darcy had said nothing during his short stay to break the engagement. The day after her arrival Agnes went to pass a few days with Lady Poultney, who was holding great state at the capital, her husband's rank compelling every evidence of social concession from the British minister and his suite.

It was the bitterness of wormwood to the haughty patrician when she learned that her son's betrothed was under the roof of the vulgarian, but she smiled grimly in the assurance that such errors should not be tolerated when the marriage knot was safely tied!

Lady Molly heard, with great good humor, of her enemy's coming, and made much of the *pas* her rank gave her in the *salons* where she encountered Mrs. Warchester. She was not long in discerning Agnes's secret, and, true to her frank nature, taxed the maiden with it.

"And Prince Darcy, where is he to find rank and

riches to satisfy my lady, his mother?" she asked the blushing coquette.

"I don't think Darcy cares much for his mother's preferences in the matter. If he has a heart, I think it was given long ago to some one else—at least, he never seemed to me much of a lover!"

"Was it some one else in Warchester, think ye?"

"There was a girl in Warchester whose heart he held. I met her once in the Holly Hills, and she showed that she was madly in love with him. She went crazy after that, and a month or two ago I saw in the paper that she mysteriously disappeared—some thought that she had thrown herself in the river."

"In the name of God, you don't mean pretty Norah Boyne, Dr. Marbury's adopted daughter!"

"Yes, that was the girl—Norah; she was very pretty, and it would be just like such a sentimental fellow as Darcy to fall in love with her."

"And that reminds me," continued Lady Molly, reflectively, "the British minister referred some papers to me Lord Poultney a few days ago concerning one Hugh Boyne, who has been awarded a claim in northern Mexico. He gives out that he is from Warchester, and a British subject. I wouldn't be surprised if it concerns Norah and Denny in some way. Ah, there ye are, me Lord; what have you found out about the Boyne claim?"

Lord Poultney, who had just entered, embraced his wife, and, seating himself comfortably, said:

"My dear, it's quite like a tale of Scott. I never heard anything so romantic. I have seen Boyne. His papers are all in good order. He arrived in this country over twenty years ago. He fell into bad company in Warchester, and quitted the city. He drifted West as far as the Mississippi ; went down that stream with a company of what must have been pirates. The party broke up, and Boyne wandered into the Rio Grande country, attached himself to the Texan revolutionists, was given immense tracts of land near Montaluna, in New Mexico, by a Spanish hidalgo whose life he saved from an Indian incursion. Part of this Mexican grant turns out to be silver lodes, and the government has just confirmed him in the title, made out in good form to him from the Mexican Government."

Agnes had left the room when Lord Poultney entered, and Lady Molly said :

"This Hugh Boyne must be the father of that fine lad Denis, that you saw in Warchester. I hope so, for the boy's sake ; he was a manly fellow."

"He said something about a family he had left there, but I didn't take much interest in that, and didn't question him. I am to see him again, however, and will ask him."

He did see Hugh Boyne again, and the millionaire adventurer learned of the dispersion of his family, or at least as much as Lord Poultney had gathered from Lady Molly, and the stray talk that followed Denny's visit. He counseled Boyne to call on Mrs. Warchester, with whose son Denny had served in Mexico, and Hugh at once hurried to the Vanes' house, where the lady was stopping. It would be hard to recognize in the tall, gray-haired stranger who presented himself to Mrs. Warchester, the good-humored, strapping young fellow who had handed the dripping Darcy to his mother from the canal nineteen years before. Though unadorned by the graces of the world, he sat soberly in the grandeur of the Vane mansion, and arose without any sign of awkwardness as the lady, austere and chilling, advanced in stately solemnity into the room. He waited until she had sunk into a chair and waved him to a seat before he said :

"You'll hardly be likely to remember me, ma'am. My name is Boyne. I left Warchester many a year ago, in great trouble. I went away reckless, and I had it in mind never to put foot in the place again, for I was only a curse to all belonging to me. I am told that you know something of my family. All I know is that my poor wife Kate died many a year ago, and most of the children. My boy Denis, I am told, was with your son in Mexico, and that my little Norah was befriended by you—may God bless you, ma'am!"

His voice broke down, and, as he reached this point and turned partly away, he hastily doubled an ample handkerchief of spotted red silk into his moist eyes. He looked at the grave face before him. It had grown strangely old. The lips were faded to an ashen white, and the eyes dropped uneasily before the frank, grateful glow of the other's.

"It was not that I ever was a bad man, ma'am, but everything went against me. My brother James was hard and unfriendly to me, and when I quit Warchester it was for the good of my little ones, for I thought I was a disgrace to them, God forgive me!"

He was fairly sobbing now, and the stately figure was no longer facing him; she had turned her head away, and her hands were moving restlessly in the folds of her silken robe.

"But, though I have borne great troubles, and had a heavy heart in my bosom, God has not turned his face from me in the end. It's a long story, ma'am, and I've no call to trouble you with it, only you may be pleased to know that the years have brought me riches—great riches, ma'am, such riches as I never thought could come to one man. But it is more luck than deserving. They have come to me through the risking of a life I never valued,

God forgive me, and I think he has, for now I can live to do good all the days of my life, please God!"

His voice was quite choked, but there was a triumphant exultation in the idea of doing good that welled out with a rugged pathos. His listener had drawn farther and farther into the shadow. Every word sounded in her ears like a menace. How dared this vagabond, this outcast, appear before her? How dared he make his odious life, in some inextricable sort, part of the fabric of her existence? How dared he invoke God in the loathsome scheme of his destiny? How dared he imperil her laboriously-wrought life-work by his untimely apparition and intervention? Ah, if Darcy had been delayed a day! If he could be even yet safely wed to Agnes before this hideous temptation came to paralyze his purpose!

"Your story is a very strange one, Mr.—a—Boyne. I myself know little of your family, but my nephew, Mr. Marcus Dunn, can give you every information."

She rose, trembling. Hugh looked at her, abashed.

"I ask your pardon, ma'am, if I have made too bold. I came to you because Lord Poultney thought that may be you could tell me about my little ones. I ask your pardon again, ma'am, and may God bless you and raise up friends for you and yours, if you ever need it, as good friends as you have been to mine."

Great Heaven! how long must she endure this torture? Was the vagabond mocking her? Would he presently ask her to restore Norah? Would he rail at her for working that troubled brain into new madness? She retreated to the folding doors, made a stately inclination, and, without ordering the servants to show the bewildered visitor out, disappeared. Hugh was confounded and perplexed. He hastened to Lord Poultney, to whose presence he was admitted, and found my Lady Molly there. He told the story of his reception, and asked, piteously, if he had done wrong.

"Wrong, Mr. Boyne? certainly not. But you must know that Mrs. Warchester is the proudest woman in the three kingdoms" (Lady Molly was apt to use her old country colloquialisms at random), "and she was acting out her overbearing nature. If Darcy had been there he would have had hearty sympathy for you. But you needn't mind the woman! You'll find yourself the father of as fine a lad as walks the streets, and—" Lady Molly was going to speak of Norah, but shrank from being the bearer of that sad tale. "When you see Marcus Dunn, he will tell you everything. Go to him as soon as you can."

Greatly comforted by the long talk that followed, and adoring the honest woman for her evident friendliness to Denis, Hugh waited in Washington only long enough to complete the business of identification, and then set out for Warchester.

CHAPTER XXVIII.

A NEW LIFE.

THERE was a diabolism in Madame Warchester's precautions that fairly cowed Byron, whose only thought had been to get Norah back. If she were in the house, where he could look at her, see her lovely eyes, perhaps touch sacredly her golden hair, speak with her—anything to know that no other man was near her; that no other tongue was luring her artless love. But the counsels of Darcy's mother implied more than this. The girl was to be kept from the sight of strangers. She was to be guarded by a trustworthy lad—Hiram, a boy that Dr. Marbury had rescued from the Truant Reformatory, on the verge of madness from maltreatment by the keepers: he had been confided to the Warchesters when Byron succeeded to the farm. This lad, a deformed youth of sixteen or seventeen, was instructed to sleep at Norah's door. In case she became dangerous, he was provided with a slender dog-chain with double padlocks to fasten her limbs, for the prevention of flight or self-hurt, until he could summon assistance.

Both Amelia and Byron resented the intrusion, regarding the boy as a spy at first; but in the end, Byron saw the necessity of a watcher, when Norah had attempted to throw up the window; then he warned the trembling little jailer that if, by any carelessness of his, harm came to Norah, he should be sent back to the tyrants of the Truant Home. The threat of contamination to a Mussulman could not have inspired more implicit, dog-like devotion. Hiram, the boy, never let the girl's movements escape him an instant, day or night.

Amelia, hovering over Norah, saw her eyes open languidly after she had been carried into the house and placed in the high-post bed where she had slept most of her life. She stared curiously at the white ceiling, then turned her head, and her gaze wandered over the familiar objects in the chintz-hung chamber. But there was neither surprise nor recognition in the gentle, dreamy glance. Even the thin, sharp visage of Amelia, with the malevolent glittering eyes fixed upon her, aroused none of the tremor they had inspired of old. Amelia had put her on the bed just as she came, and applied the homely remedies of the country housewife to restore her. Norah uttered no cry, though Byron had prepared his wife for an outbreak when the captive came to herself. But she was now breathing

softly, and apparently conscious of her surroundings.   She
lay still so long that Amelia spoke:

"Are you feeling quite well, Norah?"

"Hush, he bade me keep the secret! He'll come and
then he'll tell!"

"I don't understand you. Who told you to keep the
secret? What secret?"—and Amelia came close to the
bed and looked at the still, solemn face.

"Ah no, the Morris-men * would work me ill if the secret were told before he comes.   Then we'll have a Mor-
ris-dance on All-hallow-e'en, and wear the rosemary and
thyme."   She broke off suddenly and began a low subdued chant recounting the joys of the true love that remains constant.   Amelia ran down-stairs where Byron sat
by the fire.

"I do believe the crittur's crazy, Byron.   She's singing
to herself, and talking all sorts of wild nonsense that I
can't make head or tail of. You'd better send for Dr.
Banham."

Byron had purposely kept out of sight of Norah.   He
had his own reasons for dreading the effect his presence
might produce on Norah's revival.   But this news was serious.   If true, the worst had happened, and he looked forward to troublesome complications.   He hurried up with
his wife and entered the chamber.   Norah's eyes met his
tranquilly, but without a gleam of recognition.

"Norah, don't you know me? It is Byron."

"The banshee, yes—I know you! You trail the snake-
wort on the lilies and make them die; you make the frogs
screech in the full of the moon, and you rob true lovers of
their lasses; oh, yes—I know you, but I've the amulet that

---

* In the folk-lore of Ireland the Morris-men are a race of goblins
that, in the common superstition, haunt the woods, and play mischievous
pranks to lovers who are foolish or unwise.

makes ye afeard : you daren't step inside the moon's circle while I am there."

She turned away from him and began her chant again. With a sign to Amelia he quitted the room, now thoroughly alarmed. The doctor was at once sent for. He remained during the night, watching her assiduously. She was perfectly docile ; obeyed every command given her, but was clearly unbalanced. He informed Byron that, if left undisturbed and humored, she would in time recover. She had met some violent shock, and she would regain her faculties by rest and indulgence, or by some counter shock, which would place her back where the chains of reason had snapped.

For weeks she maintained this attitude of unobtrusive vagary. Amelia gave her sewing, knitting, and light work to distract her. She tried to go out into the fields at first, but was led back immediately. At night, when the tinkling of the cow-bells sounded in the lane, she grew uneasy, and at length Byron directed that she should be allowed to go among them. But the deep snow and fierce blasts would not permit this long, and she was finally reconciled to the house. She never spoke to Amelia and Byron unless a question was asked her. She didn't seem to recognize them at all, and looked troubled when they strove to recall the past. When April came, and the noisy chirping of the robins sounded in the orchard, she was strangely stirred. She started from the table where the family were at breakfast, and ran down into the wet meadow, before Byron could arrest her flight. When he came up to her, she was over her thin shoes in the soft earth, entreating a red-breast to come to her.

The exposure threw her into a fever, and toward evening she was delirious. Byron set out for the doctor, but had been gone only a few moments when Amelia was star-

tled by sharp cries and a loud shriek. She hurried to the
sick-chamber, and hastily examined the sufferer. She
started with a cry of horror! When the doctor arrived, a
half-hour later, a boy baby was wrapped up in the clothes
with the mother, who sat up in the bed, murmuring softly
and unintelligibly!

Amelia stopped her husband, as the doctor hurried up
to the sick-room.

"Byron, what do you think has happened?"

"My God, Amelia, she isn't dead?"

"Worse than that—worse than that! There's a little
baby up there!"

Byron shrank into a chair, nearly falling in his amazement.

"Good God! he never could be villain enough for
that!"

Amelia's eyes had almost disappeared under her sharp
brows as Byron fell into the chair, but as he said this an
indescribable look, one would have said of relief, shone in
her face as she asked eagerly:

"He! Who do you mean; not young Darcy?"

"Yes, the infernal coward! I'll have his blood, so
help me God! Oh, the scoundrel—the coward! No
wonder that old hell-cat, his mother, wanted to get the
girl hidden! I'll make her smart! I'll make every one
of the purse-proud tribe dance to another tune than
they have been prancing to this many a day—damn
them!"

Sure enough, the next day Byron rode furiously to
Warchester, and astonished the servants by a brusque
demand for the lady of the house. He listened incredulously when the lackey told him that madame had set out
for Washington, and the Colonel had gone with her as far
as New York. He listened grimly to the information

that madame had gone to meet her son, who was expected home immediately. That was enough. Master Darcy would find a warm welcome when he came!

Byron's cradle was brought down from the garret, a wondrous contrivance of rockers, canopy, and shining posts, and the small, blue-eyed baby was bestowed in heaps of soft wraps and pillows. Norah never let her wondering eyes quit it. Day and night she hovered over the little morsel of pink and white, crooning soft melodies that soothed it to sleep. She seemed unconscious of her condition. She met the mute gaze of Amelia with an innocent assurance that fairly overwhelmed that scandalized matron.

Byron had charged the doctor to keep the event a profound secret. No one knew of it save the family, and the lad who had been instructed to watch Norah, and never let her go too far without giving warning. Until the birth of the baby, Amelia had shown no repugnance to Norah's presence, but now she urged Byron to send her back to her friends, arguing, very justly, as Byron admitted, that her story would be misunderstood so soon as the neighbors came to know that she was a mother and not a wife. Byron agreed that, so soon as Mrs. Warchester returned, Norah should be sent away.

Mrs. Warchester did not return directly from Washington. She remained in New York until late in April. When the day for her coming was made known, Amelia, who saw as little of Norah as she could, came to her as she sat cooing to the baby, and said, without any preliminaries:

"Norah, you are going from here to-morrow!"

"Going! going where?"

"I am sure I don't know; to the poor-house, I suppose. You can't expect to be kept like a lady all your life. You'd better pack up your things as soon as you can. They'll take you away from here to-morrow!"

She turned and walked primly from the room without looking at the terrified face she left behind her. Now, if Amelia had racked her brain for the most terrific threat in the range of human cruelties, she couldn't have named a terror so overwhelming as the word "poor-house." Even to the unbalanced mind of Norah this was a reality so dire that her clouded brain seized it with all the distinctness of a clear intellect. Indeed, to a sound brain it would have been less dreadful, for her mind, filled with gentle perversions, immediately clothed this loathed and dreadful unknown—a dim reminder of the terrors her mother suffered—with all the panoply of woe that filled the minds of those that entered Malebolge. With this mantle of terror upon her, the craft of the mad began to work in her brain. She must fly! She must put herself out of reach of the dreadful men who were coming to take her.

He was somewhere waiting for her. His plight was hidden under the acorn-cups by the brook! If she could reach that, she would be safe. No baleful spirit could touch her there! All that day she watched eagerly. No, there was no chance. Byron was in the garden; the men were trimming the orchard.

All night she sat awake, and watched by the baby's cradle. The cocks were crowing blithely in the barn-yard when she fell into a doze. The exhaustion of terror held her fast, and when she awoke the sun was high, and the birds were piping melodiously. She got up, haggard, hopeless, desperate. Everybody was astir. She had allowed the morning to slip by, and in the realization of it she sank sobbing beside the baby's cradle. The little fellow awoke, and set up a faint cry. This distracted her for the time, and she soothed and fed him.

Every sound in the lane, every step on the stairs, made her shrink in a panic. But noon came, and there was no sign of the dreaded keepers. Alert to every stir in the household, Norah heard Amelia telling Hiram to go to a neighbor's on an errand, and then, as soon as dinner was done, Amelia put on her straw hat and walked over to neighbor Nelson's. The men were working in the brook-meadow. Presently Byron came from the barn with a horse saddled, stopped in the kitchen a moment, and then rode off toward Warchester. The spy was gone; now was Norah's time! Baby was wrapped warmly, and, with nothing else to impede her flight, she stole down the stairs, and crept on her knees along the currant-bushes in the garden until she reached the orchard; here, hugging the thick alders, she was safe.

In ten minutes she was in the beech woods, and she could push along fearlessly. The sun had gone under the clouds, but she didn't mind that—she was free! The birds sang to her in welcome. The squirrels ran along the low fences, or halted for friendly chatter as she came close to them. Once a great yellow butterfly hovered over baby's head, and she made a gesture as one who sees an omen. But now she had grown weary, her steps were uncertain and dragging. She sat down in a little thicket of dogwood breaking into bud, and uncovered baby's head that he might see the birds. The place was so peaceful, and the gray sky so solemn, that the confidence she felt shone in her face. As she sat cooing to baby, the sharp. report of a breaking branch startled her. She clasped the infant, and arose to fly. As she gained her feet Hiram stood in the path before her. He had a light chain wound about his arm, with a padlock in each hand.

"Well, Norah, you have taken a pretty long walk; isn't it time to come back? The folks will be wondering what has become of you!"

She looked at him with heaving bosom and wide staring eyes, but made no answer.

"Come, Norah, it'll be night by-and-by, and we must hurry and get home before the folks get back. They won't like it if they find you've gone so far away; come, let's go!"

He made a step toward her as if to take her arm. She bent over suddenly; there was a large flat stone at her feet; this she picked up, holding the baby with her left arm. Madness, rage, desperation were in the eyes that had never been seen ungentle before.

"Don't come near me! leave me, or I'll beat your head with this." She lifted it high above her head, and the lad started back in terror. He turned at a safe distance; she stood there confronting him, and as he halted, made a step toward him, and he fled still further. While his back was turned, she darted into the bushes, dropped the stone in a soft bed of moss, and fled with the fleetness of an Indian, for she was well used to penetrating the thickets. Hiram, trembling lest he should lose her, and quite as terrified to come near her, followed, keeping track of her movements by the breaking of the twigs, and sometimes catching a glimpse of her as she emerged into the clear fields. He had not seen her quit the house, but discovered the gray shawl against the alder bushes. He knew there was no one in the house, and Byron had cautioned him not to lose sight of her when she left her room; so he followed, hoping to meet somebody who would aid him to keep her until he could go back and fetch help.

She kept on with amazing endurance. Sometimes he lost sight of her, and then he came upon her seated in covert; but he kept out of reach and hearing. The gray sky grew overcast with threatening clouds, and he knew that rain must come soon. She seemed to know the way, for she avoided the vicinity of houses, and pursued wide circles to Warchester and the neighborhood of the Holly Hills.

Low rumbling thunder broke on the air, and flashes of lightning glared through the somber branches of bare chestnuts and oaks. It was almost twilight when the pursuit brought him to the brook that flows into the river below the Holly Hills. He could see Norah quite plainly as she came into the pretty glen, where a small boat-shed protected a little wherry used by the Warchesters in cross-ing the narrow stream. She seemed to know the place well, for instantly she removed a stone from a wilderness of plants, and eagerly groped about. In the vivid flashes he saw her slip something in her bosom, and then lay the baby down on a mossy knoll. Then she disappeared an instant, and as he came in sight of her she was plucking trailing vines and mosses, and when she had her arms full she spread her shawl, and sat down beside the baby, winding the tendrils about his neck and arms.

But they were cold, for he began a feeble cry. Then she took her shawl and covered him with it, murmuring words unintelligible to the astonished listener. Presently large drops of rain fell, and, looking about her, she picked the child up and stepped into the boat. It was fastened to a staple, the three planks jutting out just far enough to cover it. She slipped the baby under the tiller seat, and laid herself down, covering herself with the shawl. From her shuddering starts Hiram could see that the lightning terrified her. As the flashes became more lurid, and the detonations fiercer, she crouched in the end of the boat with her head muffled.

This was the watcher's chance ! Crawling over the mossy bank, he reached the boat ; the chain had been provided for manacling, and in the darkness he seized her elbow, and before she could rise or shake him off, the clasp, closing with a snap, was on her arm above the elbow, and the end fastened to the staple in the bow of the boat.

She broke into a hoarse scream, but baby setting up a lusty plaint, she stopped and turned to soothe it.

"Don't be frightened, Norah; no one is going to harm you. Just stay quiet in the boat. I will be back soon with a wagon to take you back." And Hiram, elate with his master-stroke, set off for the nearest house to summon aid.

He sped swiftly toward the tall chimneys of the War-chester mansion he had remarked before the twilight darkened into the early night that the storm hastened. He reached the stables, and saw a light inside. Shouting to attract attention, one of the stable lads came to the door and held up a lantern, peering over the boy's head.

"W'at is it? w'at yer want, sonny?" the man asked, in tipsy wonder. "Come in outer rain; come in, blast yer! Don't you see I am getting wet, and the whisky's a'most gone!"

He laughed tipsily, and pulled the terrified boy in.

"Ain't ye got no mouth, eh?—speak up, damn it all! Ye's among folks now, and can say all ye like, if ye don't drink too much."

As this jocose period ended, the rain made such an up-roar on the roof that Hiram could hardly distinguish an-other tipsy voice in the din and darkness.

"Aren't ye ever comin' back, Jake, I say? I want another swig."

Seated on wheat-sacks ranged beside an improvised table, the second man held a handful of cards, his body swaying to and fro as Jake resumed his place. Reminded of his mission, Hiram told of the girl in the boat, and the need of taking her to shelter. The men, intent on sharing the contents of a flask secreted between the sacks, leered solemnly at the lad, and Jake said :

"Foolish girl ; oughtn't to go out in rain. Better go home to her mammy, eh ? "

This started a shout of laughter from his companion, and the two fell to playing cards again, unmindful of Hiram. He slunk toward the door, and essayed to open it ; but the wind held it firmly, and whistled through the aperture his feeble efforts made.

"I say, sonny, if you don't let that door alone I'll lock you up in the loft."

Hiram retreated in terror, and sat down cowering on a sack. What would become of Norah ? He waited in a fever, the time seeming much longer than it really was. In a few minutes the rain seemed to have ceased. The men were interrupted in their maudlin game by a clatter outside the stable-door and the tramping of horses ; the door was flung open and a voice cried :

"Hey there you, Jake ! Muster Darcy's come back and wants these horses warmed up and blanketed."

Hiram darted from the open door and fled toward the house ; the hall-door stood open and he heard voices.

"No, Mr. Darcy, Madam Warchester and your father are in New York ; we expect them every day. Indeed, when you came, we thought it was your mother and the Colonel ! "

"Very well, Mrs. Reed, prepare my room ; I have business down street, and will be back in an hour or two ! "

Hiram darted up the steps crying : "O Mr. Darcy, the young girl that your mother told me to watch over is down at the Holly Creek boat-house and—and—"

"What girl, my boy—what do you mean ? "

" The girl that lived at Marbury, Norah—"

" What ? "

The tone was so fierce, and the movement so threatening, that Hiram darted back, thinking all the world had
gone mad. When Darcy had re-assured him, he told of
Norah's plight, and besought the young man to set out
with him to the rescue, for there was no knowing what
might befall the poor girl.

Darcy listened in dumb horror and despair. He had
been turned back from the journey to Mexico by the merest
chance. An order recalling him had come into his hands
just as he was taking ship. He had at first determined to
pursue his journey to his regiment, but suddenly he was
seized by an unconquerable desire to set his eyes upon his
home ; to see how it fared with Norah. His soul had
been torn with anguish when he thought of her. He had
a vague purpose to come home and carry her off to the
lovely Southern lands he had been campaigning in. There,
far from the sordid ambitions of his family and the hollow pretenses of civilization, he would undo the hateful
wrong he had done ; he would make her his wife before
the law, as in the tumult of his passion he had made her
before God.

What infinite mockery were all his hopes and his mother's ambitions, compared to the happiness of this innocent
child, wronged with such dastard wrong by him who should
have been first to safeguard and shield her ! He had been
a miserable man since the day of that wicked wrong-doing, and the misery of it had made him long for death,
when Denny's innocent hand came between, to prolong the
vengeance of outraged honor.

But now Norah was living—Norah was in distress—
Norah was near him. He need not even be seen in Warchester. He could go to the rendezvous she had uncon-

sciously given, take her in his arms, and fly to seclusion and restitution. He need no longer shrink from his mother's eye. He need no longer quail when Denny looked the adoration of loyalty and innocence in his averted eyes !

Hiram was feebly awestruck by the vivacity that came into Master Darcy's manner. The young man had the air of a lover summoned to the tryst. He hurried to the stables, ordered the men to prepare the saddle-horses, and to make no mention to any one that their young master had returned. He would call for the horses in an hour or two, and, until he returned, no one was to leave the stable.

He knew the spot Hiram described very well. It was near by that Norah had gone through the fairy ritual the very day he bade adieu to conscience and honor. He knew a short path, and could be with the victim in ten minutes. Forgetting Hiram, who skurried after him unseen, Darcy set out through the dripping foliage, and with eager steps flew toward the ford.

CHAPTER XXIX.

NORAH REACHES HOME.

MEANWHILE, alone in the night and the storm, Norah is solving Darcy's problems decisively and unexpectedly. In her weary brain there is but one picture ; in her ears but one threat.

"Take her back." That was all that Norah understood of Hiram's speech as he chained her. Take her back ! In her wild brain that meant the unknown, and therefore the terrible. The agonized cry that broke from her arrested the stumbling steps of the boy, perplexed by the darkness and the strange place. He turned to go back ; the echoes froze his blood. When he came to the water's edge he heard a panting, gasping sound, as of one in a death agony. Then an ominous grating and wrenching. He turned in affright, and plunged through the thicket.

Norah, with bleeding hands and maniac desperation, tugged at the chain, but it was firm and resisted her frenzied wrenching. Worn out, her hands torn and bleeding, the night-chill freezing her uncovered neck and arms, she sunk limply into the bottom of the boat, her arm held tightly in the iron clasp. Her terror of the lightning was forgotten. She looked with wide, unshrinking eyes about her as the blinding flashes followed each other swiftly. Ah! in the bottom of the boat lies a dull, notched hatchet. She sees it in the sudden glare. This she seizes; she knows the boat well. The chain is fastened by a rusty hasp to a post on the shore. One wrench with the handle as a lever, and the chain falls with a protesting, lingering rattle into the water, and the heavy hatchet descends on the frail planking.

"Ah! now they shall not take us back. Now we are in running water. Now we are free!"

She pushes the little craft from the bank; it slides slowly out into the narrow stream, and, the current catching it, in a moment it is gliding softly between the dark shadows toward the river. Kneeling on the stern, with her hand on baby's breast, Norah prayed in a voice that men near the creek recalled for many a day, freeing her sad, troubled heart in a rhythmic plaint that might have been a Druid priestess's death chant.

There was but one oar in the boat, and that a broken one. It drifted down the broadening stream into the river. Into the river? Yes, Norah was free now! What that meant to her poor weary brain, to her bleeding heart, it is hard to say; for, if she had still the power of reasoning, she must have known that an oarless boat in the river meant the cataract! But she sat quite still. The boatman at the bend saw the frail craft, and thought some adventurous fisherman at work, the figure sat so immovable.

The boat was beginning to feel the movement of the current that sets over the upper dam when he saw it through flames of forked lightning. She stoops down to see if baby is at peace under the tiller-seat. Heavens! water is gurgling in on the bottom of the boat, for, when she let the hatchet fall, it had cut through the thin timbers. Now a full realization of mortal peril came upon the poor troubled brain. She seized the broken oar, and, with the strength of frenzy, paddled the boat toward a pretty overhanging rock, where reeds and lilies grew in rank clusters, where the stream, though swift, was shallow. It was a long, exhausting effort, but they were not yet safe. Slipping from the boat into the water, she essayed to drag it nearer shore, her poor limbs torn by the rocks, and her feet bruised by the sharp pebbles. But the current was strong even here. If she could move nearer shore, and reach the low sandy bank, she could take baby out and reach the solid land; but that was far off in the dimness of the night, and every moment the force of the current increased as the boat neared the cascades.

Far in the black night, outlined against the blacker sky, the specter of a line of giants arises before her—stakes left by the workmen repairing the dam. If she could but run the craft against one of these, there would be no further danger of being swept down to the falls! Now she could hold up no longer; the water grew swifter, and kept her from the shore. Ah! she has lost her footing, the boat careens, and baby sets up a piteous wail. She clutches desperately, but the boat alone holds her up now. It is half filled with water, and sags far to one side. She tries to shriek; the water fills her mouth. She recognizes the dark outlines on the distant shore; the boat is just abreast a deep cove that indents the bank. Oh, if she could only regain her footing long enough, all would be well. Ah! God be praised! though the water is up to her arm-pits, she feels the blessed bowlders again under her torn feet; she holds the stern up while prow sags under.

"Ah, baby, be peaceful, and don't distract me now! The good God has held out his hand!"

Yes, the good God had mercifully stretched out his hand. In an instant the circling eddies carried the stern shoreward, and the mother, with a tight clutch on the rudder, is dragged after it. But presently the clutch relaxes. On the shore a man, walking under the black sky, starts as a long gurgling cry seems to smite the night from the sullen river. The chain alone holds the mother to the support of her child; but the chain, that is so fragile that human eyes can not see it, so strong that Infinite might alone can uphold it, has snapped! The moon, that presently emerged from the sodden clouds, shone down on the skiff swaying slowly in the eddying circles of the little bay, anchored to the dead mother whose solemn eyes looked up peacefully through the pellucid waters, and seemed to shine with the ineffable light of those who die in the gentle hardihood of unspotted innocence.

.   .   .   .

It is not, I think, for me to further point the moral of this sweet, solemn life. While my pen traces these lines, the lovely face rises before me, as you see the sad maid-mother in the temple of a divine, an immemorial worship—a Murillo adored and wrought it out in love and reverence. As that face shines out in memory, through the aromatic incense of the great temple, in a fantastic, troubled way, I confuse the two, or rather identify them.

Well, it is not the time to moralize; if the tale has been set down in just measure, no moralizing is needed, and we must hasten on to the sequel of mingled melancholy and merry-making.

In the first hour of dawn a long, thin flame of scarlet tipped the waters of the Caribee, and an early fisherman, adjusting his line, heard a cry that he took at first for a cat-bird. But the wail rose, and was full of the vitality of human pain. He turned toward the tall reeds, and looked along the face of the blushing waters. A dark line, as of a sunken skiff, broke the curve of the roseate ripples. He reached it with a few strokes. The stern of the boat was tilted in the air; the bow seemed anchored. The cry came from the box under the stern-seat. He had to break the frail hasp, for it was locked. He turned the slat back; a baby, swathed in flannel, blinded by the sudden glare, doubled its little fists and stared peacefully into the astonished face. He lifted it carefully, and ran to the nearest house. This happened to be Denny's cottage, and Larry was in the little garden, spading. He took the baby, wondering, and carried it to Aunt Selina. She did not at first remark the little one's wraps, but, when the babe had been properly cared for, as only a mother knows how to act in such an emergency, she examined the clothing, and her eye fell upon the shawl. She uttered a faint cry.

"Why, Larry, these are Norah's; I have seen them on her. I helped her make them. Where, oh, where did the man say this child was found?"

The man was in the kitchen, regaling himself with a bowl of fresh milk, and he told the story over again.

In agitation, Larry hurried to the water and rowed to the half-submerged skiff. It was still securely anchored, and the fisherman suggested cutting the rope ; but as he slipped his hand down into the water the line was found to be a chain. He pulled vigorously, but it was more than he could draw alone. Larry leaned over the boat's edge, and peered down among the tangled flora of the river-bed. He started with a ghastly cry.

"There is a dead man there ; I see his eyes—look !"

Sure enough, folded in a filmy sheet of soft green, the outlines of a pale face could be seen, two wide-open eyes staring tranquilly upward ! There was a broken pile that rose almost to the surface of the water—the cove had once been surveyed for a landing. The sunken end of the boat rested on this, and the body was in some sort fastened to the slender shaft. The water is not deep, and Larry, throwing off his coat, slips in at the sunken boat's bow. A slender chain bruises his ankles. As he steps further, he sinks to his middle, and something sways against him that sends the blood curdling through his veins.

"Give me a hook !" he cries hoarsely. He lifts the chained arm to the surface of the water, and then almost drops it as the outlines of a white bosom gleam just below the surface. A streaming veil of hair covers the face ; both hands are clenched on the chain that falls from the boat. It is as much as both the strong men can do to lift the body, and when it is laid in the boat Larry's companion says :

"She must have got out of the boat and passed around the sunken stake to anchor the craft. Ef the water hadn't been deeper here than anywhere else, she could have managed it without losing her life. She gave her life for the little one."

The cruel chain had cut into the tender flesh, but the water had washed away all traces of blood. While the other rowed the boat to shore, Larry readily broke the chain, and when they touched the bank, he picked the body up and flew to the cottage. He laid his burden down an instant to recover breath. As he did so the door opened, and Aunt Selina asked eagerly :

"Where is she—where is she ? O Larry, why didn't you find her—don't you know ? "

As she spoke, Larry had pulled her gently from the door and pointed to the dark mass lying on the veranda floor. To his amazement, Aunt Selina broke from him and bent over the body with loud cries.

" Ah, Norah—Norah—is this the way you come to me ? Ah, Norah—speak to me ! It is your old aunty ! It is your mother ! Ah me—ah—ah ! "

" In the name of God, Aunt Selina, what do you mean ? " Larry, bending down, picked up the body and, uncovering the face, reeled against the door.

" Put her on the bed, Larry, and run for the doctor, and I will do everything else ; she may not be dead—we may save her ! "

The fisherman broke the iron clasp with a chisel, and Aunt Selina, making use of him to bring her hot water, disrobed the cold form and applied every remedy she knew to the end of resuscitation. When the doctor came, twenty minutes later, he pronounced all efforts useless. She had been dead many hours. In his wrath and grief Larry could hardly be restrained from doing violence to the fisherman, whose slowness he blamed for the death. It took all of Aunt Selina's pleadings to keep him from killing the "murderer," as he called the frightened dis-coverer of this piteous handiwork.

The baby puzzled Aunt Selina. What could it mean ? Why should it be wrapped in Norah's belongings? How came Norah in the boat before her own door? Had Dunn any knowledge of her movements?

At noon, as Larry lay prone upon the floor, moaning in helpless rage and anguish, a horseman rode furiously up to the very threshold. His clothes were muddy; his eyes haggard; his voice thick and imperative.

"O Byron, my son," cried Aunt Selina, starting.

"Mother, where's Norah? Was it you who lured her from me? Was it you who carried her from Marbury? Don't trifle with me! I have ridden the fields all night, and I'm not in humor for silly tales!"

"O Byron, my son, lower your voice; still the evil rage of your soul; look, there is Norah!"

She had led him through the narrow doorway to the little parlor, where the pale, dead face laid peaceful and smiling on the pillow.

"Dead! my God, dead! What have I done? It is murder! I swear, it is murder! Yesterday so fair, so strong, in her room at Marbury, and now, dead! It is murder! do you hear me, mother, it is murder! and that villain, that black-hearted son of the Warchesters, did it!"

Byron fell in the chair in a paroxysm of blasphemous execration that terrified the mother and even aroused Larry to attention. An awful fear had begun to freeze the current of Aunt Selina's blood. The shadow of an odious deed, the miserable memory of things she had seen at Marbury. She shrunk from her son in terror! She believed his presence in the sacred chamber desecration, and, laying a shaking hand upon his shoulder, she said, tremulously:

"Come, Byron, this is no place for you. Let the poor brother be alone with his dead!" She took him by the arm and led him from the room, closing the door behind her.

"Now, Byron, my son, you were never base or cruel; tell me what all this means. How the poor child, twice dead to us, came into your keeping, and came from your hands a corpse ? "

"From my heart, mother, when she quit me she was as well and as strong as she ever was! I don't understand you ! "

"My son, she fled from Marbury once before. It was not to escape Amelia's shrewish tongue. It was to escape what, to her pure nature, was worse than all forms of suffering the God-fearing are called on to endure. She was drowned, she was chained to the boat! Who chained her? Some one who had worse to conceal; was it you, oh, my son? I have borne miseries, I have had my old heart wrenched within the last few hours as I never believed it could be wrenched and remain in my body, but all I have suffered is the mercy of heaven compared to the agony of the doubt your words leave in my mind ! "

She fell on her knees and raised her hands.

"My son, by your father's grave, answer: Did you wrong Norah ? "

"Ah, mother, before God, this is not true ! "

Then he poured out the story of Mrs. Warchester's coming; her plea that Norah would come to ruin at the hands of her son. Here he choked, and then went on to the miserable end.

Now the baby was no longer a mystery to Aunt Selina. She was doubly relieved, for the doubt that had filled her soul with death had been worse than Norah's loss. She kissed Byron when the tale came to an end, and said solemnly :

"I thank God with a contrite heart that the sin of the hapless child's murder is not on our hands, and I hope that you may be forgiven for the instrumentality you have been in her persecution. She knew little joy in her blameless life, poor child, and, dreadful as the end is, we may take comfort in the thought that it was under our roof she first knew happiness, in our hearts she first found tenderness, and in our love she was as our very own flesh and blood."

The sunlight broke through the windows in crimson banners as they once more entered the little room. Mother and son knelt at the bed of death, and the violet eyes of the dead, wide open, seemed from their limpid, untroubled depths to reflect grace, mercy, and peace upon their troubled hearts.

It seemed quite natural, to the mourning group that sat bewildered in the cottage, that Marcus Dunn should take upon himself the burden of the dead. He had heard the awful story, and hurried to the cottage incredulous, but fearful. Yes, there she was, peaceful, tranquil, and, oh! so beautiful. He doubted if the tender soul were ever fitted for the world's hard ways and obtruding cares. He could hardly believe the gentle heart was not beating, and its impulses mirrored, living and loving, in the radiant eyes so wide open and dove-like. He gazed into them, and saw the fearlessness of her soul's purity. As he leaned over the dead, Aunt Selina came in. She had long before penetrated his secret. She held out a small silken amulet that had been found on Norah's bosom attached to a ribbon around her neck. She explained this, and said :

"There is a bit of writing in it."

"Writing, Mrs. Marbury?"

"Yes, something that explains—explains Norah's loss of reason."

He took the little memento ; the thin surface opened readily, and folded inside he found a scrap of paper. It was in Darcy Warchester's handwriting, and the words were :

"DENNY: If death should come to me while at the war, I write this to make known to you that Norah is my wife in the sight of Heaven as she shall be in the sight of the world if I live. DARCY."

Then Marcus was told of the baby, the finding of which had not been known in the city, as Aunt Selina had said nothing to the physician or to Larry. It was brought into the room with the dead mother. Marcus looked at the crooning little waif, blue-eyed and pink, plucking its draperies with fat fingers.

"Yes, it is a Warchester," he said bitterly, "and it begins its mission early."

"Its mission, Mr. Dunn? I don't understand you," said Aunt Selina, puzzled.

"Never mind, Mrs. Marbury; it was a wicked and cynical thought. We'll take care that the boy shall not have the Warchester pride."

Marcus took the bit of faded paper and with it a golden tress from the maze of Norah's hair, and put them by with the mementos of his own mother. The little boy was given to him until Darcy should return; and it was agreed that Denny should never be told the secret of the child's birth unless Darcy commanded it. Larry suspected nothing, for he never thought of the babe in the bitter trial of his sister's tragic death.

CHAPTER XXX.

CONSEQUENCES.

NORAH's body was laid under the cedars in Mount Holyrood, at the edge of a pretty copse, where the white star-lilies grew thick under the shadow of the great War-chester obelisk. The *cortege* was very simple, though crowds stood respectfully bare-headed along the streets, as was the kindly custom in those days when the dead passed to the grave. Larry and Marcus, Aunt Selina and Manly, sat in the mourning coach. With them came the Blythes and the Marburys, Dilly being too much prostrated to take part.

Returning from the cemetery, Byron drove to the War-chesters. Although Madame Warchester had reached home the day that Norah's body was found, Byron had not gone to her. His heart was too full of rage and grief. But now he would wreak his wrath on this heartless patrician, who had decoyed him into this guilty coil. He would see whether the hard heart held no reserves of tenderness; whether death could not enforce the common sympathy of an equal humanity.

Madame rustled into the reception-room before he was seated, and waved him condescendingly to a chair, while she, with an affectation of preoccupation, looped back the heavy curtains, keeping herself half facing him as she said :

"So poor Norah is dead. I am told she made way with herself."

"No, Madame Warchester, there's no such comfort as that, poor as it is, for us. We murdered her!"

She dropped the silken loop she had partly adjusted, and turned fully upon him with cold questioning in her gray eyes.

"Do you mean, Mr. Marbury, that the girl was cruelly treated in your keeping, and threw herself into the river to escape you?"

"I mean, Madame Warchester, that you drove her mad by what you said about your son! That a child—your son's child—was born to her, and that the thought of a life of shame drove her to desperation! That's what I mean!"

Byron's voice was low, but there was a threatening intensity in it that startled the mother as much as the revelation of Darcy's criminality.

"A child!" she whispered, "Darcy's child! How do you know it was Darcy's?"

She said this vaguely, tremblingly, and low; the very walls must not be desecrated by this hideous secret.

"How do I know, Madame Warchester? Don't you know? Didn't you know it when you lifted her from the floor in her home? When the boy was born I remembered the look in your face when you dropped her on the sofa, and told me to carry her out. You knew it then! If I had known it, your fine gentleman of a son should have made her his wife, if I had to carry her to Mexico, or he would have had a bullet in his worthless body, the heartless villain!"

Never in all her life had her ears been affronted by such language. She shrank back, raising her hands piteously, and Byron's kind heart relented. He added, in a softer tone, "But he left a paper."

"A paper?" she gasped, "a paper?"

"Yes, a paper owning that in the sight of Heaven Norah was his wife. It was found in the baby's clothing."

"Owning that Norah was his wife! In the sight of Heaven?"

Yes, those were the words he had written her himself, in that memorable letter that drove her to action. What did they mean, she asked herself, quite forgetting the stern face scrutinizing her.

"And the paper you have, Mr. Marbury?"

"No, but you need give yourself no fear. To save Denny and the family, the paper has been buried where it will never be seen, unless your son denies it. No one in Norah's family knows of the birth of the child. My mother thought it best to keep the knowledge from them, at least until your son's return. That's what I came to say to you. The Boynes do not suspect Norah's love for your son, and, unless you reveal it, no one will ever tell it to them."

Ah! she breathed again. There was some decency in this low blood after all. Darcy was not to be dragged through the mire; the family was not to be smirched. Her fervent gratitude quite transformed her. She studied the frank face with softening lines about her relenting lips. Plainly, the gentle blood of Dr. Marbury was re-asserting itself in this degenerate son. But Byron was in no humor for the diplomatic expression of her gratitude that followed. He arose abruptly and bade her good-by, saying, bluntly:

"I am doing my mother's bidding; what we do is for the Boynes, and not to spare you or yours!" She did not rise as he quitted the room; she bent her head in royal protest at such heresy as consideration for the low-born Boynes. The danger was over. Darcy really was free—rid forever of this odious association. No future complication could bring the girl or her family as a menace to the smooth existence of the Warchesters. She had acted wisely. Darcy would have been mad enough to give way to a morbid sentiment, and chain his life down to the level of this low-born love. Now life would again be all serenity. Darcy would forget the miserable episode, and, with Agnes at the head of the house, the glories of the Warchesters would be perpetuated.

She moved about the house with such buoyancy, such

renewed youth, that the Colonel remarked it, and spoke jocosely of the benefits of travel, while Milly, who had just returned from a trip abroad, claimed that it was her mamma's relief at the recovery of her daughter to take the burdens of the household from her shoulders!

Mamma beamed serenely, and raised her eyes to the portrait of her son smiling from the wall, and then she was clamorously beset by the spoiled darling with soft plaints of her partiality for the prodigal.

Now the marriage she had set her heart upon could be brought about at once. Darcy should be ordered home. Her friend, the Secretary of War, Governor Darcy's close ally, would see that this was done. Why hadn't the foolish boy waited for her in Washington? Where could she reach him now? It would take months to send to Mexico. She gave orders to dispatch an express at once to Washington, to have her son sent home, and, easy in mind, waited the future. She could have wished that she had never been forced into relations with this Marbury person, for, though the son of the Doctor was certainly "well born," he was vulgar, and of the habits of the common people.

Meanwhile, the tragedy had set the city agog. Scores of people recalled the lovely girl who had made the "Blue Jay" a magnet to the sober young fellows of the town, who had gone to the simple tap-room for the pleasure of a glimpse of the demure maiden stitching in the parlor, and telling tales to the open-mouthed Manly. Then a sinister rumor of foul play took hideous shape and circumstantiality. Domestics at Marbury and Warchester House compared notes. Visions of the frightened girl in the lanes and fields were one after another recalled and compared. Byron, maddened by neighborhood gossip, told too much or too little. Curious crowds hovered

19

about Denny's cottage until Marcus, to save Aunt Selina's reason, closed the place, carried Larry to the Blue Jay, and sent the old lady to Marbury until the heart-breaking curiosity should die out. But these measures only added to public doubt. Charges of the gravest nature took shape and purpose. The rich Warchesters were held blamable for the tragedy. Their high-stepping son had made the poor girl his victim. What more natural than that the family should seek to be rid of her without much thought as to the way she was taken from their sunshine ?

In some intangible way Darcy's apparition in the Holly woods on the night of the dead girl's agony became vaguely rumored. A gardener near the Holly Creek ford recalled shrieks prolonged and terrifying, which, as his wife was lying-in, he had shut out by closing the windows of his cot.

The boat was examined carefully, and the gash in its bottom was pronounced the work of deliberate design, for a blade, evidently sharp and thin, had been first plied between two strips, had torn the calking, and then left a narrow slit—enough to sink the craft in a given time. But the conclusive evidence of baleful, premeditated murder was the chain fastened to the wretched victim's arm above the elbow. The black welt of it was cruelly plain on the white flesh when the grave-clothes had been put on the body But ghastlier, and crueler than all, the little babe had been found *locked* in the cupboard under the stern-seat !

Yes, murder of the foulest sort had been done; murder that called for the active pursuit of every man who hoped to rear daughters in purity, or sons in honor ; murder that called to the God of the fatherless, the justice of the upright !

Marcus himself, torn by the conflict that racked his heart-strings—the death of the girl that had come to be his joy, that had given him months of sweet trouble ; that had lighted, by the glance of her innocent eye, the lamps of his fading youth; that had buoyed him with the aspirations only second to the immortal longing—Marcus, bending under this burden, had not at first realized the obvious in Norah's plight when found. The horror of the rumor began to possess him! The impalpable form of it— the hideous outlines that shone fitfully through the dissonant clamor—he put away from the sight of his mind, so long as he could justify himself to himself in the evasion of what, day by day, hour by hour, uprose in the menacing specter of moral and legal retribution.

In the Warchester house the death of Norah had passed away as a topic, save in the solemn whispers of the servants, who shuddered as the serene mother busied herself in the duties of her sphere. The Colonel had been "aging to the eye," in the expressive phrase of the domestics, for days under the undivided burden of the hideous atmosphere of suspicion and reticence in which he found himself immersed in his business. People avoided him. If a group were engaged in vivacious tattle, or the ominous monotone that implied sinister revelation, his coming was a signal for instant silence or dispersion. He had gone, in the infirmity of helpless rage and hot indignation, to his wife's nephew, Marcus Dunn, to learn his redress for such odious though passive disparagement. But no one who saw the reserved, cold man that day ever forgot the mute woe he carried away from Marcus's consulting-room. He masked his grief at home, and Mrs. Warchester conjectured that it was the imminent loss of the great Myrickson suit that was turning the dark locks white, and furrowing the white, aristocratic forehead.

The Colonel had known only in the vaguest sort of a way that his darling Darcy, the indulged prince of the house, had become enamored of the pretty Norah. He had given the matter little thought. As I have said before, the "*droits de seigneur*" existed in fact, if not in form, in this country ; as well understood, if not acknowledged, as in France or any monarchical society inheriting the evils of feudalism. He would have seen nothing very odious in Darcy's amusing himself with a pretty girl if it were done with gentlemanly reticence. This was a privilege he was born to, as young men are born to hereditary law-making in England, and oligarchic administration in other countries. He had paid little attention to the intrigue because his wife, whom he adored and reverenced, had assumed the management of the affair.

When clamor had reached a crisis, or rather brought vague suspicions to a definite head, the Colonel came home one day, deeply agitated. He led his wife into the drawing-room, closed the door, and asked huskily :

"Elizabeth, much depends on every word you say. Tell me first, because—because you may have to tell it to less trusting ears—tell me what are all the facts in Darcy's unhappy affair with this dead girl Norah."

"Ah, my dear, has that odious business come to you again ? I had hoped it was ended, and that you would never be troubled by it. I told you of Darcy's weak infatuation. I didn't tell you the extent of the danger, but I took measures to save him from folly and the family from dishonor, and I succeeded."

"I don't know as to that, Elizabeth. The town is agog with scandalous hintings and disgraceful innuendoes. I have sent for Marcus to take advice. He will be here presently, and we must take some stand, or I fear we shall be involved in this hideous misfortune."

"Involved! what do you mean? What have we to do with the death of a vulgar foreigner?"

The Colonel started up and paced the floor, glancing through the window impatiently. His wife followed his movements with restive incredulity. What could it mean? Was she never to hear the last of this hateful scandal-mongering?

Marcus came in presently, and sank heavily into the seat the Colonel pushed forward.

"Well?" the latter ejaculated.

"It is true! I have questioned the men, taken their statements in fact before a magistrate, and a warrant has been issued—" Marcus, who had barely saluted his aunt, hesitated, and looked in troubled inquiry at the Colonel.

"My dear, perhaps it would be better to let Marcus and me talk this matter over before we—before—" He hesitated, and looked piteously at his wife's nephew. Mrs. Warchester arose and swept to the door.

"If your inquiry concerns any responsibility or handi-work of mine, I should prefer being present. If it refers to strangers, I will retire by preference."

She waited, glancing haughtily at her nephew, whose gaze was fixed on the floor.

"Aunt Elizabeth, I fear that you must hear this bad business, and God grant that this hearing may be the last of it! Much depends upon you. Much is at stake. Summon all your self-control, summon all your fortitude, for an evil destiny is hanging over your house!" He faltered as he saw the proud light fade in the haughty eye. She came back, and, seating herself by her husband, said simply:

"I hope that I have so lived that I can hear all the world says of me and mine without fear and without shame. I beg that you will not soften what must be said through

any mistaken consideration for my woman's weakness."
She slipped her hand into the Colonel's, and confronted
the face of anguish before her.

"Aunt, for two days I have been on the verge of madness. Dreadful rumors followed the finding of the body
of the poor girl Norah Boyne. These were all vague and
unsubstantial until the town magistrate examined Byron
Marbury and the fisherman near the Holly Hills. Much
of the tale they told, you already know. I do not believe
that you know that on the night of the girl's death Darcy
was here—was with her."

"It is impossible! It is a calumny! If he had been
here, his mother would have known it. If—"

"Alas! he was seen by the two stablemen; he was
seen and spoken to by the boy Hiram. You were not yet
arrived home. Darcy went to the Holly Creek boat-house.
He was gone from about nine in the evening until midnight, returned to the stable soiled and worn out, slept
until daylight on the couch in his own chamber, and then
set out without a groom, leaving word with the men to
make no mention of his presence."

"But, if he were here—if, for reasons of his own, he
hurried away when he found we were not at home—what
is there wrong in that?"

The Colonel with a groan rose, and, clasping his hands
over his head, walked up and down the room.

"O Aunt Elizabeth, that it should be my lips that
breathe the blasting news to you! O Colonel—Colonel
—I can not—I can not—you must take this cruel burden
from me!"

Mrs. Warchester arose and laid her hand on her husband's arm, keeping her eyes fastened on Mark. Two or
three times her lips moved as if she were uttering words,
but no one heard them; they came finally:

"Is he—is Darcy dead; has he been murdered?"

"Ah! God help us, worse than that, worse than that!" the Colonel cried, wringing his hands.

"Worse—worse—worse than death to a Warchester—dishonor!"

She raised her head in proud incredulity. "No, no, I won't believe it."

A sudden movement in the portico diverted the over-wrought faculties of father and nephew at the instant. Two men with the insignia of the local court were parley-ing with a domestic. Marcus arose and hurried out. Mrs. Warchester watched the group through the window, chained to the sight by a numbing horror that grew until her eyes refused their office. She sank into a seat.

"Husband, in God's name, what does this mean? Spare me, be merciful, tell me, anything is kinder than this suspense!"

The Colonel came over and, kneeling before her, drew her head upon his shoulder. "Yes, it is better to know. Our son, our innocent, spotless Darcy, is accused of murdering this poor girl, to conceal the evidence of his passion!"

For an instant she sat quite dazed; then, to the shocked, inexpressible amazement of her husband, she broke into a frenzied shriek of laughter, so harsh, cruel, feverish, that he thought her mad. He put his hand on her mouth to stop the unseemly sound to the ears of the horrified do-mestics, now crowded in the hallway.

"Betty, for my sake, for our son's sake, don't, don't. God—she is mad!"

This sobered her; she arose and stood before him now, her air contained, her voice in its natural key.

"No, I am not mad. I should have gone mad if you had tried me a moment longer, but the relief was so great that I couldn't resist laughing. My Darcy a murderer! When they make me believe that, I shall go mad indeed."

Darcy could not be found. Marcus, associating Governor Darcy and the greatest legal firms in the State, undertook the defense. The law's delays covered weeks, and before the trial was set the basis of the case was in the main the facts Marcus had laid before the Colonel. Darcy's whereabouts were not traced until two months after the issue of the warrant. The news reached him on arriving at the camp on the Rio Grande. He traveled by the swiftest conveyance, night and day, and delivered himself to the authorities within the time marked for the trial.

Meanwhile, all the facts which have been set down in this tale were sifted and embodied in the case for the prosecution. Byron Marbury's testimony of itself seemed enough to convict, though his hatred of the young man weakened it somewhat. But the two tipsy grooms corroborated and supplemented so directly the assumption of Darcy's rival, that the panic-stricken friends of the prisoner gave up hope. It was shown that Darcy had the strongest motive for making way with the girl he had wronged. He had been engaged after his amour to a rich young woman who was to extricate himself and his family from financial difficulties. The miserable mother, put upon the stand, was forced by ingenious cross-examination to make the case even stronger by acknowledging her interposition in betraying the poor girl from the home her brother had provided.

The great lady, now the mother, the solicitous mother, with swollen eyes and quick-coming breath, extorted, during those three hours' examination, a pity and admiration she had never won in her days of domination and grandeur. There was not a dry eye in the room as she told the tale, breaking down again and again, at the enforced betrayal of the sacredness of maternal confidences with her darling, pale and resolute in the prisoner's box before her. She told how he had been decided and eager to marry the unfortunate girl; how he had come to her to avow the determination; how she expostulated and reminded him of the covenant made long before with another; how this pathetic outpouring of mother and son had been overheard by the wretched victim, and how the blow had shaken her brain. That even in this state her son had still determined to marry her, and so wrote from the field of battle.

She read his letters on the subject, and there was many an admiring glance at the stout lover when she came to the sentence:

"Believe me, dear mother, there is no honor that can be compared with a tranquil mind. I love Norah, she is worthy a king's love. She is worthy a far better man than I am. I mean to give her the only honor that I can bestow—the title of wife! Reconcile yourself to this, and give your soldier boy a welcome with his bride, when I come home presently."

It was the knowledge that he meant this—it was the conviction that he would make the poor mad girl his wife —that impelled her to call in the aid of the girl's natural guardian, Mr. Marbury, and put the demented girl under his legal care. In all the agony and shame of this public place she preserved faculties so clear that the cross-questionings did not elicit the weak points in this adroit plea.

The case for the defense was, in brief, the mother's narrative and Darcy's statement. He had arrived in Warchester unexpectedly the night of the death. The boy Hiram had told him of Norah's being at the boat-house. He had no idea that she was under duress of any sort. He supposed that it was one of her habitual freaks. He had hurried to the spot; the rain had ceased: there was no sign of Norah. He had wandered through the places she used to haunt on the Holly Hills, but, finding no trace of her, he had gone to the cottage and had seen through the windows Aunt Selina and Larry. They were reading tranquilly, and he had no doubt that Norah had retired.

He had been in great perplexity as to the course he ought to pursue, and went to his own boat-house, where he sat pondering until midnight. He had no idea when his parents would return ; he was sure they would remain in New York, as the arrival of the vessel on which his sister was expected was uncertain. There were bitter disappointments in store for them, and, since he had heard nothing from Norah, and was ignorant of the birth of the child, he had determined to return to the army, to confide the whole story to his dearest friend Denis Boyne, by his help convey Norah South and marry her, where the event would be less of a trial to his parents. He had, unknown to his mother, formally released his betrothed, a young lady to whom he had been pledged almost since childhood, and who, happily for herself, had never given him her heart. He had taken horse and continued his journey to his regiment, and the instant the fatal news had reached him he had hurried back.

The narrative convinced many, but the case for the prosecution was so strong in every point that it was to the discrimination of the jury alone the counsel looked for rescue. The prosecution showed that the girl had come to her death by drowning. That she had been chained to the boat. That the bottom of the boat had been slit by a sharp instrument to insure its sinking. That, in spite of this, the girl might have escaped if the chain had not held her in the water, when she found the boat sinking. That the only person in the world who had any motive or interest in making way with the victim was the prisoner.

The dreadful ordeal lasted a week, and late on Saturday night the judge charged the jury. All that night and all Sunday the family and friends sat in panic of swooning agony in the sheriff's back parlor, waiting. Every clang of the iron doors sent the blood in freezing currents to their hearts. All Sunday passed. Monday morning the jury filed in. Warchester had never had a murder trial before, and the whole town was in the solemn chamber, or outside, waiting the verdict.

When the foreman arose, even the Judge leaned forward in agitation. The answer to the clerk came low and painfully:

"Guilty!"

Every eye was turned to the marble effigy of what had been the mother! She swayed forward, until Marcus caught her as she was about to collapse. But it was only for a moment. Presently she whispered hoarsely to Governor Darcy. He seemed to remonstrate with her, and then arose and asked the judge to suspend sentence. The defense desired a new trial, and the grounds were presented. The prisoner was led away, but the crowds remained all day, discussing in low tones the judgment that had fallen on the Warchester pride, the leaden-heeled justice that had caught up with rank and wealth and privilege, to avenge the humble and weak and friendless.

CHAPTER XXXI.

SORROW'S CROWN OF SORROW.

HUGH BOYNE reached Warchester while the story of his daughter's death was the topic of the town. He was

shown into the room where the dead girl lay by Aunt Selina, and started with remorse. It was his own Kate, as
he had known her twenty-five years before, when hope
was in her heart and the love-light in her eye. He could
not believe she was dead until his lips touched the cold
forehead. Only half the tragic story was told him—Aunt
Selina thinking it wiser to leave part of it until Denny
came. In time he set out to find his other children,
Agnes and Mabel. But his brother James being dead,
there was no trace of them among those he had known
nineteen years before.

Mabel had gone from Warchester years before, with
her new parents, and was at that very time married and
settled in a great milling city in the West. The Vanes
alone could have identified Agnes's parentage, but they
would have shrunk from it if they had been called upon,
which, as Hugh had no clew, was not likely to happen. Of
James Boyne's wife he could get no trace. She had gone
to Michigan on the death of her husband, and as none of
her relatives lived in Warchester it was impossible to track
her. The Marbury farm, where his children had been
reared, where he heard that Denny and Norah had passed
years of happiness, Hugh bought from Byron, who longed
to go back to the joys of the town. Aunt Selina was to be
the mistress so long as she lived, or, if she preferred, make
her home with Boyne and his two boys.

"I don't know about that, Mr. Boyne. I think when
Denny comes back you will find he will have another mistress to share his home!"

Hugh looked at her inquiringly.

"Oh, Denny has been in love all his life with a pretty
maid in Marbury, and, now that he has a rich father, I
think he will find no refusal in the family."

Denny all this time was in Mexico, unconscious of

the wreck of nearly all he loved most in the world. Marcus had dispatched messengers in vain. The column to which he was attached had penetrated far into the interior, and it was not until the influence of Governor Darcy had prevailed upon his friend the Secretary of War that a furlough was sent and orders to expedite the young man's journey northward obtained.

In spite of every effort, the whereabouts of the boy Hiram Gaskell could not be found. Marcus felt that upon this link depended Darcy's life. Every resource was employed to discover him. Rewards that would have made the boy rich were posted in every post-office, and the primitive machinery of the police system called into requisition. The argument for the new trial was heard, and the decision anxiously expected. Marcus was sure of the result; but unless Hiram were found he felt apprehensive of the verdict in the second trial.

Madame Warchester, in the interval, had insisted on sharing every effort of counsel. She had taken part in all the consultations; had examined every step of the route the dead girl had passed on the last fatal journey from Marbury to the Holly Hills. She had cross-examined Amelia, and extorted every detail of the girl's life in the old home after her return, and, though Amelia cunningly concealed the artifice by which Norah's brain had been finally and irretrievably shaken, the mother, savagely alert for the safety of her son, detected the discrepancy, and charged it upon the shrew. Amelia broke into tears of cowardly terror. She confessed all, under pledge of keeping it from Byron, whose wrath she had come to fear in the morose aspect he had assumed since Norah's flight. The dog-chain, too; she had given that to Hiram one night when she found Norah tampering with the locks.

Then the patient mother pushed her scrutiny to the

Holly boat-house; the boat itself was investigated. The shallow waters were dragged, and the hatchet found under the submerged end of the boat, where Norah's dead body had been discovered imbedded in the green water-weeds. The lawyers listened in anguish as the mother, turned advocate, reconstructed the story. They could give her little hope. All this had been substantially set forth before. Even if the new trial were granted, they could not encourage her in the outcome.

The dreaded and hoped-for day came. A new trial was granted on technical grounds, and, for the first time since the deadly strain had been put upon her, the devoted mother broke down. She was carried from the lawyer's office prattling the idle fancies of a madwoman. But she revived, and was all herself again, when the task still confronting her came back to her tortured mind. She spent long delightful hours with the son, whose eye looked the innocence she had never for an instant doubted. She caressed the handsome lad, and filled him with something of her own amazing confidence when she said:

"Darcy, it was your wicked mother who brought this upon you. It is your repentant mother who shall snatch you from this hideous peril. I have a resource that shall save you. Others may have loved you: your mother not only loves you, she lived for you—lives for you—for, if you were dead, I should not live! The blood of Alice Lisle is in my veins; she died for those she loved! Do you think, Darcy, that I would do less for my boy?"

"Mother, you must not think of the future in this solemn, tragic way. Innocent men have died before now. I have done wrong, but I have not committed this crime. If justice demands my punishment, it is no stain on you

—but—but—'' He broke down ; the hardest part of the punishment had already been his. He had been fouled by suspicion, desecrated by prison. He could never hold his head up again among men. The forces of the mother's perverted and fantastic pride had spent themselves now. It was she who had been content to rescue her darling at any cost, while he, though not indifferent, shuddered at the future, blackened by the near shadow of an awful vengeance.

Worse news still than the lack of the boy Hiram preluded the second trial. Intelligence had come from Washington that the detachment commanded by Lieutenant Denis Boyne had been ambuscaded and massacred in the wilds of New Castile, before the order for his return had reached headquarters. The grievous news was kept from Darcy, but it told on the mother. Those who had known her in happier days were shocked as she entered the courtroom when the case was called the second time. The dark eyes were sunken and dim, the wavy black hair thickly snowed with white, the clear complexion faded, and the cheeks wrinkled beyond the lines of age.

Strong as was the new testimony for the defense, the prosecution met it step by step. Byron, to save himself, was forced to give stronger emphasis to his story. The mother's discovery of Norah's situation the day she was abducted from the cottage was brought out in appalling relief. This point alone seemed to decide the case. Even the absence of the lad Hiram was made to tell against the unhappy prisoner, and, when the judge summed up, it was remarked that his leanings, which, on the previous trial, had seemed in favor of the prisoner, now took an intent against him.

The jury was out three days. Warchester was a place of mourning and suspense, for Darcy's conduct during the ordeal, and the memory of his boyish goodness and generosity, when he was the petted prince of a great race, came back to the people, and there were fervent prayers on many a lip as well as the mother's that the generous boy might be proved guiltless. It was midnight when the foreman of the jury sent word by the sheriff. There was little doubt in the judge's mind of the verdict, and, to spare the mother, he took the bench at that hour.

Scanning the faces of the twelve, Marcus knew what the answer was to be. He caught his aunt's two hands in his own, and whispered:

"Dear Aunt Betty, don't stay here. Let me bring the result to you in the sheriff's room."

She sought his averted eyes, which were swimming in tears, and became rigid.

"They are going to murder him!" Her voice was thick and tremulous, but her hands were firm in the hold she had on her nephew.

"Ah, Aunt—"

There was a sound of mumbling. The clerk was droning the hateful formula. All senses were suspended until, through the whir and sounds of doom, came the blood-curdling word:

"Guilty!"

Darcy raised his head with a gesture of the mother's old pride. He sought her eye. It was glazed and hard. She pushed Marcus's restraining arms from her, arose, and tottered to the rail by her son's side. The under-sheriff looked in perplexity to the judge, as he gently strove to disengage the arms she had thrown around her son. He desisted when he caught a kindly beam in the magistrate's eye. There were only counsel and the prisoner's family in court, Hugh Boyne, Larry, and the Blythes.

With Darcy's head pillowed on her bosom, the mother

raised her haggard face to the judge, and said in tones of blood-curdling calmness:

"A mother's pride, born in her blood, has brought this sinless boy to the edge of the gallows, but a mother's cowardice shall not permit his sacrifice. I call all here to witness that I am in my right mind." She looked steadily in the face of the judge, surveyed the startled countenances of the group below, and stroked the tawny locks pressed to her bosom; then, fastening her eye once more on the magistrate, she continued:

"I have often read of a chain of evidence so strong that the innocent could not escape. I little dreamed that my own darling would be such a victim. Have patience," she cried appealingly, as the judge moved uneasily in his seat, "I shall not keep you long, and what I have to say will convince you that I have a right to speak." She stopped, raised her head, and, with a shade of the old regal way, said:

"Darcy Warchester is guiltless of the girl's murder. It was I, Arabella Elizabeth Warchester, who made way with Norah Boyne!"

"O mother, mother!" Darcy clasped his hands over the self-accusing lips, and strove to smother further utterance. But the proud head refused the shelter of his protecting arms. Meeting the startled gaze of pitying incredulity on the judge's face, she raised her voice in solemn asseveration:

"It was I that did the murder, and I have the proof! When the court needs it, it is ready. Come, my son, we must exchange places. My wicked pride has cursed you long enough."

But the strain was too much now; she would have fallen had not Darcy supported her, and she lay limply across the rail, when Marcus came to carry her out. Sentence was again suspended, the judge agreeing with counsel to investigate the extraordinary admission.

Counsel was assigned the new prisoner by the court, to act in conjunction with Darcy's, and further proceedings postponed until the sanity of the self-accused could be tested by experts. This ordeal passed safely; the mother was equal to the further torture of cross-questioning, and captious doubt raised at every step of her narration. It was she who had placed Norah at Marbury. It was she who had, by holding out a delusive hope of a meeting with Darcy, lured her to the Holly Creek tryst. It was her hand that had cut the slit in the boat. It was she who had manacled the girl's arm. It was she who had fastened the baby in the box under the seat. It was she who had paid the boy to watch the fugitive, and force her if necessary to the boat-house. She had pretended to be in New York, but had in reality left Washington on the heels of her son, who was coming to Warchester to fulfill his pledge to the betrayed girl.

Not a link was lost, not a flaw anywhere in the monstrous story, save the lack of corroboration by the lad Hiram. Amelia was examined, and she confirmed the intent of the narrative by simply omitting her own share in the driving Norah away when the trail came near her own handiwork. She told no lie, but terror of Byron kept her from the few words of truth that would have broken the mother's astutely forged chain of self-crimination.

Darcy was held in suspense, while the new trial, with the mother in place of the son, was ordered for November. In spite of the circumstantiality of the mother's narrative, there wasn't a soul in Warchester that credited the self-accusation. To her husband's prayers she made no answer. To Darcy's remorseful supplication she replied only by caresses. When, however, Marcus Dunn made clear to her that Darcy could never again be brought into peril for a crime of which he had been already virtually acquitted, she broke down and confessed that she was innocent. That she had immolated herself for Darcy, and she counted the sacrifice light that saved his innocent blood from the contamination of the halter.

But, though conscious of the mother's guiltlessness, her counsel were gravely doubtful whether the subtle coil she had woven about herself could be cut or unraveled.

Lady Molly, who returned from the East at this juncture, furnished the first link in the chain of extrication. She had been in the neighboring village of Athens the very night Mrs. Warchester asserted she had set Norah adrift in the boat. They were in the same inn, and she saw Mrs. Warchester, who had remained behind in the tavern parlor while the Colonel had gone on by the coach. This was as late as ten o'clock. With this to work on, Marcus Dunn began the case hopefully.

Darcy had put no trust in the story of Denny's slaughter, and, the instant he was free, hurried down to verify the story or bring his friend home. If Denis and the boy Hiram could be brought on the scene, the mother's sacrifice would end with the rescue of Darcy from even suspicion.

It was Larry who found Hiram, skulking, frightened, and woe-begone, at the port a few miles from the city. He had fled to Canada to avoid Byron's wrath, but, finding no employment, shuddering at every voice he heard, the half-crazed lad had wandered back to endure his punishment and enjoy the plenty and ease of the Marbury farm. His narrative at last cleared the mystery, though he had to run the risk of trial for his handiwork. Hiram's testimony acquitted Darcy of even the shade of complicity. The boy told how he had heard Amelia inform Norah that she was to be sent to the "work-house," he called it; how the girl had suddenly grown wild; how, coming across the fields from the errand upon which he had been sent, he had seen Norah's striped shawl against the alder-bushes; how he had followed and chained her to the boat until he could get help; how he had met Darcy and gone back to the creek with him; how they found the boat gone, and Darcy had wandered through the woods like a wild man, calling on Norah; how, tired out, he had fallen asleep near Norah's cottage, and saw Larry bring the body in the morning. Then he had fled in deadly terror.

Mrs. Warchester, who had been permitted to occupy her own home, under guard and heavy bail, was never formally accused, and her reputation was cleared, in the sight of all men, of the crime she had charged upon herself to save her son.

News came from Mexico that Darcy had been able, by sending timely succor, to rescue Denny from his captors, who were holding him for ransom, and a few days later Marcus had a letter in Denny's own hand, announcing the march home, and his own arrival with his troop in Warchester early in the month. He inclosed a letter for Darcy, whom he supposed to be at home. Letters in his hand came also for Norah, of whose fate he was ignorant, and the wretched Larry carried them faithfully to his only friend, Marcus.

.   .   .   .

It was on just such a tranquil day as we saw in Warchester when this tale began, that the city's civic dignitaries were assembled at the new railway station to welcome Captain Denis Boyne and the survivors of the famous Marbury company from the southern wars. The veterans formed in line in the station, with Denny in all his official bravery of plumes and epaulettes, a shining saber in his hand. The whole town was in the streets. Colonel Warchester, with Governor Darcy, an "ex" before his title now, headed the citizens, and made an address as the little band drew up at the Rialto bridge, where years before Denny had first put his foot on the soil, toddling at his mother's heels. Hugh was there, too, and Larry, and Aunt Selina, and in a carriage sat Mistress Dilly, very proud and happy, you may be sure, in the glory of her soldier boy.

In the evening a great banquet was spread in the Robin Tavern, Governor Darcy presiding, with Denny at his right hand and Colonel Warchester at his left. Flowing bumpers were drunk to the heroes, and eulogiums that made Denny blush were pronounced by the mayor and other local dignitaries. There were swelling periods, be sure, in recounting the heroism of the gallant captain, who had illustrated the bravery of Erin and the patriotism of America on the burning wastes of Mexico. Denny was called upon to respond. He arose, trembling and abashed, and was understood to say that he accepted the kind sentiments uttered as the representative only of the hero who was not present. That it was to Major Darcy Warchester, the model of a soldier, man, and friend, that this tribute was due, and, with other tender and modest words, he made Darcy the theme of the feast.

Captivated by this modest abnegation, and reminded of the fact that Denny was now the son of such wealth as none of the potentates of the city could equal, the alien was clamorously saluted as a citizen of the town, who had won the toga of the patrician caste by his integrity, gallantry, and modest self-denial.

There was presently a sober wedding in Deacon Dane's solemn best room, that gave Marbury gossips

subject for many an evening's chat. Denny's claims to
Dilly were not disputed by the deacon when he came in
the guise of a rich suitor, and the hero of Warchester's
"best" circles. Denny mourned with more tranquil
resignation Norah's death, when he learned the cruel
wrong that his best friend had put upon her. There was
hot rage in his heart when he recalled the past: Norah's
constancy and spotlessness, and Darcy's dastard weakness—for Denny knew it was not libertine guilt. In his
knapsack he had long carried a letter intrusted to him
when the company was entering battle, and, surmising
that this related to Norah, he opened it, though on it was
written, in Darcy's hand,

"To be opened only when I am dead."

"He is dead to me," Denny said, bitterly, as he sat
with Dilly in the deacon's sacred parlor, where he was
now welcomed with urbane cordiality. They read the
letter together. It was a long narration of Darcy's inter-
course with Norah, from the first meeting at Marbury to
his parting in the Holly thickets. The miserable lad set
forth his struggles, his resolutions, his heartbreaking pro-
crastination and cowardice, and wound up by declaring
that so soon as he could reach her, Norah should be his
wife in the sight of man as she was in the sight of God.

Denny's eyes were dim, and he sat silent until the
darkness fell, and then sallied out to take counsel of his
woodland cronies. He revisited the shimmering glades
bathed in the autumn moonlight, where he had found his
friends and confidants as a boy. He knelt beside the
running water, haunted by the memories of Norah—the
memories of Darcy's first coming, when he stood to the
two countryside children for the real Prince Charming of
their tales and dreams. His heart softened; an impulse
of the old superstition came back, and he gazed believ-

ingly into the misty waters. He saw, or seemed to see, the living smile of the dead Norah, and in his ears the night-birds sang, Forgive for Norah—forgive for the dead!

.   .   .   .

Darcy never came back to Warchester. A year after Denny's coming, on his marriage-day, a letter was put in his hands from the wanderer. He had bought a property in the sunny lands where Denny had saved his life. He should live on the memories of his happier years, and ex-piate, as his conscience admonished him, the woes he had brought upon all he loved. He begged Denny to think tenderly of him sometimes—if he could, charitably ; if he couldn't, kindly ; and commended his boy—Norah's boy— to the kind hearts that he knew cherished it. And often, thereafter, Denny was depressed with the sadness of the days that had been darkest—a glimpse of that crown of sorrow, which is the remembering happier things !

THE END.